1541

THE CATACLYSM

by

ROBERT WILLIAM JONES

ISBN: 978-1-09-340567-5

Table of Contents

For my sons, Thomas and James

Prologue

Tyburn, December 1541

Thomas confidently appealed to the growing crowd in the hope that they would spare him the horrendous demise warranting his innards spilled, his privy parts severed and his body cut into sections. He had definitely had his money's worth out of the said privy parts, in fact, they almost singularly, had brought him there but he wished to hang on to them as long as possible. This appeal was rare, the King's sentence was almost always absolute. However, you could think of the dashing Thomas Culpeper as a sixteenth century celebrity. Young, handsome and linked to scandal, his historical significance had been played down and the available evidence of the last year of his life and his arrest, was, at times, questionable.

It was a cold December day and he had been drawn on a pallet by a horse to the place of execution alongside Francis Dereham whose fate was absolutely sealed. I can tell you that Culpeper wasn't looking too pretty after a good drawing through the mud and shite of Tyburn. Now lost amongst most popular histories, his contribution to the thwarting of the Cataclysm of 1541 meant that, although last minute, his sentence had been commuted to a beheading. As this was unexpected there were no formal preparations, he simply knelt down and bowed his head.

Now, history tells us that his head was removed in one clear blow but when you consider that this account was possibly written by Thomas Wriothesley, his chief interrogator, you may wish to question this. Clean? Not so. As the axe wedged into his neck bone, blood was already violently ebbing in all directions and an eerie, continuous wheeze came forth from Tom's face much like the sound of a pig's bladder being punctured by a playful child.

I was so used to this sound coming from his other end that I did a double take to see if they'd got him the right way around. An animal's death would have been kinder. I will spare you the details of the panicked axeman's attempt to clean up this bad job but at best you would probably say that his head was hacked off.

I was hacked off too, not only was I looking forward to Christmas, I'd simply eaten at the wrong time for such an event and, added to that, I'd travelled all the way from York just because he wanted me there. So, amidst the praise, I have to add that Tom was bloody inconsiderate throughout our relationship and this was no exception.

However, he was my friend and now he was gone. I would only see him bodily again when viewing his head on a pike on London bridge. I had no stomach for that particular experience or London itself although I was tempted to go just to have a conversation with him where I had the last word.

I am, of course, waxing flippant not least because of the unexpected, but drastic, transition in my personality.

In 1541 everyone experiences death and they experience it frequently but do not presume that the loss of someone loved is any easier than at any other time. Thomas was dear to me and gave remarkable service to his country, the details of which have never, before now, been revealed. What was worse was that I knew all along that this was the only possible end to the complex assignment we had, earlier in the year, found ourselves contracted to.

1: Lord Silas

Stratford upon Avon, June 1541

Although it was summer, the weather remained moody and all Lord Silas seemed to have done for months was travel. Travel, mostly, was what Silas did but, particularly today, the last part of the journey from York to Stratford upon Avon became gruelling. He made use, in part, of the great north road but, once off the known and beaten track, the journey was tough. Strong, fearless and donning the fashions of the season, Silas was every bit a Knight of the Tudor realm. As he passed through the villages, towns and hamlets of England, one after another, he could hear gasps, particularly from the ladies, as step by step he dominated the territory beneath him. Confident, he breathed an air of expectation of a welcome fit for a king. Silas was the archetypal Renaissance man.

At least this is how it all seemed in his head.

Silas's raison d'etre was to pretend to be something he wasn't and, for him, it worked most of the time. Living a life of fantasy suited him and certainly helped to get things done. On the road, he was Silas the heartbreaker and warrior. At home: the village idiot. "Village idiot" is, to be fair, unfair. At a basic level, like most people of this time, he understood his place in society and this meant that he would do stuff others wouldn't and, at low cost, but his appearance, combined with his constant air of confusion, meant that he was a source of levity to those who knew him. This was partly why Silas travelled. The only real love of his life was Annie. Annie was a middle-aged horse with the strength, dedication and attitude of a foal.

And, of course, he wasn't a Lord.

However, Silas really did wear very impressive clothes. He owned more than one skirted doublet and particularly loved to acquire new boots and shoes. He was completely familiar with how a hat would be worn as the fashions shifted and took good care over the presentation of his steed. He was comparatively tall and extremely thin so, sadly, however much he tried to woo the ladies with a subtle turn off his calf, his hose was simply too big, and the laces that tied his hose often dangled to his knees, providing a source of constant amusement to almost anyone who encountered him. In his mind he was a prince, through Annie's eyes he was a prince but that was the extent of his kingdom. He did know that what he was doing was dangerous, the feudal system of the middle ages had somewhat broken down, not least due to the devastating effect that the Black Death had on the working population, but there was still structure. Impersonating someone of privilege was highly dangerous as King Henry's sumptuary laws forbade anyone to dress in the style of a courtier or above their rank. In York he was known as "Lord Silas" but the village idiot tag gave everyone the general impression that he was harmless. However, he did, unquestionably, play this hand too many times on alien soil.

Silas spent a lot of time on the road but was quick to (well, would attempt to) make friends. However, his pretentiousness heavily combined with his uncanny ability to misunderstand almost anything said to him, often left him in the dark and others too. He had an engaging smile but this was rarely seen as his self-esteem was in short supply. As his head went down at night he was alone inside and out. He felt inferior even to his peers and often wondered what would become of him. If he managed to acquire a mission (as he loved to call them), it gave him a sense of purpose but this did not compensate for the two certainties of life. Things had always seemed to go wrong and, things will continue to go wrong. Very few people in his life would see or understand the depth of his sadness. He lived for acceptance, friendship and, one day, a relationship with the future Lady Silas, whoever that may be, for he had never had such a relationship. He had lost almost all of his hair but pampered that which remained. He would, daily, nurse a long strand of red hair that started at his crown and ended at the tip of his somewhat pointed nose. When he became pompous and, or, agitated it would dance around his face even, strangely, when he presumed it to be secured under his hat. At least there was always something interesting to look at when in Silas's presence.

One drizzly evening in June 1541 Silas entered an inn on the outskirts of Stratford. He instantly attracted many glances as his ostentatious clothes didn't fit with his general demeanour but, even so, people often thought he could well be a Duke or an Earl at first glance. That is until he spoke.

'I'm sent on a mission by God himself!!' He announced to all who were quietly drinking and minding their own business.

'Would you like some ale and food first and perhaps tie up that nag that's wandering off?' said the landlord.

Silas bolted outside knowing full well this wasn't a jest as he had done the same thing many times before. The rain was now so heavy that he could barely see and as he darted back to the entrance his head hit something hard. This too wasn't an unusual occurrence for Silas. He stepped back, looked up and saw a swinging sign that said, "ye dirtye pesant". Unusual, he thought, but probably very appropriate. He retrieved his hat and returned. Fortunately, the laughter had died down before he sauntered back into dry of the inn interior. More or less.

'Some ale and a pie please my good man' and he raised his hat respectfully. Better, he thought to himself as his hair did its first pirouette around his forehead. And then peace. The crazy beanpole with baggy tights had given up they thought. Until

'I'm sent on a mission from God himself!!'

'Bollocks!' said a valued patron.

'I beg your pardon, how dare…'

'Bollocks. Sent you a letter did he?'

'Listen here my man.' Silas retorted.

The landlord's wife chipped in if only to calm things down a little.

'We think we know what you mean lovey, but saying God has spoken to you would be considered heretical around here.'

'I didn't speak to God…' he said apologetically leaving everyone confused. Another one of Silas's great failings was that he would forever take the bait when it was offered.

'Was he not in then?' quipped a farmer near the fire.

Silas thought to himself, what a pudding prick I am. Why do I always have to do this? I do have to try to be more discreet. So he was quiet for a few moments and mulled over his entrance techniques whilst he took the first very welcome bite of the conglomerate before him that masqueraded as a pie.

Everyone settled and stopped taking any notice of the new guest but the silence didn't last long. Silas jumped up, his plate spinning in mid-air before clattering to the floor.

'I seek your blessed island!' he shouted suddenly, leaving

even himself wondering why the hell he had. This was so ridiculous. The current villagers were now dumbstruck and checking whether they were sufficiently armed. There was no laughter this time and the landlord's wife told him in a very sort of "there, there" way that there weren't any islands in Stratford upon Avon. Why did he do things in this way? It was part of the drama, the facade of Lord Silas. Silas really did see the world as a stage long before the other guy was even born. What he didn't realise was that his act was crap. He had tried his hand on the boards but it just didn't work out. If there was an object to his side he would bump into it as he would something above. The floor wasn't safe either, the thinnest rug would have him on his face. Added to all this unrehearsed clowning was his habit of often introducing his own lines and his own character, that being Lord Silas, so he never lasted long amongst any single troupe.

On this occasion, Silas was most embarrassed because his mission was, very serious, and he genuinely had a really important job to do. He had, yet again, gone about all this in the wrong way. However, as they no longer felt threatened it wasn't long before he was completely accepted into the small parochial group if not only because they had been in need of a new village idiot after the last one dropped a half-groat in the wishing well for good luck and decided to follow it in. It certainly helped that he bought everyone a drink at a cost to him of four days wages.

Before long he was alone again except for one man of good age who thought that there might be something about this madness. Silas didn't know if this man's advances were altogether safe. He had an unfortunate way of grunting and grumbling his words out and carried a large and very sharp dagger that looked as though it was used often. Throughout the conversation, this man gripped Silas's leg tightly. To make matters worse he told Silas that he was called Runt. Who on earth would let themselves be called Runt? thought

Silas and then he remembered that, due to the limitations of how little he could write himself, that, when he did write his name, he had spelt it Silias and took him years to work out why everyone in York was shouting "silly arse" as he walked by. Runt's probably not that bad, he thought. It also didn't help that this man's breath was so rotten and all his teeth were black or missing. In a day and age where halitosis was almost good manners it was fair to say Runt's total ignorance of dental hygiene was extreme. Silas's face definitely wasn't pretty all screwed up. He held his breath as best he could and tried to concentrate on the conversation.

'I think you probably started off on the wrong foot mate.'

'Oh, I always do.' Silas started to smile. Partly because this looked like the first real human engagement he was to have in a while and partly because holding his breath started to seem silly and it amused him like it would a child.

'What's this all about then? Message? God?'

'Oh, I'm not allowed to say. It's a secret mission' he said as seriously as he could whilst exhaling.

'You bloody joking?!' shouted Runt. This startled Silas. 'You just told the whole village your plan!'

'I know, I do keep doing that' said Silas. 'I am seeking an artefact'. Did I really say artefact?' He thought.

'I really can't say what, but it lies on an island directly north of Stratford on the Avon'.

'Well, I'll tell you for nothing I think you're barmy… unless…' Silas's heart missed a beat.

'There is a village four miles north and, nearby, there's a huge farm run by a friend of mine, Richard. He oversees lots of lands and to the west of it, there is a massive lake. I suppose in the centre is what you might call an island.'

Silas thanked him in the same way a child would thank someone on receiving a present. It never occurred to him for a second that it was probably all nonsense. He then thought that this sudden friendship was a little too friendly and, again, checked the grip Runt had on his thigh. Is this the dirty peasant referred to on the inn sign? supposed Silas, and then struggled to concentrate.

'I'm up there tomorrow, Saturday, and you can ride alongside my nag and cart if you wish. Bring some food for the journey.' At this, Runt sat back and gave Silas his leg back.

Delighted and relieved, Silas picked up the plate from the straw floor, the pie he'd dropped, the chair he'd knocked over, picked a piece of the inn sign out of the back of his hair and then brushed some beer off Runt's shoes. Runt growled, so he left it there. Silas turned to take a small candle from the landlord's wife hoping to get his head down but, as his left foot negotiated the first step, he heard the inn door slam shut. Someone was preventing Runt from leaving. That person was the same one who had ridiculed Silas when he had first spoken and Silas decided he must be called "Bollocks" simply because of his unrepentant and constant use of the word.

'You're not leaving here 'til I get what I own Runt' said Bollocks.

'By God's blood, you'd best let me out or there'll be trouble for you Blythe, you evil bastard' retorted Runt. He has a name, after all, thought Silas. So much for bollocks. Silas was aware of a tremor in Runt's voice which told him that this was a real threat. A voice in Silas's head suggested he intervened but another more wobbly voice interrupted and said don't bother.

'You'll get what's yours tomorrow, you have my word on it' said Runt and this, thankfully, seemed to appease the thoroughly unpleasant Blythe.

'Last day, last chance' said Blythe and he let Runt go. He then swung around to give Silas a deathly stare which had Silas promptly at the top of the narrow steps before he could give it a second thought. At the top, he found a small, narrow room. You could barely call this a room but there was an excuse for a bed in the space he had found. He lay down. The bed ended where his knees began but he found that he could get all of his lanky frame in there if he pulled his knees up to his chin. Not the least bothered by the interesting collection of insect life in there with him, he sincerely thanked God for the blessings of that day, for new friendships to come, and hope for protection on his mission, happily dedicating his life to the Lord. The real one, that is. He rested his head and slipped into a dream in which the crowds cheer Lord Silas on the completion of his mission, festooning flowers at Annie's feet.

It seemed almost instant that Silas could hear a cock crowing and detect chinks of light fanning out from the cracks in the shutters. Yesterday was a good day he thought. He'd got this far and, for once, no one had battered him. Moreover, he may well have made some new friends. Full of optimism, he rushed outside where a horse and cart was waiting for him but to his surprise, it wasn't Runt holding the reins, it was the landlord's wife who had sought to comfort him the night before.

'Morning dear!' she shouted, 'best get cracking, it's a long journey. I've got some berries and bread inside so we can eat on the way'. Silas was a little taken aback wondering why Runt wasn't going with him. He considered making some grandiose statement again but realised he didn't have to make an effort to win this woman's kindness or understanding so he simply asked why.

'Master Runt's where he's meant to be today – working.' She said 'And am telling you, my lad, he'll be nothing but trouble if he was sitting here instead of me. We only visit Richard's farm once a month and half the stock seems to go missing when Runt's on the errand. We suspect he may be a regrator!' Silas was quite shocked at this. Apart from beggars and Spaniards, regrators were probably amongst the most hated in England. They adopted a practice of buying, or acquiring, goods and selling them on, sometimes at a higher price.

'I'm also more than a little worried about these so-called secrets you keep, they'll be all over the County by tomorrow if you say any more. You can leave your horse here and pick her up when we return, she'll be fine.'

It wasn't often that Silas insisted on something but this morning he had to, he didn't go anywhere without Annie so, astonishingly, he managed to negotiate. Maud, for that was the landlady's name, seemed happy to comply and Silas knew that Annie would love pulling this little cart. It was also a bonus that he didn't have to travel a slow four miles with a dirty peasant's hand on his knee. He then had a stark thought and considered that Runt's hand could well have gone on a journey of its own. Silas shuddered and then shut the thought out.

This rotund woman called Maud was possibly the nicest person he'd met in some time and reminded him of his mother who had heaped kindness and love on the young Silas particularly when so many started to make fun of him. He so missed his mother and he absolutely missed kindness.

It was a fine day so the opportunity to break their fast was enjoyable. Maud told him about Stratford, and the inn, and about Will the landlord, how they met, their relatives, their relatives - relatives, the weather, their animals, how you make a pie, how you make two pies, how to serve ale and some other stuff as he couldn't concentrate any more. She then broke away from the mundane and said,

'I don't know how much of this "mission" is in your head or is real, but people around here will kill for less than a shilling so I wouldn't say too much if I were you, although, I have to say, Richard is every bit a gentleman and I imagine he'll be helpful.'

'Truth is Maud' he said, 'I've only got a little information so it's been very frustrating. I have, honestly, been commissioned by a prominent member of the church and

I'm assured that the task at hand is of the greatest significance. This is all I've got'. Silas took out the smallest piece of parchment which had on it a few words in Latin. Most were incomplete.

'Ha ha ha!' Maud laughed so loud that Annie's head whipped around and the cart wobbled. 'It's not much is it?!' said Maud.

'I know' replied Silas 'But can you make any sense of it?'

'Sense? What on earth would make you think I could read lovey?' She laughed again. 'I'll tell you for nothing it's not very old, I thought it was going to be some ancient map drawn by Romans or sommat.'

'Oh no' said Silas, 'we know it's been written in the last few weeks, that's why the Abbot said it was so urgent'. Oh no, he thought, said too much again. It was a habit he could do little about. There was, however, one personal secret Silas would never divulge so he congratulated himself for getting through another day where that said secret wasn't shared with the world.

'Abbot is it?! thought 'enery and Cromwell had done away with all of them.' Silas went quiet, he'd been told to use discretion and, again, wasn't.

'Oh don't worry dear, I'm not one to say anything but you will take care won't you? Keep your tales to yourself for a while – eh?' He nodded, realising that this woman had a big heart and couldn't care less if there was a revolution as long as the pies were ready for 6 o'clock every evening.

'Thank you, Maud'.

'Pleasure… My Lord' she said respectfully,

The incessant, but surprisingly pleasant conversation, along with this woman's company, made the journey seem short. They had taken a shortcut through a forest and it had Silas thinking of the challenging terrain he had encountered on his journey from York. Perhaps I am brave after all he considered, realising fully for the first time the extreme risks he had taken on this current mission alone. There can't be many people who would take this on, he reasoned, leaving him feeling a little daft rather than brave.

Annie stopped suddenly of her own accord and snapped Silas out of his deep thought. They had emerged from the coppice and the summer light was instantly warming and inspiring. Even from a distance of half a mile, he was overwhelmed by the scale of Richard's farm at Snitterfield and, as they got closer, he gained a better understanding of how busy this time of year was for those engaged in husbandry.

'He must be very rich' said Silas. Maud laughed.

'Well, he may be rich in many ways, and he's certainly blessed, but he's a tenant farmer! He doesn't own the land.'

'Oh I see…then why do you come so far to buy produce Maud?' he replied.

'Well', she said, 'he's family and, if I'm totally honest with you Silas, he can be generous if you know what I mean.' She winked. 'Our little enterprise wouldn't survive without his "goodwill" and, we all love to see Richard and the family whenever we can'. She thought for a moment. 'I doubt very much that he has your buried treasure but I can guarantee you the most satisfying welcome and fresh food on that table, my lad, as soon as they know we are on our way'. This day just gets better and better, thought Silas.

Richard greeted them at the gates.

'Who've you got here then Maud?' he said with a broad smile on his face.

'This, Richard, is my very good friend Lord Silas.' (This time her wink was directed at Richard away from Silas's glance). Richard had a quick look up and down at the visual statement that Silas's gait, expression and clothes were making and he understood straight away.

'Welcome my Lord!' he said and even bowed. 'Will you be joining us for something to eat?'

'Well…' he hesitated, 'Well…and if it's not too much trouble…erm…that would be just fine Sir' Silas said. I shouldn't be calling him Sir if I'm a Lord, he thought, reminding him that his life as an impostor often created more problems than it solved. He craned his neck and took an audible intake of breath.

'Of course, we would love to dine with you on this fine day my good man'. His eyes then danced around their faces to see if he had pulled it off. They were impressed leaving Silas puffed up and proud. Before they finished chatting, the whole family had temporarily left their chores and run to come and meet the stranger. The children warmed to the celebrity instantly. Children and animals just seem to have a sixth sense when it comes to trusting people. They could see that Silas had a good soul and he did, unquestionably have a good soul, it was just a shame that such a twit was at the front of the queue when God was dispensing it.

Silas was introduced to Richard's wife, Abigail and then his children: Anna, Margaret, Robert and Richard and was then informed that there were 4 more in the house. They had 8 children under the age of seven which had Silas thinking that the country life must be very good for you. That very day, Abigail, having been up since sunrise, had dressed the children, fed the family, made butter and cheese, tended to the chickens, geese and pigs and she wasn't even halfway through it. She was visibly a lot younger than her husband, he being in his fifties and her looking as if she was still in her twenties.

They talked, they eat, they drank, they eat again and they talked some more. Then they played games, Richard playing Henry V with the rest of the family performing as the English army at Agincourt. Maud had to remind everyone of the time and asked Silas if it was alright to share his story with Richard. Silas, in response, made it known that he couldn't wait to see this island. However, Richard was a little confused, he wasn't sure if this was being done to placate an idiot or it was a serious request. Either way, he was fine with it and pointed out the impressive lake and the very small and insignificant mound in the centre with an equally unimpressive bush growing out of it. Moreover, he offered to take his three eldest as well as Silas in their small rowing boat to "dig for treasure!"

Silas's heart was banging out of his chest for, in truth, he didn't know what to expect but one thing was for sure, he had complete faith in this being the right place. Once there, it became clear that, realistically, there was only one spot free enough from roots where it would be possible to dig. Anna and Margaret were given the task of digging. After ten minutes they had struck something hard. The excitement was evident on the face of young Robert and also on the face of, the even more immature, Silas. Richard's expression didn't change. The absolute revelation of what this was, seemed to take forever with Anna now giving a continuous commentary.

'It's something dead…no…no…it's a knife…no a book…a ship's anchor!' Then she pulled it out. There was silence as the object was unrecognisable, although the tension was palpable. Silas was sure that Richard was trying not to laugh which left him very confused but suddenly the silence and the tension were abruptly concluded.

'My box!!! Robert screamed, 'You buried my box?!! I've been looking everywhere for it.' Ann, Margaret and dad were in tears and bent completely double with laughter. Silas didn't have a clue what was going on.

Richard had made a wonderful wooden box for Robert to keep his little wooden figures in but Robert didn't look after it. In fact, he hadn't even noticed it was missing. So, what better opportunity to finalise their conspiratorial prank than during this unexpected expedition.

'Oh, I'm so sorry Silas.' Richard could see the deep disappointment on Silas's face, not comprehending how serious this was.

'You won't find anything here, no one goes on this land or lake, but us. Come on, let's go back and you can drink some more before you journey back.' Robert was happy to take his box to be cleaned up and, eventually and reluctantly, joined in the jape.

Somewhere amidst the disappointment, Silas realised that he had let himself follow an obsession and, again, felt a little stupid. He felt stupid quite a lot. Wonder why? Other thoughts flooded into his head. The King himself was presently setting off on his progress to York. This mystery of his had to be solved before the King arrived, it had to be. The Cataclysm was imminent. I'm no wiser, thought Silas. However, he tried not to panic as he had no wish to ignore this wonderful family that were showing him so much kindness and, as he did, a butterfly descended and sat on his right shoulder and folded its wings vertically to indicate that it would stay a while. That's the second time this week that's happened, he thought.

It was a credit to them all that nobody made fun of Silas following the dig and Richard tried as sincerely as possible to offer suggestions about this mysterious island. As the cart was loaded, and Annie happily joined them for her jaunt back, they were passed some bread and berries. What abundance, thought Silas. He turned and saw Abigail offering him the kindest smile and wave.

'Now we've met, we're friends forever My Lord and, if you can get help with your writing you must write to Richard and let us know how you get on' she said. Silas suggested that they pray together which particularly touched Abigail as all his petitions were for the family before him and his new friend Maud rather than himself. Richard personally returned Annie from the stables and hitched her to the cart. There were many goodbyes and Silas felt the warmth of friendship as they trundled away.

'What lovely people' Silas said to Maud.

'As they say, once you've met a Shakespeare you've got a friend for life' she replied. What a funny name, Silas thought.

2: Edward Fawkes

York, July 1541

York! At last, I had arrived in this breath-taking northern City, a pulsating paradox of beauty and filth. As I approached the walls that led to Micklegate that were seemingly endless both skyward and to my left and right, I became overwhelmed by the constant traffic trudging through the mud, blood and excrement that flowed continuously from the town. Men on horseback, traders carrying goods, beasts galore and pilgrims that had come from far and wide. Once at the gate known as Micklegate Bar, I intended to follow someone through as my destination was close by. Absolutely everything here was dominated by the huge and beautiful, cream coloured, magnesium limestone, Cathedral known to all as York Minster as it was, by definition, both. Even from this distance, this was a heavenly vision, proof for certain that a higher power was unquestionably the architect of all things. It was a statement about the order of things in Tudor England and, although undoubtedly a symbol of religious power, it offered solace, redemption and security even when viewed from five miles distance. Uncannily, the Cathedral stood as a City within a City having its own boundaries, observing its own laws, having its own shops and even employing its own constable. The many satellite churches impressed me as did the tall buildings and guild halls now adopting brick, stone and glass and owned by the most prosperous in the City but it's all a completely alien place to me. York was a patchwork of bright colours, architectural delights and some of the worst smells imaginable. There was a lively hustle and bustle. Generally speaking, everyone I encountered either held a professional position, had a trade or simply worked for someone.

I found people polite as they interacted with each other and they had a sense of place. This was a well-ordered society with a King at the top and, not long ago the Pope would have been as equally important in the English psyche, but this has changed dramatically in recent years due to the Reformation. When asked, most people could tell you that the King was the eighth Henry and was known typically for changing his thoughts, views (and certainly his mind) particularly whenever it involved his spouses. They only knew what he looked like from his face on coins, but certainly, here in the distant north, people were little impressed by him. There was a historical and measurable contempt between North and South, Northerners almost considered as barbarians by their London counterparts but conveniently important when taxes or wars cropped up as they often did.

So, that's the tourist version. So far so good.

Conversely, my most immediate impressions of this great City were the smells. If I'm honest with you it's the part I struggled to deal with most as there was little escape or relief. I looked behind me beyond the City walls and could see animal remains and a variety of Renaissance litter and faeces that had either been discarded from buckets and barrels or planted in situ. Don't presume for a moment all the waste is from animals. Anything unwanted had been left outside the walls and it festered there. A mother and daughter skipped along the City wall passing a man artistically expressing his relief as he had a dump, but they barely flinched. I bloody flinched. I was out of there in an instant. He was no distance from the moat's public privy but had clearly decided this was a more suitable spot. The overwhelming smell of burning helped a little to defuse all this but not much. There seemed to be a lot of burning. There were a lot of smells. I didn't like the smells.

I could see some citizens that were sensible enough to adopt petals and posies but, as I couldn't get hold of any, my initial encounters were continuously unpleasant. Bacteria in all its glorious forms was here and having an all-night party but simultaneously completely absent in the imagination of the sixteenth-century public.

The church was incredibly important in the mid-sixteenth century but, although I saw some priests I encountered just a single monk who appeared lost and completely at the end of his tether. People were avoiding him. The Reformation, which led to the destruction of monasteries, abbeys and convents had turned England upside down economically and socially and was, in part, the focus of my mission.

I did have time to acclimatise. It was part of my job and part of my mission to blend in. The warm day did little to disperse the thick soup of odours but it did raise my spirits. I am small so go relatively unnoticed as I make my way to my assigned destination, a gruelling journey of two hundred yards, although I am increasingly aware of my vulnerability. And, this also means I manage to avoid loud citizens selling anything from a pigs tongue to a room for the night. I instantly recognise the northern dialect although the variety of accents and tongues (not pigs) are astounding. Remnants of Norman French, interjections of Latin and some words and phrases I simply did not understand, despite my research, are used commonly.

The Barbican and high walls of Micklegate left me in no doubt of the present and historical significance of York. I scuttled in behind a trader who was granted access to the City. Strangely, once inside, I felt secure. There was a warmth unconnected to the summer's day that told me that this would become my home. I could see wooden buildings stacked together at right angles to the City walls in which tradesmen spent their long days grafting.

I slowly progressed along the footings totally engaged by the surprisingly harmonious sounds of hard labour. The third lean-to along belonged to a middle-aged man with an obvious but painful gait that had probably advanced significantly this last five years. A lifetime of carpentry in all weathers, temperatures and altogether unpleasant conditions had left his breathing, stature and temper in decline. I say middle-aged, that means around thirty.

I recognised him immediately, he is wearing a woollen jerkin covered by a well-worn, leather apron. Grumbling as he placed a large piece of timber, that looked as though it wouldn't be out of place on the hull of a warship, his workshop was strewn with part finished objects in wood ranging from candlesticks to ornate wooden panels. He had probably got little to show for his years of service but this is what he knew and he had food and somewhere to sleep. For most people in 1541 life was no more complicated than this. Death would come but it did to everyone. Death was a regular experience and, for most, simply an expectation.

His sudden cough was so loud that it startled me and the fart that accompanied it sent me retreating two of the yards it had taken me half an hour to travel. There was a pile of sawdust with a cobweb stretched across it like a damask curtain in which I found solace and comfort for I had no interest in Godwin. However, my timing was perfect as I could hear whistling outside. It was an immature and timeless whistle but a happy one and shortly a face appeared at the shutter. It was good to set eyes on someone so young, energetic and full of optimism.

Although Godwin made no attempt to look at his young visitor, there was an exchange in conversation. The phrases most recognisable were "late again" and "cheeky bastard" but it was clear that it was all water off a duck's back to the lad. The lad was Edward Fawkes, nine years old. He was from a family that was already respected in the City. His father, William, was a notary and advocate at the cathedral and it is expected that one day Edward will succeed him. However, his father, William insisted that Edward had an education that involved getting his hands dirty, for soon he will attend grammar school. So there he was. He had dark bushy hair and wore hose, everyday legging wear for men and boys, and in front of his skirt, he had fashioned a small purse into a codpiece clearly to give the impression that he was older. Truthfully, it looked a bit comical. His doublet, although slightly too big, was impressive but it was evident that all his clothes were slightly tattered and put on today just for manual work. He wore a hat. Every man wore a hat, it would have been considered impolite not to. His smile was heart-warmingly innocent and it instantly declared sincerity and trust to a stranger like me. Turning up was no chore for him and there was something about Edward that told you he simply loved life and any degree of cursing or reprimand from Godwin had little effect.

Again, they exchanged words and it became clear that Godwin was happy to have a break and leave his young apprentice in charge.

Of all the things I had to do over the next few months, my next task was to be the most difficult. I waited until he ceased humming and whistling and then waited a bit longer.

Eventually, he drew a breath to launch into another tuneless ditty.

'Edward' I whisper. 'Do not be alarmed. I am a friend, but when you see me it will come as a great shock to you so, do not shout out'. Even to my very own ears, this sounded ridiculously cheesy and I visibly cringed. I felt as though I should have had wings and talking to shepherds on Christmas Eve.

There was a silence that seemed endless. Should I say it again? I thought. Wasn't like this in rehearsal. More silence. So much so, I could practically hear him thinking.

I opened my little mouth for take-two but, as I did, he whipped around, saw me and, quite unimpressed, he quietly said,

'God's teeth. A speaking mouse.'

This response left me somewhat dumbfounded. How many speaking bloody mice has he confronted? I thought, and even though I was immensely grateful that Edward wasn't startled, and even more grateful that he didn't make a big fuss, I couldn't prevent myself from thinking, surely I haven't chosen the village idiot? Sadly, that encounter, to my chagrin, was yet to come. Our eyes met and I realised that this was going to be much easier than I imagined. Edward and I have our first conversation, it isn't long but I'm astonished at how compliant he is. He did struggle somewhat with the notion of confidentiality but eventually, the penny dropped, I informed him that, for now, I could not communicate with anyone else but him and that he mustn't reveal this peculiar discovery.

I instantly found Edward charming and he put me at ease. On hearing that we were on a mission "commissioned at the highest level" he seemed to grow a couple of inches and happy to do anything I asked of him.

'I'll make you a little home' he said. I was delighted by his kindness but also immediately concerned that I would speedily become his pet so I interrupted him.

'I have to ask much more of you Edward. I need a small vented box in which you can secret me, if and when, I travel I also need to have somewhere to hide and something useful to do when you're not around'.

'I've got it' he said, 'there's a space behind that wall no bigger than a wardrobe, I'll make sure you get food and water and I'll fit it up as a workshop with tools you can use!' He laughed. I laughed. It was amusing. The idea that I would have a bespoke mouse-sized workshop was quaint, to say the least, but, if he could pull this off, it would be perfect. Already it was as if he knew my brief, part of our task would be to fashion a Tudor Rose boss out of timber in secret. A boss was a decoration placed where beams intersected in the ceiling vaults of the Minster and, ultimately, this simple ornament would make a dramatic difference to our mission. I did have the skills but hadn't a clue what I could or could not do with these newly acquired claws.

'Excellent!' I said 'and a shutter on the window… and a bucket with water in…and a lid…to be replaced daily!' I thought it may be rude to mention smells in case he was offended. He happily agreed. The only thing left to impart that, contrary to all rule of nature, was that he had before him a talking field mouse that wasn't nocturnal. So far, this was easy and I had no reason to doubt either his simplicity or sincerity. I had learned two things about my new home: I liked Edward, I hated smells. Our conversation was cut short as the familiar cough, groans and farts of Godwin could be heard approaching the workshop. Edward speedily hid me in the space aforementioned. My workshop, a dark, dirty and dank hole was, for now, my home.

3: Brother Bernard

Northumberland, May 1541

Bernard scrambled up the rocky slope cautiously, fully realising the danger he was in. The incline, now covered with grass, smooth stone and sand was not easy to negotiate. It was a fine day with a cool sea breeze that did little to temper his conflicting and overwhelming emotions. Physical pursuit was certainly not his forte but he was determined to scale this daunting and familiar hill to see what lay at the apex and, in recent months he had been no stranger to physical challenges. Soldiers. He could hear guards engaged in idle banter about their boredom and joking about why anyone would think that this sodarse of a place (as they referred to it) was of any value. This angered Bernard and also broke his heart, this place to him was as important to English Christianity as anywhere on Earth.

One of the King's morons was below to his right so Bernard lay still periodically as the said soldier turned to empty his bladder on the beach. The overwhelming feeling of disgust and injustice only helped to propel Bernard to the top and he landed flat, exhausted, on the wet grass. The abbey was still there and, more or less, intact but constantly guarded because it now belonged to the crown. A handful of fat and pretty useless guards protected it although there was little left to secure as all the contents had been sold off. The Reformation in which Henry the eighth had appointed himself Supreme Head of the Church of England had caused havoc to the religious community and would, eventually, affect society as a whole. Bernard could see surveyors in the distance, confirming that the rumours were true, the abbey would be demolished to build a nearby fortress. He then knelt in prayer despite the danger his exposure would bring.

He put himself completely in the hands of God and he feared no more. As it rode on the wind, his Latin prayer sang to the Heavens.

'Dear Lord, I bear my soul to Thee and offer my most humble self as Thy most committed servant ready to give all I have to Thee Lord. You are above all things and know the secrets of all hearts even these misguided creatures that surround me. They have lost their way and I pray for their souls. Our Holy Houses are being destroyed as I speak and I have gained knowledge of even worse to come. What I have discovered about the imminent deeds of this bearded and lustful devil incarnate will corrupt the very sacrifice made by our Lord Jesus Christ for all time. I beseech Thee Lord to bestow on me the strength and wisdom I need to thwart this evil plan and avoid the Cataclysm. I live constantly in Thine promised hope and love and accept the plan you have for me. In the name of The Father, The Son and The Holy Ghost. Amen'.

He could hear his petition echo and carry across the hill but then it suddenly stopped. Everything stopped. He felt a sudden change. Bernard thought he had hit his head on something and was then aware that he couldn't see. An uncanny dizziness overcame him. His limbs had paralysed leaving him completely confused. But, he was moving. Am I falling? he thought and then realised that he was both spinning and sliding. Glimpses of light seeped in, the landscape swiftly delivering flashing snapshots as his body violently changed direction and his eyelids flickered. Bernard tried to make sense of it but could not. His heart told him that this experience was not of God. And then he blacked out.

Bernard was right. One of the soldiers, astonished that this stupid old monk had the audacity to return to the priory, had reached for his crossbow and fired his least valuable quarrel (a short bolt) and mercilessly shot it at close range into Bernard. The momentum sent the monk reeling backwards and left the company of guards guffawing.

The soldier that was on the beach had now scaled the hill but flatly refused to go back down after Bernard leaving his colleague, the culprit, to negotiate the slope downwards utilising his ridiculously oversized upper body and skinny legs. It may have been wise of him to ask his colleague why he had returned. In this part of England, the tide was renowned for coming in at a pace and, by the time the guard reached the bottom, his feet were in the sea and was rising up the face of the cliff by the second.

'Papist bugger'll be washed out to sea by now' he shouted up to the increasingly disinterested thugs and made a complete fool of himself trying to return to the top. The respect due to him by his conspirators was so little that thirty minutes later he arrived back at the abbey face completely exhausted, filthy and wet and they laughed incessantly. This was so funny, they thought, that the best thing to do was push him back down again. Nothing was taken seriously by these thugs and they cared little for the old monk.

When Bernard opened his eyes it was dark except for moonlight. He was now certain about what had happened to him. He had a bolt through his left shoulder and was scratched and bruised by the fall. He hurt everywhere but instinctively put his fate in God's hands, grateful that he had lived and acknowledged that he had been through worse and survived. He had been fortunate enough to slide down the slope in a narrow stream of mud, grass and sand that had dropped him into the mouth of a cave that was still over the waterline. My box, he thought. Where is the box? He carried a box with him which was of great value. If it, or its contents, were damaged then all was lost. He strained to feel around his waist. Not there. It was dark and, although leaning in any direction was painful, he felt around the cave floor. There! He could feel it and the sound that then emanated from it, as he clasped it near to him, assured him that all was well.

It would be hard not to respect Bernard for he was a Christian. No. What a mean to say is that he was a follower of Christ, which is different. The Reformation exposed systemic corruption in the existing church and there was a consensus, almost overnight, that all monks were up to no good and there was, certainly, evidence to support this belief. But Bernard? Not so. Many like him were resolutely devout and served society in so many beneficial ways. Brother Bernard loved Christ and he loved what Christ had taught. Love your enemies, forgive everyone, offer redemption, heal the sick and feed the poor and he did not doubt that all mankind was on the same journey, preparing for a place in a better world. Although he resented the Reformation he understood and accepted that, within the church, men had tried to replace God and the kaleidoscope of nonsense created by mankind, not least the idea of purgatory, left him in a minority fighting for the principles that his faith had been based upon. His sixteenth-century version of inclusion and diversity made him very unpopular with those who wrote the rules and who had used them to control the populace. He knew, without any doubt, that within the Gospels were the answers to society's problems.

Although his name was taken from the very founder of the Cistercian monks, Bernard was a devoted Benedictine and carefully followed the rules of St Benedict particularly those relating to humility, community and hospitality. He was a man of complete spiritual integrity and he would fight for what he believed in until his very mortal coil was no more. He knew now that this was getting nearer by the hour. He even understood why he had so quickly become a figure of fun to the idle soldiers. Brother Bernard was old and, as only months ago, he had been taken in the Tower itself, his body was now a burden, broken and weak. He continued to wear his dark monk's habit now appearing to sympathise with his physical condition as it was ragged, torn and dirty. There was no need for him to don his capuchon as he wanted to feel the breeze on his face and absorb all that surrounded him, possibly for the last time. It was folded back along his shoulders supporting his long grey hair and beard.

Depending on your stance, Brother Bernard was a rebel. Refusing to sign the act of succession and denying himself a "keep quiet" pension, he had been to hell and back just to see his beloved priory again. He had been a fugitive since the imposition of Cromwell's treason act that had seen major political players, not least Thomas More, put to death. His final quest was to rally support at this abbey where he had hoped, naïvely, for ecclesiastical support and, if that was not possible, to issue his final petition to God on the site. His hopes of praying within the walls dashed, he was still content, secure in the knowledge that God answered all prayers for all patient men and women. He now had one last task before him. He prayed that he could be given strength and enough time to carry this out before he was, once again, detected but, as he did, he fell back into a dark sleep.

'Coo, coo, coo'. A familiar and soothing sound came

from the box and awoke him, it was day again. Faith is alright, he thought, but I must take her out and look her over. He clawed the box nearer to him, the sand resisted his pull but soon it was next to his right leg. It wasn't by any means a small box, looking like it had been made for two birds rather than one. He pushed the box up onto his knee and, with his right thumb, released the simple, single clasp on the front. He gently grasped his dear pigeon, Faith, and did his best to look at her from every angle possible. She was fine. Bernard never simply thought that God looked after him, he was certain of it. He accepted the struggles and cruelties of life but knew that, despite this, the Almighty's support in all situations was consistent. He kissed faith.

'Coo coo, coo' she seemed to respond and he placed her carefully back in her box.

He thought about the boat. He then decided to carefully examine his wound. There was very little blood, externally at least, but he knew that to live, the bolt had to come out and there was no chance of that. His biggest enemy now was the pain he felt and the immobility that came with it. Even so, he attempted to crawl, securing the pigeon box to his back with his waist rope. Simple as it sounds, this took him almost thirty minutes utilising his good arm. His small but barely efficient rowing boat had been secreted away from the view of any hilltop guards and he knew also that he couldn't be seen from where he was. If he could get to the boat and then to the mainland, complete his final task, nothing would matter after that point. He accepted that death was imminent. Yes, the mainland. For this was an island, the same island Silas would later seek and Brother Bernard was, indeed, the Abbott that Silas had referred to although he wasn't, and never would be, an Abbot.

His crawl was pathetic. Even the most hardened hearts would have wept for Bernard as he barely moved at all in the direction of the boat but, ultimately, he did reach it. He threw himself into the vessel, released the box and prayed again as he untied the boat. Even he knew that a miracle empowering him to row was expecting too much. However, providence did slowly float the boat on the tide toward the nearby mainland shore.

By this time the guards had seen the boat and set off in speedy pursuit. You may ask yourself why on earth they would be bothered. Was it vengeance? Had they been tasked with capturing this solitary monk? Nothing so straightforward. The quarrel had to be accounted for and retrieved. Any bluster about shooting down a rebel monk would have to be accompanied by some evidence especially when using what was now regarded as a hunting weapon. These soldiers were sparsely supplied and would very much have liked the idea of owning an arquebus, or hagbuts as Englishmen called them, between them but guns were so new that only regular and specialist guards of the King would be trained in their use. Added to that was the reality that they were useless in the rain and it seemed to rain almost all the time on this northern island. So, confidently, after the bolt, they went as it was easier to leave their incompetency hidden and pretend this whole episode never happened. They too had a boat, larger, more efficient and they could row well. As Bernard reached the shore, they had almost caught up with him. The same over-eager guard took out his crossbow.

'You idiot! Don't make the same mistake again' said his superior.

'He's within reach' said the older and only slightly wiser soldier. Bernard threw himself, box in hand, out onto the beach. With no hope of going any further, he ensured that the message, that he had scrawled on a small piece of parchment the day before, was in the cylinder attached to Faith's leg. He crudely tied it on leaving it flapping and unsecured. He held her gently for the last time and bade her give flight and instantly she was away over the two

31

boats and leaving a message of her own on the guard's heads. Faith sped skyward and Bernard's soul floated gently upwards after her.

He had found his deserved peace at last.

When they reached him, the two guards angrily grabbed his corpse by the throat.

'Bastard's dead' said the first.

'Cut out the bolt' said his colleague and he did so in the most grotesque manner. Once he had cut into Bernard's, still warm, flesh the anger grew within him and he started to curse, spit, stab, cut, kick and thump like a man deranged. The other guard simply watched at first and then laughed.

'Strip him of his clothes!' he shouted and then took up some branches and broke them into equal lengths of about a foot long. They used these to deliver the final, abominable humiliation leaving the most appalling sight and Bernard's remains drenched in blood. The quarrel was washed in the seawater and returned to its home. For them, everything was back to normal after a slightly eventful day.

Three fishermen watched the whole episode from a distance but did not, and could not, do anything to help. However, as the soldiers disappeared into the distance, the fishermen ran over to Bernard and covered his remains with nets and his torn habit. They didn't know who he was but it was clear that he was one of the many monks that for decades had helped to feed their poor and tend to the sick in their village. Already hurt because of the intrusion of these southern thugs onto their soil, they chose to do what they could for Bernard's body.

The youngest, Peter, wept. He looked upon a Godly man and, although he had little knowledge of state or church, he simply knew that what these southern guards had done was wrong. Very soon Bernard was decently covered, his bodily state restored with just his head showing. Peter mumbled some Latin words he'd heard when last rites were read for his father as he lay dying. His efforts were child-like, a mix of English and Latin, and rambled somewhat, but there were love and power in his monologue. He asked for passage and acceptance of this brother's soul in Heaven and asked for forgiveness of his sins. When he had run out of ideas, Peter looked up and saw that the two older, hardened, fishermen were also weeping. One of them added a passage he had remembered from Matthew's gospel,

'Blessed are those who are persecuted because of righteousness, for theirs is the kingdom of heaven. Blessed are you when people insult you, persecute you and falsely say all kinds of evil against you because of me.'

As they carried him to the dunes for a Christian burial, Peter noticed a small blank piece of parchment that fell from Bernard's habit. He picked it up and slipped it into one of his pockets, simply as a sign of respect. The others didn't comment.

Brother Bernard would have been more than satisfied with this impromptu requiem mass and particularly amused at the idea of Peter the fisherman burying him.

4: Elspeth and Wynnfrith

York, July 1541

My relationship with young Edward was as solid as I could have wished it to be. I had now had over a week of endless questions, very few of which I had answered. Give him credit though, he'd been landed with a talking mouse waxing lyrical about state, church and a dangerous mission, so questions in abundance were expected.

We had made considerable progress. My workshop was magnificent. This amazing boy had laboured every spare minute to furnish me with comforts and had fashioned various tools that I could use to, initially, carve and paint the Tudor Rose boss. When the streets were clear on a summer's morning, I could fully open my shutter and look upon the beauty of York. I was even getting used to some of the smells. Well, a bit. I would work when Godwin wasn't around and discovered my new love of sleeping which, seemingly, comes with the being a mouse thing. Our security, however, was brittle. If discovered, too many questions would be asked about the workshop which would have been destroyed probably with me along with it. It was unbearable to think that Edward was in danger and I frequently felt guilty about this.

I had divulged some facts to Edward and, in complete honesty, he now knew as much as I did. Our mission was becoming more urgent by the day. The King had left London over two weeks ago to head north and, ultimately, would arrive in York. This wasn't the King, his horse and an overnight bag, by the way. He had an entourage of thousands meaning that the whole court, and the army, what it owned and what it ate was on a progress northwards, in part, to assert his authority following rebellions against his religious supremacy. Our work had to be concluded by the time he landed. Edward truly was a blessing as he followed every do and don't I threw at him and I had total faith that I could go about my business using him as my mouthpiece. So far, no one else knew of the talking mouse. That was to change dramatically if only I would have known what was to come over the next few weeks.

It was Tuesday morning at six o'clock. A fine day, but it had rained the night before so there was a serene rising mist that filtered the sunlight into a broad, warm, pastel palettes. At last, I was going to get out of my non-proverbial hole for a while. We had set off from the workshop, Ed hastily on foot and me in a little box filled with straw with some holes for air and some other holes so that I could see what was going on. Getting out was a treat and I was now getting my very own tour of the City, albeit bumpy and without commentary. We set off downhill along Micklegate, past the once-thriving Benedictine monastery on our right, now sadly destroyed, and over the river into thick of it. I now had a spectacular view of the Minster, a marvel of medieval architecture with so much to look at that my eyes could not keep still. Over five hundred feet long and over two hundred and thirty feet high it boasted buttresses, stain glass windows, towers, grotesques and gargoyles. I truly was in awe of it.

I was, at last, acclimatising a little to the odours and the visual contrasts. However, I couldn't cope with the swaying motion of my box, let alone Ed's incessant whistling, and soon I had a headache.

'Stop bloody swinging about so much!' I shouted in desperation.

'Quiet mouse or everyone will hear' he said with authority. God no, I thought, he's getting strict with his "pet" mouse.

'Nobody can hear me over the horses and tradesmen shouting, and don't get stroppy with me lad, just stop swinging the damn thing!' He laughed and swung more. Little bugger, thought I. I haven't seen him like this before, he's getting his own back. Or so he thought until there were four shades of puke and poo running out of pet mousey's little box and down his skinny leg. He knew we would be meeting some ladies soon so he promptly stopped to change my straw and clean up a little. This got him back at my eye level.

'Stop being a smartarse and get us there.' I insisted gruffly. He laughed again and took more care.

I was able to direct him in and out of narrow snickleways and down toward the Minster via the Shambles where the butchers were already at their work. The City had received orders to clean up for the King's visit and there was evidence of some loyal citizens doing just that by putting sand down but, for the greater part, northerners didn't give a shit about fat Harry's weekend break in the north. We arrived at Bootham Bar. We were outside the precinct of the Minster, although we stopped to peep into that other world beyond the liberty which was that of the

Minster and its populace.

Here, there was a mixture of artisan workshops, small dwellings and washing houses. Contrary to my belief about Tudor hygiene, there was seemingly enough washing of clothes taking place to provide continuous work for washerwomen. So, we were about to visit a busy, but relatively domestic, wash house.

'This one?' asked Edward.

'Yes, just walk in and remember everything I've told you.' He was, unsurprisingly, very nervous. This was a dark, cramped and damp space and made my little workshop look like a palace. There were buckets a plenty, some filled, some half-filled with water from the river. Even I could work out that this would be quite a haul daily for these two industrious ladies and that filtering out the filth would have taken twice as long.

'Morning good ladies' said Edward very politely.

'Can't take any more today my lad, take us a week to shift this lot' came the first, sharp, reply

'Oh, I'm not here for washing.' He now started to sound a little nervous. Edward, like me, was a little taken aback by what he'd seen. I knew full well the identity of these two young women and it turned out that Edward had seen Wynnfrith before when he was very young. What struck me more than anything was the realisation that I was, in every respect (except for speech), a field mouse so, unlike young Edward, looked upon these two with a completely objective eye and the virtues of both shone like the sun itself but in unique ways.

I had the idea that they were sisters but I wasn't sure. They were certainly looking, behaving and speaking as an experienced duo and were also my assigned contact at this point in my journey. However, they knew nothing of me so this, particularly through an interpreter, was going to be a challenge. Elspeth, on the left, as we entered the washhouse, was the tallest. She was slim with exposed, and extremely short, blonde hair and her whole demeanour spoke of authority and confidence which possibly gave away too much in that she also appeared educated and out of place in this glorified shed. Around twenty-five years of age, you could easily believe her if she told you that she was a direct descendant of the Vikings of York, then called Jorvik, and everything about her spoke reliability. Wynnfrith was the smaller of the two, pretty and dark-haired, again uncovered but long and tied at the back. Usually, this would inform us that these were both unmarried women. Wynnfrith didn't speak as much but was not the least held back by her apparent palsy. Not the palsy that was often used as a generic term for illness at this time but palsy of the brain, possibly caused at birth. Sixteenth-century society would have been cruel to little Wynnfrith but, to see her, you wouldn't know it. She too was confident and, even though she had some involuntary movements and her speech was mildly affected, it did not keep her from saying what she thought. From a mouse's point of view, these two women were immediately inspiring and I was eagerly looking forward to collaborating with them.

'Hop it and take your shitty mouse with you' said Wynnfrith. Perhaps the collaboration will take some time, I thought. In fact, I was a little hurt until I saw her snigger. Wynnfrith was going to be the cheeky one. Thank God, I thought, we're going to need some light relief on this quest.

Edward took a deep breath and announced,

'I'm here to talk about the Cataclysm.' Whoa!! I thought. No messing about Ed and, despite the fact I told him not to use that word, he had decided to lead with it. At least he'll get a response. Almost before he had finished this brash sentence, Wynnfrith had slammed the door shut and locked us in.

'Now I'm only going to say this once to you lad so it had better sink in. You don't want, no, you really don't want to, be using that word anywhere, especially in public and not with such drama' said Elspeth.

'But…' Ed nearly got another sentence out but she immediately interrupted him

'I'm doing the talking now young man and you're doing the listening. If you turn around, I'll let you out and we'll say no more about it, let's just say I have no idea what you're talking about.' Wynnfrith interjected,

'You're Fawkes's lad aren't you? What you doing sneaking around washrooms talking such nonsense? What would your father say?'

'I have a contact, a secret contact, who is extremely knowledgeable and can help with your mission' muttered Ed nervously.

'I suppose it's the mouse' joked Wynnfrith. Elspeth laughed.

'You'll have to do a lot better than that young un' said Wynnfrith closing in on him.

From my preparation, I believed that the sisters would be more receptive to supporting us but admired their unwillingness to trust strangers. At this point, Ed showed some initiative. He took out a small piece of linen with three words written on it. The three of them exchanged bewildered glances that said "you can read?" from one side and "you can write?" from the other. There was, albeit completely silent, a conversation between the two ladies. They suddenly became animated, each securely grabbing one side of an old barrel that gave the impression of having been there for decades. Underneath was straw, lots of it, and when this was brushed aside, a door in the floor was revealed. Elspeth grabbed the ring handle and pulled it up whilst Wynnfrith lit two candles and beckoned Ed to go down the steps.

'Leave the rodent here' she said. However, there was no hesitation from Edward,

'He comes with me or I'm not coming.' He had said this with such an air of importance that they, again, both looked at each other, shrugged and beckoned us down. I could feel Edward's fear. This was not good and a little too secretive for my liking. As they had asked Edward to go first I couldn't help thinking that they were either going to lock us down there or that there was someone else lurking below.

Once in the cellar, they sat us down which helped to calm us both a little.

'I don't know what you know' said Elspeth 'but you are touching upon the most significant threat we have probably ever seen in England.'

'Or beyond' said Wynnfrith. 'So, if we risk talking all sorts of nonsense with everyone who walks past with a rat, we'd be dead within the week. You're going to have to tell us everything you know first lad.' Ed opened his mouth, hopefully to deliver what I had trained him to impart, but was interrupted by the most outrageous sounds from above. Bang! Bang! Bang! Someone was at the washhouse door. More than one person. Then shouting.

'Open up in the name of the Sheriff of York!' This was heard clearly in the cellar. I confess that I went completely cold. There were two Sheriffs, William Watson and William Harper so this could have been either or both and I had no wish to find out which. We were getting nowhere and to be caught so soon by law officials would be a tragedy. My next thought was of Edward, he didn't deserve any trouble, I'd practically guaranteed that we would be able to maintain a low profile throughout our investigation. Crash! The door had been forced open. What followed was a great deal of shouting and movement of heavy footsteps and I knew, as the door could not be covered whilst we were still down here, they would soon find us.

'Here, a trap door.' Right on cue, I thought and I heard the soldier grab the handle. We were petrified, hardly breathing and now completely in the dark except for a crack of light through the cellar door as the candles had been blown out by Elspeth. Creeeak! This would be it.

'He's here!' said one of the voices. We were stunned. Who was he referring to?

'There in the corner under that pile of linen!' he added. The cellar door was dropped. What followed was a series of dramatic shuffles and scuffles and a yelp from a man who was seemingly now being punched and dragged out of the wash house.

'Here's the beef he stole too' shouted another. They were seeking a thief and, although I felt for him as he was dragged away for even further punishment, I was so relieved for the four of us and the cause. Unfortunately, it also meant the end of any discourse and, as we sensitively rose through the floor, Wynnfrith checked that all was clear. Elspeth told us to leave.

'I'll arrange a meeting and we'll speak again. Not sure we can trust you yet but not a word to anyone and, I'm keeping your scrap of linen. Absolutely no talk of this at all!' We were happy to get out of there although I was concerned that this thief, whoever he was, had heard too much in his innocent attempt to hide.

Edward walked calmly and naturally away from Bootham Bar and we talked about what would come next. Our breath was stolen as we looked up, and up and up, even more, until our eyes reached the top of the twin towers at the fore of the Minster. This, by the way, wasn't voluntary. This building would take a hold of you even if you'd seen it a hundred times. Magnificent in every respect, this intergenerational masterpiece was a triumph. But, our sightseeing wasn't to last. Out of nowhere came a boot, a big boot and it rendered Edward helpless as it made contact with his head. Oh no, I thought, as if things couldn't get worse. They did get worse, a lot worse.

'Talking mouse, is it? We'll see about that' the thug muttered as he whisked me away, left Edward barely conscious, and eventually imprisoned me in the direst conditions.

I found myself jammed between two stones in a wall where contaminated water ran in and I was offered little food or respite from this narrow space. My thoughts were of Edward and what had become of him and the completely pathetic role I had played in this mission to date. I did, however, understand why this thug was keeping me alive, and within days, my first fears were realised. As we left this squalid hole, I could feel that I was in an enclosed box and we were heading for the busiest part of the City. I think I would have felt a little better if his actions weren't as predictable, I was to be put on show as an oddity.

'Today, ladies and gentleman, you will witness the most astonishing event of your lives as you will see, for the very first time...a talking mouse'. I could now see a little through the crude joint in the corner of the box. Mmm, I thought, a crowd of five, apparently not going as planned. I was further puzzled as to why he was so sure of my gift as he hadn't made any attempt, so far, to have me speak.

'In half an hour's time, I will tell you the tale of this wicked creature and how he came to be here.' A dickhead he may be, thought I, but there's nothing like a touch of the diabolical to get the juices flowing so he had even gained my interest in a somewhat perverse manner. The sun rose higher in the sky. We were the main event with the Minster itself as a backdrop and I could tell that an audience had gathered. I intended that, throughout my quest, there would be only one person who would hear me speak. That had already gone awry. However, the thing I desperately wanted to avoid was any talk of either magic or evil. Either would get little mousey fried but brain cell here had decided this was going to be his unique selling point. Although I now began to see a little more, I instinctively knew that we were in the square to the south of the Minster and the recently established church of St Michael le Belfrey where, ironically, Edward had said he would one day wish to get married and have his children baptised. The swirling wind was relentless. It seemed to me that this was the most breezy location in York and it interfered with his already desperate presentation. What he was doing was not, by any stretch of the imagination, legal but nobody seemed to be bothering very much. As we were just beyond the boundary of Minster law there wasn't much they could do either.

He dragged me out for all to see. He presumably expected a gasp but, to be fair, all they could see was a dirty mouse on a box.

'This is a talking mouse.' That was enough, before us were already fifty shades of village idiot and they were hooked.

'But, before you hear him talk, I'll tell you how his dark disposition came about.' Disposition? Where the hell did he learn a word like that? I saw a priest at the back watching with interest but that interest wasn't in the show itself but specifically in me. Bayard, for this, was the street entertainer's name, held back a little as he didn't want to be fried either.

'This mouse is possessed!' Oohs and Ahhs and a sharp intake of breath from all. Some even took a few steps back.

'This mouse was next to Mark Smeaton when he was executed and the devil himself, now owning his very soul, put that soul into the mouse for the whole of eternity!' Some of the audience did look terrified. No wonder it was so easy to control the Renaissance populace, I thought. They were buying it wholesale. Mark Smeaton was, allegedly, one of Anne Boleyn's lovers whilst she was still married to the King and, he was the only one to confess, after the most abominable torture that is. So he was, as far as they were concerned, a downright bad un.

'Talk, demon rodent!' he shouted. Not bad I thought, could have done with some backstage noises and a bit of smoke but not bad.

'Taaallk!!!' Mmm. No way mate, It's not happening. Just

as the crowd seemed to lose some interest he took a flaming great pin and stuck it in my arse. I squealed. For some this was enough but he wasn't happy.

'I said talk!!' He did it again.

'Bugger off you fat bastard! I'll pull your gizzards out! Just let me out of here and I'll show you bloody evil!' I'd lost it. So much for not giving into torture. Two pins in my arse and I'm anybody's apparently.

I can't have been heard by more than a few at the front and many at the rear were laughing as they didn't know what the hell was going on but it certainly wasn't the show they were expecting. One guy was rushing to the front and I quickly envisioned a few possible scenarios. He's unhappy with Bayard's show, he wanted the mouse for himself, he wanted to kill the mouse or... Punch! He lunged forward and floored Bayard shouting

'Ought to be ashamed of yourself!' and, as he turned, I recognised him as Godwin. My heart sang. This half-crippled belching, farting, grumpy carpenter had turned out to be the hero. Momentarily I wasn't the least bit bothered why he was there, I was just glad he was. There was little protest, the majority of the crowd presumed Bayard a fraud anyway but to smooth matters over, Godwin theatrically pulled back a makeshift curtain and rail to reveal, what I presume was, an accomplice.

'This is the voice you heard' he cried to the remaining audience and most wandered off disgusted. The guy behind the curtain had simply been a jester awaiting his turn to perform. Godwin whisked me away before anyone actually noticed except, perhaps, for the sinister priest still watching with intent. More interesting than the sombre priest was the poor creature that was accompanying him. Dressed as a peasant he was old and, although he constantly rambled, I guessed that he had once had considerable intellect. We passed close to them both

'Water...my brother...Para...' he muttered.

'Mad…keep away from him…could be catching.' I heard one woman say to another. Mad he may have been but he had gained my interest.

It was now late in the day and, as he walked, Godwin said nothing and I thought it very wise to do the same. We ambled amongst small dwellings which were a mixture of small quaint shacks and slums. He was taking me home. It was the most basic house you could imagine. In a time where rich people had their eyes on tall and elaborate chimneys, Godwin simply possessed a small hole in the ceiling to relieve smoke from the fire. Beyond that, it was simply a room with a platform half-way up the east side. There must have been a reason why such a skilled carpenter wasn't established as a master craftsman and afford a few small luxuries but I never once asked him why this was.

'Home my dove' he called out and a rotund wife with a warm smile greeted him. I tried to count the children but it wasn't possible. Surely they weren't all his? One was around eighteen years old and another a baby. Not that worn out then, Godwin, I thought.

'Here's our pet mousey I told you all about that works with young Edward'. The younger children petted me which wasn't at all offensive as they were all so gentle. Today, I seemed to wander from one confused thought to another. How did he know about me? What did he know? Why did he save me? I was jolted out of my wandering thoughts as he had taken me up four rickety steps to a space with a small bed in it and then, very surprisingly, made a pathetic little acting voice

'Hello Lizzy, it's me, Micklegate mousey. I've come to hug you and make you better.' I forgave him this performance instantly as, before me, was possibly the frailest creature I had ever seen. I imagine she was around six years old and she would have weighed next to nothing. She strained a smile and stretched her arms out for me. She cradled me in her emaciated arms. Lizzy was so tender with me that I was happy to oblige and be the aforesaid Micklegate mouse although, inside, my heart broke. I was sure Lizzy wasn't long for this world. For fifteen minutes or so, Micklegate mouse and Lizzy forgot the ills of England and gave each other comfort. And, as I unfurled my head to look upon her cherub-like face, I noticed that a small butterfly had settled on her shoulder. At nightfall, Godwin placed me in some straw at the foot of Lizzy's bed and I slept like I hadn't done in a week.

When I awoke we were already on our way to work. I was so frustrated that I couldn't speak, I had so many questions. As we arrived, I could see that Edward had already opened up shop. Oh thank God, I had felt so bad about what had happened to him. All of a sudden Godwin became quite authoritarian.

'Right you two. I know you take me for a fool and now I'm getting on a bit and I can even understand that, but do you really think I wouldn't notice what you'd done to my storeroom'. The "storeroom" being the hole which was converted to make my workshop.

'I thinks you're both involved in some proper dangerous business but I don't want to know. You (looking at me)… I knows you can speak. I can't think of any reason on God's good earth why you should, but you do and…I don't want you speaking at me!' Understood. He turned to Edward.

'Your father is a well-respected fellow in York and he trusts me to take care of you and do that I will. If you're going to get caught up in anything daft tell old Godwin first!.. Oh…' he looked at me again, 'and you can make my little Lizzy happy once in a while too.' Also understood and welcomed. I nodded. Nodded? What was I thinking off? A mouse that now nods. Edward poured thanks and guarantees and apologies on Godwin and all, for now, was well.

That evening I was so glad to be home. As I calmed

myself I chuckled at how my most base personality had come to the fore as I'd assumed this role, using language and a turn of phrase I just hadn't accessed before. "Fat Bastard"!...I giggled to myself but gradually turned to more serious matters. I thought of Godwin and Edward, of Elspeth and Wynnfrith, of the thief, the priest and of Bayard but mostly of Lizzy. How cruel life can be, I thought.

5: Faith

York, May 1541

There were puddles practically everywhere. It had rained for days in York and a citizen-waste soup meandered through the snickleways, alleyways and streets. It hampered but didn't stop, the enterprises of the day as people went about their mid-day business. Some activity overflowed from the market as this was Thursday, so the area became quite crowded. Some more modest traders tried to find their way into the smaller, narrow alleys to avoid the warden who was present to collect revenue from regulars. There were pigeons in abundance along Whitnourwhatnourgate but the Sheriff himself had ordered two of his lookouts to be watchful for a particular carrier pigeon as he had been given word of its potential purpose. These two disengaged and unappreciative characters saw this as a needle in a haystack assignment but did have the upper hand in that they knew that Faith had been seen flying awkwardly over the rooftops of Durham, and later more locally, with a cylinder uncomfortably spinning around her feet. They were given the impression that she would be easy to spot as they knew her destination and that was, the aforesaid, Whitnourwhatnourgate and what a street Whitnourwhatnourgate was. Nothing could be more frustrating than pigeon watching all day, it's hard on the eyes and you frequently get messy. The rain didn't help. Crowds didn't help. The noise didn't help. They decided to take turns, one hour on, one hour off in the hope of dealing with the monotony.

'Who else would be engaged in such a shitty enterprise' said the first. The reply from his co-pigeon fancier wasn't fit for recording, let's just say he also wasn't too happy with their latest employment. However, they both may have been surprised to learn that they weren't the only ones watching the skies around Whitnourwhatnourgate. Those who knew Faith could spot her amongst thousands and those who knew her value were to lay in wait for days without a word of complaint.

There were several people present that morning all convinced that they were being discrete, sure that they were hidden amongst the populace. The least discrete were the Sheriff's lookouts who dressed as shoppers but pretended to be tradesmen and so, inevitably, looked like misfits. Locals and regulars could tell there was something fake about them, not least their craned necks and constant complaints. There were others, however, who had given this task a little more thought and preparation.

One walked with a stooped back and a stick, wearing their capuchon to hide their face and they took time to purchase a few relatively insignificant items. Another was not in disguise, going about their business as they would anywhere else but succeeding in becoming a part of the huddle around small stalls and resisting the temptation to constantly look upwards. Even for these two more diligent spies, it wasn't the most conducive environment for bird spotting. Added to this were those chancers who simply wanted to stuff any pigeon under their cloak to take home for supper which was, within the confines of the City walls, illegal. Suddenly a juggler appeared, loud and nauseating, confusing matters even more. To be fair, he was a crap juggler spending most of the morning chasing his balls around the market, if you'll forgive the expression. Who on earth would want to juggle when it's persisting down with rain anyway? This hyperactivity put those watching out for Faith on edge and there was a tight atmosphere developing although most people couldn't work out what it was.

'Bugger off pudding prick!' Shouted a merchant having had simply too much of the juggler and promptly kicked his backside. The poor, incompetent juggler fell into the mud, stood up, and then tried to regain his composure. Sympathy was in short supply this grey and noisy day so many others turned on the self-professed entertainer and chased him out of the area. This sudden flurry put our watchers on edge and pigeons fluttering in all directions. As some turned to witness the ungraceful exit of the juggler, they noticed a distressed but determined bird that was practically spinning as it came down to earth. This happened right in the middle of all the market activity and attracted a great deal of attention although some people simply pointed and stared. This now played out as a game, each of our four characters waiting to see if anyone else had spotted Faith. Suddenly one of the Sheriff's clumsy lookouts pounced on Faith and wrestled her still. He yanked the cylinder, now in a state of poor repair, from her leg leaving a deep wound. Then he threw the bird down injuring her further. His colleague puffed himself up with a sense of accomplishment as our other two characters momentarily slipped into despair. Everyone else made very little of these events. Once opened, the agent exposed the tiny piece of parchment to the elements, raised it to read the message that this diligent pigeon had striven so hard to deliver.

'God's teeth!' he declared 'It's bloody blank!'

'We've been here five hours for a blank parchment!' harmonised his accomplice and they wasted no time getting out of there attempting to rip the parchment as they left. That was until these idiots realised that it was almost impossible to tear parchment so one, very angrily, took his dagger and cut it up. It was now in four pieces and drifted in as many directions on the breeze before the rain pushed them to the ground. The hooded, stooped figure edged forward and simply knelt a little further, picked up two of them and, on looking up, realised that the other, lurking, gentleman had picked up one piece. The fourth was nowhere to be seen. Even at this, she was happy so she then strayed away from the crowd, glanced briefly at her two prizes, concealed them and walked back to the washroom. Faith had come home to Elspeth who, on this occasion, had had to work alone as Wynnfrith was so easily recognisable by her gait. Elspeth bundled Faith into a blanket that she put under her cloak and started to move away. She didn't know who the stranger was who had taken another one of the scraps but she was sure that, like her, he understood it to be common knowledge that messages could be sent in secret simply by applying citrus juice, usually lemon, remaining completely invisible until heated. She was, however, puzzled as to why the two dolts hadn't thought of it. She bent her head to kiss Faith and whispered,

'God bless you, Brother Bernard. We'll get to work straight away and we'll be seeing you soon'.

By the time Elspeth arrived at Bootham Bar, she was drenched and anxious for the welfare of Faith. Yes, the bird was essential to their cause as a carrier pigeon but Elspeth and Wynnfrith cared for her deeply as well. Elspeth arrived home, for home was also the wash house and pushed her hood back so that she could see the door handle through the rain. The two sisters lived together having lost their previous way of life and their abode. Not being the type to desire many possessions, they were content here and it offered discretion. To date, no one had bothered them and they only had contact with those they wished to. Why look for Faith on this day? Just over a week ago, a small note had been pinned to the door of the, now empty, house that had belonged to Bernard's sister, Cecelia, who had disappeared not long after Bernard had. Barely legible, the note gave notice of Faith's return. Elspeth instinctively ranted about the idiot that had put it there for all to see. But the promise, at least, did come good.

'Elspeth!' Wynnfrith cried and the door opened, she was concerned for her sister's welfare, whether she had succeeded or not. She refrained from mentioning the prize until she had put Elspeth in the warmth and carefully taken Faith in one hand to examine her.

'How bad is it Wynn?' asked Elspeth.

'Her leg is torn but she's remarkably well otherwise' and Wynnfrith set about the application of some crude sewing of the wound as Faith tried to wrestle away from her. The bird was distressed and, in turn, this had the same effect on the girls. Afterwards, Wynnfrith sat by a small fire and gently cradled Faith. Elspeth described the events of the morning without even touching the scraps of parchment but was reservedly elated, she regarded her adventure as a success. As she dried out, they both laughed at the buffoons that had been employed by the Sheriff. Then, a moment of realisation could be seen on Elspeth's face, 'What if they are really blank?!'

'They might well be' said Wynn calmly, 'do not be anxious sister, The Lord will make a way for us, he has to. Are they dry?' Elspeth looked at the two small scraps that she had laid out to dry inside the entrance to the washroom. They looked pathetic. So much trouble over something so innocuous, they thought and paused before they took this leap into the unknown.

'I can't help thinking, from what you've said, that Brother Bernard must have been under some duress' said Wynn.

'Yes, The way in which the cylinder was attached to Faith was crude. Do you think someone else has got to her first?' asked Elspeth.

'We won't know, dear Elspeth, and we may have to consider that it's a message sent by a third party to confuse us.'

They looked at each other recognising that they were deliberating too much so Elspeth took the parchment pieces over to the candle. Amazingly, the lemon writing had withstood the battering and a drenching over 140 miles of flight. At first, all they could see were disconnected blotches. This had seemingly been written under some stress and, although the journey had somewhat spoiled the results, it had given them some comfort that this had, indeed, been manufactured by Bernard. The marks were inconsistent but, eventually, they discovered something legible. They repeated this painstaking process with the second piece, about the same size, but they had already worked out that, disappointingly, the pieces didn't fit together.

They placed them on a small table by candlelight and, for what seemed like forever, said nothing. They had a habit of looking up, and at each other, at the same time. This synchronicity was noticed by all who knew them and most presumed each knew what the other was thinking. They were probably right. Initially, they couldn't make head or tail of what they saw but intelligently tried to build on the knowledge they already had:

Something Cataclysmic was imminent in England.

It would start in York.

With the right knowledge, it could be stopped.

Bernard was the only person who, as far as they knew, was party to the whole plot and Bernard was putting a trusted team of agents together and, at the moment, they seemed to be the only two.

They wouldn't see Bernard for another month at least.

'Any ideas?' said Elspeth to her sister.

'Nothing, not like this'. The "like this" meant that there was nothing cohesive about what they had. There, clearly in Latin, were recognisable words but, even pairing them up, left them with a conundrum. Latin wasn't a problem for these two. As women they were equal in commitment, will and determination to any man on earth and the presumption that one was hindered by her medical state was folly, as these two were equally impressive. They stared and looked. Examined and pondered. Sighed and tutted. Gritted teeth and paced the room. Piece one, once translated, said this:

ord must be saved
isle to north of Stratford on

and the second read:

the Avon
and in the Minster
Here the catacly

It was, therefore, reasonable to assume that there was something on an isle north of Stratford upon Avon. However, as well-educated and worldly-wise as the sisters were, their knowledge of islands was poor and, at best, the most accessible maps were still unreliable. The reference to the Cataclysm told them no more than they already knew and the Minster wasn't a great surprise as they knew of the connection between York and the looming Cataclysm.

'We must approach Robert' said Wynnfrith.

'Oh Wynn. We simply don't know if we can trust him. If anyone is in the King and Archbishop's pocket it would be the Lord Mayor. We should if we can proceed, proceed alone' replied Elspeth.

'My dear sister, we don't know which way to turn! Without Bernard, we are completely isolated and he did say that we should look to Robert if all else fails.' Wynn was adamant.

'You do know the risks Wynn? said Elspeth. 'our lives are on the line.'

'Our lives have been on the line since day one. We both gave up everything for this cause and we can't get any further without some risk' replied Wynnfrith.

'I can identify the man who took the third piece, I'm sure that if we could access it we would be much clearer' interceded Elspeth, for good reason trying to divert the conversation away from Robert Hall. Wynn wasn't giving up.

'That's something we can certainly pursue but we need to seek counsel from Robert as soon as we can!'

'Fine! But if he puts his hands on anything but the door handle this time I swear I'll chop them off along with some of his other Mayoral valuables' asserted Elspeth angrily. She then caught Wynn trying to stifle a laugh and they both spluttered out laughter and hugged each other for reassurance.

'Coo, coo, coo' came from behind them. Faith was on the mend already.

6: Mayor Robert Hall

York, June 1541

Elspeth deliberated for a further few days and then allowed Wynn to venture out. This was a much finer day than when she had waited endlessly for the return of Faith. She took a short, steady walk to Goodramgate and straight into The Holy Trinity Church. Holy Trinity is conveniently part concealed. Not through invention, although you would think to look at it someone had stuck some houses in front of the church to hide it. Not so. The church had, long ago, built a row of dwellings on its grounds to rent out. Some thought that Our Lady's Row was ancient and they were, certainly, amongst some of the oldest buildings in York. It did, however, mean that it was easy to slip into the church gardens unseen and therefore, ideal for Elspeth and Wynn's clandestine plans. Along the route, Wynnfrith cautiously checked to see if she was watched or followed and did the same as she arrived at the passage along Goodramgate. She took a moment to admire its simplicity, sitting as it did in the shadow of the imposing Minster. Again, checking that she was alone, she entered and knelt by an arch that separated the nave from the aisle and placed her hand on the lowest part of the stonework. Diligently and silently, she found a familiar section of masonry that could slide inconspicuously in and out. As it came out, she placed a small piece of paper that also incorporated lemon ink for its message. Just a second or so to slide it back and her work was done.

Holy Trinity was unusual in its layout. It had an inner chapel isolated from the main church so that, historically, lepers could worship there and they were able to watch the service through a hole in the wall that was called a squint. Wynnfrith thought she saw some movement beyond the squint and this momentarily distracted her.

Without warning a voice beckoned her.

'Good day maiden, would you like me to join you in prayer?' Wynnfrith jumped but made sure to keep her hand where it was, at the same time as looking up. It was the priest. She had little choice but to respect both him and his office but was startled by this sudden appearance. These were difficult times. By now churches should have been completely stripped of their valuables and decorations but this was still, somewhat Catholic. Wynnfrith couldn't presume for a moment what this man's allegiances were, let alone how she should address him so she guessed.

'Oh thank you, kind Father, I'm praying for good harvests this year and further respite from the plague'. Wynnfrith's hand started to hurt, it was trapped and this, combined with the daily reality that kneeling was extremely painful, compromised her demeanour. The priest seemed kind but incisive, there was something about him that cautioned Wynn.

'You are surely blessed' he said observing her involuntary movements. Wynnfrith was taken aback by this, some of these movements aren't involuntary, she told herself, I'm in agony! Moreover, she had lived life with the expectation that every other person would condemn her disability as witchcraft or, at best, something she surely deserved for "being wicked" but the priest had said the opposite. By now her hand was wedged in the stone. It hurt, her leg was squashed and her anxiety started to show. He took her left hand and introduced himself.

'Father Matthew, child.' It was expected that there should be at least a modicum of fear when in a priest's presence but there was none here, just lots of concealed pain. She wasn't scared of him but very scared of being found out.

'If I can't pray for you today, perhaps I can help you up?' This was her opportunity. Before Father Matthew could get around to her side, she quickly let go of the message and pushed the stone back into place with her right hand as he guided her up by her left.

'Thank you so much Father' she said breathlessly and turned toward the door a little too quickly.

'I do hope to see you here again, child.' She turned as she genuinely didn't wish to seem rude and was already feeling somewhat guilty for the abuse committed on his wall.

'I will pray for you and your sister' he added, as she got to the door. This sent a sudden chill throughout her body which, combined with the pain and her physically awkward exit, almost broke her will. She hurried out into Goodramgate and her mind raced. Who is he? What does he know? How does he know about Elspeth? Does he know about the message hide and the Mayor? Already a good five hundred yards away, she collapsed onto a wall on the east side of the Minster and wept. The responsibility heaped on these two young women was enormous, they had made next to no progress and Wynn now felt someone was onto their plans.

On the best of days, Wynnfrith attracted attention. The weeping did little to help so she quickly regained her composure and bolted home as fast as was possible.

Elspeth's first words were,

'My dear sister, what on earth is the matter?' Wynnfrith relayed the whole story. It was always Elspeth's intention to be strong for her sister and, particularly on this occasion, she took care to outline the positives.

'It's hard to believe he is our enemy if he spoke such kind words, Wynn. Could it possibly be his way of reaching out?' Wynnfrith agreed and suggested going back but Elspeth swiftly dispelled the notion.

'We stick to our plan. We have to presume that your Father Matthew knows nothing about the secreted message and you'll return Friday to pick up Robert's reply.' Wynnfrith agreed knowing that she wouldn't sleep at all for the next three days.

Those few days were intense. Wynnfrith, in particular, wanted to ask around about Stratford upon Avon (and islands) but she was reminded by her sister that such a course would only serve to invite curiosity, they had to be patient and they had to be calm. At night Wynn would imagine every possible scenario of her impending encounter with Father Matthew. In some, he was an ally putting himself at the service of the two sisters. On one occasion her thoughts drifted and lapsed into a nightmare where Father Matthew had a hidden dagger beneath his vestments and plunged it into her right hand whilst helping her stand up. She woke in a sweat. It was Friday morning. She got dressed and immediately set off on her quest. Why did the journey to Goodramgate seem three times as long? Why are there so many people? Why do I feel so cold?

Before she knew it, she was at the church door but realised that she was frozen, unable to take the next step. Breathe Wynn, breathe. She pushed the door open slowly, politely and quietly closed it behind her and turned to look to the altar on her right-hand side as she entered. No one there. So far so good. She approached her intended destination and knelt, this time taking more care over her position so that she could get up in a hurry if necessary. Her heart sank as the encounter replayed. There he was again, Father Matthew. He pleasantly shouted,

'Good morning my child.' Wynnfrith had spent days winding herself into a frenzy so she was now in a heightened state of anxiety. She opened her mouth to speak but was interrupted by a third party except that the sounds she heard were almost unintelligible. She could make out the word "Father" and "rope" but, whoever this was, was beckoning Father Matthew back. He (for it sounded like a he) was so persistent that Matthew had no choice but to turn back. This was all that was needed for Wynnfrith to move the stone, grab Robert's reply, put back the stone and leave. Bang! The door slammed behind her as she left and, again, because of Wynn's indomitable caring nature, she felt guilty at her lack of respect and manners. Relief. She headed home at some pace but not before she had checked that this was a reply and not the message she had left. Success! This was not the same piece of paper.

Around the candle, the girls waited for Robert Hall's reply to appear. It was brief. "Meet Shambles hostelry Sunday after mass, I will wear a broad Lincoln green hat."

'What a peacock!' blurted Elspeth 'even has to put on a show when he's in disguise!'

'At least he will meet us sister, and only a two day wait, I'm so tired of waiting, sitting around.' responded Wynn.

'You mean all the waiting around between incessant washing!' Grumbled Elspeth, 'He'd better be of some use!' Wynnfrith tried to calm her sister,

'No matter how distasteful this is, he's the Lord Mayor. The Lord Mayor of York and, unless we are misinformed, he's on our side. Take heart sister, we will make some headway come next week.'

You would be right in wondering why on earth there would be an inn on a street known for butchers and piggeries. Well, strictly speaking, there wasn't. There was, what you might call, a meeting place for gentlemen, well, men. It was accessed via a very small alley between two stinky butchers shops and its unofficial name was 'byte me bunne', a place where you could dip your bun in your beer or, you could have a beer and dip your bun in or, just have a bun or just a beer. You could also take part in numerous extra-curricular activities after the stalls and shops had closed. A crude name admittedly and one that usually only passed the lips of the most coarse men of York but a name, nevertheless, a little less amusing than the name of its proprietor, Mrs Grindem who was, not surprisingly, part bun maker, part beer pourer and part almost anything else you wanted her to be. She was the sole proprietor and the entire workforce and entirely illegal. Mayor Robert Hall liked everything Mrs Grindem had on offer and it cost him next to nothing to purchase the whole place for a few hours, but shame on him for showing Elspeth and Wynnfrith such little respect. Having said that, they would be completely alone for their meeting and if anyone within the walled boundaries of York could be relied on to keep quiet it was Mrs Grindem. Oh, the secrets she could tell.

In the following days, the two sisters deliberated on the best way of approaching the broader subject of the Cataclysm and their recent discoveries. They complained about the Mayor's wandering eyes and, even worse, his wandering hands, his complacent attitude to imminent events and wondered, yet again, if this was the right course of action. Nevertheless, they had to move forward and they had no other pathways.

Mass came and went and it was time to meet. Elspeth and Wynnfrith were both disgusted at the sight of the assigned venue which found them wading through yesterday's offal. They then squeezed down the narrow alley once sure that they couldn't be seen, pausing to consider how the Mayor's carcass would get in it. A water damaged door creaked open and jammed half-way. They were expecting to see the notorious and well used and abused Mrs Grindem but were surprised when it was Robert himself in a bloody silly green hat. They knew the Lord Mayor reasonably well, and by his first name, as he was a relative, albeit distant. He quietly beckoned them, took them to a cramped and cold rear room and sat them at a table which had a crude bench on either side. They noticed that this dingy space had no windows but two other, narrow, exits. Wynnfrith found it very difficult not to imagine the deeds that may have gone on behind those doors or, even worse, where she sat. They practically lip-synched his first five words for, in this setting, those words were always the same.

'You know where I stand!' he asked emphatically but rhetorically. They both nodded. As far as any espionage (or what the sisters regarded as good works) were concerned he was not for persuasion. Where he stood was this: Robert was a wealthy local merchant trading successfully in both lead and glass (Elspeth thought of asking him to do something about the dark room they currently occupied) and he wished to stay rich and privileged. If an ardent Protestant asked him about the papacy he would nod and agree until the cows came home and, yes you've guessed, it if he were to be approached by a Catholic the same would be true. He would, in later years, be described by The Archbishop of York as "no favourer of religion". He also had no love for the King, which was odd as he modelled himself on Bluff King Hal himself i.e. a fat, pompous, dictatorial, rich bastard, but knew he would have a duty to grovel when the King arrived in York as all were expected to apologise for the northern resistance of recent years. He did care about the warnings. He understood the Cataclysm to be real, significant and long-lasting and he also knew that it would not result in him retaining his undeserved privileged position. So, he would establish contacts. That was it, he put people together. If his name was ever to be mentioned he would deny all and, he definitely would not get involved with anything practical. If anything, he constantly claimed neutrality.

However, for Elspeth and Wynnfrith he was a lifeline and quite frankly, all they had. Robert's eyes were on Elspeth before she sat down, his attitude to Wynnfrith different and this was, in part, due to their past relationship. Some may consider his advances harmless but our more experienced ladies knew this was the thin end of the wedge and put him in his place.

'Business only thank you cousin!' said Wynn assertively and he feigned disappointment as if he were a child. He was smart enough to know that these two would take no nonsense so sat down and asked how he could help, possibly still hoping there may be something in return. They told him everything including the scraps of parchment and the priest. They trusted him, partly because they had no choice, but mostly because he had shown no signs of betraying them thus far. He promised to look into the priest's identity, why he was taking an interest in the sisters' affairs and agreed that they needed to have someone else investigate the clues on the parchment. He leaned forward, serious and intent as the bench groaned under his weight. The girls successfully stifled a laugh. He whispered,

'I have just the man, he's available immediately and you can trust him with your lives'. The excitement on both their faces was instantly evident and they too leaned forward.

'You can truly trust this man?' asked Wynn.

'Absolutely, on my life' he replied.

'Are you able to give us his name here and now?' she persisted.

'Ladies, I have the pleasure of informing you that I can put at your very service the much sought after Lord Silas himself!' The change of expression on both their faces was immediate and striking. The girls then looked at each other and then back at the Mayor.

'You're joking?' said Elspeth quietly and she looked deep into his eyes for a flicker that might give him away.

'You're not joking! God! You mean The Lord Silas who isn't actually a Lord but is, in fact, York's most famous idiot?' Wynnfrith calmly interceded.

'Please tell us you're not serious Robert.' He slapped the tabletop with his glove indignantly.

'Have you ever met him?!' he said.

'No.' They said in unison.

'So all you know of him is rumour?' This calmed them a little and, particularly as Christian women, they felt a little ashamed of their outburst.

'I'll be completely honest with you cousins, he is a fool, at times a complete simpleton and his pretence at being more than he is, embarrasses him and those around him but can't you see? It's a perfect cover. Silas has been working for me for years now and no one even suspects' his head went down a little as he felt some shame. 'And….err…ahem… he's very cheap' said Robert.

'There we have it!' interrupted Wynn. 'Cheap does it every time.'

'Now look here…' blustered the Mayor defensively but was stopped by Elspeth's respectful tone.

'All right, all right, we'll meet him, and in good faith but please make it soon'. The Mayor's eyes were now transfixed on Elspeth's bosom. This didn't go unnoticed by anyone in the room and what made matters worse was that he had started to, very slightly, drool.

'Eyes on my face, and both your hands on the table if you please!' insisted Elspeth. Wynn tried not to laugh. He capitulated immediately which now empowered the ladies in this negotiation as he tried to redeem himself.

'There's more' said Robert 'you now need someone on

the inside at the highest level.' This shut them up. At least temporarily.

'You mean King and Queen highest level? The Royal Progress highest level? How on Earth?....' marvelled Elspeth.

'I'll say no more today and I won't move on this until I know more but there are those that we can trust and will help. Mind you, I'll only set up contacts, no more.' They agreed yet again to this incessant mantra but otherwise, they were stuck for words and were, of course, very scared.

'We'll say no more now and we'll next meet Thursday after curfew at the wash house, we can't come here.' They agreed, pondering as they always did as to why the Mayor never made any attempt to disguise himself fully and quite impressed that Thursday would be no exception. He would find good reason to be in the vicinity of Bootham Bar on Thursday evening whatever it would take.

7: Hope

Wolverdington, June 1541

Following such a disappointment, you would have expected Silas to make a hasty retreat from Stratford upon Avon. He had every intention of making speedy progress but with only a mile between him and Richard's house, he noticed an awkwardness in Annie's trot. Annie always came first, he would never see any harm come to her so he stopped on the outskirts of a village to look her over. Shoes. He hadn't checked her shoes in weeks. Fortunately, there was only one shoe that needed replacing but her left fetlock was hurting and the shoe had worn at both the heel and the hoof. Yet again Silas reprimanded himself. Poor Annie, how could my obsession with my mission leave you like this? But Annie was fine, loving the attention, although the shoe really did need to be replaced. As he looked ahead he could see the welcoming silhouette of Wolverdington. Surely I can get the shoe done here and then I'll be on my way, he thought. Luckily, the farrier's was the first place he saw on the edge of a row of wattle and daub cottages. For once Silas was in luck, no awkwardness, no questions, no making fun, the farrier agreed to have the shoe changed that very afternoon and cheerily advised Silas that he could get fine lunch at the local inn. Even better. This seemed a respectable hostelry with a decent name for a change, "ye pilgrims reste". If there were a Renaissance league table of pubs this would definitely be in a different league to "ye dirtye pesant" and "byte me bunne". Mind you, so would every other inn.

He always dreaded his entrance. The least he could expect was stifled chuckles and he was tired of being such an easy target. He decided to walk in confidently and simply ask for a drink. Heads did turn but his reluctance to deliver the, now famous, grandiose speech certainly helped him. Yes, people noticed he was odd but, within reason, minded their own business. There was a solitary bench in the corner, away from others, and he relaxed with his drink knowing that his dear Annie was being looked after. He deserved an hour or so of peace so, to take his mind off his most recent failure, he let his mind drift back to when he first met Elspeth and Wynnfrith. What a warm and lovely thought.

He smiled at how proud he had been when Robert had told him about the mission, how honoured he was to be part of it and how excited to work with these two formidable young women.

Come the day, he was terrified. He knew what people thought of him and he knew also that he would not be the ladies first choice but, in his head, he envisaged many noble deeds and conquests to come. It was this faux confidence, always, that was Silas's life force. For Elspeth and Wynnfrith, the wait for Robert and Silas to enter seemed endless. They could hear constant muttering outside the door. What if they don't like me? What if I'm dressed incorrectly? What if I say the wrong thing? What if. What if. What if. To give Robert the credit he deserved, he did spend some time reassuring his young appointee but was now losing patience. He threw open the door and Silas after it. Once in, Silas had decided that, yet again, he was just going to go for it. He was to make a grand announcement and then step forward to kiss the two maiden's hands.

'Good day to you my fair ladies. I am…at your very service…Lord Silas!' He bowed, took a bold step forward, fell on his knees and bounced awkwardly down into the cellar landing, fortunately, on a bundle of dirty clothes and amidst the other cellar mess.

'Wynn! I told you to keep that shut at all times!' reprimanded Elspeth.

'So sorry sister, she replied. But it is pretty hard to miss' she replied, now looking at Robert whose expression was now one of complete hopelessness. The girls genuinely intended to offer Silas assistance but he had already crawled back up, his wispy lock of hair full of straw and rat droppings and a ladies petticoat wrapped around his chest. Adopting his well-tried routine, Silas just carried on as if nothing had happened. Robert physically took hold of him, placed him forcefully on a stool and bade him not to move until they had left. What transpired then was a mature discussion about all they knew including what the "ord" was that "had to be saved" as written in the first sentence on the parchment but they decided that they should, for now, concentrate on what concrete information they had. Silas's brief was straight forward: he was to gain by any means necessary more information about this island, seemingly north of Stratford upon Avon, but he was not to mention the Cataclysm, the King, the King's progress, the parchment, Brother Bernard, the priest, the pigeon or the sisters. Silas gave them, in return, a knights' assurance (although he wasn't a knight) and the two ladies were, albeit momentarily, confident that something may progress at last. They were to meet weekly to speak of any progress not knowing that Silas was going to bugger off to Stratford without telling them.

Lord Silas let out a big sigh once outside again as this had been incredibly daunting for him. Robert smiled, patted him on the back and they walked a while in the moonlight, alone except for the constables charged with maintaining the curfew who, in recognising the Mayor, turned a blind eye. To be clear, the main purpose of the curfew was to ensure all fires were out in the City before dark, mostly for safety reasons. Added to that was the sensible premise that anyone wandering about in the dark must be up to no good. As they strolled, Silas talked endlessly about the sisters. He had never seen such short blonde hair on a lady, almost shaved. Such intelligent girls, they made him feel so comfortable. Remarkable courage, and strength of character. By now he was rambling so much that Robert stopped and looked him in the eye.

'Haha! I don't believe it, lad! You, Silas of all people, you're besotted!' Silas very quickly tried to wriggle out of this, women didn't like him and he would be horrified if he'd given the wrong impression during the meeting but Robert wouldn't allow him to speak.

'Well, well, good on you lad and...I don't blame you for a minute. I'd give half my fortune for an afternoon's roll in the hayfield with young Elspeth. But that's never going to happen, not with any man Silas.' Silas then found his voice.

'No, no, I have no such intentions, you misrepresent me, Sir.'

'Oh!' said the Mayor. 'You mean' He stopped again and Silas was blushing so much his hair disappeared into his face. Silas stopped Robert from saying any more,

'I am discovered, sir, please do not utter a word to anyone.' And then silence. They sat down together on a church wall. Robert had it in him to be compassionate and so he placed his arm around Silas in the hope that it would give him the confidence to talk.

'I won't say a word my dear Silas but, truthfully, it's good to see you like this.'

'Thank you, my Lord. I am almost lost for words, I am entirely captivated by Wynnfrith. Wynnfrith, Wynnfrith. I shall say her name every second. Don't you think she is remarkable…and…and...so beautiful?'

'Beautiful she is my lad. This will be our secret but, perhaps next time you visit, try to stay on your feet for five minutes?!' They both laughed and when they stopped laughing, Silas realised he was completely breathless and his stomach was churning. One little lady can do this to me? he asked himself. Oh, dear. Perhaps I'll be ok tomorrow. He had a question for Robert.

'Before you leave My Lord, tell me, what did you mean about Elspeth and "any man?"'

'Oh that. Don't you know? Elspeth was, and always will be, a nun. Married to Christ my lad!' Silas was quite shocked, not least because so many nuns were driven into exile, pensioned off or much worse after the Reformation. And then he saw Elspeth as she was, a rebel against the Reformation and his admiration for these sisters became limitless.

They parted company and Silas tried to digest everything that had happened and that had been said that morning and strolled home drunk on this newfound passion. He stopped, turned and ran after Robert,

'Sir! Sir! …And Wynnfrith?...' Robert laughed again,

'You're ok lad, she's no more than a maiden ripe for the picking!' He turned and walked away. Silas's daft little heart danced all the way home.

Silas had drifted so deeply into this daydream he hadn't realised he was muttering Wynn's name as he sat in the corner of the pub and this, not surprisingly, attracted attention. It raised a few smiles but nothing more, Silas had found a little oasis along the way of his troubled venture. Or so he thought. Over to his left was a table with five men, two engaged in heated, but respectable, debate. It didn't trouble Silas very much as no one was bothering him personally but he couldn't help himself from eavesdropping. He understood from their discourse that these two were called Farrimond and Ham, which amused Silas as it sounded as they should run a high-class abattoir together. The fact that they referenced each other by name indicated that they were, despite the rumpus, good friends.

'I'm telling you, none of this has anything to do with Martin Luther or those who protest against Rome, it all started with that Boleyn, cow's udder she was, when she got her evangelist claws, all eleven of them! into him. Twisted the fat bugger round her fingers she did, teasing his bits and insisting on him marrying her. He would have walked through fire for bloody Anne Boleyn. Put a spell on him!' This was Farrimond's continued rant, clearly referring to Anne's influence on Henry in the decade now passed.

'Too easy! Too simple…look, apart from the nobility, the people bleeding us common folk dry have been those in the church. Monks with mistresses, wealth beyond your imagination in monasteries and cathedrals. A piece of the cross itself sold outside every abbey in England. Enough to build a boat!' retorted his mate.

'Oh, I'll give you that. Holy men and women completely bent, rogering anything that moves, and the rest of it, but she was his bloody mistress, he's had loads of mistresses! If she'd just have known her place. Our queen, our real queen, gone. Died the most humiliating and lonely death, cast aside like an old garment! She was his dead brother's wife and the Pope himself said it was ok for Henry to marry her but no!! Harry knows better. He now knows the bleedin' Bible better than anyone!' Farrimond blustered, wearing his affection for King Henry's first wife, Catherine of Aragon. And on it went. One of the group prodded Ham as someone across the room was taking too much interest in their conversation. These were dangerous times and this was very dangerous talk but, everyone did it, everyone had an opinion. You just had to be careful about when and where you expressed it and, of course, the drink didn't help matters. They were wise enough to take the volume down and then blustered on about how Anne Boleyn, Henry's second wife was solely responsible for the Reformation in the church and how God had punished her with a miscarriage on the day of Catherine's funeral.

'He's been bloody obsessed with having a son. Now he's got one it's something else, he's out of control' said Ham.

'He's just weak. Wolsey, More, Cromwell to name a few, toying with his every thought. They claw their way up like rats at a butcher's window…' Farrimond interrupted

'Yeah and Wolsey just a butcher's son, Cromwell the son of a blacksmith!' They all laughed.

'True brother, there's breeding! and the power they had too! They couldn't trust him and he couldn't trust them and now they're all gone. Her and all, along with her lovers!' said Ham. Farrimond then offered some defence of Anne.

'Come on, surely you don't think all that's true? He just wanted rid of her and when he wants rid he gets rid!'

'Well, who knows. But what I do know is that we all suffer for it!'

Silas had heard this many times and in different ways up and down the country except the details tended to be thinner in the north, Henry generally getting a constant bad press. It was true that that as early as 1529 there were notable protests against the existing church and the writings of Martin Luther had intrigued intellectuals across Europe. The change in attitudes to the church in Europe was well under way long before Henry wanted a divorce but it was certainly good timing as far as he was concerned. Henry still regarded himself as Catholic in the true sense of the word but, nevertheless, he was now the equivalent of Pope in

England and the Pope had no legitimate influence. Anne failed to give Henry his heart's desire, a son and heir so, once he had seen her off with several trumped-up charges, Henry found his true love, the gentle Jane Seymour, who, on giving him his long-awaited heir, passed away in childbirth. This loss, along with Henry's unfortunate jousting accident earlier in 1536 left him a changed and extremely difficult man. So, the rumour was out. He was out of control and easily influenced by others in his vulnerable moments, dictatorial, tyrannical and accountable to no one but God himself. Some thought that he had given in to madness, believing himself a deity. This was only slightly tempered by gossip that his latest victim, Catherine Howard, had him behaving like a schoolboy again. What man, even a King, in his fifties, would be foolish enough to think a dalliance with an eighteen-year-old both publicly acceptable, good for the country and wise after a lifetime of trying to get the better of the opposite sex? The Cataclysm itself had started as rumour but Silas was amongst a select few who now knew it to be real. As yet he was not sure what it was or how it would manifest itself but was convinced that it would massively overshadow Henry's previous radical behaviours. This was why he had to make more progress with his investigation and why he muttered a little prayer for guidance at this point.

Another, quite upbeat, character sat down and, as they greeted him, he immediately interjected.

'All right, let's give this bloke a fighting chance here. You all forgotten the prince who became King in 1509? Good looking, a brilliant scholar, could speak several languages, an expert in theology. Musician and champion in the jousts? Worked so hard to stabilise our alliances, kept peace in England?' Some laughed but most groaned and jeered as they all knew there was at least a sprinkling of "devil's advocate" in his offering. He was, of course, right. This King was no idiot and they all knew it but he had let circumstance control his decisions and this was to affect the ordinary man and woman for so many years to come. The newcomer also delivered a very reasonable line of argument in defence of Henry that finished with,

'Imagine if you had his responsibilities but no real friends, no single person you could trust, and those you employ to advise you, just feather their own nests.'

They argued, petitioned, pontificated, deliberated, criticised and drank. This argy-bargy went on and on as people of all times and places are inclined to do when faced with irresponsible leaders and it seemed that it was becoming naturally exhausted when suddenly, one of the group asked his "expert" colleagues a quite profound question that particularly piqued Silas's interest.

'And, in all of this, what happens to our faith? Our relationship with the Lord? One minute we're told to worship this in this way, and a week later, worship that in another way. What happens to your every day, God-fearing man?' He had, unwittingly, hit upon a concern that affected all English citizens now. After all, the English mostly were devout followers of the faith but were getting confused as to what the faith was. Following a short silence in which this conundrum was being absorbed, a lone voice answered.

'Now that every one of us can read, or have read to us, the Gospels in English. It's all anyone needs: to remind ourselves daily that our Lord Jesus died to save us, leaving a message of hope, peace, forgiveness and love. So much of the rest is twisted by those in power to confuse, control and scare us.'

It wasn't deep theology but it was sincere and it was also the truth. The positive message of Christ was getting lost in man's attempt to make it better serve his selfishness and, already, there were deep divisions in the brand new church in England. Everyone turned around and almost every person in the pub went quiet. Silas himself was very impressed and he sat there thinking that this was an impressively positive contribution until it dawned on him that he'd said it. Did I really just say that? They're all staring at me. Where did that come from? His mind was in a spin, his stomach churning and his heart beating out of his skinny little rib cage.

Done it again, he thought.

He did, of course, mean what he said but if every Englishman went around exposing their heart to all, there would be few Englishmen left. Silas's loneliness had delivered him a very personal relationship with God and he, for one, was sure that this, along with his Gospels, was all he needed. Not wise to say it though. Momentarily he had become an evangelist, and even he was wondering what had happened to Lord Silas the village idiot. He prepared himself for he was sure that a very swift apology should follow but he simply didn't get the chance. Apart from a few, disinterested patrons, everyone cheered or, to be more precise, offered a variety of guttural noises of approval. Fists were slammed on the table, beer was spilt and there was a measurable mood of comradeship amongst the drunks. A good number of these characters would have been able to do a reasonable counter to his point of view but, on the whole, they couldn't be bothered. Seemingly, peace, passion and being pissed were pretty compatible. Silas audibly exhaled in relief but his nervousness was, for the most part, completely unnoticed.

'Now there's a man as speaks common sense!' said Ham emphatically.

'Come join us, Sir. Get this man a beer.'

'Most sense I heard all night' said Farrimond, 'A true agent of the word!' Silas was doubly delighted, not least at the reference to him being a Sir. This expensive doublet was speaking volumes after all. As he stood, he remembered that he'd had two beers already and so exercised his finest stagger in the direction of the, already crowded, table. His little knees were unsteady and rattling in his, still too large, hose and he also decided to spill beer on his legs which didn't altogether best represent his male physique. One of his worst nightmares was getting his codpiece stuck under the table as he sat down and tonight was no exception but, as the crowd thought he was intending to be funny, this also went down well. He was welcomed, greeted, slapped on the back, punched in the shoulder and offered more drink but then, out of nowhere, he felt a firm hand grip his left arm. It was the farrier. Annie. He'd forgotten about Annie.

'I'm so sorry....' apologised Silas but was promptly interrupted by the, still very accommodating, farrier.

'She's all done my Lord, fed as well and resting. Catching no harm, you just go get her when you're ready.' Silas was in such good spirits he thanked and thanked again, the obliging farrier, paid him and bought him beer. He joined them and told Silas that his name was Thomas. Silas really liked this man, a gentle giant who by now, was looking out for him. There were now eight, worse for wear, men around this table and by all accounts, having a bloody good time.

The conversation drifted here and there and Silas drifted in and out of consciousness but was instantly alerted by the topic of choice by Ham. Ham was teasing Farrimond about his devotion to his pet bird, a pigeon. This was, at first, a most regular jape but the said Farrimond found himself under pressure to repeat his unusual tale regarding this pigeon.

His inebriated condition did little to provide clarity but it was clear that he had recently stumbled upon a homing pigeon whilst near the school in Stratford. Silas, wishing to boost his newfound popularity even further, considered mentioning that Wynnfrith had a homing pigeon but then thought better of it. It transpired that Farrimond's pigeon had a neatly secured secret message on its leg when he'd found it and he'd had the good sense to warm it over a candle to reveal the words.

'It even said who it was for.' Expanded Farrimond. 'And, let the Lord himself be my witness... I asked everywhere as to the whereabouts of the owner but people either didn't know or they blanked me at the mention of his name.'

'What name?' came the chorus from those who hadn't heard this tired tale before.

'Why, Bede of course. Bede like the ancient monk.' Farrimond was a better storyteller than he gave himself credit for as this was received with oohs and ahs. He was pressured to reveal what the message said but, as a seasoned professional, he wasn't doing spoilers. Well, not yet at least. However, what came next astonished Silas.

'What a bird I tell you, what a bird! I could see her coming as straight as you please, a direct line south to the very spot where I was standing.' Of course, he was questioned as to why on earth he knew this but, fortunately, more than one witness at the table could vouch for testing this pigeon on several occasions.

'That apart' and he paused to invite maximum intrigue. 'you'll never guess where she'd come from? Only the Holy isle itself!'

'No! Never! You don't say' and other collective noises of either genuine or feigned astonishment vented forth from the sozzled gathering.

'Lindisfarne itself' expanded Farrimond 'Christianity came to England through that very isle thousands of years ago!' Just as he was starting to look extremely knowledgeable and, although it would have been nice to think that Christianity had been in England for thousands of years, perhaps he should have stopped to think that the very year they were in, 1541, was in fact, 1541 years since Christ was born. He was right about the other part. Christianity was around to some degree when the Romans occupied Britain but it was King Oswald of Northumbria who popularised Christianity in the northeast during the seventh century. He settled Aidan, and twelve other monks that had been brought from Iona, on Lindisfarne isle where they built the first abbey.

Silas was desperately wishing he hadn't had a drink. South. From the north! Island. Holy Island! Pigeon. Stratford. North! Island! He so wanted to shout out. He so wanted to celebrate his discovery. Well, a chance discovery. He wanted more. For once he bit his tongue. Everyone here would happily spill the beans about their greatest sins after another beer so he decided to sit and listen. As was usual for our hero, he fell off his stool, spilt his drink, ripped his sleeve, ripped someone else's sleeve but, today, that was all right as everyone around the table was doing the same.

After the fascination with monks and pigeons died down somewhat, there were still calls for the rest of the tale.

'Well, as far as I'm concerned, Hope is mine now' continued Farrimond.

'How do you know its name, she tell you?' joked one of the drinkers.

'It said. The message ended with: If this bird, Hope, doesn't reach her destination …blardy blah blah…so, you see she's mine now.' Silas was having trouble coping with this. There must be a connection! Wynn and Elspeth have a pigeon called Faith and this one's called Hope?

'Rest of it didn't make a lot of sense, just said "have prayed for your escape and recovery, landed on Lindisfarne, put all faith in the nun, meet at the bar" and signed, Bernard.' Ham responded,

'Pretty dull end to the tale, my mate, but the Holy isle stuff was exciting. I'll give it to you, she's a smart bird, pity you'll have to go all the way to Lindisfarne to get her to home again!' They all laughed, as far as they were concerned the bird was a dud.

However, Silas was in a high state of anxiety. Far from

home, his head was spinning with confused thoughts. He was completely amazed that Abbot Bernard (for Silas was still mistaken that Bernard was an Abbot) had more than one contact. Was the nun Elspeth? Was the bar Bootham bar? Who on earth is Bede? And more to the point, what the hell did any of it mean? He could be sure that he would return with his head held high and he thought, also, he could reasonably assume that Bede, whoever he was, had either gone missing or was dead. Silas was delighted and, as far as he was concerned, it was a complete coincidence that he had stumbled across this information.

In time, some considerable time, everyone seemed to drift off and Silas found himself offering friendly farewells to his newfound pisspot comrades. He made a proper show of himself navigating the short distance from the table to the farriers, in fact, it took him about twenty minutes to negotiate two hundred yards. Thomas the farrier or, not surprisingly, Thomas Farrier as he was known locally, had got there ahead of Silas and offered him the reins. He was certain to bestow endless thanks on Thomas for his kindness to Annie and gave the sort of farewell that implied they would meet again. As the noble Lord Silas set forth to continue his life and death mission, he slumped over Annie's neck happy and pissed as a northern fart. Miles passed before the beer started to wear off, the headache sang dirges inside his little skull and he took more notice of what was going on around him. He had to stop to empty his bladder, bowel and stomach, amazingly, almost simultaneously. He found a nearby stream in which he cleaned himself up and tried to cool his head. What would Wynnfrith think if she saw you so? What would Elspeth do if she knew you had learned so much and then forgotten it?! Many other dark thoughts seeped in where fluttery birds and happy thoughts had so recently been.

He looked at Annie. She had been beautifully cared for, her coat brushed, a perfect shoe fit, well-fed, watered and, the saddle had been polished. Thomas is amazing! he told himself and further inspected the leatherwork around the horse. As he did, a letter fell out from beneath the saddle. Silas's reading was good enough to recognise his name on the front and the modest seal of the farrier on the back.

8: Bede

Oxford, March 1541

Yes, the King was great at making changes and dictating what everyone else must do but he very rarely considered the consequences of his crazy plans or ever even planned ahead. Is it likely that a whole nation would change its relationship with the church, the pope, monks, nuns and yes, God overnight? Well, of course, they would, because he said so. However, he didn't give enough credit to those gritty northerners who had been so valuable when his coffers needed filling or when a battle had to be won. It is unsurprising, therefore, that everyone didn't give way to his every whim and the shock, in particular, of the raids on monastic possessions, buildings and their orders led to the notorious Pilgrimage of Grace of 1536. Directed by some of the most prominent noble families of England such as the Nevilles and Percys, this rebellion of faith soon spread in all directions from Yorkshire and Lincolnshire. The Pilgrimage of Grace demanded a return to Rome and recruited Lords, priests, monks and peasants and, surprisingly, was reasonably confident of success due to its growing numbers. They were, in particular, aware of Thomas Cromwell's dark influence on the King and demanded his removal as well as a return to Rome.

Henry's initial response was to send troops north but struggled to match the 40,000 strong movement. He decided to resort to diplomacy, conceding to their demands and offering pardons. Or, at least, that's what he said. Digging himself deeper in this hole, he now had to decide what to do with those who had been part of this revolt. His progress of 1541 was his way of showing who was in charge. His slow journey north was escorted by thousands including a significant army and aimed ultimately to humble those may have considered crossing him.

But long before 1541 he began to torture and execute almost anyone he pointed at. In 1537 Thomas Percy was hung, drawn and quartered for his treason.

Henry's headcount was now growing by the month and, he continued to have people executed on a whim. Mercy petitions were endless and would touch even the hardest of hearts but had little effect on Henry once he had made a decision, so God help anyone who ended up in the Tower. No one would want to end up in the Tower.

Brother Bernard ended up in the Tower. He had been transported from York after being identified as one of those Benedictine monks who would not agree to the succession and had been known to speak out against it. Yes, York. As a rebel, he could only survive by hiding away which he did at his sister's house in Whitnourwhatnourgate. She worked such long hours that she was hardly there so it made an ideal discretion except that Bernard was both too proud to stop talking about his beliefs or stop wearing his monk's cassock. Initially, Elspeth would do the same, that is, wear her nun's habit and that is how the two struck up their alliance. Being a woman, the population of York was less sympathetic and that was when she used her birth name once again and embraced the role of a washerwoman. Eventually, Bernard was to be captured as was his sister for hiding him. They would never see each other again.

Initially, alone with a single guard, Brother Bernard's company would multiply like cells each time they reached a new hamlet, village, town or City.

As the carts trundled along roads barely fit for purpose, more carts and more soldiers appeared, more prisoners, more cries of pain and hunger. Those who made too much noise were punished and, on the excruciatingly long journey to London, they often sat and slept in their own waste. They were little bothered by verbal abuse, now labelled "heretics", "devil worshipers", "papist whores" and anything that suited their captors. People in hamlets and villages were encouraged to deride and throw refuse at the prisoners and demonstrate their allegiance to the crown and the Supreme Head of the Church of England.

Bernard had no care to live or die and his heart was crushed for what was being done to his faith, his order and his beloved country. He would often fall into a stupor expecting the end to come. He was no longer young and felt that, besides prayer, he had no resistance. However, he was human and was constantly being reminded of the terrors of the Tower via the taunts of the soldiers. One morning his cart stopped completely. In the near distance, he could see the church spire and rooftops of the beautiful town of Oxford. It emanated comfort, sanity and normality but any ideas of being able to get from his current position to that comfort would be nothing short of miraculous. In reality, it was also a melting pot of controversy and many of its abbeys had already fallen, but Bernard would have taken its unpredictability in preference to anything his current situation offered. Infrequently they would be given water. But not this time. No water. His cart was full, it stank and every fibre of his being hurt. Even so, his captors decided they could fit another prisoner in the cart. They had taken a route not far from Stratford upon Avon and picked up a few monks, already shackled and still clinging to their beloved Thelsford priory albeit in ruins. Amazingly, they managed to cram this additional creature in. He groaned and leaned on Bernard. Bernard did his best to look this unfortunate character up and down and decided he would be most comfortable if he cradled him. It was instantly clear that this gave the man some comfort despite his blatant injuries. Little was said. Not that they were allowed to speak but there was still an uncanny sense of camaraderie amongst the bedraggled victims. Miles and miles passed, the light disappeared and the only benefit of being so crowded was that it kept out some of the cold. There was an eerie silence except for the soldiers making camp and boasting of their conquests, presumably about how many ageing, shackled monks they had defeated in battle that day. Then Bernard heard an unintelligible sound. It became clearer. A small voice said

'Thank you, Brother'. Bernard twisted his head and saw that it was the last addition, this battered man beneath his arm.

'Bede' he said.

'Ah, The Venerable Bede' replied Bernard attempting a joke for, indeed, Bede was the stuff of ancient history being one the founding fathers of Christianity in Britain. A small gruff noise came from Bede acknowledging his humour.

'May I pray for you Brother Bede?' said Bernard.

'I would so much welcome that brother, but not aloud, I wouldn't wish you to be further beaten, pray in your heart if you please.' Bernard had been praying incessantly in his heart for months so a little postscript for his newfound friend wasn't a problem. By the 1500s there were numerous factions of monastic orders and, it probably won't surprise you to hear that, sometimes, they agreed on very little. This, now, was of such little consequence that Brother Bernard wasn't the least interested in Bede's order or anything else.

'Our Lord suffered worse' croaked Bede, 'let them do what they will' and then he simply went to sleep. Bernard too slipped into an uncomfortable and inconsistent nightmare that seemed to last for days.

The next thing he knew, he was being offered water and it was Bede who was cradling him. There was a third person just behind them both at the cart's edge who had died that day. It would have been unwise to say anything as it would have invited a further flogging so it was another half-day before the carcass was hauled out and consequently offered a little more room. The guards were both incompetent and cruel. There was no rhyme or reason to their erratic mishandling of their prisoners and abuse ranged from perpetual humiliation to murder. They took glee in watching each other drive daggers into random body parts of their victims, the aim being to puncture and penetrate as slowly as possible. They would take bets on this. Few victims would survive even a leg wound of this nature. Brother Bernard would never be able to clear the image of one such torment from his mind. Early on in the journey, a companion had been randomly dragged, hair first, from the vehicle into the midst of the drunken rabble. These weren't punishments, just the result of a perverse game to while away the journey. Part of the fun was observing a victim's reaction as they faced mutilation or death which, as the diversity of human nature dictates, could be unpredictable and, seemingly, entertaining to the thugs. One Cistercian monk had to bear a blade being painstakingly driven up from under his chin, through his jaw and as far as his brain. This monk was unbelievably stoic, accepting his death with a Jesus-like resolve that every Holy man would wish for but Bernard wondered if, when his time came, he would be able to do the same. The guards knew that almost any cut was fatal, infections were rife and there was no care given for those who were slowly dying, it simply made the carts lighter and meant less work. As long as they had a reasonable quota of surviving prisoners by the time they reached London, they would get their payment.

One soldier was an exception, in more ways than one. He was younger than the others, much slighter in build, inexperienced, and was troubled by the violence. Four days into Bernard's journey he could hear a whisper, presuming it was one of his co-captors.

'Fathers…Fathers…some water.' This was repeated so quietly that it was somewhat dream-like but it was enough to get Bernard to turn his head. As he did, he couldn't help thinking what an absolute mess had been made of the Reformation in England. This poor lad doesn't even know the difference between a priest and a monk, enough to get him killed. Death through ignorance thought Bernard. And, sure enough, young Eirik, sneaked some water to them both. Having a Viking name in the mid-sixteenth century was rare. Eirik had come from a long line of Viking stock and did have a Christian name but chose not to use it. None of this much mattered as all the other guards just called him Dung.

People often ask "where is God when…" and this would have been Bernard's answer. God was there, in Eirik's heart and in the water. Often simply in the small things, and Bernard was damn glad to see God this day. Bede spluttered out a few words,

'stop my son, you put yourself in danger…nothing for us now.' Eirik ignored him but did keep a nervous, watchful, eye on his colleagues. What followed astonished all the monks in the cart. Eirik leaned in and, with his thumb, gently cleaned the eyes of every brother. They had all been practically blinded by the conglomerate of filth that had accrued amongst them on this infinite journey. Bernard took his hand and offered a blessing but Eirik took it away as he knew it would draw attention. It is fair to say that this young and noble man of integrity saved many lives. Sadly, the question was what for?

This remarkable clandestine altruism continued day after day until even the minimal difference in water ration was noticed. Disappointingly, it was someone who Eirik regarded as a friend that uncovered his good works and who thought to gain favour amongst the more brutal guards in reporting this misdemeanour. To be clear, these soldiers were nothing grand like Gentlemen Pensioners or Yeomen they were simply mercenaries. Brutes. They would kill their grandmother for the right coin so, in most situations, their anger dictated their decisions and actions. What followed was a great deal of shouting, threatening and Eirik being dragged this way, then that. Being punched by one, kicked by another and spat at repeatedly, they then decided that it would be completely legitimate to hang him from a tree. The monks that were able to make any noise at all protested but only invited laughter at their pathetic pleads and this was mostly, if not completely, ignored. However, seemingly as if it were the last call before death, they successfully raised the volume and, if any sense could be made of this cacophony at all it was

'Take me instead…take me instead…'. Surprisingly, the gaffer was taken with this. Not moved mind you, just interested. He walked up to the cart in which Bernard and Bede were.

'So all of you papist shites will give your lives for useless Dung here?' Pathetic as it was, they acknowledged and verified his question.

'Well, well Dung, what sort of favours you been offering these sheep shaggers then?' It was rhetorical and invited more raucous laughter from the mercenaries. He took the rope, already wrapped around Erik's neck, dragged him to the cart and, although there was no room at all in the cart now, threw poor Eirik on top of the prisoners. They all groaned and, although manacled, they attempted to protect him immediately and, whenever they were offered any water rations, it was passed immediately on to Eirik.

There were a few days when the weather was more favourable, the soldiers periodically distracted, and the monks recuperated a little. Bernard found that he had the chance to hold a conversation with his new friend and they mostly talked about how they had arrived at this point. Bernard explained that those monks from his abbey in Lindisfarne, who had refused to go the way of the King, were branded rebels and were hunted down. They had made a pact to return to the island when everything had settled down because that's what they believed would happen. Surely the King couldn't sustain this nonsense? There would be a day when it was all back to what it should be. Then, they would re-establish the abbey and its good works. Bernard told Bede about how he had managed to hide for a while at his sister's home in Whitnourwhatnourgate in the City of York where he had trained a homing pigeon. At this point, Bede stopped Bernard in mid-conversation, seemingly astonished.

'Who would believe such a thing? I have my very own sweet pigeon, Hope, that I cared for when I was banished. What creatures they are' said Bede. He then went on to tell his own story, not dissimilar to Brother Bernard's. They exchanged the addresses of their hiding places and their trusted colleagues as if it were two people on vacation swapping addresses. Their respite was short-lived as the rains came, the guards became irritable and the rations were almost gone.

The rest of the journey was extremely unpleasant but uneventful except they were surprised to eventually make London. They could see its walls in the distance. Neither Bernard nor Bede had seen London before, nor had any desire to do so, and they were astonished at its size and how busy it was. Although far away, Bernard managed to correctly identify Westminster Abbey, one of England's oldest Benedictine houses very recently disestablished and he was encouraged to see it intact although he had no hope that the building would be there for much longer. As they got nearer there seemed to be people everywhere but the one thing that commanded their attention, as they blinked away the dirt from their eyes, was the Tower itself. Their cruel travelling companions had gleefully described this daunting hell on earth in every detail and, this included, what it looked like. By now they felt little fear, in a state beyond exhaustion and they used every degree of self-discipline to deal with their pain. All the same, it was an awesome sight. However, just half an hour later they were surprised as they seemed to be taking a detour. Instead of heading straight for the City walls and the Tower they were now travelling south-east toward the Thames. Having reached its banks, they were dragged and tipped out of the carts and lined up at the water's edge. Still tied to each other, they were able to look down, and, what was a drop of about ten feet, seemed like a chasm. Before they knew it they were ungraciously pushed into the river. Not surprisingly, a few welcomed this, hoping for a swift demise but this was not the intent of their captors. This human merchandise had to be reasonably presented when delivered to the Tower and this was the mercenaries' genius bulk-cleaning solution.

As most of the monks were tied to at least one other person and some of them wished to live and some wished to die, there was violent and erratic movement and many just disappeared into the filth of the Thames. At this point, the gaffer gave a panicked command to get them out. Easier said than done. As the soldiers ran down the embankment, they floundered grabbing ropes, clothes, arms and then noticed a body swimming away at speed. At first, this was difficult to comprehend until they realised that young Eirik hadn't been tied to anyone else and had got away. The first few prisoners were now recovered and on the shore cheering "God speed!" after Eirik for which they were, again, duly assaulted. He truly was an excellent swimmer and soon disappeared into the distance. Two of the monks were lost and two seemingly dead. Those two were cut adrift. The stupid soldiers argued amongst themselves as to whose fault this was but were now grieving the fact that they had arrived in London with less than sixty per cent of their original captors. The most serious consequence for them was that they would lose money. Rebel monks were relatively low down in the order of retribution but some would still need to be tortured and put to death to create an example for anyone with similar sympathies who may have considered acting on them.

The prisoners shivered, groaned, coughed and some cried, this already seemed like torture and they all prayed for it to end. Boats arrived. At least there was plenty of room in them. The boatman scoffed.

'Lost a few again, have you?' The gaffer let forth all the profanity and blasphemy that he knew but then realised that this boatman would happily turn back and report their poor management at the Tower if he didn't take care. Bernard commented to Bede that the boatman was different. There was no cruelty in him, just doing his job and, although five of the soldiers remained on board, this was possibly the most peaceful hour they had had in a month. Bernard quietly said a prayer for Eirik and for the boatman. Bede said a prayer for the mercenaries in which he forgave them and asked God to do the same.

The Reformation, in part, was a movement to get rid of corrupt church members and, there was no doubt that some were living the good life at the expense at others but, for those who had truly dedicated their lives to God and the betterment of life for their fellow man, monks were brothers absolute. They had a connection beyond the understanding of most laymen and such a bond was now eternally sealed between Bede and Bernard. As their boat gently rowed toward its destination they knew that they had found a mutual strength gifted from above and certain that, whatever became of them it would be part of God's plan.

9: Father Matthew

York, July 1541

I seemed to do a lot of sleeping and was constantly reminding myself that, although short, mice had bloody good lives. Godwin had, in his kindness, decided that likkle mousey would like some cake now and again. You can imagine what a treat this was but even I knew that this wasn't exactly accepted staple diet for mice. It was, however, very good of him and I loved being in his home. I was now tucked up in little Lizzy's arms and fully understood what it was like to be a pet. She continuously poured love and affection on me and, hopefully, I was offering something in return. Part of my brief: don't form attachments. What? How on earth do you do that? If you met Edward you would say he makes you smile, makes your heart glow, how do you switch off from that? And Lizzy. I ask you, I'm watching her dying and I'm not meant to take notice? Who writes these dumb rules. Yes, she is really poorly and, what's worse is I know what's ailing her and, what's even worse than that, I know the cure but can't help. If there is any way around it I will, definitely, help. Her father, Godwin, was assisting her to sip a warm drink containing herbs and, before I knew it, he had gently whisked me away. He never spoke to me directly, almost as if he wanted no part of this weird talking mouse stuff that's going on. He was kind with me, and to me. Eventually, he settled me into my workshop for the start of the day. Today, though, was a very special day. We were to meet Elspeth and Wynnfrith and there was some hope of progress in the air.

As soon as we reached the workshop, Godwin welcomed Edward and his little head, wearing a broad smile, peeped through into my hole-in-the-wall apartment.

'Excited?' he asked.

'Possibly more frustrated Ed, I'm desperately hoping that the sisters have more to give us and that, together, we can make some headway. The last visit was a complete and utter disaster!' I said somewhat grumpily. I was there for a reason (and I don't mean that in the same way our intrepid monks might) but literally I'd been dropped in York for a reason! I'd been put there for a very specific purpose, to monitor, understand and take part in any attempts to avoid this imminent Cataclysm. So far I'd spent most of the time sleeping and the rest either being petted, locked up or having pins stuck in my arse. I snapped, momentarily, out of my negativity. The sisters alone inspired confidence. They knew what they were doing and, by now, must have made more, worthwhile contacts.

'You coming then grumpyarse' said Edward with glee.

'I'll grumpyarse you' said I 'you'd better not let Godwin or your father hear you speak so and…while we're at it…no swinging about, no talking and watch out for muggers.'

'You got it boss' he replied cheekily and before I knew it we were on our way. As we passed the Minster guess who was there giving his best bullshit? Yes, Bayard the master of popular public oddities and entertainments. Ed looked nervously on as it was clear Bayard had seen us but he took no notice as he was busy with his most recent expose. Believe it or not, he had lined up, all of King Henry's illegitimate children. All sixteen of them apparently and, he could tell you all their mothers' names too. Yet again, there were plenty of paying customers that fell for this crap but, boy, did he overdo the redhead thing. Powerful genes that Henry has, to be sure. God knows where he'd got this lot from but I was increasingly concerned for their welfare as some of them were very young. I realised how distracted I had become. Concentrate, soon be there. Edward, true to his word, hadn't spoken but, as we approached the door of Elspeth and Wynnfrith's washhouse, he paused and the sudden slant of his head suggested that we should stop and listen as there was an unholy rumpus going in inside. If I'm honest, we did try eavesdropping but before we could get close enough to the door hinges, we heard Elspeth scream,

'Just get out! And give us time to think you clot!' And, as the last word was still ringing in our ears, a man was bodily pushed out of the door and past us, falling into the straw on the threshold. Ed took great care to place my box down and was particularly considerate in positioning me as I now had a ringside view of events.

He respectfully rushed to help the stranger to his feet and very graciously said,

'My Lord Silas. Are you hurt sir, may I be of assistance?' Up to this point, I knew nothing of Silas except for rumours that incessantly circulated York. Was he a Lord? Was he the village idiot?

The jury was out, you simply took him as you found him. Let's face it, we're all judgemental and I was, unashamedly judgmental. Nice twit. That's what I thought.

Nice twit, and, to be honest, it's still what I thought after I'd known him a few months. It was both endearing and entertaining watching Edward fawn over this very important idiot. But, I simply thought, if he's important to Ed, he's important to me. Silas responded to Edward in kind and assured him all was well but unable to say anymore as he was a secret agent. Not secret anymore, I thought. The door was thrown open again and Elspeth's voice, yet again, bellowed out of the wash house.

'Get back in here you useless lump and you too!' referring to Edward. 'What is it with that damn ferret?!' Elspeth was indeed angry as this was possibly the worst language you would ever hear from her.

What was incredibly reassuring was that both Elspeth and Wynnfrith were both in a no-nonsense mode so, within minutes, she made it clear that we were now all on the same team, that is, excluding me of course, being no more than a visiting rodent. Elspeth's temper gave a lot away. Still furious at Silas's unexpected disappearance, she didn't give anyone else a chance to speak. Silas was silently thanking God that he had called at the travellers rest on his way back from Stratford or he would have had nothing to impart except for digging up a toy box with some kids. Like all sensible men, he stayed quiet until he felt that Elspeth's energy levels were waning. Believe me, this took some time, she must have had gunpowder for breakfast, thought I.

Poor Silas was now practically shaking. As always, he had dreamed of a hero's return and even though a bollocking was very much an everyday occurrence to him, he felt he had disappointed Wynn, the very girl for whom he had harboured and nurtured such deep feelings. As I looked at her I would say she was giving nothing away but was, very much, the level head in the room. She put her arm around her sister and tried to calm her.

'Shall we see if, together, we can measure progress sister?' Magic. I noted immediately that Wynnfrith had a very special influence on her sister and knew we may have to call on that in the future.

They decided to tell us everything they knew. They told us about Brother Bernard, what they thought the Cataclysm was and what would trigger it. What they had assumed from the pieces of parchment from Bernard, and promises from the Mayor, Robert, about involving agents at a higher level. By the time the sisters had finished speaking there was a complete calm in the room and all eyes were on Silas. He apologised for his escapade, assuring all gathered that he simply wanted to expedite the investigation and deliver speedy results. In truth, he seemingly just wanted to impress Wynnfrith. A gentler reprimand followed and he promised not to do anything so independent again. He then told us the, apparently over dramatised, tale of his discovery regarding the pigeon called Hope that did, indeed, only fly north to south from Holy Island, Lindisfarne. He told them also that the bird had belonged to Bede but no one knew anything about Bede.

The heat was off Silas, he had, remarkably, delivered although, momentarily, they still couldn't make sense of what they had. After what seemed like a very long silence in which everyone took turns looking at each other but saying nothing, Elspeth noted,

'Well, we all knew Bernard belonged to the Holy Island abbey at Lindisfarne so it's not really telling us much!'

'No' said Wynn, 'it's more than that, it's clearly about something there or something that has happened there. Think. Our scrap parchment says "ord must be saved" clearly meaning something or somebody from the abbey needs to be secured.'

'A sword!' exclaimed Edward.

'Yes!' agreed Silas 'An ancient Viking sword that will save the nation from King Harry's evil deeds!' You could rely on Silas for the dramatic and, this was certainly a very useful contribution as the idea of a sword just didn't seem to connect with either an abbey or, indeed, Brother Bernard at all. I looked around, amused by the contortion of faces, the faces you see when someone is trying to remember the name of a long lost acquaintance. Silas was even grunting as he did it. They were clueless and, as I considered what an unbearably long journey this was going to be, I said,

'Word! It's the Word that has to be saved! Bloody obvious if it's a monastery! Word, word, word!'

Oops.

Everyone froze including Ed. I looked to him first and could tell that he wished to tell me off, he must have been thinking about the extensive efforts he had made to keep this quiet, and I'd blown it. Everyone else had backed off a few steps, Silas shivered and then nervously farted. I could see Elspeth draw a breath and expected a real drama.

'I told you it spoke' declared Wynnfrith calmly. So, they had picked this up on our last visit, I thought. I wasn't too bothered that I was out, in fact we would all benefit if I could contribute without using Edward as an interpreter but, again, I was dreading all the nonsense about witchcraft, "work of the devil" and so on. Before another word was spoken, Edward stood and told the tale of how we had met and how I had been sent "with the highest authority" to assist in the avoidance of the Cataclysm. He seemed to talk for ages! And, they listened. Moreover, God bless him, he told them that it would be offensive to imply any evil here. I was so proud of him. They certainly took note but on his conclusion, Elspeth said,

'Well, how come it can talk then?' It? It!? Had she not listened to anything, that's the secret bit! Edward reiterated the confines of our agreement and, as I turned to Wynnfrith, it was clear she was interested only in my answer.

'Word, yes it has to be.' Now, to be clear, in this context "The Word" could either mean the Gospels or Jesus Christ himself which both scared this motley group and empowered them at the same time. The only physical connection to Christ would be the host and I found this very unlikely. The host is the term used when people take bread and wine at communion. It's literally seen as being a part of Christ as he asked his followers, at the last supper, to remember him in this way. Silas was about to announce his intention to reinstitute the crusades, search for the holy grail, the lost ark of the covenant and some other nonsense when there was a quiet knock at the door upstairs.

'We have to stop meeting here' said I, rather sarcastically. I suggested the strategy of hiding was getting a little worn so Elspeth went to answer the door. To be clear, already there were four people and a mouse crammed between barrels, linen and buckets in a cellar so I was desperately hoping this wasn't turning into a party.

At the door was the man who had competed with Elspeth to win the parchment on Faith's return. A conversation ensued that could not be heard by us in the cellar but lasted over ten minutes. Trust was and was going to be, the greatest issue moving forward. We simply could not take under our wing just anyone who thought they had some information that would help us. Once uncovered, we would all be dead meat and there would be no one to avert this disaster of which we all spoke.

But trust this man, Elspeth did, and she didn't give trust lightly. This surely was an incredibly eventful day and nerves were yet again frayed as a man came down steps.

'Father Matthew!' exclaimed Wynnfrith. Elspeth did a double-take.

'You're Father Matthew?!' she then turned to the others.

'This is the man I saw at Whitnourwhatnourgate waiting for Faith to return' said Elspeth and it was also the priest I had seen watching Bayard's pathetic expose in the Minster square but, wisely, I kept my mouth shut, my secret had travelled abroad enough for one day. Elspeth sat him down on an upturned bucket and told us of their conversation at the door. In short, he did, absolutely, know of the Cataclysm, of Brother Bernard and, there in his pale hand was a piece of the very same parchment that the sisters had.

'May I?' said Elspeth.

'It's yours, my dear.' Said Father Matthew politely. They put what they had, three pieces together, on the floor. This didn't add much but it added enough. Translated, it looked like this:

hath spawned a plan
Eadfrith's hand and
Command, the Word must be saved
isle to north of Stratford on the Avon
and in the Minster
Here the catacly

There was still a great deal missing but the word "Eadfrith" jumped out at us all. I knew instantly what this meant and, for the first time since arriving, actually prayed that someone else did too.

'There's a tanner down Petergate called Erdfirth' blurted Edward.

'And….' commenced Silas, possibly going down an even dafter route, but thankfully he was then interrupted by the priest.

'My children. This puts us in a much stronger position. I will explain. The very object that we must secure is none other than the Lindisfarne Gospels themselves.' A little light went on in Wynnfrith and Elspeth's noggins but not even a flicker in the vicinity of Silas and Edward.

'This beautiful and glorious book represents the very foundation of our faith in England. Eadfrith was the very man, along with his brothers, that created it and, as well as telling us the story of Jesus's life and ministry in Latin, notes were later added in Anglo Saxon. It is indeed one of England's greatest treasures. Eadfrith was Bishop of Lindisfarne in the seventh century and, on its conclusion, this magnificent tome was bound in leather, gold and gemstones. It is regarded as one of the most breathtaking artefacts of western art and faith. I once held it myself and assure you of its power and its beauty.'

'So, to Lindisfarne I go!' shouted Silas as he stood. Silence. He sat down again.

'It's not there my son' said Father Matthew.

'Then where is it?' said Edward innocently.

'It's not been on the island since the ninth century, the Vikings saw to that. Raids from the west meant that valuables from the abbey had to be removed and, since, they have been at a priory in Durham.' Silas leapt up again.

'So...'

'Please sit down' said Wynnfrith, knowing exactly what he was going to say. This cut deep. Silas was desperately trying to hide his obsession with little Wynn and even this little suggestion seemed like a reprimand.

'It's not in Durham...' Continued the priest.

'How come you know so much?' asked Wynn who then thought to herself that she was sounding quite abrupt, almost like Elspeth.

'Simple child. It's all gone. All of it. All of it from everywhere. Cromwell's had the lot.' They knew instantly what, and who, he was referring to.

Thomas Cromwell had been dead just over a year and, yet, his name still struck terror into the hearts of most Englishmen. A cunning and ruthless lawyer, he had acquired so many titles whilst in Henry's favour that it would have been onerous to list them all but he was, unquestionably, by 1534, the King's chief minister and principal secretary and he was entirely, for a spell, the second most powerful man in the land. He was a major player in the Reformation and consequently credited with securing Henry's marriage to Anne Boleyn. He soon fell out of favour with Queen Anne and so had little difficulty in orchestrating her downfall and execution. However, as with all of the King's most trusted counsellors, the novelty wore off. Following Jane Seymour's death, he arrogantly choreographed a betrothal between Henry and Anne of Cleves, a complete disaster resulting in the eventual annulment of the marriage. After a spell in the Tower, Cromwell was beheaded on 28th July 1540.

When Father Matthew said that "he'd taken it all" he was referring to the aggressive plundering of monastic wealth from 1536 onwards. Cromwell was diligent enough to ensure that these riches were flowing in the direction of the crown although everyone knew that this money was often used as "persuasion" to bring stubborn people in line with the new way of things. He also made sure he looked after himself. Would every item have been logged and accounted for? Not likely, and it is certainly probable that, before the Reformation, there was no comprehensive catalogue of church property at all so, consequently, there was no method of verifying exactly how much fell into Cromwell's grubby hands. Rumour had it that Cromwell, for whatever reason, had decided to take the Lindisfarne Gospels into his care and many believed that the book hadn't got as far as the King.

'Where does that leave us?' asked Silas innocently.

'We need to track this Holy book down. You can be sure that the King and those closest to him will want to secure it too. If only we knew its significance' said Father Matthew. 'We can no longer meet here, it's too dangerous' he continued 'and, we need to be much more discrete about who we can, and can't, trust.' That's bloody rich, I thought, he creeps in here out of the blue without any warning and he's lecturing us about discretion!

He then said,

'I'll speak to Robert and he will be in touch regarding

our next conference.' He knows Robert too, I said to myself in a notably stroppy manner. Then, remarkably, another revelation but from Edward,

'If you mean Mayor Robert, I know him' he said calmly.

I was, of course, flabbergasted but not able to ask him how.

'He's my uncle.' Of course, I thought he was joking but, as it turns out, not at all. Ed's aunt was married to the Mayor and this is why Wynn knew Edward. I was starting to feel proper left out of this family.

'And what of Brother Bernard?' asked Father Matthew.

'We know nothing and we have no way or either contacting him or finding him but I just know he will get to us if he can' answered Wynnfrith at which the priest adopted a sombre expression. I looked around, I wasn't the only one who had concerns about our most recent member, he was hiding more cards than he was showing. I was becoming irritated. You can't bite your lip if you're a mouse, not without serious consequences that is, but I did stay quiet and leave judgments and decisions to everyone else. He turned to leave and suddenly turned back, clearly he hadn't finished,

'The talking mouse may come in use too' he commanded, and then he left.

'You're bloody kidding me, I've sat here holding my breath for half an hour whilst Father windbag bleats on about some blessed book and he knew about me anyway, how could he..' Ed interrupted,

'Bayard, the stage, remember?' Of course, he was there silently creeping around. I was still pretty furious he hadn't said anything sooner. As I looked upward the girls were giggling, really laughing in a way I hadn't seen before. Silas looked sheepish. When people laugh he would always presume it was always because of him. But it wasn't.

'Your pet mouse is so funny, what's he for again?' Wynn said to Edward. He laughed too, then Silas joined in. So I decided to put my foot down (or would have done if I still had a foot).

'Now listen up you lot and listen carefully!' I launched into my most effective reprimand. More laughter, I wasn't going to win this one and realised that, although at my expense, this merriment was certainly helping to bond this team. Team! That was one of my jobs and I had forgotten. If I was to get any sense out of this lot I would have to wait so attempted some cute standing on two legs stuff, some scratching around to at least demonstrate that I wasn't always angry. Why was I like this? The mix was so powerful, I was having so many days where I had forgotten my former self and completely become lost in this adventure. My personality was so different. Curmudgeonly northern, and often foul-mouthed, rodent! And, most of the time, I loved it, I didn't waste words and most people knew instantly what I was getting at. At least, for now, everyone was happy, I politely asked if I could now contribute. Wynnfrith was still sniggering a little and I could see that this, in turn, was making Silas's day. He was now endlessly staring at little Wynn and I made a note to self to advise him that this wasn't necessarily the best way to win a maiden's heart.

Thanks to Edward, I was now completely out of my box and on an upturned barrel and even I realised how ridiculous I must have seemed. As I looked down I could see the damage Godwin's cake binge had caused, my little fat belly resting on my feet. This did, however, hide my embarrassment if you get my drift, as I was always completely naked except for when I was in the workshop wearing my rodent-sized leather apron. I tried very hard to ensure that this ridiculous exhibition didn't minimise my determination.

'From now on, please, don't add people into our group as if it were an embroidery group (this already offended the sisters, must dial it back some, thought I). I came here to offer my knowledge and service in this greater matter and part of my brief was to reveal my power of speech to just one person. Now you two ladies, Edward, Silas, Godwin the Carpenter, Bayard the bastard entertainer, the priest and all his mistresses know!' None of them did sarcasm it turns out, so my exaggeration was wasted.

'Sorry. I actually have no knowledge of the priest having mistresses (this was going to be hard work). However, we can use our growing numbers to our advantage but need strategies that guarantee secrecy.' Edward then suggested that we needed a name and I was, again, quite rude implying we weren't playing at Robin Hood but then it did strike me that we should have an identity. Numerous flaming ridiculous suggestions came forth like vomit from a drunk. "The Lindisfarne Gospel defenders" was the offering excitedly introduced by Edward.

'For God's sake Ed, I'm not sure that the name of the gang should advertise one of the things that we're keeping secret!' He looked quite put out and I could tell that, yet again, the group, thought I was being very rude. Much too sensitive this lot.

Then Silas decided to pitch in. We had no hope whatsoever of hearing anything meaningful but, it seemed only fair to let him speak his little mind. Sadly, almost everyone tuned out completely due to the very low expectation of anything worthwhile being delivered as he started to ramble about his drinking companions in Wolverdington.

'Silas, my friend' I said, 'you've told us all about this and it certainly was useful.'

'No. No, you don't understand. When they first spoke to me and, as they complimented me on my contribution to the conversation, they called me something quite unusual.' I would imagine that wasn't the first time he's been called something unusual, I thought.

'Agent of the Word' he said with some authority.

This stopped us in our tracks not only because it adequately described what we were and what, for the time being, we were about, it also made us think that his encounter was more than a coincidence. Wynnfrith smiled at Silas.

'Wonderful, that seems so appropriate' she said. Silas blushed. He really, really blushed so he then stood up and this, of course, came as a warning to all that he was about to deliver something grandiose. Elspeth hurriedly moved objects out of the way for his safety.

'My ladies…I am you're very…at your service…your most obedient..' and this incomprehensible gibberish gushed forth from the lanky beacon for several minutes. His titian hair sketched its way across his accentuated features and eventually settled calmly on the rear of his scalp. It was a moment, at least, where I was able to measure some growing affection and, dare I say, respect for Silas as everyone just sat back and listened. He sat down. I looked at Elspeth, it had all gone over her head and she remained thoughtful for a few more moments.

'That's it then. We are the Agents of the Word.'

'Agents of the Word' we chorused. It did seem somewhat childish but, for five minutes, we were the new knights of the round table and there was, undoubtedly, a warm sense of camaraderie.

I picked up the conversation.

'We must be so careful from now on, our practices must remain completely clandestine and, whether there are others like us up and down the country or not, we must tighten our grip on any information that we have as a group.' I spent a few minutes explaining to Edward and Silas what clandestine meant and then suggested that all tangible information passed between agents should carry our sign.

'There's something else' added Silas, 'the kind farrier that replaced Annie's shoe left a note in my saddle.'

'What did it say?' I asked, trying not to reveal my frustration at his timing. He paused, then decided he would try to blag whatever was on this cloth he had just removed from his purse. It was clear to me that Silas still couldn't read and, although I think everyone in the room had also I detected this, I saved him the embarrassment by asking him to pass it to Edward. It simply read, "we are with you". That was it.

'Let's take it at face value. If he is an ally he will get in touch again'.

'About Agents of the Word' said Elspeth, 'what is our sign to be?' I knew what she meant instantly. We had to get better at keeping conversations and information within the group. I told them in detail about my workshop, home, hiding place and how I had, at my disposal, a range of tools and time to create a unique seal.

'A seal?! interacted Silas. 'Kings, officials, Mayors have seals.' Ed further impressed by telling us that his father had access to a seal. I assured them that I could fashion a discrete seal and make enough matrices (the stamps) for everyone to use.

'Won't a big wax seal be suspicious?' said Wynn.

'It would.' I replied, 'but these won't be big and I'll make sure that you can use the stamp to print with almost anything.'

'How soon?' asked Elspeth so I guaranteed that this would be a priority and all would be delivered within the week. Our meeting was growing to an end and, certainly, the Agents of the Word were looking like a unit. As we all watched and admired how Wynn doggedly negotiated the steps up from the cellar without complaint, I heard Ed whisper to Silas that he would teach him to read. Elspeth turned to me and whispered,

'you will be our greatest asset mouse, I can see that now.' Ultimately, despite the next month feeling as though I had contributed little, she would be proved to be right. We were all excited for our next meeting and were feeling confident again.

We left and, not for the first time, noticed a blonde-haired young man, of athletic build, hovering quite innocently near the washhouse. He moved to speak to Edward but Edward, not surprisingly following his previous experiences, decided to march away. I mentioned this but Ed just brushed it aside and said that he must have been waiting for the sisters. We spoke no more about it and headed   back.

10: Nick

York, July 1541

I had worked hard all day in the workshop and settled to sleep. As I did, my mind drifted to a far but familiar place. I saw myself in a different guise, not a mouse but a man. A learned man. He says that he is a leading practitioner in the field of historical analytics. Yes, Of course, that was me. I had been asked to give a lecture to an audience of over two thousand impatient enthusiasts of historical science. Regarded as an expert in my field, I was always very happy to inform people who, generally speaking, had a similar analytical mind but I had no patience with notions of time travel and historical fiction.

I could see myself in front of thousands but I didn't seem nervous. I approached the lecture, proud of the progress that my sector had achieved in the century and a half since this discreet body was formed to offer a holistic approach to collating historical evidence. I was working in historical analytics and thanks to the advances in both digital, holographic and quantum technology we had drastically altered how we now dealt with historical fact. I started to speak, confidently.

'This lecture is not uniquely about black holes, singularities or our general interest in dark matter and dark universes, although I will spend some time giving you some detail about how the numerous discoveries from the days of Hawking onward have helped us to understand the universe we live in, the ones we don't and how this informs our understanding of what previously we described as "the past.". Together, we are all history enthusiasts so, believe me, when I tell you that today I have no intention of offending anyone's sensibilities and hope you leave here much better informed and excited about our imminent quest.'

It was the word "quest" alone that invited instant, supportive and enthusiastic cheers. It's quite foggy in my mind. This isn't a dream, it is too detailed but much of it just translates as nonsense to me. The thought of eating supersedes this nonsense. I concentrate.

'In some sense, history doesn't really exist. Until recently we have had no way of touching it or referencing it directly but, surprisingly, every hour we engage as a society, and as individuals, with historical notions and considerations, brushing against it constantly in the form of entertainment, reference and as a comparison to who and where we find ourselves in the present. But this has often been done in a fanciful way, projecting modern politics, ideals and fashions on another age; misrepresenting intention, building an evidential tower out of three or four bricks of information and sometimes, conjuring outright lies for the convenience of a few. Elbert Hubbert famously said, "History is gossip well told". Napoleon agrees: "History is a set of lies agreed upon." H.L. Mencken describes the historian as, "An unsuccessful novelist" and Will Durant tells us "Most history is guessing and the rest is prejudice." So how should we regard events passed and how can we possibly give them some meaning? After all, for generations, most of the population have considered history as fact.'

I broke away from this silly thought, snuggled into the straw and thought again of Lizzy, was there anything anyone could do to help her? I started to get confused and struggled to understand this boring narrative in my head. And then it came back, I could see myself striving to sound important.

'Our traditional approach as historians would be to access and collate any information we could and the most conscientious historians would rely, usually, on primary sources to create a fair and balanced interpretation of events. However, long ago, it became clear that even the most dependable photograph and film footage could be doctored leading to mass conspiracy theories – almost about anything. A case in point has to be the NASA missions of the 1960s and 70s that was supported by extensive documentary evidence but some people, as is their right, chose to question the evidence. An even greater enemy of totally reliable historical narrative has always been the bias in which history is written. Would a British or French account of Trafalgar be the same? On the bigger issues, yes, but the detail can offer confusing contradictions. When Abraham Lincoln was shot on 14th April 1865 in Ford's Theatre in Washington DC, there was absolutely no shortage of witnesses. It would be hard to imagine a more public setting. However, our understanding of the events is a consensus of witness statements rather than the absolute truth. Statements from those in the audience conflicted so much with each other that it left investigators completely confused.'

Grains, straw, warmth, new friends. These things, quite rightly, wanted to dominate my thoughts. I fought to get a grasp of this recent memory but it all seemed so dull, unnecessary and irrelevant and then I could hear my voice again. My voice? It was different, I was undoubtedly now a northerner, a northern mouse I suppose but that's not what I'm hearing. I tried as hard as possible to concentrate.

'It's simple, isn't it? Where humans are involved there isn't just a margin of error but also the misinformation we get due to people's need to dramatise, embellish and claim part of an event as one's own. In fairness, people's memories sometimes are simply not reliable.

So, up until the past hundred years, the study of history has been little different from a complex court case and the best we could ever hope for was enough evidence to reach a reasonable consensus. Proof in itself is very rare in most aspects of historical research as it is in life.

It was as late as the 21st century when the bones of Richard the third were discovered, and an age-old argument about his physique was settled. Unpopular Tudor press labelled him as a stooped villain but so many of the accounts were written after his death by his enemies, at a time when he no longer had any support. In 2012, his bones were discovered in a car park and science, confirmed by matching DNA from his descendants, gave up the truth about his body and his death. He did have curvature of the spine (scoliosis) and there was considerable evidence of "humiliation injuries" inflicted at the time of, and after, his death which probably said more about the Lancastrians that killed him than Richard himself.

The application of forensics aided us in being "much more sure" about certain aspects of his life and death. That phrase has become the unofficial motto of our department, all of us understanding that it's often dangerous to be completely certain of anything. That's why historical research throughout the third millennium has been correctly regarded as science and our technology has allowed us to further investigate the unknowns.'

What a windbag. Is this truly me? Must concentrate, I'm struggling to remember why I'm here but, much more powerful is the urge to sleep, ignore, it. I find I'm not the least bit interested in history.

'To be clear that is all we do. Our agency is an investigative enterprise and it is there simply to inform. Our unique departments comprise of highly trained experts with a single aim of filling in the gaps and clearing up uncertainties. At this point, I know you want me to address that term we all hate but you love to use!'

I remembered those gathered, starting to laugh and there are a few cheers of anticipation.

'I can tell you unequivocally there is no such thing as time travel! There is…no…Time Travel!'

It was said light-heartedly but there were few friendly groans of disapproval.

'However, it is a flattering notion and what we do here is probably as close to the fictional perception of time travel that there is. So what is going on? As many of you are aware, the last few hundred years have taught us much more about dark matter and quantum juxtaposition. Put simply, we know that past perceptions of the supernatural, alien culture and extrasensory experiences have more than likely been based on some fact. Us, together in this room, here, at this time, represent just one page in an almost infinite book. There are so many other pages. What we have been able to do is to reference some of those pages even if they are regarded normally as outside our current time and space. We can glimpse the past and, yes, even interact. However, our "presence" in events of the past is little more than a virtual reality experience. One, I grant you, that is now astonishingly real and rewarding. Remember the first time we were able to get hazy images of Victorian London and how excited the previous generation was at this revelation? We have come such a long way evolving a detailed code of practice, only pursuing specific areas of interest or contention and developing a recruitment plan for our pilots that from start to finish takes eight years even before a trial assignment'.

I'm a hologram? An avatar? A "pilot"? What a bloody cheek. I'll avatar this numpty. Why am I having trouble remembering and why is all this so incredibly bloody boring?

'Our most astonishing discovery? You can imagine that our greatest concern was that even the slightest amount of interference would affect historical events. We simply didn't know at the time that this was nonsense, it's science fiction. Let me give you an example. Imagine operating in fourteenth-century England. Our pilot's interaction with a young girl accidentally causes her to fall into a cold pond in Winter. Subsequently, she becomes ill and misses the opportunity to start work on the farm next door having been replaced by another girl. One way or another it seems this was meant to happen. Did we interfere? Yes. But it makes no difference, she simply wouldn't have got the job on the farm.'

I was startled and broke out of this. I can't help Lizzy, I thought. My interactions seem to have influence but events won't change despite my illusion of presence. I was now becoming more confused. Of course, I must at least try to make her feel better, more comfortable? I was at odds with my own theories and losing interest in my former life very quickly. No matter how I tried to sleep, my own, former, droning voice picked up where it had left off.

'How does this work? Truthfully, we are nowhere near understanding the complexities of these issues but it surely is an incredible advocate for what was once called fate. So, let me ask you – if you could be around just before the Titanic sank or the Amritsar massacre or before Shipman met his victims or before Dantz attacked the Mars shuttle, would you intervene? Of course, you would. That moral drive is so powerful within us that we want justice at any cost. It's perfectly natural to think in this way. But think this through. If you are the one shouting "iceberg!" before anyone else can even see one what do you think is likely to happen? The Titanic had received ice warnings long before it floundered and they were still ignored. Fred Fleet, with the best possible view on lookout, only saw the offending berg seconds before it struck so what hope would you have of being believed? Your next logical scenario is to think that you could replace him on lookout. What would you do with poor Fred? Imagine the sequence of changes possible for you to legitimately be in the crow's nest that night. As I talk, you're constantly creating juxtapositions of how this can be done. Believe me, we do the same but, so far, our interventions haven't made one bit of difference historically – as far as we know…'

There were cheers from the audience again.

'In any case, we have no wish to intervene. Interact, yes, but we work to a precise set of dos and don'ts, regulations that have been approved by every legal body imaginable and, these are constantly being reviewed.'

This is what I did? But it feels like the past. Of course, it's the past, it was last month. I'm now struggling to understand what has happened so think hard about what came next.

'Another myth – we are time-hopping every other week. In the last 5 years, there have been just 2 assignments and I have been preparing for as long as I can remember for my imminent mission. There are no adventures, each mission is a carefully thought out response to a historical anomaly and, believe me, we have sustained incredibly complex missions from which we have learned nothing.

So, to the process itself'. Wild cheers and applause continued for a few minutes so I seemingly waited for it to die down. What a dick, I appear to be grandstanding for God's sake.

'It's a mixture of the incredible and the ridiculous and, I know it has been responsible for much lampooning in the media. Magna Carta is at the core of the process. Not, of course, the historical Magna Carta but the amazing interface built by the Brunestein brothers; our very own digital dark matter search engine...'

I snapped out of my recollection. Search engine? The Brunesteins? Sanity intervened for a few moments. Must have dozed. I am Micklegate mouse. I'm sentient, I care for people. Edward, Godwin, Lizzy. Confused. I was so very confused but then my previous vision was back yet again. The auditorium. The audience was now watching a 3D presentation of the process and it occurred to me that they were little interested in the science. It was the drama and risk that interested them. They experienced a comprehensive display of how pilots are acclimatised to the biogel, the fluid in which they survive whilst on a mission. Although housed in a man-made womb, the pilots float throughout the duration and the biogel provides every need including exercise. Magna creates a streaming interface between the pilot and the desired destination. I have to accept that much of the attendees are nerds and the same questions crop up time after time.

'No, there is no way you or I or anyone can see what is going on besides the pilot so, within reason, we are left with the same historical conundrum, i.e. we have to rely totally on pilot feedback.'

The straw is so comfortable - must store some more food before we venture out. It's then I realise that this is the mix. The mix is when virtual reality becomes so real that a pilot becomes completely consumed by it. It's getting hard to fight this, I like my bed, my food and particularly enjoying meeting lady mice. I would happily lapse into this identity but my memory keeps prodding me. Dr Nick Douglas. Of course! That's who I am. Oh, that's who I was. I think. That means I'm not even really here. But I am. Don't want these thoughts again.

'Thank you so much ladies and gentlemen' I said out loud. I could hear Edward laugh in the distance. He's not distant, he's right next to me.

'Oh Edward' I said, 'didn't see you there.' He carried on laughing.

'You were saying the silliest things, do mice have nightmares?'

'Yes, yes, a nightmare Edward, wizards, magic and dark coffins, so glad it's morning!'

'Me too Doc!' he scoffed.

I couldn't risk this happening again. My colleagues behind the biogel casket have no way of knowing what goes on in this alternative world of mine so it's really important I don't get completely consumed. The one topic I did try to avoid at my lecture was that of accidents. In the early trials, there had been numerous cases of irreversible brain damage. I remain aware of the risks and accept them but must concentrate on my mission. I laughed, what ridiculous notions! The devil himself has entered my very thoughts. I am Micklegate and just need more sleep.

11: William Fawkes

York, July 1541

As we moved away from the washhouse, I became increasingly aware of the countless dangers that York presented to a creature of my size. Without Edward, I was completely helpless and vulnerable. There were beasts everywhere with little sign of order or control and, it wasn't just the large animals like oxen, pigs and horse that threatened, it was that impending notion of becoming entangled with one or more of the rats that terrified me. Truthfully, I was extremely concerned and my innate sensibilities didn't help, I simply didn't like the constant ill odours and the pushing and shoving that took place in the ever-narrowing snickleways. We entered Grope lane. If you think that's quite a crude reference, you should hear the more commonly used extension that accurately describes its purpose. More than anything, I still couldn't get why no one was doing anything about the filth. I had to accept that there was, in this age, no knowledge of germs but why didn't they tackle the smells and general tidiness of the streets? Instantly that put me in mind of the orders that York citizens had been given relating to that very issue. Still, not much sign of locals tarting up the town for Harry's visit I thought. Suppose, on that issue, I don't blame them.

I was having a series of personal issues. I say that like I needed a therapist. Perhaps I did. But it's hard to describe. Some days I had lost all sense of my former self, others I'd lost the plot completely. No, seriously, there have been times when I'd completely forgotten my brief and then, most days, I was simply Micklegate mouse. Added to that, I was daily becoming more and more aware of dangers both immediate and impending. To the self-appointed Agents of the Word, my value was only in my intellect, a heads up on historical events and my uncanny and unparalleled ability to fit into small spaces. That had become clear concerning the Tudor Rose ceiling boss that I was carving for the Minster as I had realised that I could fit into the back of it and that this was no coincidence.

Young as he was, passers-by showed deference to Edward as he was, unmistakably, no street urchin. Today, acknowledging the seriousness of our meeting, he was dressed as he would as if he were with his father attending official duties. He was very smartly wearing his best hat and skirted doublet with a thin cloak as it was warm outdoors. His gait gave him an air of authority that belied his age. This certainly made our passage through the City much easier and, besides the smells, much more pleasant. I'm not apologising for mentioning smells again, it's my story and I just didn't appreciate the peculiar and persistent peasant pong.

It was both busy and noisy but not so noisy that we couldn't hear the drama behind us between Grope lane and the Minster. There was the Sheriff of York, other officials, some armed, a man clinging to his horse and an almighty bout of shouting. As all respectable northern citizens do, we stopped to have a nosey.

'Must be something serious' said Edward to himself 'looks like an arrest.' Fascinated as I was, I knew that the sensible thing to do would be to get away, avoid attention. But no, off he skipped to see what was going on. I was absolutely determined, this time, to say nothing but struggled to keep quiet and ignore events as we both suddenly realised that at the centre of the action was none other than Silas. It was he who was being accosted by officials. As we eavesdropped, it was clear that one of the armed men represented the Sheriff of Warwick. There had been a murder...near to Stratford on the Avon... villager called Runt...Silas to be taken in. This was serious stuff, one of the men even carried a firearm which was still a rare sight to most common folk. Silas's speech was completely unintelligible and he was on the verge of a breakdown. He looked, by his very nature, guilty. Of course, he wasn't. Edward whispered to me,

'What shall we do?'

'Nothing' said I, for I knew that we were of no use although I did wish to hear more.

'Get closer Ed, we need to take in all we can, then I'll know how to help him.'

The arrangement was that he would be detained (tortured to you and me) in York Castle whilst an investigation took place. Silas looked a mess. He had been terrorised, threatened, harangued and accused in a very public place and the crowds were growing by the second. I heard him ask for sanctuary and, although York was legally one of the sanctuary Cities, it could not be claimed by a murderer. The mumbling soon grew into moronic chants and heckling. Many citizens didn't like him anyway and he was now struggling to behave in a dignified manner. There were so many reasons why we didn't need this attention right now and we certainly didn't need any Silas-type confessions. I had only known him a few hours but wanted to rush in and save him as I had very quickly become fond of this strange and vulnerable character. Edward and I had to watch as they took him away. It was heart-breaking. Children were straggling behind shouting "Lord silly arse!" And, even worse, starting to kick him.

'You don't think he could possibly have…' asked Edward innocently.

'Look Ed' I said 'the only thing Silas has murdered recently is the English language with a few crimes against fashion thrown in.' Edward smiled and, momentarily, was reassured. I whispered to him that we would surely help Silas but, we would need support and we should aim to use our heads, and not our irrational emotions to solve this problem. Moreover, it was paramount that we got our derrières out of Grope lane immediately. However, just as we were ready to scarper, the officious procession came to a halt. A King Henryesque type figure approached the Sheriff of York and simultaneously placed his hand, reassuringly, around Silas's shoulder. Bugger, can't hear anything! I thought to myself but Ed came into his own by providing a commentary,

'that's my uncle, the Mayor, Robert, who the priest and the ladies spoke of. He's saying they can't do anything without his authority.' At this point, the temperature rose and words were exchanged but Robert had a firm grip on Silas.

'Get closer!' I whispered to Edward and, as we were very much in the vicinity of the action, a soldier commanded the very best of York's riffraff go back to their homes and businesses.

'Let me out!' I beseeched Edward.

'You crazy?' he said 'you won't last five minutes out there!'

'Just do it!' I demanded and asked him not to move from the spot where he now stood and observed. Brave, you're thinking. Not really, I was shitting myself. No, literally, you can do that if you're a mouse. To be honest in York, in 1541, you can more or less do that if you're a human if it so pleases you. I scurried along as close to the buildings as I could. I had a sense of being invisible, incognito. That was until a kid kicked me for fun. God's teeth, it hurt! But it did, at least, project me in the right direction. I was now up to my ears in shite but determined to find out exactly what was happening. I had just got close enough to hear what was going on when I saw a horse's hoof coming right down on me. I was now trapped in every direction, feared the worst and prepared for my early exit from this amazing but confusing adventure. If I'm honest, at this point, I closed my eyes and opened my bowels yet again. I was to regret this as the hoof gently guided me back against the wall, into my own mess but protecting me at the same time. It was Annie! I wanted to thank her but was simply too humiliated about the cowering, pooing thing.

I was so close now. Tempers had calmed, the freak show had stopped and the conversation was civil. From what was said, Robert would take custody of Silas whilst a proper investigation took place. Silas was still trembling and rambling on about "Maud" and someone called Shakespeare, a name so odd that the Sheriff suggested that he'd made it up.

If I had had any previous judgments about this Mayor they had suddenly been dispelled, he certainly looks after his own, I determined. His arm was still around Silas (and believe me, Silas needed it) and they headed in our direction. I started to panic again as my protector was also, unwittingly, my captor. Robert took the reins of the horse and gently pulled her away, turned to me and said,

'balls of bleeding iron, young mouse. Iron balls!' I really didn't know how to respond but before I knew it he had waved Edward over.

'Get the mouse in your box and get yourselves, home lad.'

'Yes my Lord' replied Edward graciously and with gratitude. I can tell you I was so happy to get back in there and heading south toward the workshop.

For some reason that I simply couldn't fathom, Ed started to hum and the hum became a song.

'This is the ballad of a talking mouse.

Micklegate mouse who lives in walls.

Micklegate mouse that courageous soul!

All of York call him Iron Balls.

Iron Balls oh, Iron Balls.'

I needed to have a serious talk with this lad once we're back, I thought.

My eye caught a stone, a part of a wall much like any other, except it had weathered away leaving a bowl shape that had collected rain-water. I was absorbed by the glinting sunlight dancing about on its surface. Ah, calm, at last, I thought. That was until I was out of my box and taking an involuntary bath in the very same exotic whirlpool. Edward had grabbed me roughly by the neck and dunked me in and out several times. Although I couldn't argue with the necessity of this, I was well pissed off and the more I protested, the more he laughed.

The rest of the journey almost didn't seem to take place as, before I knew it, I had dried off in the heat of the sun and we were back at Micklegate Bar. I don't think I've ever been so pleased to see home. Home, yes, this was home and I couldn't tell you at what point it had become home. Godwin had a strange habit of acknowledging me but ignoring me at the same time although his almost constant cacophony of bodily noises could, on many occasions, masquerade as a greeting. On this day, without saying a word, his coded wind emissions said "you're taking too many chances you two and there won't always be people to bail you out. And there's work to be done. Do you think I have to do the work of three now?" And on it went, well at least in my head it did. One thing I was sure of, I was damn glad to have this big guy on our side even though (like Mayor Robert) he wished to remain on the sidelines. Mmm, I thought, Robert is struggling already to stay out of affairs despite his firm rule and, as I merrily settled to my work, I started to worry about Silas. Whatever was to transpire from now on, one thing was for sure, we would all have to learn patience. Anything rash would uncover our mission and put one another in danger so I transferred all my anxiety to my enjoyable task of making the wax stamps.

I was almost completely in the dark. If I were to open my shutter people would get the shock of their lives and soon I would be, yet again, York's performing rodent. However, I could see through to Godwin's workshop and sometimes I would watch him at work. He was a fine carpenter and Ed made a diligent assistant. He was teaching Edward how to carve a design into a chair leg. Such skill, I thought and pondered on how a character like Godwin who was very important as far as I was concerned, would get completely lost in historical records. My old self took over and asserted that I was in the presence of real history. Sod Kings and Queens and people killing one another! Give me real people any day.

Then, we had (well, they had) a visitor and it was apparent that it was someone known to them both. The conversation was civil but also business-like and Godwin called the third person 'Sir' throughout. It was only when Edward used the word 'father' that I realised that this must be William Fawkes. William was, without question, a respected member of the York Minster administration. As a notary, he would be dealing with many of the legal issues that fell into the remit if the Archbishop of York and would be aware, through his daily assignments and general conversation, of every bit of gossip and nonsense that went on. There was a quite warm and mutual respect between Godwin and William despite them standing on opposite rungs of the social and economic ladder. They chatted politely about Edward's progress in this, his life experience working with his hands, and also exchanged brief stories about their families. He referred to his wife informally as Ellen and Godwin, in return, refrained from conducting his bodily orchestra for five minutes. However, as dads do, William's conversation took a darker turn and his tone became more stern. He had received word of Edward, more than once, wandering through the City and, with all things, a mouse! William Fawkes wasn't angry but was essentially warning Edward that he could potentially bring the family name into disrepute added to which was his concern that Ed was skiving from work. Godwin not only assured William that Edward was running errands, he also promised that he would take personal responsibility for his welfare. I was shocked as Godwin had only just stopped short of complete deception but, this did, reaffirm the fondness he had for Edward and his understanding of the cause. However, we all knew that William Fawkes was an incredibly smart guy (see what I did there?) and, more than likely, he knew exactly what was going on. The bigger issue was which side he was on. I ran this thought over in my head a few times. In the thick of it, history that is, there simply isn't this side and that side, just extremes and many shades in between. So, I suppose what I meant to say was, we weren't sure where William's sympathies lay and I did, at least, appreciate how difficult his role must be dealing with legal issues in a time when the Christian church was experiencing an aggressive change in management. He did come over as a very reasonable person and, from first impressions, I liked him. The farewells were amicable and he re-joined, what I presume, was his clerk waiting outside, and walked steadily back toward his place of work. He had barely gone ten yards when a fat head appeared through the hole in my wall and shouted,

'all your bloody fault this!' Godwin was, of course, quite right and not only was I was starting to worry about what I'd got Edward into I was now feeling bad about dropping Godwin in it too. I did the right thing, stayed quiet and absorbed myself in my work.

When I was at my work I was incredibly happy. Edward and Godwin provided me with everything I needed and, if I couldn't manage or complete a task they would always help. That afternoon the mouse workshop turned into an efficient wax seal factory. I diligently hammered stamps out in copper, time and time again, ensuring that there were no inconsistencies and that these were small enough to be concealed and detailed enough to make a small but recognisable seal. In one day they were made, tested, packaged and hidden. Following the morning's adventure and many hours toil, I was completely buggered and lusted after my pile of straw on the floor. I could hear Godwin packing up for the day, Edward having left long before. I then expected either a grunt or the sound of the door lock being engaged, or both, when Godwin's face appeared like a harvest moon once again.

'C'mon mouse' he beckoned and I was soon back in my box and on my way to see Lizzy. As long as there was some kip involved, I was very happy with this new arrangement.

Godwin aimed to be home before curfew and, as he grumped, coughed, belched and farted his way through the City, I was enjoying this quieter evening environment and had a chance to breathe in the atmosphere of this stunning province. Joke about smells coming? No, I'll leave it for once. His abode was deep within the snickleways and I definitely would have had trouble trying to find it alone. It was incredibly modest and I was reminded, once again, of how humble the everyday citizen's life was. Family greetings and food were waiting for Godwin. It occurred to me, and this wasn't uncommon, that they ate a lot of grains and, for whatever reason, unlike some of their peers, didn't mix many berries with it. As for meat, well, I presumed there just wasn't money for it. As I thought about this a little light went on in my minuscule grey matter and what the little light shone on was a correlation between Godwin's guts and Lizzy's illness.

I realised how stupid I had been in not preparing myself for this visit, particularly failing to put Lizzy and her condition at the centre of my thoughts. This was an altogether different sight to the one I had enjoyed when I first visited Godwin's home. Lizzy was no longer at the top of the stairs but laid out in the centre of the main room and all the family were around. She had worsened considerably and, as he placed me gently in her folded arms, I could see the extent of her affliction. How I would love to portray a quaint scene of a devoted Renaissance family comforting their dying daughter but this wasn't what greeted me. She was much worsened and distressed. She had difficulty breathing and, at times gave way to involuntary giddiness, spasms and screamed out declaring that insects were crawling around under her skin. I could detect the first signs of circulatory problems and, in its totality, this was heartbreaking and difficult to watch. Saint Anthony's fire. That's what they called it. I call it ergotism but in 1541 there's little relief and no cure.

I believe that my presence did bring her some comfort. It was probably for the best that I couldn't speak in this present forum as I'm not sure what I would have contributed. Now, to be clear, death would be no stranger to this family. They had many children which indicated to me that they must have had at least twice as many, to begin with for all of these to survive. That didn't mean that they were blasé. I was in a room filled with broken-hearted, hopeless people. Godwin and his spouse debated when was best to send for the priest. Particularly with this condition, I knew that the introduction of a priest could create all sorts of problems but, last rites were still seen as essential by many if the soul was to have a hope of transcending heavenwards. His youngest son scurried off as he would be the least likely to be seen during curfew. The priest, of course, was allowed to administer at any time.

As we waited I saw the culprit on a wooden plate by her bedside. Her diet was not the same as Godwin's after all. Lizzy had been given a special treat of bread. She was the only one eating it, presumably to get her better, but it was doing the opposite. Claviceps purpurea. There's the cause. A fungus, ironically often caused by contact with rodents, develops in rye and this is what had been used as an ingredient in the bread. My first thoughts were, thank God she's the only one eating it. My second thought was they must have bought the bread somewhere and others will be affected. The priest arrived. I chastised myself for thinking any ill of Father Matthew for this was a different creature altogether. Overweight, untidy and very drunk, he jumped on that old possession bandwagon immediately.

'Beelzebub himself is inside this child and must be removed! She will be taken from this place.. blardy blardy more hate and nonsense.' It was impossible to listen to and I would have intervened if it wasn't for the determined and sensible protestations of Godwin and his wife. An unbelievable rumpus ensued and I simply knew that if the priest managed to access his superiors, little Lizzy would be burned at a stake before she naturally expired. I felt completely useless.

The door swung open and Edward Fawkes stood there. Godwin could not conceive of the son of a gentleman being in his home and wasn't sure how to respond.

'Young sir. What brings you here?'

'Why, your daughter master, and also to remove this oaf before he does any damage!'

The priest vented all the anger he could summon at young Edward and, stoic as I would expect, young Ed practically took no notice.

'I am the complete and only authority here!' blustered Father nob head (not real name).

'Not any more' said young Ed and, as he moved forward into the already cramped space, a tall and shadowy figure emerged from the snickleway. It was Father Matthew, who, for whatever reason, apparently out-ranked this buffoon. They exchanged words but the drunk did submit to the superiority of our most recent visitor. Father Matthew then confidently, and rather impressively, banished this dud priest altogether from the situation.

He delicately took hold of Lizzy's hand and bade us all pray. Although she was still visibly distressed, she quietened immediately and he then gave quiet instructions to all in the room which was an incredibly effective calming strategy. On his direction, we sat by candlelight (three in all which must have been costing Godwin a fortune), knelt and prayed silently. Another knock on the door. If it wasn't for the gravity of the situation this would have been farcical. Bayard! The showman who Godwin had punched. What on earth was he doing here? Which was more or less, if you remove the colourful language, what Godwin said to him.

'Just please give me a moment to explain.' Godwin shouted him down thinking that this was unbelievably inappropriate. He continued 'I heard about your child. I know this, seen it I have, all over. A liar and fraud I may be but I've travelled you see. Everywhere you see and I knows this. Saint Anthony that is there, and I've brought you this herb mix.'

'Let him bring it' said Father Matthew knowing full well, that there could be practically nothing that could make her worse. I knew, of course, that this wouldn't make any difference perhaps apart from it being a placebo but was, admittedly, stunned by this act of goodwill and repentance from Bayard. They let him in and the herbs were administered. Godwin's wife told Bayard he was welcome to stay. The hush descended again on this little space and a woman entered stealthily almost without anyone noticing and, unbelievably, things had become so crazy that she stood on one side of Lizzy administering the herbs whilst Father Matthew was around the other side praying quietly. Our priest must have alerted Elspeth and asked her to help.

I knew the herbs were useless and, if I'm honest, I had already lost hope. Bayard did know his stuff. He told them to throw away the bread, and any from the same source, away and Godwin did just that. It became so peaceful. There was a cooperative and heartfelt will to keep this little girl alive. Candles, people kneeling and quiet prayer. A room filled with love. It was incredibly touching particularly as I saw Godwin and Bayard sit side by side in prayer. And then everything went quiet. Very quiet. I presumed Lizzy had left us but I was still rising and falling on her chest. She had gone to sleep, bless her. An unexpected, peaceful sleep. We kept vigil all night although, if I'm truthful, I kept dropping off. There were about three spells during the night when she cried out, rubbing her arms to discourage those insects she felt were crawling beneath her skin but she did get some respite and some sleep. I was awoken abruptly early morn as, ungraciously, Godwin stuffed me in the box and away we went to work. Now, there was only Lizzy's mother sitting by her bedside, everyone else had gone. I was astonished that she was still alive and, on our journey, was warmed by the unselfish acts of my friends, and Bayard, during the night. Love is so powerful I thought. Powerful enough for a miracle? Well, who was I to say? I'm just a mouse.

12: Peter

Bamburgh, June 1541

Peter relaxed as he absorbed the stunning view across the bay to Bamburgh from his fishing boat. Today was particularly calm and, as they rowed out to fish, the north-east sunrise was inspirational to him. There were three others in the boat, two were his brothers and the other his step-father. Content as he was, Peter often yearned for adventure. Older and wiser members of his family thanked God for every uncomplicated day. They desired a good catch, good health and were happy, simply to face a new day alive and to be left alone. Adventure, no thanks. The problem for Peter, being a teenager, was that life had become very repetitive. The only real excitement he had ever experienced was when he had found the body of

Brother Bernard but no one spoke of it. He was smart enough to understand that too much talk brought trouble but he had been constantly worried about the incident and felt particularly guilty at keeping a personal possession of Bernard's for a while, Peter treated this scrap of parchment as a holy relic but it troubled his conscience that he was keeping it secret. Having said that, he hadn't got a clue as to what to do with it. You can't just throw away a blessed parchment, it could have been part of the Bible for all he knew.

The ever-increasing weight that this issue placed on his soul started to make him feel unwell. He confided in his older brother, Phillip, but his brother looked at the scrap and laughed. Beyond that he showed no interest whatsoever, he simply suggested that he threw it away. The more Peter thought about it, the worse his obsession became. He knew it was only a matter of time before he was going to ask practically anyone he could until he was given a satisfactory answer or his head would burst. As he lay awake the very same evening he prayed about this burning issue and decided that he may be able to trust Gilly. Gilly wasn't a real name, it was an affectionate name given to the man to whom they took their catch daily and decided the worth of the fish. He would buy it off you and take it to market. People said he'd been doing it so long he had grown gills.

Two days later, Peter begged his step-father to give him sole responsibility for taking the day's catch to Gilly. Surprisingly, he said yes as it was a small catch and relatively easy to transport, but insisted he'd get a clout if he didn't secure a fair price for it. Gilly was a fair man and had built a light-hearted rapport with young Peter but Peter was dreading asking him for advice. Why did he want to ask Gilly? Well, Gilly openly talked about national affairs, the King, his ministers, the Reformation. To many, he was the daily news even if he did often get things wrong.

Gilly chuckled at Peter taking on this manly task but resisted any temptation to take advantage.

'A fair catch! And quality fish too young man!' And he gave him a reasonable price.

'Next!' Here was the problem, it would be ages until Gilly had finished, so Peter had to work out how to wait, interject when convenient and also to avoid being late home.

Gilly always worked in a break at some point so, as he sat, Peter approached him.

'You still here young feller?!'

'Yes sir, I would seek your counsel.'

Gilly wanted to chuckle at this notion but simultaneously loved the idea of being the town's sage so asked Peter to sit beside him and told him that, today, counsel would be free but he had many a person waiting for his invaluable advice. Where to start? Thought Peter. He decided to just jump in and tell the story of the monk's death.

'Brother Bernard, m'lad that is and, if you hadn't described him so well, I'd have just told you it couldn't be him. Captured long ago, he was, for challenging the King's position as head of the church.' Gilly was now whispering 'as Godly a man as ever walked these shores young Peter. Nursed my good wife every day when she was dying, in between all his many other duties, that is. I thought him dead not long after his arrest. I had word that he had hid in the City of York for a while. That's right, in the daftest sounding street you've ever heard off, whatsmenourthisngate or summat. He wasn't well then, a nun was hiding him, taking care of him. What I can't tell you is why he'd be daft enough to come back up here. Nothing here for him.'

Peter decided to go a step further and tell him about the parchment.

'Be a secret message that will.' said Gilly. Peter paused

for a moment for he was now old enough to realise that, sometimes, adults would embellish a tale just for the sake of it and Gilly was no exception so he asked him to explain.

'Our good friend Brother Bernard was a rebel. A rebel against the King and the changes in the church. He would communicate with other rebels using coded or invisible messages sent by pigeons.' Peter knew that there must be truth in this as he saw a pigeon fly away as Bernard lay dying. He now had a job on his hands stopping Gilly speaking.

'Bring your scrap to me and I'll tell you what it says. Won't make any difference, anyone he would be writing to will be dead as well by now.' Peter now had very mixed feelings. Firstly that he'd betrayed his dead friend, secondly that he had told Gilly too much and thirdly that he would now be sharing Bernard's personal secrets with a third party. He sighed, realised that he didn't have much choice and was sure that very little could be written on this little piece of parchment anyway. He did take great pains to thank Gilly. However he looked at this, it was a kindness and he had learned a lot. It would be another week before his step-dad would let him take fish to Gilly again. Keeping all this to himself was going to be very difficult.

A week of sleepless nights. Seven days creating endless hypothetical scenarios in which he and warrior monks defeated the fat King. If he had known the real truth, it would have horrified him. The process was much the same as the previous week: get a price, wait for Gilly to take a break but this time Gilly took him indoors into a poorly lit corner where he lit a candle.

'Let's have it then young un!'

Peter handed over the scrap.

'Can barely see it!' scoffed Gilly. He pinched it between the finger and thumb of his left hand and waved it around about half an inch from the flame and there, gradually, letters appeared. Peter was mightily impressed by this and asked him if it was magic and Gilly explained, quite sensibility, how it worked. To Peter, Gilly had become the all-seeing, all-knowing village guru but what they discovered made no sense at all.

Satan's Brother
most evil. By
God's

But, it sounded pretty serious. Gilly decided it would be unfair to over-excite the lad so told him it was some religious nonsense written by a dying man.

'It must have been part of the last message he sent' asserted Peter and Gilly, in all good conscience, had to agree with him.

'But listen, lad' said Gilly 'you have to let it go. He's dead now and I can promise you that even if his old pigeon had a destination there wouldn't be anyone left alive to receive it now. Let it go young Peter.'

Peter meandered home with his face in his boots and still unable to avoid gestating numerous mythical adventures in his head. In all of them, he came out as the hero. He was now old enough and smart enough to know that there had been sufficient trusting for now and may have to do as advised and let it go. He couldn't imagine anyone from where he lived journeying to York, surely it was on the edge of the world and surely people couldn't speak the same tongue? He stopped at the point on the beach where they had buried Bernard, said a prayer and asked for guidance.

He was late home and was questioned by his step-father. He handed over the coin and said nothing beyond a sincere apology. He walked to his bunk, stuffed the minuscule parchment between two timbers on the wall so it couldn't be seen and went to sleep. He promised himself he would think on it no more.

13: Thomas Cranmer

London, April 1541

Brother Bede and Brother Bernard now found themselves guests of the King in the Tower of London itself. Even for the constant and professional staff of the Tower, the Yeoman of the Guard, these were confusing times. They cared little about why someone was locked up or awaiting trial but did establish an unspoken code of honour and one such test was when they were eventually asked to torture a woman, Anne Askew, and refused and Thomas Wriothesley himself did the deed. They were also open to bribes, or payment for services, depending on how you looked at it, but did regard themselves as honourable men. Those prisoners of high or significant standing were known to have quite comfortable lodgings but this would come at a price and it could also be used to pressure them to conform. Withdrawal of "privileges," normally taken for granted, could be devastating to someone confined long term and an easy way of obtaining information.

One long term guest of the Tower, already in residence when Bernard And Bede arrived, was Margaret Pole, imprisoned for her Papist sympathies and particularly for her connection to the Pilgrimage of Grace, the northern revolt. Now in her late sixties, this seemed particularly cruel but few who crossed Henry were pardoned. When Henry was young he had celebrated Margaret as a fellow royal but in these later years, she was given no mercy as she refused to change her views. During her final years that were spent in the Tower, she was given no concessions, not even being allowed to have a change of clothing.

The Tower was usually reserved for people of high standing and power but the massive resistance to the Reformation, questions about Henry's title as head of the church and also his dubious marriage to Boleyn in the previous decade, generated a backlash that Henry was determined to quash. So, if rank was of any value at all you can imagine the conditions that greeted our monks. The head of any rebellious monk on a spike would, without question, send out a powerful message to all and the information they would impart under duress may well have been invaluable.

At this point, both Brother Bede And Brother Bernard cared little for life. Their pain was unbearable and, for such committed Christians to give up hope in this way, tells us that things had to be extreme. They still had value. Their torturers wanted more names, possible plots, hideouts and information. Although the King's journey north was advertised as reconciliation, in reality, he would have no one left alive who opposed him.

They had been incarcerated only a few hours when Bede was dragged down a broad stone corridor dripping with fetid water. He was already wet, cold, sore and broken. He was then pushed down the circular steps of the tower in which they were now held and was manhandled into chambers bedecked with instruments of horror. He was thrown into a chair and promised a quick death if he gave up the names of those in Stratford upon Avon who were rebels. He could only strain out a few broken words but managed to tell them that he was the only monk in that area that opposed the King and he was happy to die if this was deemed a crime.

As per usual, there was a sinister commissioner present and he was the one who always asked the questions and he, or a clerk, would record events or, at least, record their version of events. The strain of previous experiences was even showing on these seasoned professionals.

'Stupid and pathetic papist shite! You think we're idiots? No one works alone. Ever! I will bloody cull you all. Bled us dry for years you have, so, how about you take a turn. I'll give you just one chance to make it easier for you and your pretty concubine upstairs!' In the room there were two Yeoman Warders who laughed at the thought of Bernard and Bede being lovers, but at least it did signal to Bede that he may be able to make things easier for his friend and Brother in Christ, Bernard if he could only think of the right words that did not conflict with his conscience.

'Be the breaks for you! No messing now monk.' And a warder went to grab the foreboding implement used for cracking teeth, commonly known as breaks. It was standard procedure to simply taunt prisoners with tools of evil at first but, on this occasion, there was no time-wasting on the behalf of the guard. He was ruthless, one tooth cracked after the other. The aim was not to pull teeth out, but to break them in two, inflicting optimal pain. This man had been doing this for years and felt nothing personal except, on occasions, a degree of pleasure. Bede had no energy to scream, the noises he made were similar to a dog whelping and it was pathetic to hear. Cries, screams, protestations, prayers, pleading and crying could be heard incessantly resounding throughout the thick stonework every day in this place and no one who worked there could give a fig. They were doing the King's work so there was nothing to deliberate upon. You do wrong, you end up here. Simple. Bede's resistance was incredibly low and the torturers, despite their ruthlessness, were experienced and knew that a lost prisoner was lost information. They decided to give the monk some brief respite as he was losing consciousness, intending to show him the manacles when he came around. Manacles, can't be so bad surely? You just hang there by your wrists. At least you're left alone? Not at all. These were used to elicit total and perpetual pain and meant little or no labour on the part of the guards. As they relaxed momentarily and Bede slumped into a shattered and bloody heap, the door flung open unexpectedly and a warder, clearly their superior, dragged in a pathetic, skinny figure. Through the haze of blood, sweat and filth that covered his eyes, Bede could make out the outline of a young gentleman, his fine clothes now in tatters. This guard politely nodded at the commissioner and the clerk and then demanded that the warders drop Bede immediately.

'Wriothesley, Cranmer and Somerset are about the building. Sharpen your ideas, they are looking in on prisoners.' He threw the hapless young gentleman to the floor.

'This man should have made his confession before yesterday! Move yourselves, you useless bastards! What the hell's going on? Wasting your time buggering an old monk?! Get about the King's business!!'

Angry as he was, he was scared as well. Any one of the aforementioned could have this warder's head removed on a whim, absolutely no one carried an exemption card and even those Henry regarded as close friends, like the publicly popular chancellor Thomas More, had ended up in the

Tower and then losing their head.

They hurriedly dragged Bede out in a disorganised frenzy and took him along the rough course from whence he came and then threw him on top of Bernard in an already cramped cell. What followed was a spell, probably as long as three days according to Brother Bernard's calculation, when they were simply left alone. Unappealing and congealed gruel, a poor excuse for food, was thrown in every so often but, otherwise, they had been overlooked. They managed to regain a little physical strength but could barely stand the constant sounds of torture and death. Howls and groans and screams. Begging, promising, asking for their King, their friends and their mothers. Praying. Constant prayer. Shouting and profanity. And then silence, usually at night, and then it would start again. It's hard to imagine why people would resist admitting to anything that these brutes asked for but, astounding as it seems, many brave souls did just that. To grasp this you have to understand an age where your conscience is your very soul, your very self, and the most important part of your being. Thomas More himself inferred that stripped-down, that's all we are. Our beliefs and principles. Once you give those up you have given up all that you have left of yourself. So, like many others of faith, Bede and Bernard could only offer what they believed to be the truth because, of course, like almost all the population, this life was but a preparation for a better one and a clear conscience was a clear route to Heaven.

Bernard became the carer as, by now, Bede was substantially frailer than he was. Together they would pray for death or, alternatively, the hope of a miracle in which they were released or escaped.

Although it's hardly a term you would see often written about a Renaissance gaoler, this lot were overworked. They were overworked and confused. The Tower, once a well-oiled wheel in the machinery of medieval justice, was now a place where too many demands were made of the building and those who worked there. What was worse was Henry's disposition in which he constantly changed his views like the wind. Yes, he'd cut off all ties with the Pope, but after 1540 he started to become concerned about the growing Protestant wave in England as he still considered himself Catholic in the proper sense of the word. It's no wonder that warders were asking for very specific instructions when crushing out confessions. This over-occupation was, of course, bound to work in the favour of our two monks as, they were at least for now, small fry.

They knew that they had almost been forgotten and chose to give up on death and try to plan for something more positive. Eventually, the door creaked open. A guard was instantly repulsed by the oily thick odour that came from this disgusting little space and the monks themselves. He covered his face and then re-entered, but not alone. On chains were eight male prisoners of mixed age, size and social status. Bede and Bernard made a pathetic attempt to help, console and speak to these poor victims but were held at bay by the instant furore of the Guard.

'Who the bloody 'ell is this?!!' he said angrily, almost sure that this cesspit was entirely empty.

'Remove them immediately!' he commanded his subordinate and the monks were dragged out before the others were able to enter. For now, they were dumped in the corridor. Challenging this particular warder was not a good idea and this was a very tough induction for the new guests.

The pushing, shoving, beating, shouting and arguing seemed to go on for ages and Bede and Bernard just weren't sure what to do. Of course, the brothers weren't to know, but they were presently in the Salt Tower without any bearings whatsoever. The Salt Tower was on the south side of the fortifications where the moat was narrowest and where, beyond, was the river Thames but, from where they were, there was no view of the exterior or any sounds to indicate that they were near the water. Nevertheless, they crawled along the corridor away from the ruckus that was still taking place in the cell that they had vacated. This was no dramatic escape bid, they could barely move and had no plan or idea as to what they were doing and presumed that they would, sooner or later, be apprehended.

They found themselves at the foot of some spiral steps so, with few options, did their best to negotiate the climb. Half-way up they stopped, exhausted. There was a sizeable recess in the wall where bowmen would once have stood to fire arrows downwards toward potential invaders. Through this chink in the wall, the monks were able to get their bearings and, ridiculous as it seemed, kindled some hope. They collapsed and rested for a few moments as they could see or hear nothing that would pose a threat. All that could be heard were the birds and sounds from the river, boatmen shouting greetings and directions to one another as they went about their daily business. They took a few seconds to enjoy this oasis of normality. Then, the silence was broken. They realised that they were leaning on a large oaken door which, because of its state of ill repair, they presumed was not used. They heard conversation, a grave conversation. These weren't guards. Bede whispered to Bernard and explained that the Tower, over time, had become a honeycomb of lodgings, torture chambers, cells, offices and even living quarters. Until 1509, the King himself had resided here. They were instantaneously aware of the danger they had put themselves in. At first, they had no intentions of eavesdropping as they were preoccupied with their predicament but, as the conversation took a more sinister turn, they strained to listen.

'Whatever your thoughts gentlemen, he's losing all reason and his health is failing. His current mood is raised simply because he has married a girl. Why, practically a child! He makes a fool of himself when in her presence, an old man feeding his vanity. Without us, he has no direction.'

As yet Bernard and Bede had no idea who was this was but it was evident they were referring to the King.

'You are too bold Somerset! We are here to advise his Majesty not to direct him. However, Wriothesley and I respect your position as uncle to the new King…'

He was abruptly interrupted.

'Your Grace, may I remind you that it is still regarded as treason to contemplate the King's death.'

'Nonsense!' said the first, we're all gentleman here with the fate of a whole new world on our hands, the King incapable of making rational decisions regarding state or faith.'

This was starting to make sense. These were the people that the warder had referred to earlier. Somerset was, in fact, Edward Seymour the brother of Henry's third wife Jane Seymour. Sweet Jane who had died giving birth to the future King, presently Prince Edward. This not only meant that Somerset was now one of the most prominent and powerful figures in the realm but also essential in mapping the course of the next reign. "Your Grace" was non-other than Thomas Cranmer, the Archbishop of Canterbury and the architect of the new faith in England. The third, Thomas Wriothesley, or Earl of Southampton, was now one of Henry's principal advisors. A motley and powerful crew indeed who were now clearly intent on national stability on their terms as long as they kept their celebrity status and continued to live in a prosperous manner.

'If we choose to take your path my Lord, we would need to know that you offer security' said Cranmer.

'I am certain of the way forward and entirely persuaded by our discoveries and this will deliver riches never before dreamed off. However, this much I cannot do alone. Our plan guarantees the King absolute power and, for Prince Edward permanent seniority to the Roman Pope' assured Somerset.

This was a sinister and deep plot that Bernard and Bede had stumbled upon. Then there were footsteps. Footsteps that were descending the spiral stairs toward them. They had no ideas and no plans for escape which was heart-breaking as, at this point, they felt very strongly that God had a new purpose for them. They huddled as best they could, in foetal positions, to hide in the shadows. Two men were coming down the stairs at a pace also engaged in a heated discussion. Unbeknownst to them, one was non-other than John Gage, Constable of the Tower. This was an almost unique day. Anyone else would have spotted them but these two officers were so intent on their destination and discussion that they sped by. The monks, relieved, instantly returned to following the conversation behind the door.

'This is a brave move, my Lord. We are rewriting history and re-writing our faith…' said Cranmer but was hastily interrupted by Wriothesley.

'Tut, Your Grace, no time for weak bladders! This is a pact that must be sworn between us this very day and we must stand firm. You will gain much from our treaty. Can I remind you that two of us overheard the King in prayer and this is not only his heart's desire but what God hath commanded of him.'

'Yes, Yes but surely there's a matter of some doubt, even with His Majesty, as to whether this is true providence' said Cranmer reluctantly knowing that his soul was now in peril for what they were about to do.

'The Lindisfarne Gospels, the copies and the newest work are now secured, squeezed from the clammy grasp of Cromwell's dead hand and contingencies have been put in place. We know that the change will be considerable and the populace must be entirely convinced of the authenticity of the changes. We don't want a bungled repeat of the Reformation from which we all still suffer' declared Wriothesley.

Archbishop Cranmer turned to Somerset,

'and you, my Lord. Are you prepared for this? You will be in the prayers of millions for all time and if it fails you will be damned for all time.'

'Absolutely' he said, 'this is what God and the King himself believe to right and good, it cannot fail. We already have agents throughout England waiting for the signal and diligently seeking those rebels who may get wind of our design.'

'And you Wriothesley are you willing to sacrifice all your diligent efforts to secure peace with Spain?'

Silence, presumably a nod from Wriothesley.

Then the Archbishop declared that for now there should not be, apart from the extensive plans that had been collated, any written record of this meet but that they should collectively swear an oath to this new treatise that was to be called the "Clarification". So, after a minutes quiet, they each recited an oath that set out what the clarification was and this was so long that it lasted over ten minutes.

What followed was a never heard before catechism that the three recited together. This sea change in state and religion would make the Reformation seem like a small rise in taxes and potentially turn Europe upside down. And then they left, thankfully through another door.

Bernard turned to Bede who was weeping. Bernard was speechless. How he wished this was a nightmare. Five minutes passed before either was able to speak. For those who believe in the power of the Holy Spirit, there was no doubt that during that moment it had descended on these two humble servants of God for they were filled with a renewed sense of purpose and strength. If they had to fly out of the Tower to stop this these monsters they would. Eventually, Bernard spoke,

'Brother, this is, in its totality, the work of Satan himself. Diabolical in its conception it is Cataclysmic and will destroy all we know. Even if we can get to just one person who is willing to oppose it we must'. He then looked at Bede. He was broken physically and mentally, like himself, filthy and bloody.

From this point on the monks refused to have the term "clarification" on their lips as this was in itself a lie and they would refer to the impending event as "The Cataclysm".

Beyond that, there wasn't much thinking to do. The choice was to either descend to certain apprehension or go upward into the unknown. This wasn't a great option for they were both in very poor physical and mental condition but, fortunately, their spiritual health was as good as it possibly could be. They scrambled and crawled upward, the spiral design making the task much more awkward. The stone felt cold and hard beneath their knees but, together, they made progress and eventually could see the top of the Tower. They weren't to know it, but they were now in the Cradle Tower and were as near to the Thames as you could get and, it had the narrowest area of the moat of all of the fortifications. They found a platform and rested, stunned that, still, they had not been discovered. They saw an opening which, at first, appeared to them as a black abyss but, as they had few choices, chose to investigate. There was practically no light in this room but they could make out abandoned instruments of torture, ropes, weapons and furniture. They had unwittingly stumbled on an abandoned storeroom. It wreaked of neglect, dust, cobwebs and dead rodents and appeared completely mismanaged, that is if it was ever managed at all. Potential escapees on finding this would have been elated at the discovery of weapons, but they meant nothing to these two monks. As they looked back, and downward, they realised they had passed a metal gateway halfway up the Tower which looked like it definitely should have been locked. Could it be that with all the rushing about, panic and confusion of this day that it was unwittingly left open following the Constable's descent?

Brother Bede and Brother Bernard didn't even bother to ponder on such issues as in Bernard's newly inspired mind, a plot evolved. He picked up a metal implement. He presumed it to be a weapon although he could not name it. He supposed it looked like a claw, a metal claw, it was substantial and quite heavy. Indeed, very heavy for two monks who were on their last legs. Bede slumped into a dark and sooty corner whilst Bernard started to tug on ropes and then cut a small length from one using a rusty dagger. He held the shadowy dagger up to his eyes and was reminded of how he abhorred violence. He let it drop to the floor, they wouldn't harm another person under any circumstances so this was of no further use to him, his sole purpose was to recruit help and stop this diabolical design which they had so recently uncovered.

He leaned over Bede who could barely make out his companion's face in the dim light. As he got closer, Bede could just about see that he had a good length of rope wrapped around his waist and shoulder, two shorter pieces and this ridiculous unidentified rusty claw-like weapon.

'We must make it to the top of this tower brother' said Bernard.

'You think of escape?' muttered Bede 'go my friend and God speed, I will die here a happy man if I know you have tried to get away.'

Bernard seriously considered this. Life and death not being the issue, rather one of them alerted the nation to what was about to happen. Even so, he decided that they could possibly double the chances if they could get to the top. They debated this for some time but Bernard decided to take charge and again, together, they negotiated the last flight. This took much longer and, once out in the fresh air, they took time to draw new strength. As long as they kept low they were unseen so Bernard told Bede that they would wait until dark before moving again. During this time they designed a plan that they could agree on. If only one of them survived, they would attempt to get word to those they could trust about this "clarification" which they now described as a dark Cataclysm. They acknowledged that if they had to resort to written messages that they must be cryptic and in Latin. If Bede survived he was to alert his trusted contacts in Stratford and then make his way in disguise to York. If Bernard were to survive he would go do the same but he swore that first, however difficult it may be, he would gather together his brothers in Lindisfarne and use them to recruit further support.

As night fell they were so much more invisible and Bernard went about his scheme. After another hour had passed, he showed Bede the rope with the claw on the end and explained how he intended to throw the rope beyond the moat into firm ground and, by wrapping the short rope over it, would slide down and, as long as they could clear the moat, they would be only a breath away from the Thames. For the first time in weeks, Bede managed a stifled laugh.

'My, you're ambitious my friend. David against Goliath no less, and I pray you succeed for so many reasons but, this, I cannot do.'

Brother Bernard was an incredibly reasonable man but, for whatever reason, would not give up on his friend. They continued to debate this for some time until Bede agreed, conceding that he would most probably die whatever happened.

The biggest challenge for Bernard was to work out whether Bede going first would create the greater risk or the other way around, but he finally decided to go first himself, reiterating the procedure to his friend time and time again. In return, Bede assured him that he would do his utmost to succeed.

In the dim crescent moon evening, Bernard had a clear view of the moat and beyond. He threw the claw with every ounce of strength that he could muster only to hear an almighty splash as it ventured downward into the moat. He knew that this would raise an alarm and that they now had very little time. As much as he was able, in his ruined condition, he hurriedly made a second attempt. He immediately knew that this time, his makeshift grappling hook had met its target. He winced as the rope screamed through the crisp air. There was a distinct "schluck!" sound as it hit the mud. Unfortunately, the sounds now gave the guards a sense of direction.

'Go brother go!' said Bede and Bernard hurled himself out over the moat. This was, by no means, a fantasy hero scene. This man was now half-crippled, drowning in his hair and beard, and sporting a filthy, torn habit. All the same, he feared nought. He was alarmed at the speed at which this took him downwards and across the moat and it took his breath away. He fell clumsily on an, already damaged, left hip but was exactly where he wanted to be and beckoned his friend to follow. Bede obediently stumbled up onto the top of the Cradle tower ramparts, placed the short rope over the now extended rope, took both ends, one in each hand and threw himself off as if he were a stone. Now there were shouts as the guards could see some movement and they rushed to apprehend him. He moved a few yards along the rope but then started to wobble. Just a little at first but soon he was swaying about, losing control and straining on the hook that was uneasily wrestling its grip in the mud. Suddenly his arms felt lighter and he was eerily aware that the grapple had released itself and was pirouetting through the air as he fell. Surreally, he plummeted like a sack of potatoes toward the moat and heard the rope shriek as it passed him. The iron claw clanged as it hit the tower wall. Almost as if in a dream, he was following it, with his eyes, rebounding and heading in his direction. At the moment he hit the water the claw hit him hard on the skull. He went under and, momentarily, Bernard turned around, as his natural instinct was to help. Bede surfaced once and only once and Bernard could just make out the slurred words, God speed, I die in peace.

Bernard froze and yet something told him he could not dally. As his heart broke for his friend, he made for the river. This is where his amazing plan ran dry. Foolishly, he had not thought beyond this point. Despite the strength of his faith and conviction, he felt hopeless and instinctively ran toward the bank. He could still hear the shouts and confusion behind him and found himself looking at the silhouette of boats. He thought to steal a boat as he had no other credible ideas. Apart from a little moonlight, it was completely dark and he was grasping at shadows. He discovered the water's edge still unsure of his next move. For the first time since they had left the cell, he started to panic. He looked at the river before him and so wanted to be Moses standing before the Red Sea but felt more like Job. Then, he remembered what to do when fear, in all its forms, manifests itself. He decided to pray. To be precise he intended to pray but hadn't delivered one syllable when he heard a quiet voice.

'Monk. Monk!'

How Bernard had always wished that God was a northerner, for that is what he heard, but decided to give his head a shake in case he was now simply hearing things that weren't there, but he heard it again.

'Monk, here.' He heard. In the shadows he saw a small figure, a boatman signalling him to get on board. Bernard stood and leaned nearer and a hand grabbed his habit and pulled him in.

'It's me!' Brother Bernard got closer and palmed the facial features of this angel.

'It's me, Eirik.' Bernard was overjoyed and embraced the young boatman. Now, to be clear, committed Christians don't do coincidence so the monk didn't bother to ask what Eirik was doing there. As far as Bernard was concerned, he had been placed there by the Almighty, no less. However, Eirik was determined to deliver his story as he rowed away toward the dock at Limehostes. Eirik didn't have a river barge licence and he definitely shouldn't have been about at this time of night but, he was without doubt an excellent, stealthy rower. He sensibly took his time, hardly making any sound in the water and, happily, there didn't seem to be any evidence of a chase behind them. They were both trying to tell their story over one another until Brother Bernard calmed down and let Eirik speak as they would be travelling for some time before reaching Limehostes.

Eirik told him his whole story. How he had been orphaned, left to fend for himself as a boy and then taking on any work that would come his way. As far as he remembered he had never had a home and, when he was ten years of age was employed by a soldier. Well, at the time he thought he was a soldier so Eirik regarded his role as a sort of, valet or page. As the need for mercenaries increased following the Pilgrimage of Grace, his employer took him along as part valet, part guard. He admitted to Bernard that he was terrible at it. Bernard gripped him tight around the shoulders and said,

'You were excellent at it my lad. Truly, you were a light in a dark place! I wouldn't be here without you and you've no idea how important it is that I now survive.'

Eirik tried to take this compliment but the sum total of his deeds left him with a weighty lump on his conscience. He was delighted to escape and, as soon as the dust settled, Eirik had bartered for employment on the river. In a matter of days, he secured employment with a boatman, a trade in which there would always be work as the Thames was still the easiest and busiest way of travelling in and around the capital. Totally in character, he was practising his rowing skills, in a stolen boat, without permission, after curfew.

'You risk much young Eirik. If you can, by God's grace get me as far as Limehostes from whence I will make haste with my mission.'

Bernard's faith was, again, in peak condition as he didn't even have a clue where or what Limehostes was but he was out and away and that's all that mattered.

'I won't go back' said Eirik 'if I can stay with you Brother, that will be my way from now on.'

Bernard wasn't in the frame of mind to argue. This fine young Viking warrior would be a great asset if he had any chance of succeeding.

'If you are with me, kind Eirik, I would ask much of you and you will have much to remember. And, we cannot stay together.'

The docks were in sight. Bernard went to great pains to ensure that Eirik understood what was now asked of him. Eirik said he would steal two horses. Bernard agreed reluctantly that, for the cause, it would be acceptable, in God's eyes, for him to steal one horse but he, would find another way.

'Now, my very young and brave saviour, can you repeat everything I have asked of you? '

Eirik took a deep breath, now putting up his oars as they silently approached the jetty.

'There is a grave and Cataclysmic event in the air that I must speak to no one about. I am to make for Stratford upon Avon and find Brother Bede's hideout (he paused as Bernard interrupted him)...lodgings and see if Bede had returned (having seen what happened, Eirik gave Bernard a skewed look of disbelief) and, if not, to find a man called Nails and tell him of Bede's fate and to let me have the homing pigeon called Hope and if not I am to steal it... erm ...borrow it. Then to York. I will go to your, erm, lodgings to be found at what's me thingy gate (Bernard stalled and rehearsed him in the correct pronunciation)..yeah, that, and to speak to no one but a short-haired blonde lady called Elspeth and, if I can't find her to gather up your pigeon and then meet you on the

Holy Island. Blimey, Brother, that's some adventure. Can't you tell me anything more about why?'

Bernard informed him that he had said so little as he wanted to protect Eirik but did say that there was to be an event in York Minster when The King arrived that will trigger this diabolical deed. Eirik shuddered and recited it again genuinely excited at being given so much responsibility.

'In a month's time I will be at the abbey at Lindisfarne with a moral army and will meet you there and, together, we will investigate the purpose of the Gospels once protected on Holy Island and absolutely thwart this evil King's intentions!'

Eirik was both shocked and surprised at the fire in Bernard's belly. They had made an uncanny bond. Bernard had complete faith in his young friend and reiterated that he would be in danger if he said anything. Parting company was hard. Bernard's health was failing but this spurred him on to send Eirik on his way. Eirik gave his word that he would succeed but then asked how he would find Stratford upon Avon. They stared at each other for what seemed an eternity. Bernard was embarrassed by his limitations but told Eirik, that in this matter and, for the rest of his journey, he was on his own. The young adventurer didn't flinch, he already knew he could survive anywhere and was confident that he could secure paid work along the way knowing who to trust and who to avoid. For both of them, the journey would be a very long and challenging quest but it was one that they had to take on.

They almost parted but Brother Bernard had to ask one more thing.

'My dear boy, I haven't a clue where I am. I can see boats and ships and horses but honestly don't know where to start!' Bernard had almost said nothing for this truly embarrassed him. About to embark on an adventure, he was lost already. Eirik chuckled, smiled and said

'My very good Brother Bernard. Take this drinking water for I have enough for several days. I will guide you to a road, which you must follow until you reach the place where they buried St Edmund. It will take you days. I know a Benedictine just like you, he is, living in that very town.' Bernard hung on every word as Eirik as he explained about Brother Benedict who was now living incognito as "Samuel" as he was a monk not strong enough to stand up to the fear of torture and death so agreed to Henry's divorce and his status as Head of the Church of England. He told him where to find Samuel. If he were to tell Samuel his story, he would most definitely give him food, water and money.

Bernard, foolishly argued that he didn't need money but Eirik told him that from Bury St Edmunds to Yarmouth, and from Yarmouth by sea to King's town upon Hull by boat, and from there to the northeast would cost. Bernard was aghast. Sea? Boats? Coin? There must be alternatives. Not unless you get a horse insisted the young man, and, you still need money. It's the best protection there is, advised Eirik.

Eirik guided him to the road that would take him eastwards and they stood, literally, on a crossroads and bade each other God speed, good luck and goodbye.

Again, Brother Bernard reminded himself that this boy was, indeed, an angel and told him so. In truth, he wasn't far off as he had already bandaged the monk's cracked and bleeding feet and even gave the shitty smelling ecclesiastic a loving embrace before they parted. As the distance grew between them, they looked back and waved knowing that it was very unlikely that they would ever meet again or even arrive at their destinations.

At least they were well out of the frying pan. By the time summer came and Henry was to commence his progress north, he would order all in the Tower to be executed.

14: Eirik

York, end of July 1541

I awoke in anticipation. A new day, one in which we would meet as Agents of the Word for the first time and commence battle against the threat that was known as the Cataclysm. Father Matthew had designated his very own church, Holy Trinity, as our permanent meeting place and, in the next hour, the Agents were to make congress. However, as I was swung about in a most undignified manner in my box, I was, accompanied by Edward and Godwin, on my way to see Lizzy. I was so excited. Elated that she had survived but anxious to see how she now fared. It was a warm morning and I was in a great mood, certain that, in time, the Agents would thwart Henry's diabolical plan.

The first thing I noticed as I arrived was that Lizzy was no longer downstairs. Godwin took me out of my box and up the stairs to where she lay. She was sitting up in her modest bed and by her side was more of the herbal drink supplied by Bayard. She was thin and retained her scars but seemed stronger as she spoke, screaming with delight and, as I was placed in her lap, stroked, kissed and caressed me constantly. What was even more touching was the conversation. I say conversation but it was one-sided. All the same, she shared all the gossip of the household and the alley in which she lived. How I wished I could have answered her although I was still positively engaging with her and having some therapeutic effect on this little girl. I heard Godwin and his wife whispering. It became apparent that they didn't think Lizzy would live despite the respite and, if they'd have asked me, I would have agreed. Our time together was short-lived as we had to leave for our meet but I was relieved to hear Godwin say that he would bring me again soon. Lizzy, quite sensibly, asked why I couldn't live there and Godwin's bluster and nonsense about how I would eat too much, take up too much room and so forth left her even more confused. There was no doubt, however, about me staying. I was needed elsewhere.

Godwin set off for work parting company with Edward and myself as we made our way innocently to Goodramgate. We had walked out into a dramatic burst of warm sunshine which was a relief as this had been, already, an inconsistent summer. One day a deluge, the next sunshine but I loved it. I loved York. I even stopped talking about the stink. Well, a bit. On this day, I had some clarity, I was able to think about Nick, my former self. My real self, I suppose although, rocking my way along the bridge over the River Ouse, I was, one hundred per cent, Micklegate Mouse. Hell-bent on my mission, I was intrigued by my relationships and friendships that simply seemed more than virtual. According to the science they were, literally, virtual.

I wasn't even in York. Momentarily, it makes no sense to me so I shut it out, knowing full well that it's an attitude such as this that invites and worsens the mix. I realise I don't give a rat's arse about the mix. The nation needs to be saved.

We had plenty of time so meandered somewhat and, as we heard a familiar sound to the north, Edward asked if we could take time to watch. A crowd had formed and, yes, Bayard was there doing what he does best. Heads on spikes today no less, we moved in to see him perform.

'Yes, my very good citizens of York I present to you at great expense (a dramatic pause whilst he whipped off the sacks that covered the heads) the very heads of Anne Boleyn, Thomas More and Thomas Cromwell!!' Oohs and ahhs echoed around the square, potentially another success for the greatest showman. And yes, these were genuine heads although, even from where we stood, it was clear that there were two female heads and one male head. Illusion, is of course, in part, having the audience believe what you want them too so, much credit again to Bayard as no one, as yet, bothered to question this. Neither did anyone seem to question the fact that it was now five years since Anne Boleyn died so she was looking in pretty good nick. Heads on spikes? Not that shocking really. Even as far north as York this was still being used to set an example to those who may have considered challenging Henry. In fact, my home, Micklegate Bar, was a favourite site for the spent faces of traitors. My biggest concern was wondering where the hell Bayard had got these heads from. Edward leaned down and whispered something to me, asking my permission I suppose. I conceded and promised to keep this request from Godwin and, of course, Edward's father. We moved in further and Edward delivered an impromptu reaction to the performance.

'Oh no! Queen Anne Boleyn, and just as I remembered her!' The audience was immediately moved by this and a murmur resounded about the square. Bayard gave us a wink that said thank you as we sneaked away. I remembered what Bayard had done for little Lizzy and felt as though I was managing to put the pin in the arse incident behind me. Behind me? Is that funny? Not really. Not over it yet I suppose.

I was fascinated by the Holy Trinity church that was intriguingly part hidden and overwhelmed by its simplistic beauty. We were soon inside guided by Father Matthew beyond the interior to an ante-chamber which had a secret opening in the floor.

'God's armpits!' I seemingly said out loud and both Ed and the priest swung around.

'Sorry, just getting a bit tired of seedy cellars, becoming a bit of a regular thing. Can't we just meet in the church while it's quiet?!'

I was surprised to see Father Matthew smile. He went on to explain that this church was, if needed, a perfect place to hide someone away almost permanently and that we wouldn't be meeting there. I was, of course, embarrassed and thought it best to continue the tour in silence. Beyond this room was a short, dark corridor with a single door at the end. More bloody dark, damp rooms I thought, but managed to keep this thought on the brain side of my big mouth and was glad I did. As he opened the door, glorious sunshine streamed in. It was a walled garden, the walls so high that no one would be able to see us and the garden so large that we could talk in the centre unheard. Brilliant. Put some effort into this secret agent stuff has this priest, I thought. The only building overlooking the garden was the Minster but this was still some distance away. Robert, the Mayor, was already there stuffing bread into his already over accommodated mouth, looking completely complacent and then, out of nowhere, appeared the two sisters. So, our Agency was complete but I was then left wondering why there was a delay in proceedings as everything was set and was uncannily informal. For a moment I was wondering if there had been a sudden outbreak of amnesia as it seemed like we had only gathered to have beer and cake. Not that I have any issues with beer and cake, I just didn't like wasting time. Knocking. Faint at first, but I could hear knocking. It startled me, of all those already present at this dysfunctional gathering, I seemed to be the only one who understood the gravity of our position. Knock! Knock! Knock! Knock! Was I the only one hearing this? Father Matthew shook his head, a wry smile on his face, in the direction of Wynnfrith who laughed heartily. I'd never seen her like this before and, if it wasn't for my accelerating trepidation, I would have joined her. The priest turned and walked back toward the trap door. That was the point when the groat dropped for me. Silas. Who else would it be? Fugitive idiot locked in a cellar. Had to be him.

What was so loveable was that he still tried to make a Lordly entrance. This scruffy head appeared above the floor, ginger lock stuck in its mouth and announced,

'Welcome to you, my ladies and gentlemen. I bid you good day, proceedings will commence presently.'

Welcome to what? His pit? His church? (that incidentally belonged to God). Apparently, he's now in charge of proceedings. Father Matthew, probably for the tenth time, showed Silas how to open the trap door from the inside.

We all laughed. Silas too. He took heart in this as he knew his friends were laughing with him, not at him. No malice here, I thought, and we were all delighted to see him except, perhaps, Elspeth who, if I'm honest, just looked angry most of the time. She scowled at Silas as he appeared, and he saw it. Robert explained that Silas was now a fugitive. As we stood in the sun, Robert related the story about Maud, Runt, and the inn. Although, as yet, it was unclear as to how or why Runt died, one thing was for sure, Silas had said too much, too often and the authorities wanted him dead indicating to all that there were, surely, spies everywhere looking for those who had got wind of the Cataclysm. As he heard this, Silas felt empty inside. Deeply hurt, he so wanted to be the hero but his loose tongue almost always left him in all sorts of trouble. These people were all he had, one of them had even stolen his heart and, if he was castigated and banished for this most recent misdemeanour, he was certain it would be best for all if he simply took himself from this world in which he just did not fit. For Silas, this was much more of a practical deduction rather than self-pity. Unless you've ever felt this way, it would be very hard to understand. There was an almost permanent dark weight pulling down on Silas's heart and he enjoyed very few days of weightlessness.

But, on this occasion, he needn't have worried. Although there was no legitimate getting out of this situation for Silas, he had friends that believed him to be innocent and, in any case, everyone in the church garden was in the same boat as him as they were all outlaws now although Robert, in particular, probably thought he was exempt. For the first time, I caught Wynnfrith looking at Silas. I couldn't tell exactly what it was. Sympathy? Confusion? Fascination? And then she looked away. Silas couldn't face her at all as he was almost incurably ashamed.

'Will I be here always now my Lord' asked Silas.

'Not at all' said Robert 'you will be an agent in the field and you will be assigned this very day and away tomorrow!' Silas and most of those present were astonished and all you could hear for the next few moments were the birds and wasps in the garden. Almost as if to break the silence, Wynn walked over carrying a small cloth bundle and, most coyly, handed it to Silas. How she hoped no one was watching but her hope was in vain. Silas, struck by silence just smiled and then, yet again, managed to get his face to match the colour of his hair. He thought it impolite to do nothing so he unwrapped the bundle. Cake. Wynnfrith had brought cake.

For him. Why? I don't deserve it? Had someone asked her to do it? Bless her. My heart races. He tried to hide it but was completely overwhelmed and stared at his feet. I thought that I was the first to notice a tear in his eye but Robert was just behind him so, suddenly, decided to give Silas a very manly slap on the back and instantly drew attention away from him by inviting everyone to sit in the cloisters. Well, I called them cloisters, I suppose they were just stone seats. Wynn scurried to the back as though nothing had happened.

Even I couldn't have dreamed of an afternoon so full of surprises and twists to come so it's no wonder Father Matthew took time and great care in sitting us in a row as he now presented as very formal and serious.

'My fellow Agents of the Word. Today we draw up our plans which, once we are organised, will defeat this evil that faces us. But, there is so much more you should know. For a while a young man has sought to make contact with me, or should I say make contact with Elspeth.' Elspeth was initially surprised and then remembered the blonde-haired boy who she had seen hovering so many times close to the washhouse.

'Yes. Yes.' She said 'only saw him from some distance. Didn't trust him at all. Who is he, Father?'

'Perhaps you should have given him a few minutes of your time my dear as he has much to offer.'

Wynn was always telling Elspeth that she was too harsh and untrusting so Elspeth felt troubled that she hadn't seized this opportunity. The past month had been challenging and confusing, how was she to know who was trustworthy and who was not.

'Where is he?' she asked

'Here' said the priest. Hellfire, I thought, he's running a hotel for criminals! In for a long afternoon definitely. I was then amused at the priest's apparent parallels with Bayard and stifled a laugh as I didn't think Father Matthew would appreciate being thought of as a street entertainer but that's how he was coming across. Da da, I present…the next waif and stray rebel against the throne! I had to compose myself as there were now an array of dramatic expressions on everyone's faces and then, out of the shadows, calmly walked a most handsome young man properly dressed as a gentleman of the day in the current vogue. He was tall, blonde and athletic. The two ladies just stared at him. Another blow to Silas. He saw Wynn look at this Renaissance Adonis and his little heart simply gave up all hope.

Father Matthew prepared himself to make an introduction when something very strange happened. Elspeth stood and walked right up to the young man. What was much more shocking was that she touched his doublet in an age where physical contact and intimacy were respectably reserved for marriage and closed doors (or Mrs Grindem's, depending on your point of view). What on earth was going on? He looked bemused and looked over to the priest for, what looked like, help. She stared deeply into his ocean blue eyes and opened his doublet. Wynnfrith was the first to intervene. On her feet, she whispered,

'Elspeth, what's has gotten hold of you?' Elspeth was completely cut off from everything else in the world now and ignored her sister. Mesmerised, they all watched as she took her index finger and poked it into his shirt just below his left clavicle and continued to look him in the eye.

'Here. You have a red mark from birth shaped like an oak leaf.' He shuddered and spoke for the first time.

'What? Who are you?' He looked again at Father Matthew. 'Father! What trickery is this?'

He was now seemingly nervous as was almost everyone, quite sternly Father Matthew asked her to explain herself.

'James' she said 'your name is James.'

Bloody isn't, thought I. And he corrected her too.

A daytime drama followed in which Eirik froze and

trembled as did Wynnfrith and her sister. She sat Eirik down and asked if he remembered having a family. He answered no and patiently awaited an explanation. We watched, almost forgetting our purpose, as Elspeth made sense of her outrageous actions. I'd already guessed, as they had stood face to face, as I had thought that they could easily have been twins. Surely they were related, it was just hard to understand why he wouldn't know.

She explained. Wynnfrith and Elspeth had lost their parents to sickness when they were children and then split up. They had always told people that mother and father had died from the plague but there was no plague in 1525, what mattered was that their parents wanted them removed and protected to save their lives. Elspeth was put in the care of the convent, Wynnfrith was cared for by Robert's family but Elspeth had never known where baby brother James had gone and had always thought him either far away or dead. Looking around at the faces of my new found friends, it was hard to know what astonished them most. For my part, Robert had grown massively in my esteem. He may model his look on King Henry but God had given him a completely different heart. To take on a disabled toddler in this day and age was magnanimous, to say the least. Seemingly, Elspeth had claimed Wynn back after the convent was abolished. The three were split up when Eirik was just two, Wynn four and Elspeth nine. Their little brother "James" could be recognised by the oak leaf-shaped birthmark.

Until now, Eirik had been transfixed on Elspeth only. She spoke,

'I'm Elspeth and this is your sister…'

He took a step forward, looking intensely at Wynnfrith who gave away her gait by rising using just her strongest leg. He started making silent 'W' shapes with his mouth and then he blurted out ' Wi….Wil...Wynn. Wobbly Wynn. Wobbly Wynn!!' he shouted.

His sudden realisation and inappropriate turn of phrase were at first shocking to us and then Robert burst into laughter.

'That's right, lad. Wobbly Wynn! That's what you called her and it's what her dad called her. Ha Ha. Wobbly Wynn!' Elspeth and Wynnfrith were laughing and crying at the same time and out of nowhere, Wynn said,

'the baby, the baby. Oh, Elle, I thought I'd imagined it.'

Robert and Elspeth had protected Wynn from any reminders of the lost baby.

Silas was, at first, relieved that Eirik wasn't a rival but was now finding this current situation very moving and was quite overcome, not least, as he had no family of his own. I thought I would offer him my most valued counsel.

'For God's sake man! Get a grip! You're meant to be our best hope. Stop bloody wailing' I said. That did the trick, I thought and then I chuckled. I loved this new personality of mine although I doubted whether anyone else did. Fortunately, Eirik had not heard my outburst as he was too wrapped up in his newly discovered sisters. No one had told him about me yet so I decided to pipe down for a while. I couldn't believe that they had stumbled upon their brother. No, seriously, I just didn't buy it so kept a close eye on this revelation.

It was a while before the whole family reunion thing died down. The priest had promised a long afternoon of new information but this was beyond my expectations. Father Matthew then told us all about how Eirik had first met Bede and Bernard after they had been captured. How Eirik and Bernard had adventured far and wide, a tale in itself that is better left for another day and a weightier tome. Suffice it to say, that Eirik never found the man called nails but did get the pigeon from Stratford, and the one from York, and that Brother Bernard had made it to Lindisfarne. We were all agog as this story unravelled and were desperate to ask questions but Father Matthew instructed us not too.

At Lindisfarne, Eirik spent days seeking out Bernard, constantly cautious of who he talked to. He found him one day at the back of an inn, a former patient of his tending his sores and cleaning his face and beard. They were overjoyed to see one another and, although Eirik was happy to hand over the birds to Bernard, he warned the monk that all was lost at the abbey at Lindisfarne and that he should return, with him, to York City. However, it didn't stop Bernard going and he insisted on going alone. Bernard had become irrationality obsessed with his mission to return to the abbey on the island and immediately sent Bede's pigeon on to Bede in Stratford keeping Faith in reserve until he knew how things fared on the island. Eirik, now grown, more muscular and donning fine clothes agreed to keep returning to the peaks of the dunes at the mainland to await Bernard's return at which point they would travel to York together. When he last returned to the dunes he saw Bernard being buried by fishermen and noticed that the pigeon had gone. In such an event Eirik had been directed by Bernard to find "the girl who looks like a nun by the name of Elspeth in York City." Father Matthew interceded and admitted to posting the note giving warning of Faith's return, not because he had met Eirik, for this was well before he had arrived, but because a trusted friend (whose name he would not give up) insisted he did so although the priest, personally, had found it unlikely that they would see this bird again. No one wept for Bernard as we sat in this pleasant church garden. Not that they didn't care, everyone simply knew that he couldn't have survived but there was now a pall over proceedings that wasn't evident before.

At this point, Father Matthew promised that he would summarise all that, between us, we now knew about the Cataclysm and that, this very day, we would devise a strategy to combat it but there was still a secret yet to be told. Apart from a few supportive comments and my sharp words to Silas, I spoke for the first time. Every time I presented in this way, I could feel the awkwardness. After all, it was a big ask, expecting people to simply accept the notion of a mouse on a box giving orders. However, I knew there was something that Father Matthew wasn't sharing and I had to address this to clear the air completely. I referred to the day that I was, most unfortunately, upon Bayard's stage and, without any frills, directly asked the priest who the strange character was alongside him. He was reluctant to answer, now trying to persuade me that time was of the essence, but Wynnfrith chipped in confirming that she had seen someone when she visited the church. Bravely, but politely, Silas told Father Matthew that he was concerned about the strange noises he could hear at night time. Before he could reply, Eirik was on his feet, having drawn his dagger, shouting

'death to the demon rodent!' I inadvertently peed all over my box as he lunged in my direction. Thankfully he was intercepted by big Bob the Mayor. As you can imagine, we wasted another twenty minutes filling young Eirik in on the story of the curious Micklegate mouse, the most bizarre aspect of the Agents of the Word and another five minutes was spent drying out the box. Fortunately, Silas was already aware of my strange disposition thinking that there was nothing unordinary about a chatty field mouse. The priest then gave way to the pressure put upon him regarding his mysterious guest.

'My fellow agents and friends' sighed Father Matthew 'you've no idea how much it pains me to think that I have secrets kept from you. My only aim has been to defeat these mysterious and dark schemes of our evil monarch. This matter I keep to myself only to protect the man in question and, hopefully, to give him some quality of life. Please bear with me.' He then wandered off into the church from where we could hear the unbolting of a door, shuffling and unintelligible sounds. We waited in silence not knowing what to think of this additional revelation. What we were to behold would soften the heart of the hardest of men. A creature that could barely walk unassisted, he was bedraggled, old and confused. His hair and beard were both long and unkempt and he muttered nonsense with an intonation that persuaded us all that he was in pain. Father Matthew brought him out into the sunlight, he raised his left arm to cover his eyes and grunted disapproval. His head down, it was difficult to make out his face but to the rear of his cranium was an unmistakable saucer-shaped dent. Eirik, without prompting, walked over to this man and gently placed his palm under his chin and, in doing so, slowly raised his head. Eirik's speech broke as he softly said,

'Brother Bede.' There were gasps from the group as Bede had become such an important part of our story and, as people wondered how and why he was in York and thought of what to make of this, Eirik embraced his former prisoner. For everyone, seeing the injury caused by the grapple hook as Bede had plummeted into the Tower moat, both shocked and asserted the gravity of the situation.

'I found him wandering around then City still wearing his tattered cassock constantly rambling. At first, he could say much more. Bernard was the first word that came from his lips and I took him in both to care for him and to try to find out what he knew. He persisted in the expectation of Faith the pigeon and is, therefore, the reason for the notice I posted.' Elspeth angrily asked why he looked such a mess if he was caring for him.

'He won't let me near him! I swear I have done all I can.' It was, therefore, a revelation and a relief that Bede felt safe next to Eirik. Eirik sat Bede down to his left.

'Priest, pray tell us what he has given up' said Eirik. Father Matthew then passionately reassured us that he was, in fact, about to deliver all he had discovered when presenting his conclusion.

'You'd better be about it, fat Harry will have been and gone by the time we have a plan! Feel as though I've been sat here for bloody days!' I said, again not understanding where my politeness filter had gone.

'And while I'm at it can you and the Mayor please explain why, if you knew so very much including the return of the pigeon, you have played this cat and mouse game, if you'll excuse the expression, with these two maidens for so long?'

'Have you any idea what is at stake, Sir?! If we were to entrust all to all without testing the water, why the King himself could have uncovered our plans by now! You have my word that you will hear all today' promised Robert. The priest waxed apologetic, sincere too I think. Bede grunted. Silas was admiring Wynnfrith. Wynnfrith was staring at Bede. Edward was almost asleep. Elspeth was looking at her brother. Eirik was staring at the weird mouse. Robert was staring at Elspeth's rear. Father Matthew was staring at Robert staring at Elspeth's rear. I was marvelling at how tiny my privy parts were. So, I waited for things to die down a little and then decided to give the priest another sharp prompt.

'This afternoon has been mad! Absolutely flaming mad! It's just too much for everyone to take in so "Father!" I suggest you either conclude or I will employ these good people as best I can in the fight that is ahead.' It occurred to me that I may have been too hard on him and he endeavoured to redeem himself by saying,

'Please, please be patient a while longer as I have one more thing for you to behold!'

'O God no! Don't tell me you've got the bloody Pope tied up in his underwear upstairs?!'

I'd crossed the line. Wynn laughed, so did Ed, then Eirik, also Silas and then Elspeth. I looked at Father Matthew and he chuckled too. And Robert. Well, at least I'd broke the icy spell.

The last laugh was on me as he unravelled, from a large blanket, a large object. This was an unbelievable reveal. The

Lindisfarne gospels themselves, here, in the hand of the Agents of the Word. Father Matthew said nothing and then asked me, for some strange reason, to examine it. Edward carried me over and I looked over the open pages making sure that the said privy parts were now completely dry.

'What think you, good mouse?' said the priest.

'Perfect Father' I said restoring my respect for him 'entirely perfect.'

I looked around and it was clear that no one understood what I had said besides the Priest. I looked up at him,

'too perfect, it's a fake.' I was preening myself at being so smart but then saw the disappointment on everyone's face.

'This was taken from a notary of the late Thomas Cromwell. Perfect and beautiful it is but it is a copy so we now have to ask ourselves why copies are being made.'

It was then that it first occurred to me that not one of these outrageous revelations phased Mayor Robert in the least. It became clear to me that the priest and he had, until now, shared everything with each another. Poor Wynnfrith, I thought, must have been terrified planting secret messages in the church when the priest knew what she was up to all along. It may have been a good thing in the long run but I was minded to stay circumspect. Surprisingly, he asked me to secure the book so that it could be accessed in York at short notice if needed. This also told me that at least one of us was about to leave the City in a hurry.

'Yurk' shouted Bede and, although, we were all a little shocked and pleased to hear him speak, we also understood that he was probably now simply repeating sounds. What a truly pathetic sight he was, poor man.

The afternoon had been a whirlwind and we all sat there trying to make sense of it all, hoping that the priest would sum up. However, it was Robert who now boldly addressed us. So much for low profile, thought I.

This was refreshing after watching "Thursday afternoon

with Father Matthew" for hours on end and we hoped that he could condense all that had gone before into something we could all understand and work with. He started with the scraps of parchment presenting the fourth piece that was discarded on the day faith arrived home which Robert had acquired "by his own espionage." This left us with:

hath spawned a plan
most evil. By Eadfrith's hand and
command, the Word must be saved
Once on an isle to the north of Stratford on
the avon. In lucifer's hands doth now reside
and in the minster to be placed
Here the Cataclysm is assured.

'I feel there is still more missing but this, Agents, confirms that the Lindisfarne gospels, once placed ceremoniously in York Minster on the day of the King's arrival, will be the catalyst to launch this evil plan of which we still know too little. Father Matthew and I have been very careful, as to how we have interpreted anything that has come from the dear Brother Bede's lips. He has mentioned Cranmer, Wriothesley and Edward Seymour on many occasions most anxiously and fearfully so I feel that the cunning lies at their feet. He often tries to say "Bernard", "Benedictine" and "Eirik" and has panic fits about his escape, now described to us in such detail by Eirik. We have no idea how he got away and travelled so far to York. As regards the King's visit, be assured, as he makes his way north, that this is no reconciliatory meeting. He brings enough soldiers to start a war but also an army of labourers and craftsmen by the hundred so make of that what you will. And, he intends to meet the Scottish King and, as yet, we are unsure why. The monk also keeps repeating what sounds like clarification.'

Eirik enthusiastically interjected,

'Yes, Yes! That was one thing Brother Bernard shared with me. This plan, which he described as the evilest act to visit Christendom was called "The Clarification" by the perpetrators and the King. The clarification and the Cataclysm are one and the same.' Everyone looked puzzled including me. I thought about our group and was reminded of that adage that says one man's terrorist is another man's freedom fighter. I did not doubt that Henry's diabolical plan was, yet again, "clarifying" an Englishman's view of his world and his God. But was it Henry's plan? He had been shown to be gullible so many times before. Only time would tell.

Robert continued,

'the copy or copies of the Lindisfarne Gospels befuddles me although it does imply that, if this book is so important to Henry and the Cataclysm, he may well be being coerced. So, Agents! We know where and when, but little of what and why and that is where your mission starts.' He paused. Been watching Bayard, I thought and then, he launched into his orders like a General.

'Lord Eirik and Lord Silas!' Silas jumped so much that he almost fell off the stone bench, absolutely delighted that, although fictional, he had bestowed a title on Eirik and himself.

'I have had a letter from Richard Shakespeare that is written to you, Silas. Richard and his family are under house arrest lucky to be alive. This done under the pretence of investigating the murder of this simple character, Runt but it is, in reality, to squeeze out any information they may have gleaned about the Cataclysm. Rumour has it that Richard has discovered and secreted a most important document.' Silas put his head in his hands conscious of the chain of events he had been partly responsible for.

'Now, now lad, you'll be the one to save them! You and Eirik will set out tomorrow for Stratford upon Avon where you will reconnoitre with Thomas Farrier, an Agent just like us.'

A candle, at last, flickered In Silas's head. The one horseshoe, the convenient meeting with the farrier, the drunks in the pub. All of it orchestrated. But surely he had at least acquired some useful information to take back to York with him? How on earth would Annie just wear out one shoe? What an idiot I am. He remembered as well that Richard had sent him off in the direction of Wolverdington, he hadn't stumbled upon it by coincidence. Oh, Silas, always the fool, he thought. Not the first time he'd been used and won't be the last. To sweeten this slight embarrassment, by the end of the afternoon, Robert presented Silas with a new set of fine clothes in keeping with those of Eirik's and had sent Annie to be completely shoed and saddled.

Before Robert could continue, there was an issue of considerable contention that needed to be resolved. Wynn, Elspeth and the priest (and certainly the monk if he was still able to contribute) wished to establish a code of conduct for the Agents that stayed close to the rule of Benedict. This passion for peace and non-violence was sincerely admired by everyone else except Eirik, in particular, could not see a victory without, literally, some battles being won. Robert asserted that The Agents of the Word should be better than their demon rivals and espionage should trump violence at every step but also conceded that it may not always be possible.

He continued,

'within a week the King will arrive in the City of Lincoln. Elspeth and iron balls! Ha Ha! (pointing at me) you will need to be there before the polygamous bugger arrives!' Everyone who hadn't heard the incredible "iron balls" accolade previously, laughed heartily although

Elspeth and Father Matthew both looked like they were simultaneously sucking lemons whilst trying to grip a walnut between their buttocks. Seemingly, this was a most inappropriate pseudonym. Robert recognised this and apologised. Elspeth then reacted to his plan.

'What? Just me and the incontinent mouse? For what reason? I can't go immediately...what about Wynn?' She rambled on for some time as Mayor Robert tried to calm her down.

'You won't be alone' he added 'and, you will be our senior spy.'

'And what exactly will I be spying upon, pray?' now sounding quite angry.

'Queen Catherine' he said.

That shut her up. Shut us all up. She spluttered and stammered and babbled excuses. She was undoubtedly in a state of disbelief.

'I have arranged with a very prominent contact that, from Lincoln onwards, you will be a chamberer to the young Queen.' A chamberer was a station below the Queen's other maids and her ladies in waiting but this would mean that Elspeth would have direct access to the Queen.

Very softly, and now more accepting, Elspeth asked,

'prominent contact?'

'Why, non-other than Thomas Culpeper himself.' If the previous statements had rocked Elspeth, and everyone else present, this revelation almost floored her. It was beyond belief that a washerwoman from the City would have a position at court, albeit a mobile one. And, for just a moment her halo tilted somewhat as she had unwittingly let the descriptions and reputations of the rock star that was Culpeper show on her face.

'Different story now eh cousin?!' She didn't like being mocked by Robert and instantly returned to default Elspeth demeanour.

Robert took her by the shoulder.

'Cousin, you are the most formidable woman I have ever met. A woman of God, of sound principle and integrity and you are an Agent of the Word.' Everyone cheered in her support. He went on to add that she would have much support and instruction once in Lincoln and that she was also to take the pigeon, Faith, with her for communication. She then pestered about transport and other details and Robert promised all was in order.

'But you must start growing your hair! It will give you away woman.'

He then advised that he, Father Matthew, Edward (along with Godwin's good care) and Wynnfrith would continue to work in York, promising that care would be taken of my workshop and its contents including the Lindisfarne Gospels copy and my ceiling boss.

My turn. The stamps for wax seals. My design was highly praised and valued by the team and I, for once, thanked the Lord I had created so many spares! All in attendance, apart from Bede, were given one and I knew that our agents further afield would need these as well. I emphasised how very important it was to conceal these and not to lose them.

This had been, indeed, an extremely lengthy congregation and, as it concluded, everyone embraced each other, Silas being the first to get up and kiss Brother Bede on the forehead, others promptly followed suit. There was a palpable sense of shock and drama as fond relationships were broken apart for the cause. As Silas rose to leave, he knew that this could be the last time he would see Wynn, perhaps ever. He bravely took a few steps toward her but she was, suddenly, unwittingly distracted by the noises Brother Bede was making. Silas took this to be a cold shoulder and so decided to leave. However, something inside him spoke to his common sense and drew him back again and, somewhere deep within, he found the courage to return and speak to her. It was in moments like this that I most admired young Silas.

'My fair maiden Wynnfrith. Would it be inappropriate, would it offend...er...I am being too forward in asking...how would you...may I...well, may I...possibly have some effect of yours that I may keep with me over those...er...lost weeks?' Everyone was now holding their breath to see what Wynn would do. Never before in human relationships have two people been so inept at communicating what was going on inside them. It was truly painful to watch and I felt like bloody shaking them both. Shy, embarrassed, awkward and not at all understanding why he had asked this of her, she reached for her kerchief. This was not, by any stretch of the imagination, what anyone would regard as clean. In fact, it had been well used and reasonable descriptions could range from filthy to downright crusty and green in hue. Those gathered stifled their responses, even Elspeth who wished to reprimand her. Astonishingly this went completely unnoticed by Silas who believed that he had just been given a cloth of gold. He tucked it inside his doublet, bade everyone farewell, bumped into Father Matthew, apologised and left. Eirik thought little of this as he presumed Silas and Wynn long term friends. Poor Wynn, she was clueless. Apart from Robert's, very noble, efforts at fatherhood, her relationships with men had been limited to encounters with drunks that had forced themselves upon her. Even Robert, meaning to be kind, had told her that there would be no love or marriage for her and she was content in that. It would take Elspeth later that evening to explain to her sister that Lord Silas was going all gaga on her. But then, she still wasn't sure that it could be possible. So, this she had in common with Silas. There's was so much to love about both of them but neither could see it in themselves.

I heard Robert tell the sisters and Eirik that they would be having a family feast before Eirik set forth the following morning. Father Matthew said prayers and, yet again, I was left astonished at the most unexpected content. Yes, he prayed for the success of our mission and the spiritual health of England but then he said

'Lord there is only one Christian faith and these temporary issues that divide our people into one camp or another are pure evil in themselves. I pray equally for all souls and that divisions disappear.' I was sure of Father Matthew's Catholic sympathies so for him to be able to be so inclusive in an age of such religious turmoil satisfied me that I was in the company of the very best of people. I thought about the whole of human history littered with tribalism, this faith that faith, this colour that colour, this gender that gender, this country that country, this sexuality that sexuality, endless, endless wasted energies just for the sake of power, of winning, of one-upmanship, one up-womanship. Who wins in the end? I pondered.

As I readied myself to depart I was aware of hushed consternation and conversation behind me. I knew what this was and had expected it. Having said that, I wasn't readily prepared with answers so rather than face the music I just wanted to disappear. Instead, I hid in the back corner of my box. They were all involved in the conversation now and it became more heated. What else should I expect? I had offered no credible reason for my existence. A talking mouse in sixteenth-century England? It would be hard to think of one person who didn't think that I would be an evil manifestation. Bless them, they were trying to be discrete, I simply couldn't blame them for their anxious curiosity. Still, I didn't intervene. What could I do? Or say? The truth was complete nonsense, I wouldn't have known where to start. I could hear the climax of this discussion as Father Matthew took charge,

'Micklegate mouse, it is only fair, as one of the Agents, that you are part of this conference to which I shall conclude. This character' he said, addressing the whole group 'is one of us. He is an agent, he is knowledgeable and has proved himself to be trustworthy. It is my reasoning, therefore, that he has been sent to us by God in our hour of need. Let that be an end to it.' And it was. I wasn't to be questioned about my most peculiar disposition again. I do think he had gone too far though, couldn't imagine myself as Saint ironballs, but at least he was right in that I honestly meant these people no harm, in fact, the very opposite.

I looked around at these Renaissance disciples and wondered what would become of them in the quest to, metaphorically, slay the giant. I added a silent prayer of my own for these good souls. It was something I had never done before but found it gave me great comfort.

To be in an age where communications were so limited was agonising. What we could achieve in much less time if it wasn't so. We were literally using birds to tweet one another. Having said that I was in awe of my compatriots who, although it had never been mentioned, would all happily have given their lives to resolve this matter. Apart from the obvious "big stories" of the last few months, everything I had learned would, for hundreds of years, be completely overlooked. The stories of everyday heroes lost which, I found quite sad. If integrity, honesty and love were what made humans important, my friends would have had volumes written about them throughout the ages but, sadly, that's not how it works. Memories of my former life now fade. I care nothing for it and, although I know what I'm feeling is part of that process, I'm happy to be where I am, doing what I'm doing with the people I care for. I am iron balls of Micklegate and an Agent of the Word. Together with my trusted agents, I will thwart the plans of those who choose to destroy who we are and what we stand for.

15: Lady Rochford

Lincoln, 1st August 1541

We were met the following morning by Robert on the edge of town. Edward, having spent the night asking me to explain what had gone on the day before, took me to meet Elspeth at this designated site. I could tell he was now feeling a little left out and I felt it a priority to reassure him. Dear Edward, still a child, being my initial point of contact impressed me beyond my wildest expectations. Our meeting now seeming so long ago. I told him, truthfully, that without him, we wouldn't be where we were now and that his work in the coming weeks would be invaluable. He was as important to the Agents of the Word as anyone including the dashing, adventurous Eirik. We laughed at how I was meant to speak only to one person (namely him) and now the whole of York knew. He kissed me and it didn't even feel a little strange. We had nurtured an unbreakable bond.

Robert had assured us of transport and, God knows why, Elspeth had quite grand ideas of a covered carriage, horses and a driver. To be fair, the idea of travelling so far terrified her. Most people without a trade didn't venture abroad much nor did they want to but, seeing as Eirik, Bede and Bernard had set the world record for journeying around England, it was only reasonable that we should do our bit for the cause. We waited. Robert grinned. Edward seemed to have an air of excitement and expectation about him. Elspeth gritted her teeth. I had a doze and then we all did the same all over again and then, relief! We could hear a carriage. Well, a cart. A covered cart with just one horse. It pulled up and we wandered around the other side to take a closer look and by the time we'd got there, Edward was already doubled over with laughter. As our eyes slowly raised we could see, very amateurishly executed, a painted sign that said, "Bayard, entertainer to Kings!"

'No way. Not on Gods earth! I'd rather walk.' She turned to Robert who had already taken three steps back. 'Cousin! You promised!' Elspeth's face now red with fury, Mayor Robert struggled to keep a straight face. Bayard peered out from behind the nag and simply said,

'good day madam.'

'Elspeth, Elspeth' Robert said in his best, calming, nervous tone. 'You need a disguise, a cover until you get there. Did you really envisage arriving in grandeur? Be grateful that this man now supports us. I have his word that he is with the cause.'

'You never fail to disappoint Robert'. Now no one was safe from her wrath. 'What do we have?.. a liar, a damaged pigeon in a box, a diseased rodent and...' she opened the canvas and looked inside, shrieked and said 'oh my good God! Heads!!' Ed and Robert guffawed and a broad smirk appeared on Bayard's face,

'Don't mind moving the heads over madam if needs be. You don't have to sleep with 'em.'

For the first time, Elspeth was speechless. Something for which we were all grateful. After some time, some considerable time, she acquiesced and dangled her legs out the back of the cart as he drove away. Edward had placed me fondly on the front next to Bayard and we made our sorrowful farewells. Elspeth had been given new clothes in a bag and a letter of introduction from Robert. After half a mile she really did ask if we were nearly there so I tactfully took some time to explain what we had before us and that she would effectively be living with stinky mouse and Bayard the magnificent for some days to come.

Apart from the uncomfortable ride, sparse food and the unpredictable weather, the journey was somewhat uneventful. All of this, and more, Elspeth blamed on the driver although he rarely reacted. After a day and a half, he spoke to me, completely out of the blue,

'Sorry about the pin, iron balls. You know. The pin in the arse. Well, your arse. Bad that. Shouldn't have done it. Won't happen again'.

And that was more or less the limit of our conversational intercourse. It was an apology though, I thought. Fair enough. Frequently, very frequently, in fact far too often, Faith would "coo coo" which was cute at first but, after fifty miles, it became unbearable. For some reason I couldn't fathom, Bayard also thought it a good idea to place our boxes together so I would enjoy the added luxury of the "coo coo" reverberating around the two boxes. How did I wish she could talk but, I ask you, "coo coo" all the bloody time? If I'm truthful (and please don't pass this on) I did talk to her which was a sign of my increased desperation. She was smelly too.

As the roads (and I do use that term very loosely) got muddier the cart became very rickety and Elspeth complained even more. We constantly seemed to be dodging cattle and random travellers who could have either been tradesmen or pilgrims. I suggested that we check the wheels and axles but all I got in return was how this vehicle had travelled all over Europe without incident. So, yes, you've guessed it, that's when we hit a ruddy great rock and the wheel came off. We lurched to the left, then to the right and tumbled into a ditch. The side of the carriage hit the ground. I made hard contact with the wheel as I was thrown out and became disorientated but just as quickly came to my senses. Noise. Unbearable noise. It was a howling, screaming din. And then I opened my eyes. At first, I simply couldn't make sense of what was happening and then, as I looked around, I knew exactly where I was. I was in an aeroplane, one which I recognised. I was upside down so corrected myself and I saw him. It was definitely him. The maniac. This was four hundred years later, 1941, and I was looking at Rudolph Hess, the German deputy fuhrer, on a solo flight to Scotland. According to him, this was his quest to make peace with Britain. He had had the plane modified so that he would have enough fuel but it did not go to plan. What has happened to Micklegate mouse if I'm here? What has happened to my colleague whose mission this is? Charles. Yes, Charles, this is his mission, 1941. We were screaming and spinning toward the ground ready to crash, crazy Hess had already bailed out. What will happen when I crash?! It's an anomaly, of course, software anomaly. Stay with it. I looked down. I was still a mouse! I couldn't explain any of it.

Crash!!

I became, again, disorientated. Open my eyes. Must open my eyes. Elspeth, in the ditch unconscious. Where's Bayard? I looked, he was next to me groaning. I kept shouting his name. I then jumped on his fat head and screeched into his left ear

'Bayard!! You have to help Elspeth!' Over and over until he came round. He wasn't seriously hurt, just drastically overweight. He went over to the nun and cradled her head gently. Her mouth and nose had been clogged by mud so I told him to carefully remove it and, awkwardly, he blew into her nostrils. Now, whether it was the kiss of life or his breath that brought her around I don't know and didn't care but she was alive. Bastard Bayard was a gentleman after all, especially when you consider what man could do to a vulnerable woman in the middle of nowhere. Gratitude? Hang on a mo, this is Elspeth we're talking about. She complained endlessly about the cart, the wheel, the axle, his driving, the roads, the weather and the food until, eventually, he said,

'sure you used to be in a convent? Not a palace then?' And then went back to repairing the cart. Touché. I think that did humble our blonde powder keg somewhat, at least for a few hours. She was filthy and had a few bruises but otherwise was back to her every-day, domineering self. Although we had lost some supplies in the crash, there was one consolation for Elspeth as the heads of Anne Boleyn and the two Tommies went hurtling down into the chasm. What a find that would be for the farmer when he returns to his field I thought. Faith was secure in her box, in the cart, still making that bloody unbearable noise. Between us we did a pretty good job of repairing this sixteenth-century death trap and, for the first time, they had a good laugh together as they watched a field mouse working with mini nails and a hammer. Besides being filthy and wet, we could now resume our journey. I hadn't the heart to tell Elspeth that we weren't out of Yorkshire yet.

When I had time to think, I became extremely anxious. The little bit of training that had stayed with me told me that none of this was real. I was simply enjoying (if that was the word) virtual experiences. Having said that I can't tell you what a frightening and improbable juxtaposition that was and I couldn't help wondering what had happened to my colleague, Charles, during that glitch. It was incredibly scary but, I did take time to congratulate myself on being the only mouse to crap himself in two centuries at the same time. I had to put this out of my mind and fully absorb myself in the mission.

Elspeth, in every sense of the word, had led a very sheltered existence. She was now absorbed by the changing landscapes, vast open countryside and the small hamlets and villages and, of course, all roads connected towns and villages so there were things to look at and people to meet. She had only ever known York and the convent. I could completely understand why she seemed so uncomfortable, and irritable, with only a mouse and a dodgy one-man circus for company. She did, however, mellow and engaged, mostly on her terms, in conversation with Bayard. I had no complaints, Bayard was a massive asset to the Agents of the Word. He knew every byway, road and track and, even though they were somewhat exaggerated, his stories about entertaining Sultans, Kings and Emperors helped to pass the time.

Elspeth came to know that, without his keen knowledge, we were going nowhere. However, the journey wasn't without incident and, this being such a wet summer, our journey took its toll on us. We had stopped in more than one village and found most people amiable and Bayard even took some coin in Thorne as the warm but gullible, population were so excited to see a travelling entertainer. And, yes, you've guessed it, the world-famous dancing mouse raised enough funds to feed us for the next week. Even I found this comical, and happily bought into it, but he couldn't resist asking,

'You any idea how rich we could be if you'd do the talking thing as well?'

'Not happening' I said 'wish all you want, I'll be putting my talents to better use thanks.' As if he'd let it go, he rambled on about being as rich as Lords and so forth for another half an hour. However, I agreed that if it ever was going to make the difference between starving and getting bed and fed, I would happily dance. On my journey, I had discovered something equally as bad as the smells. Mud. Everywhere. Mud bloody mud. Mud in the City, mud in the countryside and along every track and road we met. How I yearned to get this over with and get inside somewhere warm. It's no use thinking I complain a lot. Put yourself in my position. Think about it. Imagine you're a mouse. The mud gets everywhere. At least people can stand up in it and keep everything from their knees upwards dry but recently I've had days on the road where I've completely lost sight of my valuables simply because of the flaming mud. Although, to say the least, it was difficult, both Elspeth and I had been given tasks to complete on the journey and, thankfully, our accident didn't interrupt the process or damage our working tools. These were both very specific and skilled tasks leading to essential support materials for Silas and Eirik and so had to be rushed cross-country to our precious allies as soon as we reached our destination. Not ideal, if we had had the time, all this would have been done before leaving York but it simply wasn't possible.

Eventually, we reached our destination. A muddy field on the edge of a wood. Somewhat bedraggled and very tired we neared Temple Bruer which was south of Lincoln, luckily Henry's progress hadn't reached the City yet. In the distance, we could see the encampment. It was huge, the size of a small City. Countless tents and prefabricated buildings. Thousands of people, horses and carriages. Guards holding pikes. None of us had ever seen such a thing. There was music, a galliard, and it made you want to dance. It echoed around this makeshift community and could even be heard bouncing back and forth between the trees behind us. It was all daunting and terrifying. Beautiful and awe-inspiring. I was personally mightily impressed by this Kingdom on the move and it suddenly put our half-cocked meetings in washrooms and churches into some perspective. We were taking on this?! I got a grip of myself. Yes, we are challenging whatever wicked practice was at the core of this expedition and we will win because we are good and because, between us, we can outsmart Wriothesley, Cranmer, Seymour and, if needs be, Henry himself. Full of myself I was almost at the point of adding a musical score to my dramatic thoughts when I heard hooves thundering toward us. We were undone, to coin the current vernacular. We were losing light. Towards us, coming at some pace, was a shadowy silhouette, clearly a male. We presumed this to be a threat at first but Bayard, of all people, insisted we stood our ground as we had no chance of out-running this charger. We were now all sitting on the back of the cart, me on Elspeth's lap, bracing ourselves. My mind then turned, again, to all those, sometimes ridiculous, notions people held about "the past." It always slightly irritated me that there is often a presumption that people were less skilled in the past but here I was watching a master horseman and recognising that this wasn't exceptional at all. He drew to a halt right in front of us.

'Maiden Elspeth I presume?' This was our contact. We were not only relieved but happy that we were now, more or less, at our journey's end. Elspeth struggled with this surprise encounter but managed to deliver an affirmative.

'Thomas Culpeper at your service!' he said. What?! This was Culpeper himself? At some risk, he had secretly been in communication with Robert and was out here alone? I had not, before, met Culpeper, and historians hadn't always agreed on his personality so this was going to be interesting. He dismounted in a very impressive cavalier fashion and came into the little light we had. He stood proudly in the mud which seemed to dramatise his expensive leather boots. Obviously, mud works for some people. Bastard. He was, indeed, very handsome with a sporting physique. He donned a most elaborate doublet of leather with cut sleeves that revealed a cotton billowy sleeved shirt. His hose was no less than an advertisement for his athletic legs and we noticed that he carried a sword. This was an age where a man's hat can say almost everything about him, Culpeper rode out this evening wearing a felt, beret style hat decorated with ostrich feathers. He did look amazing. He approached Elspeth and said,

'Your cousin failed to mention that you may bewitch me with your outstanding beauty, maiden. As I dwell on your pretty face the sun has risen yet again today.' Unwittingly, when we left, I forgot to pack a sick bucket and was now decidedly regretting it. Was Elspeth falling for this? Well, if I'm honest, she was clearly loving it, at first, that is. What happened to the bloody nun then? He was smooth, good looking and was capable of making any woman think that they were the centre of the Culpeper universe and even the bird went "coo coo." This is surely the reason Henry still kept him at court. Culpeper was youth, he was the very essence of the young King Henry. He was fun, simply good to have around and the King completely trusted him. Oh, dear. That word. Trusting folk hadn't gone too well for Henry. When he had completed his obligatory wooing, he looked around and first clocked Bayard.

'Ha! The entertainer. Good man. Good man! And where is? There madam, on your lap! Ha ha! The talking rodent! Oh my, how we've waited for this moment. Quick beast! say something before we lose the light!' I was testing out my best breathing exercises at this point aware that, particularly as Bayard and Elspeth were looking at me, I would have to deliver at some point.

'Come on mouse!' He then gave me a poke in the stomach as if it was my on and off button. He did it again.

'Listen up arsehole, I'm not another bloody plaything for your amusement! We're on a serious mission!' I looked around and saw how disappointed Bayard and Elspeth were in me.

'Haaaa! Haha! Haha ha!! Bloody marvellous! I can see

we're going to get on fine, mouse. Marvellous! Haha!' I was starting to get the measure of him and was certainly liking him better already, at least he had a sense of humour.

'Come' he said to Elspeth. 'we must make haste before dark. Your employment is secure fair maiden.' Oh no, I thought. He said "fair maiden." I really would be glad to see him go. He looked at Elspeth in a sort of "what are you waiting for" fashion. She hadn't a clue what to do. On the other hand, Bayard and I knew exactly what he expected. He hurriedly indicated the rear part of his, quite flamboyant, saddle.

'Oh no,' she said indignantly 'I won't be doing that!' Bayard and I made it clear that she had no choice, the light was failing and we were sure that Culpeper would soon be missed. She rather awkwardly agreed to sit side-saddle behind the Maidstone moocher who, as far as she was concerned, was already losing his gloss.

'And you' he demanded. Bayard and I looked at each other. 'You, mouse! Just jump up here. I'll grab the box. Everything sorted.' I seemingly didn't have a choice either and therefore did his bidding. Culpeper grabbed the bird box with his left hand and made to leave. Bayard assured us that this would be a good opportunity for him to bestow his unlimited talents on the nearby towns and villages and that, three days hence, he would be in Lincoln, by the castle. Off we sped into the hub of the camp. Even in this dim light, the colours of the flags, pennants, coats of arms and tents were blazing. A world or pageant, power and wealth created overnight in the middle of nowhere. The nearer we got the more impressive it became. Then, we were aware of the vast numbers in this encampment, particularly soldiers at arms, which dissolved all sense of awe and replaced it with the realisation that we now had our heads in the lion's mouth. As Culpeper's horse slowed to a trot, I became fascinated with this young man. What was his interest in helping the Agents? He was already rich beyond most people's imaginings having been bequeathed numerous properties by the King, including several that were previously monastic. As we arrived he hurriedly gave us instructions that included him saying that "he had the Queen's ear." More than her ear, mate, I thought. I already knew that he was close, too close, to Queen Catherine which meant that if Henry were to die, (and there was generally an expectation that he had only a few years left at best) and he was still in Catherine's favour when Prince Edward became King, he would wield unimaginable power. In this sense, he was in direct competition with Edward Seymour, one of the Cataclysm plotters.

We approached an entrance which, through any normal perception, was a building but I suspected it was prefabricated; erected on site. A very serious but attractive woman, magnificently dressed, approached us as Culpeper simply disappeared. Elspeth whispered,

'Do you think it's the Queen?' Apart from clearly being too old, the Queen wouldn't be wandering about greeting suspicious guests. And then she spoke,

'I am Jane Boleyn, Lady Rochford, Lady in Waiting to the Queen. Follow me.'

Not that I didn't fully appreciate my new friends in York, but now I'm finding myself star struck. Jane Boleyn, sister in law to Anne Boleyn and Queen Catherine's ally is here greeting us. First impressions? Still attractive but stern. Very stern. She was surrounded by other maids of varying ranks and, before I knew it, Elspeth had been consumed by the small crowd and hurried away.

'Take that thing away' she said and a male attendant rolled me up in a blanket and whisked me out in another direction. I felt myself falling onto a carpet of hay and, on looking around to get my bearings, found that I was now in a corner of the stables. Within a few minutes a carpenter was building around me what I thought, initially, was a prison but, once I had stopped panicking, realised that it was a small residence to keep my existence secret. It was quite comfortable and I was fed often and, more to the point, cleaned out. I did, of course, keep quiet, trusting that a role amongst all of this mess was awaiting me somewhere. The pigeon was above me in luxury accommodation making an almighty din and, as I looked across this borrowed barn there were homing pigeons everywhere. All in all, I decided to treat this as a weekend break and made the most of it. Within hours the work I had been so diligently engaged with on our journey was taken from me and I could literally see a rider speed off into the distance, his destination being Stratford and its recipients being Silas, Eirik and Thomas Farrier. I sent a prayer for success along with it. I'm praying as well now, soon rubs off on you this stuff.

Elspeth commenced training immediately. It was essential that she was able to pull off the role of chamberer. These were the most basic tasks but did give her access to the Queen's privy chamber, so, in essence, she was now a spy and in the most dangerous position imaginable and for her to keep up this guise, particularly at the start, was going to be very difficult for Elspeth. Even though court was prefabricated and on the move, she was exposed to so many extravagances she had never seen before. The routine, however, did remind her of the nunnery and the work was comparatively easy. She told herself that she had to acclimatise to this alien environment so as not to give herself away. She made friends with a maid called Mary but saw little of Jane Rochford or any courtiers. Elspeth had hardly settled into her routine when she was told that the progress would make for Lincoln City immediately. Before she knew it, they were on the move.

16: Richard Shakespeare

Stratford upon Avon, August 1541

Two days after Elspeth had arrived in Lincoln, Silas and Eirik were making their way into Stratford upon Avon. Tomes could have been written on the events, both significant or otherwise, that took place on the many journeys made by our Agents in 1541 but, suffice it to say that our two debonair gents got to their destination in good time without injury or major complaint.

You can also take it as read, that in any journey involving Silas, there were numerous creative mishaps as well but, surprisingly, this only enhanced Eirik's fondness for his travelling companion. To look at them you would be hard pushed to work out what they were. I suppose a sort of comedy duo would be an appropriate analogy mostly because Eirik now, by all outward appearances, was the archetypal, fashionable gentleman: young handsome and athletic. Silas looked as though he was meant to be just the same but nothing was quite working out for him in this respect. There simply weren't such things as clothes that fit Silas and, if they did, he would struggle to model them. So, here we had this unlikely pair who rode into town like brothers from two incredibly extremely disconnected mothers.

Eirik, still compassionate by nature and ever the champion of the underdog, simply saw the tenacity and well-intentioned soul that was Silas and, moreover, he made him laugh. For Silas, this was the greatest honour ever bestowed on him, to be treated as the equal of this dashing adventurer.

Somewhere beyond Leicester, Eirik started to tease Silas about Wynnfrith. Silas's pride and blatant embarrassment allowed him to successfully avoid the issue for some time and, as Wynn had turned out to be Silas's sister, he thought it most inappropriate to comment. Not one to let things go, Eirik allowed his companion to change the subject but only so that he could launch a surprise attack.

'Is she sweet on you too, friend?' Silas said nothing so Eirik kept repeating the question until he responded.

'No. No, I can't imagine she is, and who would blame her? She'd find a better catch in the river!' It was quite apparent to Eirik that, although Silas had made a fair attempt at a joke, he was hurting inside and probably always had been.

'You carry with you her token, brother! Take heart, I see kindness there. When we return you and I will rehearse you in your romance!' They both laughed. Silas's innards were forever subject to perpetual highs and lows. For a moment, he was happy again, encouraged that someone might give some imagination to the notion that Wynn could love him back and, for Eirik to call him brother, was the icing on the cake. Poor Silas, he had some cherished but fading memories of his mother but had never known any relatives otherwise. Oh, how he had always wanted a brother.

This pair followed a meticulous plan which was foreign territory for Silas admittedly but the rigour and discipline were good for him. Firstly they visited the lodging that was once Brother Bede's hideout, this being the second time that Eirik had been there. On the previous occasion, he had come away with nothing but the pigeon, Hope. Again, apart from the business of the school, to which it was adjacent, there was little noise or activity and no sign of anyone called Nails.

They took time to eat in Stratford and declared to each other that, throughout the country, there was an atmosphere, something brewing everywhere they went. They were impressively disciplined knowing that exposing their knowledge to strangers could have had serious consequences. After all, who would be able to tell the difference between Agents like themselves or those that were supporting Cranmer, Wriothesley and Seymour?

Before they even considered going directly to Richard's farm, their instructions were to seek out Thomas Farrier and Silas was confidently able to take Eirik directly to where he worked. Thomas was there and, on spotting Silas, hurried them both and their horses to the rear of his workshop.

'Silas! I thought you dead. They tried to blame Runt's death on you. It's so good to see you!' Someone else who liked Silas, what a day this was turning out to be. They then sat for what became a very serious and intense meeting. Silas introduced Eirik to Thomas and they then shared all the information they had and even told him about Bede and the story of Eirik's birthmark and how he, Elspeth and Wynnfrith had found one another again. Thomas was astonished that Bede was still alive and understandably needed time to digest everything that had been said. He strenuously emphasised the danger Silas was in as he would surely be recognised in the area. Silas took a deep breath and confronted Thomas about the day they had been in the inn. Thomas assured him that there was never any intention of treating Silas as a fool, but admitted that he had been steered in a particular direction so that he would become aware of certain information almost by accident. Richard had purposely sent Silas in the direction of Wolverdington and had interfered slightly with Annie's shoe. Silas was aghast but also impressed at such specific cunning.

'The story of Bede's pigeon gets told every afternoon at the inn, even now, so we knew you would hear it. I guessed and hoped that you were on our side so I didn't want you digging in every lake between here and York before you were any wiser or could alert agents in the north!' said Thomas, and they all laughed. Eirik then asked about Nails,

'he's the missing link but absolutely no sign of him' he said. Thomas leaned backwards and put his hand in a small wooden box, pulling out an object and held it up in front of the two visitors. It was a very large hand-made nail. They all laughed again. Of course, Thomas was Nails, Brother Bede's ally. Silas was urging Thomas to talk about the murder of Master Runt but he assured him that he knew very little besides the obvious that, of course, being that Silas had been set up. Silas looked at Eirik and this look voiced a thousand, sad, sentiments. Must I always be the fool? Why do people always see me coming? Will I ever be as others? Eirik put his hand, kindly, on his friend's shoulder and assured him of his value to the Agents. Again, Silas's barometer was on the up and so they turned to matters urgent. Thomas saw everything much clearer when he heard that the "Cataclysm" and the "clarification" were the same thing as he had heard both terms bandied about. He had overheard a conversation that led him to understand that the Cataclysm was very much about Prince Edward rather than the King.

'Is Henry dying?' asked Eirik.

'Rumours of his health abound. Some people say he's never been younger since he's started sharing a bed with Catherine! Others say his leg ulcer alone is killing him. Either way, I'm sure the scavengers are gathering to pick the bones off the old and the new King' said Thomas Farrier.

'Is it possible that King Henry isn't behind the Cataclysm?' asked Eirik.

'We just don't know but, be assured, he'll be in the mix somewhere. I do wish I could speak to Bede.' Thomas had answered in a tortured tone. Silas and Eirik were both emphatic that Bede was now beyond reasoning and that Thomas must park such hopes for good.

They talked about Richard Shakespeare's predicament and Silas asked why he hadn't simply been imprisoned or even killed outright. Seemingly, he was such a well-known and valued member of the community that, whoever had ordered this house arrest, wanted the matter kept quiet.

'That's because people will start to work out that there's something afoot if everyday citizens are hauled off to prisons' said Eirik.

'And they seek a diagram, a map that they believe was acquired by Richard, they still search the house. If they find it I feel there will be little hope for his family'.

They asked about the diagram but Thomas only knew that it directly implicated Wriothesley in the Cataclysm. Before they considered what to do about Richard, Silas insisted that he sought out Maud and find out why Runt died. Thomas Farrier knew about the supposed murder but nothing of Maud. Both Thomas and Eirik implored Silas to let this issue lie but he would not relent so, reluctantly, the three of them set out for ye dirtye peasant inn. Momentarily, Thomas and Eirik were delighted at the thought of food and beer. That is until they set eyes upon the place. The inn hadn't changed at all except it generally looked a little scruffier in the daylight. Silas dismounted and walked toward the door alone, seemingly thinking it rude not to collide with the inn sign for old time's sake. He rubbed his head and continued. His two companions had warned him not to go at all but he would have none of it. He looked around and then stopped. This was the new Silas. Well, almost. He had learned to stop and think so he did just that. Remembering his audacious and loud pronouncements from his previous visit, he simply decided to head for the bar. He recognised a few faces, others were new but there was no mistaking Maud. This is when his newly learned control went out of the window.

'Maud!' he shouted 'it's so good to see you again!' He threw his arms open and, in doing so, cleared the bar of everything that had previously been static upon it. This stirred the people in the inn, construing this as a violent gesture rather than clumsiness. Silas knew he had to calm himself. She barely looked up and then, blatantly ignored him. He noticed as she moved away, that she was limping badly. Quietly he pursued his folly.

'Maud it's me, Lord Silas!' He vented a slight chuckle, amused at his very first entrance in which he was attempting to delude all those present including himself. His face was now very close to hers, she leaned forward and whispered,

'Go away, you can't be seen here. (then loudly for all to hear) A beer sir? Be with you in a moment.'

'But Maud, you must remember, we were the best of travelling companions?' Again, she insisted he left and feigned the role of landlady and customer but he just wouldn't stop. That is until he felt a strong hand on his shoulder. It was Eirik.

'So sorry landlady, everyone. I think my friend here has had a little too much already!' He left some coins on the bar as recompense. Silas didn't take this lightly even when they got outside but his two companions insisted that they make a hurried exit. He was quite aggrieved at this unwanted rescue until his friend explained that they were all being watched and it was blatantly clear that Maud was too scared to speak. Silas stopped to think and realised that they were right and that, yet again, he had been a prize dick.

None of the three were to know that, even when Silas had first met Maud, she was in the pocket of one of Wriothesley's agents and, although she hated doing it, she was, indeed, spying on Silas. This, in turn, put Silas and Richard Shakespeare under suspicion. Once Maud had returned from Richard's farm on the day that they had dug for Silas's imaginary treasure, she was arrested along with Runt, the man who had been speaking to Silas the night before. Maud had very much taken to Silas and fallen for his fragility,

particularly his orphaned status so was unwilling to give up any information as was Runt. Runt, already ageing and nursing an ailing heart, died during the torture and so, at this point, Maud gave up everything she knew. The "island to the north of Stratford" nonsense was of little substantial use to Wriothesley's agents but it did tell them that the word was out about the Cataclysm. Silas's rhetoric about

"a mission from God himself" certainly set alarm bells ringing. Runt's death could easily be explained by this interfering northerner who had scarpered so soon after he was killed. What was becoming clear to all was that there were active cells on both sides in the Stratford area and whatever it was that Richard had come across gave even more weight to this idea.

Silas, Eirik and Thomas Farrier rested in the woods and commenced discussion as to how best to help Richard. Eirik explained how he would be able to take out guards one by one at twilight and remove the family unharmed. Silas chipped in with a gallant description of how he would fight to the death carrying out the youngest under his arm. His companions listened as it was such a long while since, as children, they had so enjoyed storytime. When it dawned on them that he was serious they thought it best to humour him somewhat. Then Thomas spoke.

'My friends. In my heart, I do believe that we must rescue Richard at all costs but please remember your oath to the Agents of the Word. We must keep harm to a minimum not just because it's the right thing, but because it leaves less mess, less suspicion and, hopefully, avoids alarm.'

You could see the other two pondering on how this might be achievable.

'Bear with me brothers' he said. Thomas then went to a large saddle bag on his horse and delicately untied a cylindrical holder made of leather. He sat with them and untied the straps, three in all. What he pulled out was, rolled up, the best quality paper available and he held it out for them to examine.

'That's not? Can't be? That's the seal of Thomas Wriothesley!' said Silas. If there was one thing Silas knew about it was coats of arms, seals and pageantry. His life long quest of becoming someone of note had driven his passion for such matters.

'Right on all counts.' said Thomas. 'Except it's a forgery and, the key to Richard Shakespeare's house.'

'Forgery? How?!' Said Eirik puzzled by this revelation.

'Crafted by the very hands of your good mouse. Well, claws I suppose. He was commissioned to draft this letter on his route to Lincoln, despatched on its completion to myself.' They laughed. Admittedly it was weird that a mouse could do anything let alone this. I must say, it was unquestionably one of my greatest achievements to date. The seal alone required very specific materials and I remarkably employed some of the finest techniques… sorry, back to the tale.

Thomas put this back into the holder and then wandered again in the direction of his horse. He opened the saddlebag that was around the other side and took out a large bundle. He carried this over to his companions and asked them to undo the string holding the bundle together. They looked, somewhat awestruck at the contents.

'It won't work' asserted Eirik 'I know nothing of the guards now stationed at Richard Shakespeare's house but this won't work,

they will need to be removed by force.'

'We know that there are three guards at least so, besides the element of surprise, it leaves us with only an even chance of succeeding if we get into a skirmish' advised Thomas 'and there's only you armed!' he added looking at Eirik.

'So there's a plan?' asked Silas desperately hoping that there was an alternative to risking his life. Thomas took care to settle them down and explained. This letter was sent directly from Thomas Wriothesley himself. In it, he demands the release from custody of Richard and his whole family as seemingly the missing document had been found. Richard was to accompany the agents in possession of the letter where he would be further questioned. Already both Eirik and Silas were showing little confidence in the plan. As they looked at the bundle, they saw expertly fashioned tunics of white with London arms front and back. The problem was that there was no standard uniform for all soldiers, many, especially mercenaries, wearing whatever they liked. The idea of uniforms was probably looked down upon by some veteran warriors as they were little use in a proper fight. The Tudor colours were green and white and very much in evidence amongst the populace of the King's progress but not everywhere. Yeomen were sporting the easily recognisable red. So, either someone had been remarkably well informed or it was simply presumed that London soldiers were present in Stratford.

'How well do you trust Elspeth?' asked Thomas Farrier.

'Completely!' They both resounded, almost indignantly.

'And the mouse?'

'The same.'

'I believe our network to be growing by the hour and that we will only be given information that is as reliable as we can expect it to be.'

They agreed that, in all cases, violence should be the last resort. They also knew that they couldn't risk being seen at all before they undertook this rescue so agreed they would execute this mission at dusk that very evening. They put on the tabards and Thomas and Eirik looked every bit the soldier. Silas just looked different. They rehearsed over and over how they would play this out until they were completely sick of the routine. Unfortunately, they had no idea how good this forged letter was as they could not break the seal. Eirik was to be the one to present the letter as he seemed to the only one to have no nerves whatsoever. Eirik thought differently, he had now seen action many times and knew that, however good their plan was, luck would also play a big part. Eirik always carried a dagger and, although it had been reasonably well secreted in his luggage, he also had a sword that he refused to relinquish. A few days earlier he had shown Silas what he had described as a baton. In simple terms, it was a well-turned length of wood for hitting people over the head with, a cudgel. As Eirik had two, Silas reluctantly agreed to carry one with him. Silas had also been offered a dagger but refused. Thomas happily took the dagger.

They rode toward the Shakespeare farm from the East as to give the impression that they had come from Wriothesley who was currently with the King near Lincoln. They stopped at the gates, Silas and Richard holding back some distance.

'Who goes there?!' shouted an impatient guard.

'A messenger from Wriothesley!' Eirik replied.

'Hardly bloody likely! He's halfway across the country!'

'I have a letter for the sergeant at arms!' This, in itself, was some considerable risk as mercenaries, in particular, could call themselves what the hell they wanted but Eirik was hoping it would appeal to someone's ego.

A large man carrying a halberd approached the gate. He was impatient and very suspicious.

'My good sir, this letter has been sent with the utmost urgency. I await your reply.' Clearly, this bumpkin couldn't read let alone make decisions so he took the scrolled paper and walked off with it. This was the worst part. They sat on their horses waiting for something to happen. They could hear little besides the birds and thought it best not to look at one another so sat, stoically, awaiting an outcome. They heard some unintelligible shouting which stopped as abruptly as it started and, then, it went quiet again. They waited. And waited more, and then it started to rain. Eventually, a second guard came out with the opened letter in his hand. He looked at the document and was, irresponsibility, letting the rain ruin the ink and he then looked at Eirik. He did this three times and then opened the gate and moved closer to Thomas and Silas. He looked at the document, he looked at them and, eventually, went behind the gate and spoke.

'Very well gentlemen. Give me and my infantry an hour to withdraw and you shall go into the house and retrieve Shakespeare and his family so that he may be interrogated further.'

Eirik could tell that he was dealing with someone with a modicum of authority and intelligence. Relieved, he took a quiet breath and spoke.

'Thank you, my good Sir, as is your pleasure, we will await further word from you.' The guard then looked at Silas. His skinny frame could no longer support this tabard shaped garment and it began to slowly slip from his left shoulder and, the more that he tried to shuffle it upwards again, it only helped to start the same process on his other shoulder. Eventually, this garment shimmied its way down to Silas's waist. The guard, again, moved a little closer to Eirik. He squinted so much his eyes were almost closed and then she said

'God's teeth. Dung! You're scrawny Dung from the prison gang. Thought you'd drowned in the Thames!' Eirik instantly recognised his former gaffer and was kicking himself for not realising sooner. He thought to lie but, despite his maturity, couldn't hide his Nordic features and blonde hair. He thought momentarily to sell an idea that he had been promoted to Wriothesley's service but simply knew it wouldn't wash.

Not for the first time, Eirik used this surprise to his advantage. Before another word could be spoken, Eirik's horse reared up and then took flight over the gate trampling his opponent. Hardly dazed, the guard alarmed his colleagues only to find Eirik's cudgel colliding with his thick head. He slumped into the mud. By now, rain was lashing down, stinging their faces and hampering their vision. Silas, completely alarmed, had frozen and the sudden thrust forward of Eirik's horse had startled him. This certainly wasn't what he had expected and found himself prevaricating. It's at moments like these when we all come to realise that we aren't just one person. Almost simultaneously hearing the case for flight, freeze of fight in our heads as our multiple alter egos put their cases forward. To the fore came the Silas that loved Wynn unconditionally, who respected the Agents of the Word and who wanted so desperately to redeem himself. At his behest, Annie followed Eirik's lead and sailed over the gate traversing across the rear of Eirik's horse heading toward a soldier on the east side of the farmhouse who was already drawing his longbow. He heard a distant shout from Thomas Farrier.

'No arquebus!' Which meant that the risk was smaller, someone armed with such a weapon could kill the three of them speedily and easily. Mud was flying everywhere from the horse's hooves and the ground was no longer firm. Hats may have been the order of the day for all involved but these were, one by one, disappearing, being trampled by hoof and foot into the fluid earth. A bowman on the west side had already managed to let loose an arrow in the direction of Eirik which sunk itself into Silas's saddle as he passed by his friend and ally. Silas now found himself just yards away from the other bowman still with a myriad of conflicting voices in his head. I must see this through. Must find the cudgel to my side. He's so young, don't want to hurt him. Hope this is all over soon. And then it was. Silas had drawn his cudgel, raised his right arm to the sky but as he went to deliver a blow, the young guard turned and fled across the field into the darkness. He heard Thomas shout more orders.

'The house! Get the family Silas!' Annie turned 360 degrees and Silas could then see in front of him Thomas Farrier wrestling in the soaking soil with one of the guards. As he looked to his right he could see that Eirik had fallen from his horse but seemingly recovering to tackle his opponent. Silas was hesitant but trusted the experience and command of Thomas. It was an instruction that the three of them had previously discussed, the family and the document in Richard's possession being of paramount importance. Once inside, he found the whole family huddled in a corner of the kitchen. There was a pause as they momentarily thought that this was one of the guards come to finish them off.

'Silas!' Richard and Abigail said, both incredulous that he was alive and in their kitchen although Silas was instantly recognisable as he had a very strange looking, bulky white cloth around his little waist.

'Follow me, don't break rank and don't react to what is going on outside.' Commanded Silas. This was the first time he had ever commanded anything. Did quite a good job of it too. Good lad our Silas. Very soon they were at the edge of the forest that surrounded the farm. There was very little light now and the rain was almost totally obscuring their vision so Silas insisted that they followed his instructions without deviation.

'Follow this path for a quarter of a mile. You will see a stake with a blue flag on it. Remove the flag. Don't light a fire. Sit and wait there until we come for you'. Richard embraced him, thanked him and then said,

'But Silas, what about the document. The diagram?'

'You don't have it?!' said Silas now starting to panic again.

'You know where it is Silas' replied Richard very calmly and then quietly took his family into the woods. At first, Silas was dumbfounded, something which had been a lifelong and regular occurrence for him. Know where it is? Why on earth would I know where it is? And then, like the sun peeping out from behind the clouds, it dawned on him.

Moments earlier, Eirik had been pulled from his steed by the bowman to the west who was almost twice his size. They now fought with daggers and anything else they could muster but there was little hope of him deploying his sword as it was still on the horse. No neat choreography here, these two were to punch, kick, bite, pull hair, spit and curse. Anything they could do to survive. Thomas, engaged in his own battle, looked over and saw blood on both Eirik and his opponent, their clothes ripped and muddy. Thomas, by now, had had enough of this unchallenging wrestle so drew his dagger and, by raising his right elbow above his head, brought his blade down, plunging it into the guard's neck. His whole body started to tremble as he rapidly succumbed and, although he was losing blood rapidly, Richard mercifully withdrew the dagger and forced it under his opponent's ribcage and into his heart at which point he immediately expired.

Silas had returned at the same time that Thomas was racing toward Eirik. Eirik was now being overpowered and was on the ground with the thug on top of him who was reaching for the hefty halberd that he had dropped when he had picked up his bow. By the time Silas and Annie got to him Thomas had heavily bludgeoned this fourth and final opponent and pushed him off young Eirik who was overtly suffering. They could hear Eirik whispering his gratitude and they were, of course, delighted that he had survived. However, it was only when they pulled the guard completely off Eirik that they could see the damage he had done to their friend. Eirik had suffered a serious wound to his chest which, even in this poor light, was visibly pumping out blood. Thomas rushed to stem the flow and check his other wounds all of which were nowhere near as serious. Eirik lay there filthy, bloodied and shirtless amidst the horror and panic. However, Silas couldn't fail to notice that there was no oak leaf birthmark on Eirik. Confused and anxious, Silas didn't know what to do. He felt a pathetic pull on his arm as Eirik willed him to come closer,

'I'm sorry brother.' These were Eirik's last words before he lost consciousness and, even before Silas could compute this, Thomas ordered him to get on with his task. The map, plan, document, whatever it is, I must retrieve it, thought Silas. He found the boat tied up and rowed to the little island in the centre of the lake, dramatically dug with his hands where, as he expected, he found young Robert's box with the document safe and dry inside.

Not knowing whether he was dead or alive he could see that Thomas had slumped Eirik over his horse, mounted his own horse and was heading off. Silas rushed to find Annie and followed on. As he passed the guard at the gate Silas noticed that he was recovering so happily put his cudgel to use which, besides helping his companions get away, gave Silas much satisfaction.

After they had picked up Richard and his family, they trudged through the rain and mud toward Wolverdington harbouring mixed feelings about their encounter. A disaster because their plan had failed and people were hurt, victory as they had freed the family and acquired the document, but, ultimately, a heartbreak as they were going to lose Eirik. Silas would have been willing to do anything to save his friend but had a heavy heart when he thought about how he had deceived not only the Agents but Wynn herself. Silas didn't question Eirik's motive. That was blatantly clear. Like him, his lifelong desire for a family had overwhelmed his sense of reason and decency. Silas presumed that Eirik had overheard the "wobbly Wynn" tale from Robert and decided that this, at last, would be his long lost family and end that emptiness he had carried for so long. Even so, could he not see how dangerous this was? Silas couldn't bear the thought of delivering the news of Eirik's death alongside such a tale of deception to Elspeth and Wynn. And then he remembered that it was Elspeth that had, supposedly recognised Eirik, or James? Not the other way around. What was going on? Mused Silas. He decided to forget the issue for the time being.

By the time they reached Wolverdington it was extremely dark and they were all incredibly filthy and hungry. Whispering their way through the dark, Thomas Farrier guided them to a prepared safehouse, his home. Thomas lived alone and always had done. This was a handsome abode not commensurate with his social status and, on arriving, Richard Shakespeare, Abigail and the children could not believe their luck. They showered praise and thanks on Thomas whilst he hurriedly put Eirik on a bed and authoritatively and sensitively issued orders. In no time at all water was boiled and cloths and blankets were brought in. Abigail offered to help. He refused, asking her to light a fire and prepare food and beds for the children. Silas watched in admiration presuming that Thomas must have had some military experience as he hadn't even broken into a sweat let alone raise his voice. There was just one thing that Silas found very curious. Thomas asked him to stay and witness that he had only tended to Eirik's medical needs and that he had not "touched him in any untoward manner." Silas hadn't a clue what this meant but agreed as it seemed to be important to Thomas. He took care to remove his shirt entirely and then carefully cleaned the blood, mud, grass and sweat from Eirik's torso. Not only did he not have the birthmark but ironically now had a deep cut where it should have been.

'Amazing!' said Thomas suddenly, showing some emotion for the first time 'his bleeding has stopped and I think this wound might only be in the muscle. But, he has lost so much blood. Look, he's almost blue.' Certainly, Eirik looked barely alive. Still unconscious there was some bleeding contrary to Thomas's hopes but there was certainly some evidence that it may clot.

'Will you have to sew it up?' asked Silas.

'Too bad my friend. Why, all he'd have to do was breathe and this will open up again. Can't do much now but, if he's still with us first light, I'll sort him out.' Silas feared that this was possibly too risky but had followed the lead of Thomas Farrier so far and decided it was best to trust his expertise. Everyone in the house cleaned themselves up as best they could and, except for Thomas Farrier himself, managed to get some sleep. He had assured everyone that the soldiers would not find them in Wolverdington because, as yet, there had been no suspicion attached to the town.

The back of the house led directly to Thomas's workshop and, as Silas woke, he could hear Thomas busy already. Silas went in to look at Eirik, frightened of what he might find. He peeped around the door only to find his body gone. His innards felt like quicksand and his heart raced. Thomas had removed the body in the night presumably to save them the pain of looking upon his battered, still body. Silas sat for a while and pondered over the last few months, how little the Agents had actually achieved and what it was costing them already. He silently wept then pulled himself together and wandered out to thank the noble Thomas for all he had done. To his astonishment he had laid out Eirik on a workbench and, before he could even muster the energy to ask Thomas what on earth he was doing, Thomas whipped around brandishing a length of red hot metal. Silas hopped backwards and let out his best effeminate scream.

'I need to burn his flesh, seal the wound for good.' Silas wanted to ask whether he was alive or not but then realised it was a stupid question. Delighted and hopeful, he asked Thomas how this worked and he was given a detailed reply whilst, for the last time, Thomas put the rod into the furnace. He withdrew it and then held it up for Silas to see only to immediately press it down on Eirik's chest. Eirik squealed. His flesh sizzled and smoked and there was no mistaking that disturbing smell of burning flesh. Medical knowledge was limited but if there was one thing that was a certainty in the sixteenth century it was that fire purified. Sometimes it purified so much it completely took people from this world but, in this situation, Thomas Farrier was confident that it would stop the bleeding and the pus. Silas was shocked. Not at the procedure, or the scream, but because Thomas had made a brand in the shape of an oak leaf. He turned to Silas and said

'This one's on me, you needn't ever speak of it. Sometimes life's just too short for the truth.' Silas did not know what to think. He was instantly aware and troubled by this further deception but simply couldn't cope with any of it. He wanted his friend to live and be well. Silas had forged a bond so strong with this young adventurer that he couldn't imagine going home without him.

'Nursing and prayer. Food and drink and nursing and prayer' insisted Thomas at which point he tidied his tools and walked over to where Eirik lay. Leaning over him, he gently picked up Eirik and put him over his left shoulder. Silas looked at Thomas's muscles. He was used to big men,

Bayard and Godwin were big men but much of it you could put down to too many pies. Thomas Farrier, around forty years of age, was all muscle, huge and Eirik seemed like a child on his shoulder. He carried him back inside and carefully laid him on a bed.

'Now Mistress Abigail' he said to Richard's wife 'you can be nurse. My work is done.'

Abigail was happy to hear this as she was most troubled at the idea of this big man tending to the boy although she had to concede that he had done a spectacular job.

Apart from Abigail and Eirik, they all found themselves in the main room where Silas amazed at Richard's ability to tell stories. He limped around as Richard the third to the delight of the children and, as Silas looked on, he thought that it would be a wonderful thing if the general populace could witness such a thing and then, on reflection, couldn't see any monetary value or fame in the performance of stories. Richard noticed that Silas and Thomas were watching and, slightly embarrassed, laughed and stopped despite the children's pleading and protestations.

'Gentlemen!' He said and guided them to a table. Once at the table, he craned his neck and said,

'carry on with your studies children' and, bless them, they did just that. Well, apart from Robert who was almost uncontrollably curious as to why his box was full of mud and on the table. Richard carefully opened the box and rolled out the document that had been described as a map, a plan, a diagram in fact, what you will. It was, actually, all those things and, to Richard, it was a complete puzzle.

'This was stolen by one of our agents from Wriothesley's luggage as he travelled but I'm afraid, my friends, I cannot make sense of it.'

'The Minster. York Minster' said Silas. 'This is the Minster as if you were to look down upon it. As if you were hanging from the vaulting.' Temporarily, Silas had taken the lead as the other two knew little of the Minster. The plan was as he said, a bird's eye view, the Minster looking as intended: a giant cross.

'But what's this?' asked Thomas. It says "angels" and "Mother." This was of some comfort and relief to Silas as, still, his reading wasn't as it should be.

'Yes' interceded Richard 'that will be Jesus's Mother, Mary.'

'A show?' added Silas 'part of the parade, pageantry and ceremony on the King's arrival?'

'Who knows? But there! The book! That must be the Lindisfarne Gospels on the altar' observed Thomas

'but it has an enhanced diagram next to it. What is all that?' None of them knew. It looked like a complex doodle that made very little sense. They deduced that the "doodle" seemed to indicate some machinery built about the altar stone but, beyond that, they could make no sense of it. They could make out rows of scaffolding. Then, the document did what all documents do when they have been rolled for a while, it slipped their fingers, snapped into a roll again and fell to the floor. Richard's son John politely picked it up and handed it to them and then went back to playing with his father's gloves, he was seemingly obsessed by gloves. The document was now in a slightly awkward and askew shape as it had not rolled itself up perfectly and it was there, very faintly, that they thought they could see more markings on the obverse side. The candlelight by which they had been studying the document had partly revealed some secret handwriting and further exposure to the heat revealed a location.

'Why, that's less than two miles from here' said Richard somewhat astonished 'It's a barren heath west of Wolverdington'.

'Copy house!' remarked Silas. That's what it says! A copy house!' For once Silas was now ahead of his colleagues as Richard and Thomas looked at him puzzled.

'Surely that's where they are making copies of the

Lindisfarne Gospels?' He added. They gasped at this revelation and slapped Silas on the back which, however much it massaged his ego, almost knocked him to the ground. Almost as if they were insane, they decided to go there, and then, to Norton Lindsey, with absolutely no plan or preparation and very little common sense. What they did have was an address and the patience to, again, wait for nightfall. They took with them weapons and Thomas's trade tools. Remarkably this unremarkable building was not guarded. It appeared small, insignificant and, unoccupied. Could they really be so lucky? Thomas, now quite confident after his recent encounter, insisted that he would approach this small, barn-like structure alone. It stood completely remote surrounded by water no wider than a common stream, it was odd in its setting and, once dark, completely invisible. Off the beaten track, it was unlikely that anyone would stumble upon it. Neither was it old. Built within the past few years it had a solid wooden door that was, seemingly, impenetrable and the only window it had was enclosed by a thick wooden shutter. Thomas waded through the mini-moat, hardly a deterrent, and felt around the frame of the shutters to test its integrity. With the aid of a blacksmith's hammer, he deduced that he could weaken the daub around the window so hammered, pushed and pulled out pieces of the daub and threw them to the ground. After only twenty minutes the farrier had punched a hole that went all the way through to the inside. His two allies, realising that he had managed to get so far undisturbed, decided to assist and, in no time, they had made a hole large enough for Silas to squeeze through or, at least that was the theory. He stripped down to his undershirt and hose, indeed a sight to behold but, skinny as he was, his boney hips were slightly wider than the rest of him so Thomas and Richard decided to pull him out and try him the other way around. In doing this, they unwittingly made the hole much bigger so practically threw Silas straight back in through it. It was so very dark. Richard and Thomas were comically whispering instructions to each other and to Silas although these were in vain as they knew nothing of this building's interior either. Realising that there was some moonlight, but on the other side of the building, Silas suggested that they started to punch a hole in the other wall so that they could properly utilise the little light there was. Exasperated and feeling as though they had completely lost all dignity, they acquiesced and started work on the opposite wall. God only knows how they avoided detection but they persisted undaunted. Suddenly, Silas heard a large lump of daub fall onto the straw floor and the moon did, immediately, illuminate the room. They decided that it would be wise if they were all inside so this hole became even bigger.

And there they were. A dozen writing desks on which copies of the magnificent Lindisfarne Gospels could be made, the standard of artwork and lettering so high that it was most probable that retired monks had been forced to do this specialist work for Wriothesley. Something that would have taken at least twelve months with many monks contributing to this mammoth task by working shifts around the clock. For the first time, Silas, Richard Shakespeare and Thomas Farrier felt as though they had made a real breakthrough as, there, almost as if they had been dumped, were eight completed copies of the Gospel which only left one more proverbial box to tick before they could return to York with the best news. At the end of this pathetic and darkroom was an old thirteenth-century wooden cupboard. It was, of course, locked but not so impenetrable that a blacksmith's hammer couldn't breach it. Richard did not hesitate and the cupboard was destroyed in minutes. There it was. The original in all its glory. Thomas started to collect them all up and asked Silas and Richard to get the horses. Getting these back to Richard's house would be a challenge as they were large, heavy books but they needed to take possession of them instantly. Thomas did a thorough check to see that there were no more copies and then, they left. Unbelievably, they had pulled this off without any conflict. How proud Wynnfrith would be, thought Silas and then remembered he was now naked.

'Now there's a treat for my good wife' teased Richard and Thomas guffawed at this sorry sight. Silas had no response as they had to get away but, suddenly, also realised that he had left his clothes behind so, ill-advisedly, leapt off his horse and ran back for them. Perhaps it was a measure of how confident the other two had become that they laughed heartily and incessantly as his boney arse wiggled back down the road.

'If the circumstances were different what an astounding jape it would be to leave him here!' Added Thomas and then laughed as they waited for Silas to return.

On their return, they deliberated on several matters. What were the copies for? Why wasn't it guarded? What on earth do we do with them? Sensibly, they wrapped the original book in fine blankets and temporarily secured it in a chest and then they burned all the copies except one which they kept as evidence. Abigail was up, diligently attending to Eirik but all the children were sound asleep. By one single candlelight they continued with their plans rather than put their heads down and agreed that, with haste, Silas, Thomas and Richard would go to York. Eirik, although still unconscious, was slowly healing so Abigail was to send Eirik to York as soon as he was completely well. Richard took to his bed with his wife and the other two slept where they sat.

Abigail made breakfast for all at first light and, almost before the last mouthful was consumed, there was a deliberate and sinister knock on the door.

'Please be calm my friends' said Thomas 'this is an ally and he will, single-handedly, return the Gospels, the copy and the document to Father Matthew in York at the greatest speed. We will follow on.' They thought this quite unusual as well as sudden but had every reason to trust Thomas Farrier. Silas noticed that everything had been packaged up and took pride in the fact that the very first Agent of the Word wax seal was employed. There it was, unmistakably atop the bundle. The door opened and there stood a tall and imposing figure dressed completely in black. Black hat, black scarf covering his face, black doublet, shirt, hood, boots and, yes, even a black codpiece. Silas looked at him analytically. Unwittingly Silas was always measuring himself against other men which was quite sad as he almost always judged himself to be less. On this occasion, he thought two things. Why can't I look like that? And, what an impressive sight this man was. Abigail clearly thought he was an impressive sight but tried hard not to show it. To be precise though, Silas had a third thought. Mud. Why am I always full of mud and there's none on him? It's like he got dressed at the front door. This character was still as a rock, foreboding but patiently awaiting his instructions. How had he got there so quickly and how did he know he was needed? Pondered Silas.

'Moonlight!' announced Thomas dramatically.

'Pardon?' said Silas presuming that this was some reference to the previous evening.

'Moonlight, that's what he's called. Or at least he doesn't respond to any other name.' Richard handed over the bundle. Moonlight turned, placed it in a large, specially weighted saddlebag, jumped onto his (unsurprisingly black) steed and disappeared.

'Never speaks either' said Thomas and they all laughed at this ridiculous encounter that lasted no more than a few minutes. Moonlight would, however, have the package in York within days.

Richard, Thomas and Silas took care to pack what they needed for their long journey to York and gave their goodbyes to the rest of the Shakespeare family. Silas went in to see Eirik, kissed him on the forehead and said,

'get well brother, I will see you soon.' Eirik's frail hand reached out and rested on his friend's arm. Although Eirik was still not conscious, Silas decided to tell his friend about their evening escapade in which they rescued the Gospels. It was only when he said,

'it looked like a little island in the middle of the heathland' that a little bell rung in his head confusing him even further.

17: Archbishop of York

York, August 1541

Wynnfrith stared out of the window of her room that was now within the permanent residence of the Mayor of York, Robert. Instead of marvelling at the opulent furnishings and spacious accommodation she looked out onto the wet streets of the City and its hurrying citizens. She was, in fact, in a daydream, her eyes fixed and slightly out of focus as eyes do when one is entranced by the natural and harmonious movements of moving water, rain or snow. She felt small. Proud to be an Agent, she wondered how a few local people could stop whatever imminent evil threatened. She missed Elspeth deeply, knowing that her sister would wholeheartedly play her part for the cause and, as a consequence, would put herself in danger. Dear Elspeth, she had been a mother, sister and friend to her. Elspeth had already been through so much and Wynn felt the desire to share the turbulent history of her sister with someone, perhaps Silas, but knew that it would have to wait for another day. Wonderful Elle. Please come home safely, she whispered and then thought of Silas. What a funny man. Why is interested in me? Perhaps he's not. Of course, he's not. He is fighting the good fight worlds away in a place called Stratford. He will have forgotten about me by now. She felt that inward shift from sadness to a measurable pain. She'd become very familiar with hurt. Hurt had been a close companion all her life although she had become much better at shelving this emotion because, particularly when she was young, unkindness and cruelty had been an everyday occurrence. Some days her armour was impenetrable, others it was still like paper. She chose to think of all her newfound friends and how they had accepted her. She decided that she would keep faith with Silas after all simply because he was kind and then said a quiet prayer for him. She pondered for a while about the complexities of her inner feelings especially those dark ones that so easily left her feeling useless and hopeless. She thought of how, many times, an insult or an unkind word would have had an instantaneous and negative effect on her and how this would take hours or days to go away. How fragile I am, she thought, and then wondered if anyone else ever felt the same.

Barley Hall, off Stonegate, was one of the finest houses in York and, returning there after years living with Elspeth, had Wynn looking at it differently, pondering why, just by accident of birth, some people's lives were so different from others. Soon, Robert would knock on her door, break her out of these rainy daydreams and they would discuss her assignment. Yes, an assignment. Wynnfrith was now a spy and the Agents were still in need of more information to determine what would take place in York Minster once the King was in their midst. It hadn't always been easy to access the Minster. It was, literally, still an inner sanctum within the City of York and, often, the entrance was heavily filtered. However, the Reformation was to put a dent in such traditions. The King was tired of ecclesiastical privilege and would not like to arrive at York Minster to find walls around it for the benefit solely of the cleric's comfort so, for the time being, there seemed to be some easing off. She looked at the raindrops on the expensive, but small and almost opaque, glass and found inside her a resolve that had come from the same place as Elspeth's courage. How she wished she still had a father to advise her. Her thoughts then turned to Robert. What an odd character he is too, she deduced and unwittingly smiled. She saw the reflection of her smile in the pane and closed her eyes and allowed the pealing of church and Minster bells fill her with calm and joy. Her mind wandered to the times when she was a child and Robert was like a father to her. She recognised how kind he had been lately and, that now knowing him as an adult revealed that he was conflicted. No wonder, as he would have to pay homage directly to the King when he arrived in York. Robert was playing a very dangerous game.

Then came a knock at the door.

'Please enter' said Wynn politely.

'Good day to you Wynn. I have just returned from the Minster where, already, both eclectic and bizarre undertakings are underway.'

Wynnfrith turned to face him.

'Bizarre. How so cousin?' said Wynn.

'More people of significance moving into the City by the hour, many congregating near the Minster including workmen, surveyors, architects, militia. It's so difficult to work out who is who but they are restricting access' said Robert quite excitedly. 'The good people of our City look on in awe presuming that this is what one would expect from a monarch's visit but I'm certain there is much greater devilment at play here.'

'Access to the Minster?' she replied.

'Yes. It's all very confusing dear Wynn.'

'And are all these the King's men?'

'Some. Others I can recognise by their colours and arms. One was unquestionably Edward Seymour's man, giving orders, our Archbishop, Edward Lee is complying as best he can and they have respected my office so far.'

It was the words 'so far' that concerned Wynnfrith. The Archbishop and Robert, as Mayor, were amongst the most important men in York and any signs that their authority was being undermined, at this early stage, would lessen their chances of thwarting Seymour's plan. Robert, it was hoped, would become one of the Agent's ace cards.

'Presumably, I won't be going today then cousin?'

'It wouldn't be wise dear Wynn, you would stand out, we may have to rethink.'

Wynn was scheduled to attend a Mass discretely, simply to look at any changes that may have been made within (or without) the Minster. Change was expected under any circumstance as this was an extremely rare royal visit. The citizens of York, no matter how much they disliked this imposition, would expect a spectacular show. Wynn's task was simply to identify any anomalies. There was a moment's silence as they looked at each, other, reluctant to make any decisions without Father Matthew being present and, as they paused, they could hear some movement outside Robert's residence followed by a knocking at the front entrance. From this moment onwards nothing would seem normal, they both realised that this feeling of constant awareness would not diminish until the issue of the Cataclysm was resolved one way or another. From the south wing windows of his grand residence, Robert could see a figure at his front door. Relieved, he hurried down to answer. It was William Fawkes, young Edward's father and, although as yet not an ally, Robert felt no hesitation in speaking with this man, after all, they were also related. If anything, the Mayor was simply intrigued as to why he had made the journey to his house. The door opened and there he stood looking every bit the notary. Everything about him spoke discretion, intelligence and professionalism but, as yet, neither Wynn nor her cousin could presume that he meant no harm. Wynn was in a dreamy mood this morning as she stood acknowledging the formal greeting between these two gentlemen and, seemingly, time froze and it was if she had been transported back four years where she was in that twilight between childhood and womanhood. A confusing time for any female undoubtedly but, for Wynn, that transition was much more difficult.

She remembered all those years ago when Elspeth had turned up at the Mayor's house in disguise having refused to accede to any of the King's demands regarding the "old faith." How easily she could have simply retired, found a new profession but her marriage to Christ and the Catholic Church was for all time, so in her heart, she would observe all her obligations but under the guise of an everyday washerwoman. She had approached Robert, specifically about Wynn. She wished now to care for her sister and teach her. At first, Robert was outraged. After all, he had given up much to bring up this girl who could have so easily become a complete outcast. Added to that Elspeth was bringing unnecessary shame to the family. Why not simply agree by word or on paper to the King's marriage to Anne Boleyn and his status as head of a new church and, then, hold something different in her heart? Robert had asserted. Unfortunately, Thomas More, once Henry's closest friend and adviser, would not adopt this attitude no matter how many times it was suggested to him, even when he was locked in the Tower, refused books and visits from his family. Instead, he had told the King that he would not comment at all, innocently believing that this would neither confirm his agreement or denial of the act of succession and all that went with it. Unfortunately, this silence was so significant that, when he was beheaded in 1535, he had unwittingly set the bar for all rebellious Catholics. Overnight he made dying for your beliefs seem straightforward. So, Elspeth, in her own way, was doing the same and it was much easier for her to hide than it would have been for More.

After some time Robert acquiesced on the understanding that he could still visit Wynn although neither realised that this would be such a culture shock for Wynnfrith. Life had not been easy but it had been comfortable at Robert's home. However, she soon adapted and she absolutely loved being with her sister. After a few weeks, it was like they had never been apart. One evening, literally on the cusp of curfew, Wynnfrith left the workshop at Bootham Bar to deliver some cleaned sheets that were already late. She tripped, something that was a regular occurrence for Wynn, but this time she dropped the sheets. It was possibly the only time that you would have heard Wynnfrith curse. She hurriedly gathered them up and, in the little available light, she looked them over. Thankfully, the ground was dry and the sheets were unmarked but it took her almost fifteen minutes to fold again and put back into the basket. As she straightened up she could hear footsteps. Her first thoughts were that she would be in trouble as she was now out after curfew so thought about retreating. Unfortunately, it was too late and, before she could process another thought, she was staring up at two uncouth, drunken men possibly in their late twenties. There was still an innocence about Wynn so, besides being very uncomfortable with their inebriated lack of composure, she thought that little would be said and that they would soon pass her by. Wynnfrith had been so used to people either berating her or simply ignoring her that she really couldn't conceive of many other variables. This was certainly a variable. She had come across bullies before but because of her unorthodox past, she had as yet, not had that other conversation about men, even with her sister.

Before she could even conceive of getting past them, they were making the crudest, ungentlemanly comments much of which she recognised as profanity and cursing and others she didn't understand at all. They stank of alcohol and excrement. In an instant one of them was groping her, pulling at the top of her dress and grabbing her breasts. It hurt both physically and psychologically. The other man had gone around the back of her and grabbed her waist but then started to pull at her skirts. She was crying but the conditioning of curfew protocol told her that she couldn't cry out loud but the force that was being inflicted on her induced an almost unavoidable and intense squeal. As expected, she heard hurried footsteps which meant that, possibly, there would now be more assailants as there was this accepted norm that decent people didn't abuse curfew laws. As she tried to elbow away the thug behind her she strained to look ahead. It had not occurred to her that besides officers, there were those that were unofficially immune from this imposed timekeeping and so, into the little light there was appeared Robert and a man she hadn't seen before. The stranger handled and berated the two thugs whilst Robert, dragged them away and gave them both a good hiding before ensuring that they were arrested. The rest was hazy. She only saw the assailants twice afterwards, once in stocks with their crime written above them, where they were continually beaten by the public, and later when, despite Wynnfrith's pleas for clemency, following a brief spell in the prison at York castle, they were put to death. She would never forget that night and the incident that, all in all, only lasted minutes but she had learned so much: she would never be beyond men's carnal desires despite the ridiculing she often suffered and she would never be properly loved as a woman. Robert and his companion were, at least, colleagues if not friends. And finally, that his companion, William Fawkes, had saved her and she would forever be indebted to him. To many, such an alliance, no matter how temporary, between someone steeped in the traditions of the Cathedral and the, notoriously atheist, Mayor would have been, to say the least, surprising.

She found herself snapped back into reality quite rudely staring at William Fawkes as they all stood in Robert's doorway. William Fawkes's introduction was very formal. That, sort of, came with the job. Robert would have none of it and said,

'Whatever your business brother, you're welcome here!' and almost dragged him into the vast hallway where, before he could find his balance, was bear-hugged by Wynn. William didn't reciprocate simply because it was such a shock to him, both seeing Wynn living there and receiving such a warm welcome. He did sigh, and then smile, which was his way of saying thank you. Robert liked drink. He liked beer and he loved mead so, before William's backside had hit the chair, the mead was out and into the glasses. William thought of doing the whole "on official business" thing but got one whiff of the honey-sweet mead and took a sip.

'From Lindisfarne monks!' boasted Robert 'sadly some of the last they made.'

'Dear Mayor and valued friend Robert' said William Fawkes still struggling with his informality 'you may be aware of the unexpected and extravagant developments at the Minster and, dare I say, beyond. I am here at the behest of the Archbishop so that you may have an audience with him at your convenience.'

Robert knew that he had to cut through any protracted legal talk to get to the point.

'I agree. The sooner the better, and I am presuming there will soon be no talk allowed between York officials. William, you must be aware of what is going on?'

'I only know what you do dear Lord Mayor. There is much more happening here than just a state visit. I believe it is about this that the Archbishop wishes to speak to you.' William Fawkes looked over his shoulder astutely but curiously wondering why Wynnfrith was party to the conversation and so added,

'I know that there is a rebel cell within York. With respect, amateur rebels. Robert this is very dangerous. Dangerous to all of us. You need to look after those close to you and yourself.'

Robert wanted to tell William Fawkes all he knew, there and then, about the Agents of the Word and what they had discovered, but it simply didn't seem right, he would wait until his meeting with Archbishop Edward to see where his allegiances lay. He had already guessed. Anything that was impinged upon by faith, and in 1541 that was practically anything, the Archbishop of Canterbury and the Archbishop of York were the two most powerful people in the land and would be part of decisions relating to it with Canterbury only having seniority over York. If it wasn't for a proverbial toss of the coin long ago by William the Conqueror, it may have been the other way around. The Archbishop of Canterbury, Thomas Cranmer, almost certainly one of the Cataclysm conspirators, would already have met with his counterpart in York. This did little to steady Robert's nerves and so he had another, quick, drink of mead. He then simply thanked William for his consideration and turned to arranging a time. They both agreed that the meeting was urgent and that he would, that very morning, make way to the Archbishop's residence. The Archbishop's palace was adjacent to the Minster. Once regarded as a guaranteed prize for a leading cleric, such opulence was now being brought into question. King Henry was only generous to a point and, if it was the right time to raid monasteries of all their riches, perhaps it was also time to reassess those members of the clergy who were living like Kings. After all, Henry was very keen to reclaim Hampton Court following the death of Cardinal Wolsey. Robert's expectation, now, was to see an agitated Archbishop in his residence. After two more very brisk glasses of mead, Wynnfrith bade them both farewell and the two gentlemen hurried out into the relentless rain which instantly orchestrated erratic and perpetual drumming sounds on their leather hats. Robert, in particular, was always grateful for the resilient qualities of leather but simultaneously irritated by the fashion for furs which only served to bog a man down in such weather. William Fawkes and Robert spoke hardly at all and ignored the finger-pointing and glances of the public who recognised the Mayor. As they neared the Minster they could see that passers-by were now being forced to clean up the street in the vicinity, only two days ago this had been simply a request but there was a visible and stark change. A dark authority overwhelmed this part of the City and was noticed by all. Robert had not expected to enter the Minster at all but found himself guided by William Fawkes, not through the awe-inspiring doors between the towers but led stealthily into a narrow side entrance which he had never even seen before, let alone used. Through another two more doors, they entered a chamber where the Archbishop sat dressed quite informally. They greeted one another as old friends and William Fawkes bade farewell. At first, the Archbishop rambled, clearly under some strain, but didn't really tell Robert anything he didn't already know. However, his rushed entrance into the Minster did confirm that it was now crawling with all sorts of people. The Archbishop restated that York Minster would be soon out of bounds and, then, his tone, suddenly shifted.

'You and I are very senior people in York, Robert. Can I have your complete trust, my friend?'

Robert had dreaded this moment. Strong as he was, he knew that, at some point, he would face mixed loyalties. His efforts to keep himself in the shadows had won him nothing, this would be the point where, he, of all people, would become a double agent.

'Of course, your Grace' answered Robert.

'Oh come, Robert, let's be as men today. Edward please.'

It was rare that they were both on first name terms but these were rare times. Robert's first thought was "Edward", why on earth is everyone called Edward or bloody Thomas? Realising that he was drifting, he cleared his mind. He needed yet to establish the confidence of the Archbishop. The Archbishop then leaned in and whispered.

'There are eavesdroppers, my friend, take care. I have just left a meeting with the first officer of Edward Seymour, the Duke of Somerset.'

Edward again thought Robert, which told him that he was stressed. Must clear my head, he thought again. The Archbishop continued,

'Wouldn't even give me his name but he has taken me into his confidence.'

This made Robert even more nervous, would he learn more of the Cataclysm?

'Robert, whether we like it or not, you and I will have to grovel to the King when he arrives. We will be made to apologise for the rebellions in the north and pay him off. If we are to keep, dare I say, quite privileged positions, it is important that we go the King's way. If you get my drift'.

Robert nodded.

'There is to be a most special and spectacular Mass in the Minster on the King's arrival during which, according to the promise of Somerset's man, everything will be cleared up once and for all, any confusion about "old faith" and "new faith" and also, what is to come next.'

He's not actually telling me anything, thought Robert and then froze as the phrase "come next" sank in. The cleric continued,

'All That I tell you now is in confidence between you and me, no one else Robert, mind you. Not a soul!' He was emphatic, both anxious and angry. What else could Robert do but give his promise? And then, the Archbishop gave him something that tied in with what the Agents already knew.

'There will be numerous, synchronised, celebrations across the nation on the same day. In fact, the King has cancelled all plans for destruction at Chester and it is to be assigned the title of Cathedral with a newly appointed Bishop, therefore ensuring clarification in the north-west.' Of course, there are to be new Cathedrals, more Bishops in 1541, remembered Robert but he knew not what to make of it.

'Your Grace. I presume this means more significant change to come in England?' replied Robert. This was not received well by the Archbishop.

'Not a Word Lord Mayor. Not a word.'

Robert had hoped for more but was getting nothing except more worry. It was clear that this conversation was at an end whether Robert liked it or not. On reflection, he couldn't remember at all the closing of the conversation or any farewells and found himself at the front of the Minster staring in through its giant doors. He could see all the way along the vast nave as far as the quire but, after that, only scaffolding, sheets, people and areas cordoned off. The people, which ranged from military men to surveyors and carpenters to designers were carefully studying diagrams and were engaged in heated discussions. He was in a trance, so much so that it took minutes for a voice repeating "my Lord Mayor!" to filter through.

He jumped.

When he turned his head he saw a guard wearing the colours of a London soldier. 'Can't go any further sir, orders of the Duke of Somerset.' Robert was so dazed and upset at what he saw that he just grunted an acknowledgement and walked slowly away, the rain pelting him in the face and dripping off his beard and down onto his boots. He passed some citizens, refusing to take part in the clean-up and were gossiping, they were saying that the shrine of St. William was being destroyed within the Minster. He drudged to his Manor House, his head full of questions and conflicts. Is Seymour, Duke of Somerset here? What's going on in the Minster? Are they builders or destroyers? They are already breaking up the shrines. Chester? An extra Cathedral for the west. The copies of the Gospels, they are to be used in Cathedrals up and down the land, they will be the catalyst for what is going to happen!

Father Matthew said that the culprits behind the Cataclysm, or the clarification depending on your stance, were Seymour, Wriothesley and Cranmer. Of course, Wriothesley is travelling with the King and Cranmer will oversee a "clarification" mass at Canterbury. They have coordinated this for a long time. As this whirlwind of thoughts and ideas echoed around his Lordly brain a new thought interjected. If I keep faith with the Archbishop, Seymour and the King, all could be well. I may even be bestowed an enhanced pension, he mulled. Might not be Cataclysmic after all. Might just be some sort of celebration of Henry as Supreme Head of the Church of England. Yes, yes, all will be well. Just need to reassure everyone. Agents? What do we need agents for? He laughed quietly. No need to make waves. He was now doing an astonishingly good job of establishing a complete, and convenient, psychological U-turn as people often do when their personal comforts come into play. He noticed that his pace had picked up which further assured him that all was well. That was until he arrived home and saw Wynn's little face at the window.

'Shite!' he said to himself feeling slightly ashamed. He put his head down and decided to walk around the property a few times much to Wynnfrith's astonishment as it was now raining even harder.

Eventually, he entered his residence and Wynn was

waiting to dry him off. She had decided, as a kindness, to send his servants home for the rest of the day. Although it wasn't cold, she had made a small fire and she insisted that Robert sat down in front of it. As she disappeared into the kitchen, large enough for twenty people, she shouted through to him.

'Dear cousin, what a mess you are! I will have a warm bowl to soak your feet in and will have a glass of warmed wine with you forthwith!' Robert put his head down and wept, muttering repeatedly,

'What am I to do?'

By the time she had returned he had regained his composure but Wynn could see that he was most troubled.

'I won't even ask' she said 'later today, as the Agents meet, you can tell all.' She means this, as she meant most things, kindly but it cut Robert even deeper. He would have to do some serious and solid searching before that meeting. He turned to see her limping back into the kitchen and thought back to when that little girl was first motherless. It was Robert's wife who insisted that Wynnfrith was taken in, Robert pompously arguing about how it would badly reflect on his status in society. He thought momentarily about the human condition, how worldly forces often fog the clearest decisions. How precious those early memories were and how sweet this little girl had been. A real joy she was, finding humour in her particular disposition and always finding the best in other people. Robert, again, felt ashamed, accepting that the many choices he had made would have been made by most if they were in the same position but these past few months had brought him friendships with the most stoic of people with immeasurable integrity and yet, in the scheme of things, they were practically no one. One of them is even a bloody mouse, he thought. For the next hour Robert's angels and demons battled it out and, as a consequence, he was exhausted. You see, like almost all of us, he presumed that no one else ever felt this way. Perhaps they don't. Fortunately, Wynnfrith had gone upstairs when Robert heard a most unusual knock. Well, unusual to anyone else but him. From his living quarters, there was a narrow, unlit passage that led to a small and neglected door almost hidden beneath the undergrowth of the garden behind the west wing. He checked to see if there was any likelihood of Wynnfrith coming down. He removed the bookcase that blocked the passageway, stooped, and travelled the short distance along its length knowing full well what was on the other side. He struggled with the door getting no assistance whatsoever from the exterior. He dragged and pulled at the door, pushed away undergrowth and weeds until it was ajar enough to see through. Moonlight. He was the only one entitled to use this door and, with him, was a bundle that Robert knew must have come from Stratford upon Avon. He took it from Moonlight who simply turned, jumped onto his mount and sped away. He put the bundle down so that he could secure the door again. As he bent down to pick it up and then stand up again, he noticed a dark silhouette behind him which visibly startled him. It was Wynnfrith. What a day. He had had the wits scared out of him, was found out by Wynnfrith, would be pestered for explanations and, then, would have to face the Agents.

They said nothing until they were both settled in the living quarters.

'Wynn, there are things that are kept from you for your own safety. Be assured this bundle will be from our agents in Stratford and, you must never speak of that man.'

'Moonlight?' said Wynn calmly and somewhat accusingly.

'How could you, know?' replied a startled Robert.

'How couldn't we? he's been bloody lurking and creeping about all our lives but we've no idea who he is, just that he is in your employ.'

'Then that's all you need to know, girl. No one must

know his identity and you mustn't speak of him again.' Robert didn't like to speak of Moonlight at all. His presence was sinister even to those who were familiar with him. He took the sodden cloths from the bundle and turned first to the accompanying letter.

'Silas?! Eirik?!' Wynnfrith asked excitedly.

Robert skipped all the details simply ensuring that both were alive, however, his heart was racing as this information put him deeper into the conspiracy. Bit by bit he was starting to see light. He told Wynn that everything he had learned from the bundle would be discussed at the meeting of the Agents later that day. Wynn again disappeared upstairs. He was so troubled now that he considered praying, something he hardly ever did. Moonlight would never pray, he thought. He seems to get by alright without it and then, almost as if he hadn't made the choice himself, Robert found himself begging God for clarity.

'Show me the way Lord, please show me the way.' Like so many who aren't particularly well practised in the art of prayer, he mistook the silence that followed as rejection so dusted himself off and adopted a manly stance that spoke a reprimand of "load of nonsense" to God. God wasn't bothered, he still loved Robert.

The rain persisted throughout the day. During the mid-afternoon, as arranged, Wynn checked to see that the pair of them were free to leave the house unwatched. After spending the last hour drying out, Robert was drenched again although it was a brisk, but muddy, walk to Holy Trinity church. Father Matthew was finalising a funeral that had taken that much longer because of the weather so they had to hold back before entering the church grounds. Typical, thought Robert, as he was nervous and wanted to get past this meeting.

Eventually, all the mourners had left and Father Matthew suggested that they met in the passageway that led to the garden. This time Brother Bede was already there so

Wynn sat beside him and held his hand, he was now shaven and looking much cleaner and healthier. Unexpectedly, Godwin had brought Edward along but then said he would wait outside as he didn't want to hear any of the discussion. They agreed and thanked him. Father Matthew welcomed everyone, assuring them that his good friend, the Mayor, would lead proceedings. Father Matthew looked over at Robert and thought how lucky they were to have him on board. Such a strong man, he thought, I will pray to the Lord for such strength and certainty for myself. He told everyone gathered that nothing yet had been heard from Elspeth or the Mouse in Lincoln but that there was progress from Stratford.

There was a small, wobbly table onto which Robert placed the contents of the Stratford bundle. They stared in awe at the wax seal, now broken, that represented their mission. The table see-sawed and squeaked. Edward suggested putting a wedge under one leg but, almost as if it were a little voice from beyond, Robert was reminded of Wynnfrith's nickname and how she had turned her awkward gait into something positive. Would I want her any other way? No, I bloody wouldn't, he thought.

'Leave it be!' he demanded, quite discourteously and Edward shrunk into himself as the little table continued to wobble and a pool of recycled rainwater fell from the drippy Agent onto the stone floor. There's your answer and there's your miracle said God, quietly.

'Although I am hopeful of more detail from our spies that are close to the Queen and the King, I already have much to impart' said Robert. He then got the bad news, about Eirik's injury, out of the way first ensuring that he emphasised his certain recovery and then took pains to mention how Silas had distinguished himself during their melee. Wynn pretended not to care. He then turned to the Gospels. To have the original now gave the Agents a considerable advantage and he asked Edward if the original

Lindisfarne Gospels along with the forgery could be secured by Godwin to which Edward proudly agreed. He also mentioned the decorated boss, my very own masterpiece, which also needed to be carefully guarded as it would soon be put to some use.

'Brace yourself, my friends, for what I have now to share with you. The Archbishop of York has, this very day, taken me into his confidence.' All gathered were suitably shocked by this announcement and the glare that Father Matthew gave Robert left him in no doubt about how he felt about the pompous, opulent and womanising Archbishop.

'I am now in no doubt that, as our good friend Bede here has intimated, Seymour, Duke of Somerset, Wriothesley and Cranmer are behind what is to come.' There. Said it. Done it. He thought. No going back now. Thank God, I think.

Besides finding God in a dodgy table leg, Robert had almost guaranteed himself unimaginable torture and death thanks to this declaration but, at least he had stopped worrying which was much better for his heart.

Brother Bede became agitated and tried to repeat those same names and also sounded like he was saying "Prince." When he ceased, Robert continued.

'I have no idea, as yet, of the King's hand in this. Seymour, although he hasn't been seen yet, has taken control in York including destroying some of the Minster shrines. There is to be Mass, on the King's arrival, that will spark the Cataclysm. There will be synchronised services throughout England and, presumably, the same revelations. I also know that some great, and wicked deed is afoot at the Minster but, as yet, I know not what. At great risk, Thomas Farrier, Silas and Eirik have not only saved the Shakespeare family but retrieved an important document that outlines some of the plans for this most unorthodox Mass.'

Father Matthew, Edward and Wynnfrith were

astonished momentarily and then the questions started, to which, it seemed, Robert had to keep repeating "I don't know".

Then Wynn asked about the Gospels and the copies.

'This, my dear, is the one place where we are ahead of the game. They simply cannot replicate their ridiculous show in every Cathedral in the land if we have possession of these and it's very unlikely, as yet, that either Seymour or Wriothesley are aware of their disappearance. The best we can hope for now is to thwart the Cataclysm in York on the day of its occurrence but we still need more information from Lincoln.'

'Why does the monk keep saying, Prince' asked Edward.

'Sorry lad, I just don't know. I do wholly trust what is left of his intellect though. Prince can either mean the King or Prince Edward, his son. Seeing as he's just four years old it's hard to imagine his involvement' chuckled Robert.

'Is there any chance we've got all this wrong' asked Wynn 'what if everything is being done in innocence? The King may intend to treat England's great Cities to an elaborate show as a celebration of the end of rebellion and conflict. After all, he's coming all this way to visit'.

In his mind, Robert simply thought "bless her."

'Besides all the other alarming intelligence we have, something terrified the wits out of our two dear monks. And, as they are both completely selfless by vocation and by nature, it leaves me in no doubt that there is a great threat that will affect all in our great land'.

Edward then asked about the Stratford document and so Robert laid it out for all to see. Their deductions were similar to their allies in Stratford concluding that angels and Mother Mary were innocuous but simultaneously, befuddled as to what it meant if it wasn't a celebration. They were all fascinated by the contraptions and Edward said that he had seen copies of very similar drawings based on those first created in Florence by a man called Leonardo but couldn't tell them what anything was or what it did. Robert then explained, to everyone's delight, that Silas, Thomas and Richard would be joining them soon in York but, before that, they would be re-routed to Chester before returning home. Wynnfrith asked about Eirik and he assured her that he would certainly return once recovered.

'Why are they going to Chester' asked Edward.

The King has planted a new Bishop there. More a pawn than a Bishop. Our agents will attempt to dissuade him from instigating this "clarification" in the west and, they may learn more. Then they will join us.'

Robert then, most emphatically, told everyone present that it was essential that he obtained intelligence, hopefully from Lincoln, that would shed light on what was exactly to take place in the Minster. Once they knew this, they could plan to stop it even if that prevention had to happen at the same very time it took place.

When Robert and Wynnfrith returned home she, again, went to the kitchen to pamper the drenched Mayor before even thinking of herself but, to her astonishment, Moonlight was there, still and silent. She looked at Robert

'How does he do that?!' she shrieked.

'I summon him and he comes' replied Robert calmly, slightly relieved that he had one less secret to keep.

'Creepy!' she said to Robert's face and then turned to face this dark spectre 'creepy! Bloody creepy! Can't you just use the front door like anyone else!' There was no reply.

As always, he stood, as stone, awaiting instructions. By the time Wynnfrith had been in and out of the kitchen again he was gone, headed for Thomas, Richard and Silas with orders to head for Chester.

This time they both dried out completely, took broth and bread, drank mead, said nothing and fell asleep as if they had simply returned from a long walk. Robert snored as the pair of them enjoyed, possibly, the longest sleep they had ever had. For now, all was well at Barley Hall.

The following morning, deep in the snickleways, Godwin awoke and he may as well have been in a completely different country. There was a haze on the skyline, yesterday's rain disappearing as the warm sun burnt it away.

'Please Pater, today. You promised!' asked Lizzy of her father.

'I have to work girl' said Godwin playfully and then went over to bundle her fragile frame in his arms.

'Alright. Today it is my girl. The sights of York! Young Edward can manage for an hour or so.' So, off they went. This was the first time Lizzy had seen proper daylight in weeks and, for the first few hundred yards, she shielded her eyes from the welcome but unfamiliar sun. The birds sang and traders were shouting greetings to each other and potential clients. It was, so still, crisp, dry and hot that every sight and sound was heightened. By the time that she could peek through her emaciated fingers, they had neared the markets. It was interesting how Godwin was so much less flatulent when he was with his daughter, who would have thought that wind was simply a matter of manners? He was sure that, street by street, her smile got broader. Lizzy marvelled at the goods on sale and they stopped at a particular stall that sold wooden trinkets, boxes and figures. To her amazement, there was a wooden puppet of a mouse, small enough for her to handle even in her frail condition. Godwin watched and waited for her to react but, as she did, he could see the life force ebbing from her. It was a small miracle that she was still with him. They had found four people who had contracted St. Anthony's fire and Lizzy was the only one that had lived. Godwin didn't know if it was the prayers or the gunge that Bayard had given her and to be honest, he didn't care. He loved his daughter and didn't want to lose her. And then it came like a fountain of requests.

'Look! Look! Pater! It's just like Micklegate Mouse. Can

I touch it? Please? Please?'

'Well, let's see now. Can't afford to be buying puppets and I think it's a little too heavy for you my girl...' he said.

'Oh put her out of her misery man!' said the stall owner.

Godwin, understanding wholly what he meant, picked it up and said,

'oh go on then. I think I'll buy it for you.' Her face changed completely. I suppose, at first, you would describe it as shock but it would be fair to say that never before in the history of exchanges has a party in receipt been so instantaneously content. As much as she could, she jumped about in his arms and hugged, cradled, kissed and conversed with this wooden mouse. As a father, Godwin had just acquired new, unimaginable status. This, of course, had all been pre-arranged. Godwin had made the mouse in his workshop the previous week but, for some reason, it seemed to have much more value as a surprise present as they had never been able to afford to give or receive gifts in their family. Godwin cradled Lizzy and Lizzy cradled the wooden mouse. His heart filled with joy. He was then drawn nearer to the Minster as it was, now, very much a spectacle. It was unbelievably busy but with both newcomers and the people of York either being harangued into tidying their City or just looking on in awe. As they walked nearer he was sure that Lizzy was visibly excited over this recent purchase but on close inspection, he realised that her breathing was laboured. He clasped her little face in his hard and sizeable hand and saw that the rash was returning and her temperature was raised. This had come on so suddenly that he didn't know what to do. His head was spinning, searching for help that simply wasn't there and, somehow, managed to work out that his nearest port of call was Holy Trinity church and hurried in that direction. Before they arrived, Lizzy was screaming and, again, complaining of insects under her skin. She was traumatised and, in turn, so was Godwin. He threw the church door open which immediately attracted Father Matthew's attention. As he rushed out, he became instantly aware of her disposition. He told Godwin to bring her out into the light, the garden. The grass was now long and still a little damp from the previous day so Father Matthew grabbed as many vestments as he had in his possession and threw them down. As they lay Lizzy in them, they sunk into the grass and furled around her as if they were protective and loving arms. She started to calm a little but also became very pale. Godwin had become completely useless, a shaking wreck. Father Matthew had already begun speaking in Latin and, as he got to the Lord's prayer, Godwin knew that he was giving last rites.

'Father! What are you doing?!..she will recover…look…she smiles…Father!' And then his resolve weakened as he could see her fading and, that being the case, this ritual needed to take place if she were to go to heaven. And then she spoke, little more than a whisper.

'Pater, what a wonderful day. Please, can we go to market every week when I am well?'

He turned away barely able to cope with the pain in his heart.

'Yes, my dove…ev…every week…'

And, briefly, her eyes opened and she said her very last words.

'The Queen…sa…I…I saw the Queen today…at the Min…'

What followed was an almost endless, pathetic heart-searing sigh and they both knew that she had gone. Father Matthew closed her eyes and folded the vestments so that they completely wrapped around her showing only her little face now looking quite still and serene. He then embraced Godwin who was, and would continue to be, completely broken. Godwin lifted up and embraced the still-warm body of his beloved daughter, taking care to place the wooden mouse in her hands, and then took the longest walk of his life back to his home.

18: King Henry V111

Lincoln, August 1541

I had been dumped onto the back of a carriage, inside a wooden cage, approximately halfway up the imposing but impressive hill on which the spectacular Cathedral of Lincoln sat. Yes, we had arrived in Lincoln and, even though, loosely speaking, I was a member of the royal contingent, this was probably about as near as I was going to get to the royal couple. I'd never seen so many people. The practical support alone for this royal progress numbered in hundreds. Daily, Henry's staff were hunting and requisitioning food and drink at every opportunity. Farriers to tend the horses, tanners, soldiers, hunters, cooks, woodsmen and servants of all kinds contributed to this rolling hulk. The real spectacle, of course, was the court. By the court, I mean the courtiers. Peacocks and peahens by the dozen, the latest fashions from Europe on display, finished in the most expensive materials available and bespeckled by jewels, some almost beyond valuation. And, of course, the further up this dazzling and greasy maypole you were, the more ostentatious you were required to appear. I didn't have an opinion about this. Strange, you think. Is the mouse unwell? No, I just wasn't bothered and to be fair, I could see the effect it had on the local populace. They had, literally, never seen such a spectacle. Of course, there were rich people in Lincoln already, not least the Bishop and the senior officials, but grandeur like this was incredibly unusual. So, what you would see (or more to the point what I saw) is a graduation of human cattle with those at the rear end being there simply to serve and ensure that this behemoth gets from one place to the next safely and, of course, keep the privileged happy. The nearer you were to the front, the more tarted up and important you were. Those at the arse end rarely had anything directly to do with the King but that would be much the same if they were still in London.

My carriage moved. This is what happened often. Suddenly, there was something or someone in my cart that was of use so we would move up a rank or two and, as we turned a corner, I could see, rather than hear, crowds cheering and I could just about make out the King and his wife, Catherine, meeting with the Bishop and God knows how many Renaissance wannabes at the west end of the Cathedral. There was a lot of grovelling and handing over of gifts including a crucifix and the royal couple knelt on a cloth of gold cushions. I should mention that all the giving was one way. Bells were pealing. They could be heard for miles and this atmosphere informed all that something truly unique was taking place. Eventually, with formalities over, they entered the Cathedral. Show over for us. Well, at least for the time being. What did I notice more than anything? No surveyors or builders. No signs whatsoever that Lincoln Cathedral was ready for some great event or upset beyond the King's visit. Everything, so far, was uncannily as expected. The crowds got closer, we were behind four horses plus the ones pulling our carriage. They stank. Home from home, I thought, as the reality of the everyday unhygienic decided to revisit me. It had taken me this long to realise that, in my renewed state, my sense of smell was much enhanced. Be assured it would not stop me complaining. I hoped that, very soon, I would be reunited with Elspeth in a clean, secure place. We needed intelligence and we needed it fast to assist our colleagues in York. I stopped for a moment to dwell on how difficult Elspeth's position was, completely in the thick of the Queen's court on the pretence of being a lady's maid. I thought about how multi-faceted she was, in particular how she gave little Lizzy complete confidence in her most harrowing hours and how, in an age where men were meant to be in charge, she always demonstrated an ability to lead others, even Robert the Mayor. Lizzy. Dear Lizzy. I wondered how she was and, moreover, why her health had fared so well after that initial gathering at her house. I realised then how I had forged numerous new and valued relationships, not least Lizzy whom, I had decided, I would see first on my return to York. That very thought instantly put me in better spirits so I decided to think less and relax more. At least that was my plan. My box was suddenly snatched out of the back of the carriage and I felt myself swaying and nauseous as we headed back downhill and before I could even think about my bearings, I realised that we were entering a quite grand stone house but by the rear entrance. I was irreverently deposited on a table and could now see the soldier that carried me, standing guard by the rear exit. We were in the Jew's house, a name left over from the Jewish quarter of Lincoln now, none existent, that was due to the ruling in the thirteenth century that exiled Jews. I think again about how England has often struggled with inclusion. Christians banning Jews? A strange conundrum, surely Jesus Christ was a Jew? People. A door opened and

Elspeth along with Culpeper appeared. I was struck by how brave our spies had become, not least the guard who was obviously one of Henry's contingent. And, I was so pleased to see them. Immediately we were in discussion.

'What have you maiden?' said Culpeper to Elspeth.

'Practically nought my Lord. I have not been able to get any closer to the Queen and the gossip amongst the maids is almost singularly about…erm…well you know, my Lord.'

Thomas Culpeper wasn't the least embarrassed about this. I'd even hazard a guess that he loved the idea of the maids talking about his dalliances. I added that I felt I would have been more use in York than here as I was stuck all day and night in a box amongst all sorts of animals. They ignored me. Culpeper made no secret of his relationship with the Queen and he too declared that she had said little about state affairs even in their most intimate moments. However, Culpeper had a plan and, in disseminating it, I realised how much we needed him. It was decided that, at some risk and with Lady Rochford's help, Elspeth would introduce the dancing mouse to the Queen so that I would then be a party to any discussion regarding the Cataclysm. We hoped that, in time, we could even get close to the King and Wriothesley but time was, increasingly, a luxury.

For once there were no deliberations or quibbling, we all agreed that this was the necessary way forward. Culpeper spoke to the guard who simply disappeared. Elspeth left without saying a word and Culpeper picked up my box.

'You and I will have some fun my coarse little rodent!' said Culpeper with some glee and then thought he would try that bloody irritating and unoriginal trick of spinning the box around. Been here before, I thought, so I reminded him of the consequences of such actions and added some negotiation that was in his language, so to speak.

'Might be worth remembering just how sharp these teeth and claws are mate. Wouldn't want you to find me sleeping in your designer codpiece on one of the many nightly excursions you take your tiny member on'

He laughed. And laughed again. I could see we would get on fine and, even at this stage when I barely knew him, I was genuinely worried for his welfare. The King, undoubtedly, would find out about his affair with Catherine and ultimately he would die for it. At times, it was almost as if he didn't care. Unless it was an act. I asked him directly about the Cataclysm and the Agents.

'I don't want to speak out of place until we know the facts for certain my friend but, not only do I regret receiving so many monastic properties, I will not be a party to the complete destruction of the faith as we know it.'

Mmm. He knows more than he's letting on I thought. I boldly asked him about his fondness for Queen Catherine.

'Discovered! Dear mouse. I do confess, that, if the King were to die, God forbid. I would wish to be her husband and foster the most benevolent relationship with the new King, Edward.'

Living in a dream world, thought I, and then pushed a little further.

'Do you like the King, Thomas?'

'Like him?! But of course mouse! I love the man. I've been at a court as long as I can remember and he has been as a father to me. He is a man of many achievements and has been constantly let down by his advisors, wives and, supposed, friends. He has so wrestled with his relationship with God. My, I would die for my King!'

This was sincere, no doubt. Perhaps he doesn't realise that he's letting the King down too. For the first time, I thought of Henry as a truly lonely man.

Do you think he is behind this plan, the Cataclysm?'

'Absolutely not and, if he is any way involved it will be by the misguided hands of the like of Wriothesley and Seymour!'

'And Cranmer?'

'Aye, Cranmer too but he's a good man at heart our

Archbishop of Canterbury. A complete believer in the new faith but a good man. If he's involved it will be with some reluctance.'

I was astounded at how candid he was. I felt that I had learned more in fifteen minutes than I had over the past month. We must be getting nearer to some concrete evidence, I thought, and then simply enjoyed the walk to the Bishop of Lincoln's lodgings which were adjacent to the Cathedral.

Once inside we could see along a corridor decorated with portraits, the entrance to the King's privy quarters, although, this was but a glimpse, as we went up some stairs and further west to where the Queen and her staff would be staying. It was all very grand. Bedding, rooms and food were being warmed and the Royal couple's closest staff were laying out gowns and jewellery. There was a small, anteroom, off this corridor where, again, I found myself most ungraciously planted on a table. Looking upward I could see Elspeth and Lady Rochford.

'Eeeuww! Is that it?' said Lady Rochford rather insultingly.

'Yes, My Lady' replied Elspeth 'but he does do tricks and he's quite clean.'

The glare that I sent in Elspeth's direction was enough for her to have to stifle a splutter but, impressively, she carried on,

'I believe Her Majesty would delight in his unusual and brusque manner.' Brusque? Brusque? She's pushing it now, thought I. I'll have one or two sharp words to say to her if this continues. Then I realised how brusque I sounded which did, at least, prompt me to temporarily mind my manners and reactions somewhat.

'Very well' said Lady Rochford. 'Thomas, you must make yourself scarce. You have your allocated time for this evening?'

'Yes,' he promptly replied. This, of course, referring to

his assignation with Catherine manufactured by Lady Rochford herself. I realised how deep this conspiracy was when she called him by his Christian name. Then he disappeared. Without any ceremony, everything went dark. Someone, when I say someone, I mean Lady Rochford had thrown a cloth over my box.

'Hello! Stupid! Stup…i…i…d! The box has vents for a reason. Can't breathe! Hello. You really that dumb?' And then, in reply, her voice boomed as if a Sergeant at arms,

'It bloody talks?!! Why on earth didn't someone say! Have you any idea how dangerous this is girl?!'

Oops again. She was furious. Really furious and Elspeth was getting the brunt of it. A little voice squeaked out from under the cloth.

'I can be really quiet if you like?' I had seriously dropped Elspeth in it and couldn't imagine what she was going through. That was until Rochford had apparently turned her back for a second and Elspeth thumped the box. Very hard I should add and realistically, I had no grounds for complaint.

'Very well but this must be kept secret!' her face, presumably, still blazing crimson.

'It will My Lady but, as I say, he's quite difficult to handle.'

'Well, handle him you must girl! And that's an end to it. No speaking!'

'Of course, My Lady' said Elspeth and then it went quiet. Very quiet. I heard a door slam presuming they'd both left until, again, I heard Elspeth's voice.

'You stinky little turd. Pull a trick like that again and you'll end up as part of the evening roast.' I felt terrible, particularly as I heard her voice break. I had genuinely upset her. I felt as though, at times, I simply could not control myself.

Lady Rochford was soon back with instructions for the Queen's return. Eerily, once all the tasks were completed, all the household staff simply stood at their stations until the royal couple, and those closest to them came into the palace. Particularly in the dark, this silence seemed endless with only the creaking boards and crackles from the fires to indicate that I wasn't alone. When I strained, I could hear the business of the kitchen far away downstairs. It was common knowledge how much food this man and his minions got through in a day, I sat and marvelled at the work that must have gone into meeting the King's insatiable needs. Waiting, endless waiting, and then bells followed by fanfare, and then you could hear the movement of the court from the Cathedral to the palace. This was the first time that I would hear the King. I could hear him giving instructions as he was being aided, lifted as he could no longer walk well by himself. He was complaining particularly about his leg, demanding comfort and unimaginably impatient with those so enthusiastically trying to help. I'd always imagined this deep, domineering tone belonging to King Henry V111 and, so, was disappointed at the high pitch moaning that I heard which could well have belonged to a child. I only picked out a few words and these may well have been out of context but I reminded myself of why I was here. Good history is never written from a biased or bigoted standpoint. It would still be some time before I understood his involvement in the Cataclysm plans, if he had any involvement at all and, until then, I decided that I should reserve judgement.

For the first time, I was scared. At least half the population of this palace was a dead animal. Elspeth wasn't too fond of me, Rochford hated me and Culpeper thought I was his best mate. On top of that, the box needed a clean and I definitely needed feeding.

Out of nowhere, there was this sudden activity. This was most unlike the atmosphere that accompanied the King's arrival, people were laughing and skipping down the corridor. This was the young Queen and her maids. There was joy in their interaction and you could feel the relief they all felt as they had, at last, managed to escape from the Cathedral and the Mass.

I was relying entirely on my hearing but, even so, a dynamic and complete picture was evolving in my mind of how this looked. I could pick out the Queen because of the way others addressed her but, beyond that, the relationships were relatively informal. They giggled as 18 year-olds do and there was a party-like atmosphere. More astonishingly was that I could also hear young men and some of the banter was quite bawdy, Catherine, much like Henry when he was younger, wanted to be surrounded by those that stimulated her, in every sense of the word. As I heard this happy cacophony I was worlds away from ideas of a Cataclysm mostly because I presumed, they were too.

Catherine was part of a power base. Like her cousin, Anne Boleyn, she was the niece of Thomas Howard the third Duke of Norfolk. An incredibly powerful man, he must have been elated when Henry decided to marry Catherine particularly after the disastrous outcome of his marriage to Anne. Not that this was entirely by accident. The most prominent families in the land would go to great lengths to have their youngest females catch the eye of the King. Often, it was enough to have a family member as a King's mistress but both the Howards and the Seymours had hit the jackpot. It was keeping these young fillies under control and in favour that seemed to elude them. So, currently, both were in good books. Thomas Seymour because Jane Seymour was most loved by Henry, much missed since her death and gave him the son he had so long craved for. Thomas Howard was back in the picture as his niece, Catherine was now the young and devoted wife of the King. Well, so he thinks. It is therefore not difficult to understand why Thomas Seymour was going to such great lengths to secure power beyond the King's death and why it was extremely unlikely that Howard knew anything at all about the Cataclysm.

As I listened to Catherine and her contingent, I was aware of how all this was a different world. These were young people at the top of the tree enjoying life, I wondered if Catherine had any interest in politics at all.

'Send the gentleman away I must get out of this attire. I am like a hog on a spit!' Everyone laughed including Catherine. There were flirty farewells and I could hear kisses and the young male courtiers leaving.

'Why do clergy feel they have to talk without end? The old bore! After such a journey too. Why, the King was in agony whilst that buffoon went on forever!' More laughter. Catherine liked to amuse her ladies in waiting and her friends. It was then that I was aware of Lady Rochford reappearing,

'Your Majesty. I do hope this isn't a difficult time but I have well...I suppose... a surprise for you.'

'Difficult? Why no Jane. Don't stand on ceremony is it?' Then she whispered 'from Culpeper?'

'Of course, Your Grace' replied Rochford still formally. The Queen then decided that the surprise would be for her only so, temporarily, dismissed everyone else now present in her privy quarters. Catherine became extremely giddy and I could feel the tension as Lady Rochford expected the young Queen to be as repulsed as she was. I could then hear them move closer to the box, still covered. And then, whoosh! The cloth was off and I saw this little round face framed with auburn hair that expressed happiness in every nuance. She giggled and pointed and turned to look and touch Jane Rochford. I was transfixed by her youthfulness. In my present form I didn't see women as I normally would but could still see why any young courtier would be attracted to this girl. She was just so vibrant, giddy and openly lusty. As this took place, she was halfway through undressing and besides being astonished at the number of layers she was subjected to, I marvelled at the dress. God knows the number of creatures that had been culled for this appearance alone but between what was left on her and what was draped over the bed, there was evidence of sable, ermine and rabbit, possibly only sparing the poor squirrel as it was no longer quite as fashionable. Silk, satin, damask, gold thread, jewels, you name it. She wore a hood of the French type that perfectly framed her face but still revealed her copper hair. I imagine someone would dare to say Catherine was plain but, particularly decorated in this way, she was beautiful. I liked her instantly. Perhaps it was simply her youth, combined with an innocence that you wouldn't expect at such a senior level at court, and, as I thought this, I realised that I was, again, being judgemental about Henry concluding that few would condone the immorality of a grotesque man in his fifties still lusting after teenagers.

'What does he do?' she asked as a child would.

'He dances Your Grace and, I'm sure I could teach him a few other tricks' Rochford said, giving me the meanest look. Catherine giggled and did a little dance herself.

'Go on then Sir Mouse' Catherine said kindly. I paused, trying to keep count of the numerous and frequent names I had now acquired. I cleared my mind and found myself getting angry again. I had been working hard on my self-control but, in all honesty, I was still lacking in this department. I knew I had to, fully, play this role if we were to acquire intelligence but I found it so humiliating. I was underfed, dirty and the box was even worse. To push the issue, Lady Rochford put her face right up against the box and said,

'I think a galliard may be in order?!'

I stood on hind legs, did a courtesy and then froze. Now, to be clear, if you're not familiar with the galliard, it's probably as silly a bloody dance as is possible. Particularly for the male. It involves hopping and, unbelievably, leaping. All well and good in a Renaissance context where it is deemed highly fashionable but in a cage? My first thoughts, again, were simply, this is not happening. No way. But then, I saw the most ferocious grimace on the face of a woman I'd ever seen. Well, perhaps with the exception of Elspeth. So, for the cause, I went to it almost forgetting that simply staying on two legs was difficult, let alone pulling off these ridiculous moves in six-four time. Needless to say, I fell over. Often. Catherine loved it. Even Rochford broke into a smile. I collapsed genuinely exhausted only to see the Queen in fits of laughter and issuing happy tears.

'Oh Jane' she said to Rochford 'I have the most jolly idea'. My heart sank. This was not going to be good. She then reeled off so many names of people she wished to summon. After all, the royals had brought half of London with them, anything could be done. Then I was removed without a word and for hours, although I was fed, sat around in my own filth, my box covered with a cloth, awaiting the next jolly jape.

I awoke in a room I did not recognise and a kind lady picked me up and started to wash me and, as she did, I could see my box being removed. Within minutes it was replaced with an astonishing upgrade. This was an all-metal cage but with a backdrop. In front of the backdrop appeared what I could only describe as a stage and, upon the stage, a miniature throne. It was opulently decorated and, as I stared at it, couldn't work out what its purpose was but, be assured, I was very worried. In came two young ladies, apparently seamstresses, seemingly under some pressure to complete their task. I looked down and realised, probably for the first time, just how much weight I had put on. I resembled a little barrel with the, very much valued, privy parts now disappearing completely. They had fed me well whilst we had been in Lincoln. I instantly worked out the correlation between the mini costume presented to me and my expanding waistline. On it went and I was not happy. This really was crossing the line. To save time describing every detail of this outfit I would only ask that you imagine that very famous picture of Henry V111

by Holbein. Well, that's what I now had on, except everything was in white. Even a little white codpiece with a pee hole in it. To complement: at the rear, Sir mouse is modelling a similar poop hole which also accommodates the tail. Of course, they laughed, I was to be a figure of fun for everyone for these next few days. I wasn't sure yet whether this was meant to be for the King's amusement as well but it instantly occurred to me that such a trick would be a great risk and left me feeling even more anxious. So, there I sat on my throne waiting for an audience. Ridiculous.

Come the late afternoon I could hear the Queen and a collection of itinerants return to her privy chambers. Still giddy, it was apparent to all that Catherine loved to laugh and to socialise. I could hear musical instruments, they weren't playing, it was just clear that they were being carried, the string instrument in particular twanging as its owner was endeavouring to negotiate his way through this crowd of pompous inbreds without damaging his prized possession. I was extremely anxious as I was in no doubt that I was now to be put on show.

I was gently carried into the Queen's chamber where there was, already, a party atmosphere. They had returned from a sumptuous meal and I could smell the alcohol through the cloth. Catherine then made a little speech about her surprise and the room went quiet and then the cloth was off again. What I saw was a revelation, astounding. These were, mostly, young people, very good looking and each dressed to impress. This was an entirely different world from the streets and houses of York where I had, so recently, wandered. Before I could absorb the cheers and laughter I was aware of a pretty face right up against the cage and, no, it wasn't a woman, it was Culpeper.

'Is that it Kate?' he said innocently knowing full well

that Catherine knew that it was he who had brought me here.

'What do you mean Tom?'

'Well, looks a bit docile to me. Damaged. Ugly little thing don't you think?' She knew she was being teased so just giggled but I had the measure of him. He was testing me, see how far he could push it.

'Still a bit stinky. Perhaps now is not the right time?' he added, pushing further.

I'd learned a thing or two and, surprisingly, on this occasion, I wasn't going to rise to the bait. He persisted for a short while and then delivered a wry smile in my direction, winked and let it go. Good try mate, thought I. The audience was anxious to see my party piece and, before I knew it, I had a professional rendition of the galliard played by these astonishing musicians. Dare I say that they actually made me feel like dancing. They certainly got their money's worth as I threw myself into it and, admittedly, received some satisfaction from the response. I collapsed, genuinely exhausted, on my throne which prompted the most unexpected action from my audience. They bowed and feigned deference adding whispered tones of "Your Majesty" and "Your Grace" and then, of course, collapsed into even more merriment. What the King would have thought of this, heaven knows and I certainly didn't want to find out. My high-end cage also had a curtain so I was then shut away for the time being. Before long the noise died down and people moved away. As far as I was able to assume, there had been no harm done. The King would have been quite happy for Catherine to have friends, including young men, as long as all seemed above board, it was what happened afterwards that would cause further embarrassment for Henry and, unless the Queen had a habit of divulging state secrets regarding the Cataclysm also known as the clarification, I didn't want to stay around. Events, however, now took a different turn to those I expected. I had presumed that this would be the point where Catherine and Culpeper would conveniently find themselves alone but I heard him leave. The conversation between Lady Rochford and the Queen now became quite formal. I couldn't hear all of it but it was clear that the Queen was to go to the King's privy quarters. At this point I was relieved, looking forward to some well-deserved respite. That was until I heard Catherine say,

'Wait until His Grace sees this!' Accompanied by that, now famous, giggle. I was, of course, terrified knowing full well that I would be giving a repeat performance very soon and pondering on how much I would miss my head as my arse had become very attached to it. The cloth went back on. Surprise time. Again. Downstairs, along endless corridors, until you could suddenly feel a change in climate and culture. Older men mumbling in corridors, all sorts of people attending the King. The grooms of the chamber coming and going and I then heard the groom of the stool being referred to personally as he left. Yes, Henry really did have someone simply to wipe his arse and, more astonishingly, this was a highly respected post. If the King were to trust anyone it would have to be the groom of the stool who, daily, got to the bottom of all things physical and political as he would also have been party to the most confidential information. Things were, almost always, looking up for the groom of the stool.

People were going into the King's chambers and others coming out, I could feel the bustle of this business-like atmosphere and as we neared, for the very first time I heard him shouting.

'Buffoon! You arsehole of a man! Would I wish to be wearing such attire at this time?! Off with you, you dog's dick!' And this was accompanied by a thrashing around the head. I could hear this man's face being slapped. I was terrified, that was until he seemingly clocked the Queen. His voice and demeanour changed instantly.

'Ah there. My dove. She flies along the corridor to be with her King. Come along my petal. Come along. (And then a change in tone again) Leave me be!! Can't you see my wife is attending my privy chamber?! Out! Out!'

What a change in weather I thought, he's all over the place. Within a minute or less, he was alone with Catherine and I was put down again. He asked about this strange object that she had delivered and she, yet again, described me as a surprise and this was left as it was whilst they conversed.

'Let me join you on your bed, Your Grace.' And then some rustling of fabrics as she climbed up next to him.

'How is my beloved King this evening' she asked almost as if she were talking to an infant.

'Ah, my dear. Affairs of state, my leg and my sore head. They get the better of your husband. And (shouting again) these damn advisor, Lords! I'll have all their heads one day! Each one up their own arse, no thought of what I have to contend with.' His voice gradually softened. I imagined that she was comforting him as I could almost feel the beast being calmed.

'Put these things away for tonight my love, let me soothe you.' I could hear him relaxing. He muttered a few more comments about the church, the progress and York but she dissuaded him from any more politics for that night and then, as it was such a warm night, a breeze from an open window periodically blew my little stage curtain slightly and I could glimpse the couple together, although they couldn't see me. She was caressing him, massaging his ulcerated leg and, although he could ask anyone in England to do the same, he was content and transfixed by this young girl.

'Oh, my love what would I do without you?'

'I will be forever thine Your Grace. My love is yours.' As anyone would, I was now intrigued by this relationship and my initial judgements were that, although she was undoubtedly going to meet later with Culpeper, she clearly did have some affection for the King. There are, after all, so many shades of love and I could easily believe that Catherine's love for Henry and Culpeper were in completely separate compartments in her head but, unfortunately for her, that's not how it works in the real world. She was doing a very good job of calming him and then to my horror she said,

'Do you think the sergeant at arms might stand to attention tonight my love?'

God no! I thought. I haven't signed up for this! I did that thing where you stick your claws in your ears and mumble to yourself but I could then hear his voice booming again.

'God's blood! What's that whining?!'

'Patience my love…your surprise?'

And then he chuckled.

'Sergeant. Haha! my dove. He was to bed an hour ago. Defeated in battle methinks!' They shared laughter at his response and I was heartily relieved. I could now see him more clearly as the breeze had picked up. They were on a large four-poster bed with sumptuous curtains, the walls bedecked with tapestries informing of deeds of ancient Greeks. This, of course, would have belonged to the Bishop and, like all hosts, he had to walk that fine line between ensuring his palace wasn't too opulent that it would upset the King but also not too sparse as to be deemed not good enough. Henry appeared much older than his fifty years, his ginger beard now heavily greying. He was huge, almost a disfigured version of his younger, athletic self. Bulging eyes, scabby pale skin and an expression that spoke of constant pain and stress. If he wasn't the King you would probably take pity on him. Moreover, I had expected some ostentatious furred nightwear but he was wearing no more than a long nightshirt which was soaked in parts from sweat. I looked at Catherine. Whatever else you may say, she was fulfilling her wifely duties as there was no evidence of her being repulsed by this man. Maybe she was simply a good actor. She urged him to stand and come over to the cage. He was in considerable pain and I wondered if he would have been able to alight from the bed if she wasn't there.

'I do hope this raises your spirits your Grace' and the curtains were pulled apart by the Queen. Those enormous bulging eyes and wide face now filled my view. His pale expression changed to that of red currant and his cheeks were filled with air. I was mortified. For a second or two I simply couldn't tell what he was doing, that was until I heard this seeping of air from his cheeks, a little like a punctured pig's bladder and this was followed by a, sort of, laugh except it was an almost continuous 'heeeeeeeeeee' and eventually this developed into full bluster by which time I thought it would be wise to start dancing. As I did, he bounced very slightly up and down, as it was probably all he could manage, which came across as infantile.

'Little King Harry!!' He'd found his shouting voice and I had acquired yet another name.

'Little King Harry!! Ha haha! I will keep him, my love!' No, you bloody won't, I thought, even though I was mightily relieved that he had decided not to squash or eat me yet.

'Have him made more costumes like mine. He shall rule alongside me He He!' and he planted a kiss on her cheek. It was at this point that I realised just how far off course I had found myself. I wouldn't be able to carry out my mission if I became the King's plaything. Fortunately, the conversation changed as she offered to stay the night with him. At first, he was so compelled by this unusual sight before him that he failed to respond but then, in an instant, he drew my curtains and turned to answer her. He was, unquestionably, moody. Whether he was understandably moody would be a question for others but it was clear that his ill health, ulcerated leg and the trials of ruling this past and eventful thirty-two years, had taken its toll on his mental health. In years to come there would be debates about thyroid problems, syphilis, diabetes and Cushing's syndrome but, even if all or some of these, were evident, that knowledge was of little use to those who had to deal with him day in day out. He was, by now, a complete mess which alerted me also to how vulnerable he may well be and how open to suggestion he may already have been. If only Catherine would engage him in discussions regarding any future plans, I could get some intelligence to York.

'Alas my sweet dove, I must get to my prayers and I have one more meet before my slumber. You go now, tomorrow there will be dancing, feasts and gaiety.' He kissed her fondly and bade her goodnight and, as the door shut, I could hear the King struggle to find his knees to make prayer. He prayed as anyone would, and about the things anyone would, but this also stretched to affairs of state finalising his petitions with the Lord's prayer. As it went quiet, I presumed this to be at an end but it wasn't. His tone changed as it would when begging, beseeching and he talked to God about his dream and cried. Unfortunately, the details of this dream didn't feature in his prayers but it was clear that he had, in the previous year, had a dream so powerful that he thought it a premonition and, this being the case, I was sure that he must have shared it with others. A premonition, real or otherwise, by a dictator, was a very dangerous thing to be sure. His prayer ended with,

'Dear Lord. If you could find a way to show to me that what I have seen is the singular truth then I will make all the changes you would require for the people of this world.' No sooner had he managed to get himself upright there was someone at his door.

'Come Thomas, but pray keep it brief I am without strength tonight .' I had no clue as to who this was except, as he spoke, I was sure it wasn't Thomas Culpeper leaving me with possibly another thousand others with the same name. He had a business-like attitude and business-like voice and, although he showed due deference to Henry, there was cunning in his voice that I didn't like. What did I mean by this? Well, I could detect an air of condescension in his voice which I suspect the King was used to.

'You must forgive me, Your Grace, but I must push the issue of York.'

'York! York!! Are you bloody obsessed man! Do you have some whore waiting for you there Wriothesley?!' This took away my breath. He's here, Wriothesley, right in front of me and, unsurprisingly, talking about my home City. The King was fired up.

'God's left armpit man! Do you only know one tune? It feels like we've been travelling a year already. York will see us when we get there and not before!'

Wriothesley then adopted his best used sycophantic tone attempting to appease the King and, presumably, trying to keep hold of his head.

'It shames me to think I have upset Your Grace. Perhaps if His Majesty could confirm that we will be making for York after Lincoln?' This was followed by silence. I could feel the King trying to see through this weasel, he was seemingly suspicious of this relentless talk of York.

'Let it be, for now, Thomas, I'm tired' he replied calmly and sounding exhausted.

I heard a drink being poured and the room soon became much calmer.

'Perhaps Your Majesty would like to discuss plans for the Minsters and Cathedrals?' Zealously and changing humour again, Henry agreed and gave forth a grand plan for all the religious houses in the country and, as he did, I was both shocked and mindful of the need to retain this information. Was this it then? The Cataclysm? But why, then, were they calling this the clarification? It made no sense. I was left cold by this en masse callous approach to matters but did, at least, think my search for intelligence was at an end.

That was, until Wriothesley decided to stay a little longer and Henry, certainly not for the first time, discussed his dream. The dream. The dream. Everything seemed to hang on this now notorious dream. Now everything made sense. The clarification (or Cataclysm) was to be a manifestation of his dream. Rather than the recommended course of letting God decide whether a premonition was, in fact, a premonition or not, Wriothesley, Cranmer and Seymour were going to manufacture Henry's premonition for him. This was now regarded as a prophecy and a prophecy that was to be fulfilled. I was devastated by Henry's plans for England's places of worship, this left me almost paralysed and terrified for the people of England. However, it was now clear to me that no matter how diabolical Henry's schemes were, the plans of Wriothesley, Cranmer and Seymour were straight from hell itself and their conversation confirmed, undeniably, that Henry had not been part to that which we had been referring to as the Cataclysm.

I was now trapped in the King's privy quarters during which time he spoke to me incessantly. A man so betrayed by so many and so often now sought to bare his soul to a mouse. The more he spoke the more I learned of his dream and the more everything made sense. I was to be shown off a dozen times more, dressed in even finer clothes and held in the affection of the King himself.

Uncannily, as preparations were made to leave Lincoln, the Queen herself personally asked Henry if she could take his mouse to the stable ready for transport.

'He is to go to York too' she said and Harry seemed delighted.

'Very well my petal. Very well we shall rule together from York! I shall see you in that fair City, little King

Harry!! Ha Ha!' I could tell that Catherine was anxious to whisk me away and she did just that. Within the hour I was with Culpeper and, shortly afterwards, back with Elspeth. Eventually, I was completely alone with Elspeth who, surprisingly, looked very happy to see me.

'I knew nought until this morning' she said. 'I feared you dead. Have you news?'

I took a very slow breath as I knew that my next comment would be overwhelming for the young nun.

'I know all' I said and Elspeth gasped.

'It is essential we get the pigeon away today with a message for our agents in York.'

'It's all in hand. Say nothing for now, if all goes well we will be away within the hour!' she replied. I did as was told and accepted my dark but comfortable cage as we seemed to be hurried well out of reach of Lincoln City centre.

'Mouse! Brave mouse! Still with us and dressed as a…slightly…shitty courtier. Ha Ha!' This, Of course, was Culpeper.

'We must make progress Thomas, with the utmost urgency!'

'What was it like being abed with the King and Queen Mouse? Could you compete? Ha Ha!' He continued to tease me, as was his wont, for some time and I was fine with it. Dear Culpeper who had risked so much for the cause but was to lose all because of his uncontrollable affection for Catherine. It seemed like farewells took an hour and, as Bayard's familiar cart rolled up Culpeper said,

'You, fair maiden will torment my heart for the year to come' and he kissed Elspeth's hand. She reacted momentarily, saw that I was looking and then returned to her default, angry expression.

'How think you of your King, mouse?' asked Culpeper.

What a question, it was hard to say.

'Absolutely not what I expected. A very sad and lonely man, perhaps the victim of his own wickedness. Who knows?'

Culpeper helped us to scribe instructions that would go directly to Father Matthew and Faith was away to the skies in no time. In a much more serious humour, Culpeper put his face close to my cage and whispered,

'I'd like you to be there when I die Mouse. Can you do that?' What do you say to that? He knew his fate was sealed and I did, of course, agree to his request. And then, we said goodbye for the last time. I was pleased to see Bayard. I felt I was returning to my family, that being the Agents of the Word. Both Elspeth and Bayard endlessly pressurised me for answers but I knew the effect that the truth would have on them and so promised that all would be revealed at Holy Trinity Church in York and tasked myself with generating a plan that would put an end to all this madness.

19: Bishop of Chester

Lockington, near Nottingham , late August 1541

'I'm sure somebody has moved York further away' complained Silas. His two companions smiled although they were exhausted, their recent triumphs in Stratford almost forgotten as the journey was getting the better of them.

'Take heart good friend, we will make haste over the next few days. There's one thing we can be sure off and that is that Fat Harry will be travelling a lot more slowly' said Thomas Farrier.

'And' added Richard 'That donkey he's on will need rests every few miles with all that weight on him.'

'He's on a donkey?!' asked Silas, astonished at this, as he was sure that the King would be better looked after.

'Him on a donkey and her in a little two-wheeled cart being dragged along.' Silas looked at both their faces which gave away nothing. Donkey? Really? The King? And then he saw the jest as Thomas Farrier winked. By now they could laugh together. This was far away from the ridiculing Silas had known so well, this was banter between friends and he could take any amount of it.

'Soon be at Nottingham. We will eat and rest there' said Richard. As he was at the front he turned his head to speak to his two travelling companions only to discover that there were now three.

'Who on earth is that behind you?!' he said, alarmed. Silas and Thomas didn't react at all.

'No, seriously, there! We're not alone!' All Richard was getting from the other two was a self-congratulatory, but gormless, smile as they weren't falling for this one. Frustrated, he brought his steed to a complete halt and doubled back around the rear of his friends to confront this shadow.

'You?!' he said. His companions still didn't turn. Silas felt as good as he had ever done as he was not going to be outwitted this time.

Moonlight handed Richard his instructions and then disappeared.

'Done yet friend?' said Thomas.

Richard rode alongside them, insisted that they stopped and showed them the sealed letter.

'How did you do that?' said Silas as he would to a street magician.

'I didn't do anything!' came the angry reply and, no matter how he tried to convince his companions of what he had seen, they were having none of it. Their expressions became smugger and Richard became more angry and frustrated until, running out of ideas, he rode in front of the other two and stopped them in their tracks. His mood changed, they now understood his seriousness and all three dismounted, found some shade by the edge of a field and Richard broke the seal.

'It is from Robert!' he took a few moments to read the instructions, looked up and said sheepishly,

'We're to go to Chester?'

'Who's Chester?' asked Silas.

'Not a who, but now a City' informed Richard 'The King has put new Bishops, some of them once Abbotts loyal to him, in six places creating instant Cathedrals in Peterborough, Westminster, Bristol, Gloucester, Oxford and Chester.'

Silence followed, mostly because they were dumbfounded by his knowledge but also because this mystery was becoming more confusing.

'Why on earth would he do that if they are all to be destroyed?' asked Silas.

'Ah Silas!' said Thomas Farrier 'you're doing what we are all doing my friend, guessing. As yet, we don't know that destruction is Henry's plan but we do know that there is to be a major event at your beloved York Minster and, therefore, possibly others. He may be creating more Cathedrals to give this event more impact.'

'I'm worn out and I want to go home' responded Silas, childlike.

'I understand my good friend, but we must do this. Our brief is simple and, as soon as we're done with the new Bishop of Chester we will make straight for York to join our comrades.' Silas didn't hear "comrades" he just heard "Wynnfrith" and so reluctantly agreed and they picked up pace now rerouting toward Chester.

'John Bird' shouted Richard as they galloped alongside each other, an impressive sight. This attracted no response. So he shouted it again.

'What is?' asked Silas.

'Bishop of Chester, that's his name'.

'Let's hope he's not flown' added Thomas but there was no response, perhaps not the time for humour.

'Ah flown, yes, bird. Ah' rambled Silas, eventually.

To put this correctly on record, it is fair to say that this conversation was not flowing although it did transpire that Richard Shakespeare knew this man. Both impressed, they slowed and, unsurprisingly, asked how but he refused to give more detail. It was almost unimaginable that a tenant farmer would know a Bishop but clearly, they were not going to be given any more information. Over the next day or so this would crop up again and again but no more information was forthcoming from Richard.

Eventually, they arrived at the gates of Chester and, unexpectedly, followed the flow of traders, and pilgrims in search of the shrine of St. Werburgh, through the gates and toward the City. As they crossed the river they marvelled at the remains of buildings that were once occupied by Romans. Richard took the lead and, quite authoritatively, headed straight to the abbey, now a Cathedral. They were instantly aware of the busyness and fuss around the Cathedral just as it was in York. They were stopped five hundred yards before the entrance and dismounted to angry responses from guards. This had no effect at all on Richard.

'I never thought about a scribe or pen, do we have a quill perhaps amongst our luggage?' he asked his friends. Silas, now obsessed with the skill of writing brought out a quill. Richard thanked him, took out a small knife and cut his arm. He tore a blank corner from the message they had received from York and wrote on it using his own blood as ink, still not phased. He boldly approached the nearest guard and insisted he took the message to the Bishop. The guard's rude, abrupt and cynical response was interrupted by Richard.

'He will want to read this and he would have you removed completely from all duties if you don't.' Silas and Thomas Farrier were aghast not even knowing if this was a bluff. The soldier looked at Richard contemptuously, reminding all present that these three looked a messy and bedraggled sight as they hadn't seen water for a week. They unquestionably looked tired although Richard was still standing his ground.

The soldier stared. Richard stared. Richard stared so hard he could see the soldier thinking about possible consequences if he didn't deliver this pathetic scrap.

'Very well. But if this isn't above board you'll all be out on your arses…or worse!'

No discourse took place between the three of them for a while. They sat on a grass verge and practically acted as if nothing had happened.

'What's going on?' Silas eventually blurted, not able to keep his curiosity at bay any longer.

'Bird and I have had business before. Most unpleasant my friend.'

'What business?' asked Silas. Thomas glared at him knowing that if Richard had wanted to declare more, he would have done so already. So silence, yet again, followed.

More than an hour passed and a cleric came out whom they expected was passing by but, as he approached said,

'Gentlemen, please follow me.' They were taken, by the longest route possible, around the back, through the cloisters and into a small office where they could hear work being carried out beyond the nave. They were left alone so sat, enjoying the most comfortable seat they had had in a week. They heard someone approach, the door opened and there he was Bishop John Bird.

'Just you and I Sir, or not at all' he demanded.

'All, or we leave with what I know' coolly replied Richard. Bird's attitude softened immediately.

'There, there, gentleman. No need for conflict. We are, after all, in the house of God'.

'No argument from me' said Richard 'you'll find no disrespect in us.' Amongst all this, incredibly unusual, discussion, Thomas and Silas were probably most shocked that Richard was refusing to use the Bishop's title or show him any respect.

'I arrive completely in peace. I mean you no harm.' Richard asserted 'we know of the King's plan to launch some devilment in York Minster and word has it that the same thing will happen here and elsewhere at the same time.'

'The King?!' I think what you have, Shakespeare is a little bit of information that you know not what to do with' scoffed the Bishop.

'Maybe so. But I also have some information on you that I would know what to do with!' Thomas and Silas looked shocked.

'Come now' said the Bishop instantly regretting his arrogance 'we're all good men here, no need for threats.'

'No threat. I'm here to give instruction. We will, absolutely, thwart this initiative in York and, as we believe you are to do the very same thing at the same time, I'm telling you that you will look stupid if you persist in this matter and that you are to give up such plans forthwith.'

The Bishop's mood was constantly changing as this was now a game of cards where Richard was probably revealing too much of his hand too soon.

'I would say you have a little information. Let's suppose you're even partially correct. Why on earth would I disobey orders?'

'I'll give you two reasons my friend. One, I'll make it known to your superior, the Archbishop of York, about your disgraceful past. Two, we now have all the copies of the Lindisfarne gospels and the original so you won't be able to go through with your charade.'

The Bishop's mind was now spinning. This was his greatest anxiety, the copy of the Gospels had never arrived. Could they be telling the truth? He looked at the other two. One a fool the other a thug. Could they also know of his past indiscretions and offences? He thought. He worried. He pondered and thought some more. Richard was very patient.

'You have my word that, even under torture, I will not speak of our secret, even to these two, if you comply. I will give you that very oath on the Bible this very minute' promised Richard.

The Bishop let out a long sigh.

'Very well. As long as you understand that I am under some immense pressure here. You are right, I cannot instigate what I have been instructed to do without the Gospels or a copy. But, you are presuming that all this was to happen simultaneously with York. Not so, in fact exactly one week later. But…agreed…It will not be happening in Chester at all.' They then all pushed him to describe what was going to happen but it was clear he simply didn't know. He was yet another pawn in the scheme of Seymour, Cranmer and Wriothesley. He continued,

'Also, I can help you with one more thing. The King. This is not his doing.' They were astonished. How on earth could there be a major change to affairs political or religious without the crown being directly involved? Dumbfounded, they remained, for a while, just that. Dumb.

They rose to leave, Richard having made his oath. He then asked about the shrine of St. Werburgh. The Bishop confirmed that the destruction of shrines was Henry's doing and that he would do all he could to resist it.

'I do hope we can part friends Shakespeare' begged the Bishop. Richard turned away, said nothing and left with his travelling companions as quickly as they had entered.

They ran and jumped onto their horses as Richard commanded,

'To York and to victory!!'

20: Maud

Warwick castle, September 1541

Two of the men that Silas had met at the Inn at Wolverdington, Ham and Farrimond were sat on their usual stools but not, as had become their habit, discussing politics and religion. They were now taking an active part in such matters. Unbeknownst to their allies in York, the Agents of the Word had been organising themselves in pockets around England for the past year, ever since the first rumours had begun regarding this elusive Cataclysm. Now, everything had escalated. Richard Shakespeare, Thomas Farrimond and Silas were known fugitives and Wriothesley and Seymour's men were at great pains to find and kill them. They had closed in on Wolverdington and, amongst the tiny population, it would have been very easy to find Abigail, her children and Eirik and they would, undoubtedly, have shown no mercy. So, they had fled to safety not knowing, at first, what that meant despite Eirik still not being fully recovered. What, in the eyes of their hunters connected them all? Maud. Maud, who had been, against her will, in the employ of one of Wriothesley's chief agents was now the focus of these wicked men's attention. They presumed that she knew all. Who Bede and Nails were, Why Silas was in Stratford upon Avon, how Shakespeare had stolen the plans, how the attack on his farm was planned, where their hideout was and where their whereabouts was. Where the Lindisfarne gospels were, where the copies were. But, in truth, apart from the nonsense relayed to her initially by Silas, she knew very little.

But none of that mattered as she was now in custody and being tortured. The hunt for the Agents had been postponed until they had retrieved all intelligence possible from Maud. This is now what occupied Farrimond and Ham's discussion.

They looked strange seen together as Farrimond was a third the size of his friend. Ham, very aptly named, as he now looked like a hock and seemed to get bigger every couple of months leaving his hose and jerkin under some considerable duress. There are more pigeons in Ham than there were flying around the market in York. Conversely, Farrimond looked like he could well have benefitted from a few of those cooked birds coming his way.

'Well, we do or we don't' said Ham finishing off his pie.

'We do friend. Unless she's dead we should give her a chance if we can and, hopefully, we already have the advantage.'

'Alright, we have a pact then. We go this very afternoon.' For two halfwits, their plan wasn't half bad but they had only just got through the door when they realised that they didn't even have any transport. This left them again with a problem. They could borrow a couple of nags from a farmer friend but there would be questions. Stealing would create even bigger problems. They decided to go with the former idea but took along a jug of beer to soften the deal. Horses secured, they set course for Warwick castle.

Warwick castle. The two words alone invoke visions of a fortress that told tales of romance and chivalry. This was once true but it was now, like many castles, in a state of disrepair. Henry had provided some funds to keep the walls supported but it was hardly fit for residence. It was used, periodically, to keep and torture prisoners and this is where Maud could be found.

'What sort of man would torture a woman?' asked Ham.

'The very ones we are fighting and is one of the many reasons why we must win. We must win Ham no matter how many lives are lost both here and in York.'

They were scared. This type of adventure wasn't the province of farm labourers and the very sight of the castle, as they arrived, overwhelmed them. It was huge and it was high. Farrimond assured Ham that they had the upper hand and that they must stick to the plan. If they were wrong about their assumptions and the place was heavily guarded then they were done for but, at first glance, the place seemed almost deserted. They carried with them a large and heavy bundle and, for Ham, in particular, the climb was gruelling. He puffed constantly and stopped regularly but, without comment, his partner stopped with him. They found a break in the castle wall where the stone had deteriorated and simply walked in. They hid behind some old stocks and looked around the vast courtyard.

It was hard to know where to start but they were buoyed by the absence of life so far. It was a distant clanging that caught their attention and left them with two choices. Either to follow the noise or await more movement. As stealth may as well have been a foreign notion to them, they just stood and went toward the persistent metallic noises. They found themselves at the entrance to a Tower with stairs that wound both upward and downward. The noise now accompanied by murmurs were unquestionably coming from below. At this juncture they did, at least, have the presence of mind to be quiet. They knew they were heading for the dungeon and danger. This was nothing like the Tower of London. It was poorly secured and poorly guarded. They got as far as the cell door and Farrimond could see Maud and her husband and a single torturer. He felt so cold, he was no warrior and this sight made him sick to the stomach. Maud's innocent and harmless husband had had his hands removed and blood gushed forth from his mouth as his tongue had also been removed. He was certainly dead. Farrimond thought to turn and say something to Ham but he knew his colleague was busy. Maud seemed to be bleeding everywhere but was still bemoaning a long and quiet protest. She could still speak as this brute presumed to get more information from her. She had no nails on her hands and feet, her teeth were broken and her head had been shaved. Both of them were naked. Even with this one, wicked soldier, it would have been unlikely that Ham and Farrimond would have found the courage between them to take him on but, as they had discussed, they had an advantage and they were going to use it. Farrimond's only action was to keep reminding his partner to be quiet that was until he indicated that he was ready. Even this plan wasn't completely risk-free as they were relying on state of the art technology for this rescue to succeed. The door, surprisingly, was already ajar so, with one very simple order Farrimond pushed it open further and whispered

'Now.'

The guard, on picking this up, turned his head, not to see two bumpkins staring at him, but the barrel of an arquebus propped on a stand and ready to fire. Since acquiring this, Ham had only been able to practice twice so everything rested on him getting this right. There was a rather pathetic sizzle, then a crackle and then an almighty boom! This echoed around the ramparts. As the smoke cleared they saw that the guard was down, a hole in his chest from which he would not recover. They rushed over to release Maud from her chains and manacles but she resisted.

'Too late…leave me to die…can't go on…' and the rest was unintelligible.

They were having none of it. They carried her as best they could, intending to get out of there as quickly as possible. With no thought of taking the arquebus home with them, as it wasn't theirs anyway, they headed for the nearest slope downward. It was impossible for them to carry the now unconscious, Maud so simply let her body slide down the wet grass and mud toward the horses and they followed suit.

In later life, when Ham was to relay this story in the pub, at least a hundred archers were firing at them as they leapt the huge distance across a furlong wide moat but, in reality, no one followed and, for all they knew, there may not have been anyone else there.

They returned to Wolverdington for just two days in the hope of getting Maud better but they knew that none of them could stay there, so made plans to leave.

21: Lizzy

York, September 1541

Lizzy's funeral was a grand affair for such a poor family. Despite his humble protestations, Godwin had found himself amongst new and dependable friends who had grown to care for him and his ailing daughter. For the first few days after her death, he cursed God, the Church and even Father Matthew for not saving her and thought it best for her not to have a Christian funeral. This, of course, did little more than upset his good wife and those around him although the generous offer from the Mayor of a funeral fit for a lady was delivered the day after her passing. This made Godwin weep and, momentarily, count his blessings. His heart was broken and, for a day or two, he had forgotten that, realistically, she never did have any chance of survival and was angry at everything and everyone. His workshop was closed leaving the Lindisfarne Gospels, the copy, other evidence and the Tudor Rose Boss unattended. Cataclysm? As far as he was concerned this was a Cataclysm and he even tried to reason that there had been a connection between all the "Agents of the Word" fuss and Lizzy's demise. You could forgive poor Godwin for being so angry and irrational but he did agree eventually, to the altogether respectable funeral at Holy Trinity Church.

Wynnfrith sat toward the back of the church, looked down to her right, and remembered the day that she had first tried to hide a message in the stone wall. It seemed so long ago, so many things had taken place since then and many of those events, meetings and partings swirled around in her head so much that she felt faint. She stood up as the coffin was brought in. It was covered with leaves and summer flowers but, what was most striking, was that the box was so tiny. As she saw it, tears flowed down her cheeks and she then realised that, singularly, Godwin was carrying this coffin on one shoulder and this sight hurt even more. On each side, he had carved little mice at play. It was both beautiful and appropriate. Wynn looked around. Robert, Edward and his father, William Fawkes, had attended and Father Matthew was about to deliver a requiem mass. Her thoughts were so different from Godwin's, she was overwhelmed at the binds and friendships that this threat had created. Lizzy was loved, not for the sake of it but because she had been one of them. Momentarily, Wynnfrith felt alone as Robert stood to do a reading. Her eyes went down to her feet and her tears gave away her sympathy for Godwin as well as the terror they were all facing. An arm gently folded around her shoulder and she felt a gentle kiss on her cheek. It was Elspeth returned from Lincoln. She turned, delighted, and without fuss hugged her sister. As Elspeth leaned backwards Wynn could now see Bayard's hefty frame approach the coffin. He stopped, bowed reverently with his hands clasped in prayer and then, put his right hand in his pocket and pulled out a mouse, their mouse. Godwin placed me, now dressed in fineries, on the coffin and I lay there as close as I could to the nape of her neck where I used to slumber. I saw a tear and a smile from Godwin which gave me heart. As the mass came to a close everyone surrounded Lizzy's coffin and I realised that we were almost in the same positions as that night at Godwin's home when we first sent for Father Matthew. Lizzy was lovingly buried in the yard at the front of Holy Trinity Church very close to the parents of Wynnfrith and Elspeth, a coincidence which gave both the sisters and Godwin's family comfort. It was then decided that all but the family should leave. As we wandered toward Goodramgate, me now back in my elaborate cage, we understood that we could not be seen together. There were King's builders on the outside walls of the Minster so we would easily be observed. So, as we went our separate ways, to give the impression of unfamiliarity, Robert whispered that we were to meet the following day within the church and to take care to make this look coincidental.

I was relieved to hear this. It was with the utmost urgency that I needed to relay all my information to the Agents and take some time to rehearse our plan. Well, my plan.

Wynnfrith could now return to the wash house with Elspeth and, although she was going to lose those comforts and luxuries of the Mayor's residence, she would have had it no other way. The sisters shared everything that they had learned, Wynn soaking up the tales of courtiers, beautiful women and beautiful clothes, of the King and Queen and of glorious Lincoln.

'The mouse knows all' said Elspeth 'and he says it is more shocking than we feared.'

'Why hasn't he told you everything ?' asked Wynnfrith, confused.

'I believe that it is simply too much to impart to each of

us individually and I also think he is worried that we may reveal ourselves before the day.'

'That makes sense' said Wynnfrith 'I suppose, more than ever, we will now need to work as a team.'

'Yes. Yes, dear Wynn. That's just it. He says he has a plan. It's all so daunting, I sometimes wonder how on earth we got involved in all this.' Elspeth sounded more sad than scared when she said this.'

'Remember your calling and your cause sister. And that of Brother Bernard and, come to that, all of us in the north.'

They agreed to speak no more of it until the meeting and enjoyed their time together which, surprisingly, included cleaning clothes.

I asked Bayard if he could take me to my workshop and he happily complied. I hadn't got a clue as to how I would get in and was distracted by those familiar sights as we moved toward Micklegate as it seemed like a while since I had made the journey. In reality, it hadn't been long but, on this occasion, the sight of the semi-destroyed monastery so close to my workshop both saddened me and strengthened my resolve. As we neared I could see some activity and noticed, to my delight, that Edward had gone ahead. He was cleaning, tidying and generally taking care of the place. Love in yet another guise I thought, no doubt he felt that he couldn't help Lizzy or Godwin so he would do something practical to help.

'Hullo street urchin! Hope you're not stealing anything!' His head spun around and he ran out.

'Micklegate! Dear Micklegate Mouse!' Got my polite title today. He took me out, picked me up and talked incessantly about everything. I do mean everything. You'd think I had been away for months. In the midst of all of this, we had a conversation about my strange and opulent attire. Edward didn't quite know what to make of it but I did reveal that the clothes were made at the request of the King and

Queen. That impressed him so much he actually shut up for five minutes. He then gave me a guided tour and I was deeply touched by the lengths he had gone to care for the workshop that Godwin had, quite understandably, abandoned and, he had secured all the items that, potentially, could be used as evidence. And then, possibly ten minutes overdue, it started. What? When? Who? Why? And so on. It was all in vain because I had decided already that I would not be playing the part of a dripping tap. They would all get the deluge the following day. I couldn't think of anything better than mucking in at the workshop and thoroughly enjoyed it. As the light dimmed, he locked up, gave me clean straw, food and left me there, alone in peace.

My sleep was often broken. Although I had completely adjusted to my new life and mission, I was haunted by this other person, Nick who, by now was almost a night terror. I had no desire to think of it and fought this notion. I decided to stay awake and rehearse for the following day as my fellow agents would have high expectations. We were now in so deep, you can't imagine how deep, and every detail of our plan would need to be rehearsed over and over again. I started to doze but then I heard some nearby rustling and that alerted me. Small as I was, I felt the need to bury myself in the straw, that was until I could hear faint whispers. I stuck my head out to look. It was Edward, he had returned.

'Frightened the bloody life out of me Ed!' I grunted, sort of pleased to see him 'what you doing back?'

'I thought it was important' he whispered '...you should know...Silas has returned and is hidden again in the Church. He has brought with him our agent in Stratford, Thomas Farrier and the farmer that had been imprisoned. The Mayor has given them lodgings' said Edward.

'Ah! Good. Good. Then we are almost quorate. Excellent!' I replied.

'We're wha? said the confused child.

'We are almost, all, gathered my friend. This is when the Agents of the Word will come into their own. Now hurry home before curfew lad and come get me at sunrise.' Off he went, dear boy. I thought for a moment what a blessing it was that we don't know our future. The Fawkes' were such a fine family and Edward would have had laudable ambitions for his children as William Fawkes had had for his. However, sadly, Edward's son would become one of the most notorious villains of all time and his crime rooted in the very events that the Agents were now dealing with. How I wished I could help avert such things but, alas, I couldn't, I could only take part. This snapped me out of my philosophising into a reality that spoke of great responsibility. No sleep I decided. I would spend the night preparing for our meeting and refining our plan against the perpetrators.

The morrow was a warm day in September, I arose to accompany Edward to Holy Trinity Church very possibly for the last time. I was both excited and apprehensive. Between us, we had managed to accrue enough intelligence to stop this imminent event and had already frustrated some of their plans. I took pains to rehearse over and over again everything I would have to impart to my friends and colleagues praying that they would remain on board and support my, extremely dangerous, plan. Swaying? It no longer bothered me. Such petty complaints were now the province of everyday people and the Agents were, no longer, everyday people. Truthfully, I enjoyed it. How I had loved the company of these folk, particularly Edward and knew that within a week, if still alive, I would be craving our bouncy, smelly walks around the beautiful City of York.

We had arranged to achieve a staggered arrival so that Edward and I would be the first in church. Yes, today we would meet within the church. The garden had always been overlooked by the Minster but now it was crawling with people inside and out. To be clear, this church was small but beautifully designed. As I walked through the door and then looked to my right along its length, the five panelled, stained glass, window warmly invited me in. Once in the centre, I feel comfortable between the arches and, beyond, more coloured windows to my left and right. I looked at Edward, Father Matthew, Brother Bede and Silas, coloured light dappling their faces, hair and clothes. It was a serene and homely sight and I would urge anyone in search of some respite, peace and stillness to visit Holy Trinity Church in Goodramgate, York.

Father Matthew was happy to see us. Silas was breaking his fast although the priest had already taken Mass and had been up most of the night. Bede sat close to Silas for comfort, now looking in much better physical health. Strangely, we talked about the weather and the condition of the church almost as if to avoid the reality that faced us. A gentle knock. Wynnfrith's knock. Father Matthew rushed to open the door and let them both in. As Wynn approached, her eyes fixed on Silas. He panicked and so jumped up, his wooden plate now spinning on the floor and began, in vain, to adjust his clothes and his beloved strand of crimson hair.

'Sit down you fool!' I whispered 'sit down!!'

On hearing the word "fool" he obeyed as it most certainly must have applied to him and, he did, sit down, but appeared a complete nervous wreck. He looked at Wynn, and thank God, said nothing. Neither did she. Here we go again, I thought and still wanted to bang their heads together. He then placed his hand in the left pocket of his doublet and partly drew out the kerchief given to him by Wynnfrith before he had set forth for Stratford upon Avon. She squinted a little as she didn't know what it was. No longer several hues of green, it was only identifiable by its shape so, when the metaphorical candlelight started to flicker, she smiled, then blushed, then turned away. He then appeared disappointed.

'What is wrong with you two?!!' I exclaimed insensitively

and had now startled everyone in the room. This had the opposite effect on these two extremely unwilling lovebirds. This was certainly going to be a long game, I thought. Father Matthew went to great pains to, at least, get them to sit together where they both looked as if they were awaiting an interview. Further taps at the door. Richard Shakespeare and Thomas Farrier. Although half-stories had already been shared about each other's adventures some Agents were now meeting each other for the first time so several introductions were to be the order of the day. Elspeth and Wynnfrith begged them for news of Eirik and they were assured that their brother would return as soon as he was well. Silas felt uneasy as they used the word "brother" and glanced over at Thomas who gave nothing away. Silas tried to tuck these thoughts away as they created a very uncomfortable conflict within him. Then, Thomas started to relate details of their encounters but was politely stopped by the priest as, sensibly, he said that all should be there to hear it.

The Mayor arrived blustering in without knocking and complaining about how busy York had become. In reality, he had lost track of the time whilst making a very unofficial, official visit to Mrs Grindem's. More welcomes and introductions. Over the next hour, we would be joined by Edward and Bayard who entered laughing as Bayard was sharing stories of how uptight Elspeth had been on the journey to Lincoln. The expression on Elspeth's face suggested that she knew what they had been discussing. She now looked different, her blonde hair down to her shoulders and I deduced that her recent encounters had helped to soften her demeanour somewhat. However, she was still, and would always be, the devoted Catholic nun with a purpose as determined as anyone else in the room.

Once together there was a pall over the place. I think, in part, this was due to the loss of Lizzy. This event alone was symbolic, a reminder of how we are often limited in what we can do, and can't do, no matter how well-intentioned. Added to this was this feeling that we were nearing the end, whatever that meant. Things would never be the same from now on and it was unlikely that we would all survive. The silence spoke volumes about how we wanted to freeze this moment permanently but, alas, we needed to move on. I answered all I could about my silly costume which did lighten the atmosphere and I would have happily been a figure of fun for all time if we could have forgotten about the immediate future, I thought. But we couldn't.

'My brave iron balls. Where should we start my friend?' said the Lord Mayor.

'Well, I'm telling you all now that we will be here for hours. Can we make that work Father?' He agreed and I suggested that, firstly, Robert told all about his meeting with the Archbishop and what he had learned from that and then Thomas Farrier could relate further details of the adventure in Stratford, and then I would sum up. As they spoke, the gathered Agents were both aghast and impressed by what had taken place and we spent some time dwelling on those events. Then it was my turn.

'The intelligence that I now have in my possession has been possible because of a number of people who have taken unfathomable risks and I would highly commend them. Dear Elspeth, who threw herself wholeheartedly into the Lion's den, Master Bayard who was our compass and our ultimate security. Lady Rochford who covered our tracks and, not least Thomas Culpeper himself and, ultimately, the Queen.

'Are the rumours true about Culpeper and the Queen?' asked Wynnfrith sweetly.

'They are Wynn. Culpeper is a lovable delinquent and I believe the Queen has fallen in love with him. Their assignations on the King's progress along with Catherine's past indiscretions will, unquestionably, cost them their lives.' I said. Surprisingly my friends looked sad rather than judgemental, possibly because they understood the risks these people had taken on their behalf.

'Could have been worse though' I added 'Culpeper also took a fancy to your sister!' I sniggered, and there was gentle laughter and gasps around the room. Elspeth looked down and said nothing, Wynnfrith giggled for minutes. I could hear Wynn whispering "what was he like" and Elspeth kept shushing her. Silas had an instant and dramatic spell of depression as he didn't altogether like the interest Wynnfrith was taking in this rogue. They then, quite naturally, started to ask questions about how the Queen looked, her clothes, the courtiers and so on. I promised them that, on another occasion, we would all meet socially and I would impart all this information. How I hoped that that would, one day, come.

'What is the King like?' asked Edward.

'A quite sad, ageing and lonely man. Completely deranged by his obsession with the succession and power. He has no real friends or allies and is little loved although the Queen is kind to him. His mood changes by the minute and his health is failing, struggling to get around of his own accord. If he hobbled past you in the street, apart from his clothes, you probably wouldn't even notice him.'

'But he seems to have stirred trouble for almost all, even in his own country! Pray tell us now of the King's wicked plan!' demanded Robert.

'The King doesn't have a plan' I calmly responded. There was a chorus of "what?!!" So I continued.

'That's not entirely true. The King had been toying with a grand idea of completely culling all religious houses as they stand, not just monasteries. That's why there were so many surveyors and builders amongst his retinue. This would have involved knocking down all the Cathedrals completely and replacing them with houses of worship, with his image as Supreme Head of the Church everywhere. However, I heard him in discussions with Wriothesley and, besides being too costly, they both seemed to think that this would be ill-advised, almost certainly attracting increased rebellion. Otherwise, the King knows nothing of the Cataclysm. However, several shrines have already suffered as part of this ill-thought out project.'

'So this is entirely the making of Wriothesley, Cranmer and Seymour?' asked Richard. Brother Bede became increasingly agitated at the mention of these names.

'Yes, they claim that their deep and devious plot is in the King's interest and there's no doubt that they now have a growing number of followers. In reality, they are preparing for the King's death and feathering their opulent nests for many years to come afterwards.' I went on to explain that everything from the discovery of the Gospels, to the soldiers in the Cathedral and from the diagram obtained by Richard, to Lizzy's sighting of the Queen all made sense. Absolutely everything made sense. There was just one anomaly. What was to happen in York Minster would be repeated in every Cathedral in England but, not as thought, simultaneously but one after the other. The reason for this being that they had to be assured of success in York first.

They waited in complete silence for me to follow this up but I asked for a break. Not for dramatic effect, I knew that what was to come would take hours so we agreed to socialise and embrace some small talk whilst Father Matthew provided us with bread and beer.

I now found myself sat in a circle, surrounded by my friends and allies, breaking bread and drinking beer. I don't think the irony was lost on any of us. Not just the physical similarity between these humble warriors and the apostles at the last supper, but that overbearing feeling that, like Jesus, each one of us would happily have this huge responsibility pass over us if the opportunity arose. However, that was not to be. We were the only remedy to the diabolical deviance that was imminent and, I was confident we would win out. I did, however, dread having to tell them one fact that I was already certain of, so dropped the crumbs from my claws and as, best I could, stood upright and said,

'I must tell you my good and noble allies, that there will be a considerable death toll from this event. It's not something I presume, I know it.' Not one of them questioned my certainty and, although for a while, heads went down, they came up again and everyone carried on as if I had said nothing. I was struggling to keep secret just how deeply touched I was by their dedication. Our brave band had in its ranks an ageing priest, a broken monk, a dodgy mouse, a child, the village idiot, an angry nun, a farmer and a blacksmith. Not quite the stuff of the round table but I'd bet on this team against Arthur's any day.

'One more thing. There will be some of you from whom I must keep some of this secret. For the plan to work it is essential that you don't all fully understand my method. You will all be involved completely, I promise, but you must respect this.' I braced myself for the backlash. Again, nothing. What remarkable people.

'You are the most remarkable and trustworthy people one could wish to have as allies' I told them 'not least in that, incredibly, you have all accepted me for what I am. One day I hope you may understand why you have, before you, a talking mouse but, for now, I assure you that your trust will be rewarded. I will not let you down. However, I have to leave soon. This is something beyond my control so I thank you for your love, fellowship and the sacrifices you have made.' It wasn't my intention to upset anyone but I heard snivelling. It was Silas. Wynn took his hand. A breakthrough at last! I thought.

After an hour I politely asked Father Matthew, Elspeth and Richard Shakespeare to leave and they rose to do so without question. I asked Edward to find his father and bring him as a matter of urgency. There were questions about how trustworthy William Fawkes was but, at this stage, it was absolutely imperative that he was supporting us. We needed him and that was that.

As she stood to say goodbye to her sister, Wynn took a little stumble. Silas caught her arm and without any prompt or awkwardness, the same arm naturally wrapped around her tiny waist and they embraced. It was a still, warm and loving gesture and, as we stood and watched, it would have been easy to believe that they were floating for that is how it seemed. These two misfits fit perfectly together and, in their silent embrace, they spoke a thousand words. In that moment they supported each other physically and metaphorically and had been transported, eyes closed, to another realm. Love had finally managed to bind, quite securely, these two loose ends and, as I looked closely, I could see happy tears in their eyes which were infectious. There was no kiss as it would have seemed out of place. This was enough, in fact, much more than enough. There wasn't a man, woman or child in the room that didn't take something from this happy event. They broke from their intimacy, sat and held hands. Not a word had been spoken.

For those remaining, I could see the relief on their faces as I explained, step by step, what the Cataclysm/clarification would be and then took pains to explain in the most precise detail, my plan of which I was so confident. For the rest of the day, those remaining rehearsed tirelessly. The day after, between Masses, we did the same and, eventually, we parted never to rehearse again and never to make contact unless it was a simple greeting when passing in the street.

22: Paracelsus

York, September 1541

That day of the King's arrival in York seemed to come much sooner than we would have wanted but, to be fair, he had now been on the road for weeks taking many a detour in East Yorkshire to ensure that he received as much cash and as many grovelling apologies possible for the Pilgrimage of Grace. York was no exception. He was met outside the City at Fulford Cross by the Mayor, Robert and many other officials who duly submitted, said sorry and gave both Henry and Catherine gold cups filled with gold coins.

It would have been usual for them to enter the City through Micklegate Bar but, as they were entering from the east they could be seen appearing as a bejewelled hoard on the horizon slowly making way for Walmgate. It truly was an astonishing sight and no one, whatever their place in society, could fail to be impressed by this assertion of power. It would even to be fair to say that some hard-liners were so swayed by the spectacle alone that some of their views softened. It was an education in both order and organisation just to see how they made camp so quickly and make use of supplies in York and its surroundings. This was 16th September and we were reliably informed that the King and Queen would meet the Archbishop that very day but would attend Mass on the morning of the 17th. Rumour dictated that Henry desired to meet the King of Scotland in York who was conspicuous by his absence.

We, as the Agents, were now relying heavily on William Fawkes. This was a Mass by invitation only and from the rumours, I reasoned that numbers would be few but it was essential that some of our Agents were in the Cathedral at the time of the Mass. So, come the dawn on the 17th, Elspeth and Richard Shakespeare accompanied Father Matthew through the huge entrance at the west end entering the nave thanks to Fawkes's connection with the Dean. William Fawkes had managed to secure their entrance by the subtle addition of a half-row of seats where they promptly placed themselves to avoid any unnecessary attention. Richard had never seen a Cathedral this size. His glimpse of Chester was brief so he took advantage of this opportunity to enjoy one of Europe's most magnificent houses. He looked up at the vaulting and the detailed decorated bosses on the ceiling and then marvelled at the building's width, length and height. He could see ahead of him, beyond the quire, the magnificent east window, the morning light starting to peep through. As he looked along its almost endless length, he thought he could see a shimmer as you would on a hot summer's day and this helped to relax him. He then turned to Elspeth on his left and said,

'All the seats are in the centre, is that unusual?' Elspeth told him it was, in fact sometimes seats weren't used at all and Father Matthew also acknowledged this by his, now apprehensive, expression. They were also astonished that so many windows had been darkened and none of the three could reason why. It was unbelievably quiet, this eventually broken by a fanfare of trumpets and an announcement that the King and Queen were to enter. The congregation understood that they were not allowed to look the King in the face so they stood, heads down, waiting for them to complete their entrance. The royal couple knelt and then sat in front of the meagre congregation. No choir. There was no choir to be seen in the stall and none to be heard. There were Yeoman Guards in the, now famous, red livery in the north and south transepts and in the aisles, and between them stood the Duke of Norfolk and the Duke of Suffolk both glaring at the weasel, Wriothesley, on the opposite aisle. The man who everyone recognised as Seymour's representative was present too, standing near Wriothesley.

The King, surprisingly, had managed to hobble in unassisted and his attitude appeared quiet and reverent at the start of Mass. The Queen supported him as they walked.

I could also see this most clearly. Where was I? I was a hundred feet up cradled inside the Tudor Rose Boss that I had so recently fashioned and completed. People were like mice from this height so it felt good to turn the tables and here, I could see all. The Archbishop appeared along with the Dean and the Precentor. They were standing quite close to the congregation, on their side of the quire and, instead of utilising the high altar, there had been an altar placed only six feet in front of King Henry. The Mass started as you would expect with the chorus of stifled yawns already begun but, seemingly out of nowhere, the Archbishop was joined by a man with what I'd describe as one of those mad professor hairstyles: bald with a clump of hair either side just above the ears. Almost everyone woke up again. Who was this maniac passionately gesticulating? I knew who he was, he had been to England before and was known throughout Europe as the "Martin Luther of medicine" as his ideas were so radical. Truthfully, his medical research deserved respect but it was that other thing for which Paracelsus was famous that concerned me. He prophesied and his prophecies were dangerous. Elspeth had now turned to Richard hoping that he would have some clue as to who this intruder was but he was also totally confused. The place was now so heavily infused with incense it was hard to breathe.

'Behold! A prophecy come true!' Paracelsus exclaimed, frightening the bloody life out of me. I nearly fell. He now had everyone's attention and that attention was focussed on the altar. Seemingly on a cloud, the Bible rose from the altar untouched by human hand. Everyone from the King to the Agents gasped. Once airborne, Paracelsus took hold of the book and showed it to the congregation. It wasn't a Bible.

'The Lindisfarne Gospels. As prophesied in that miraculous dream of our gracious Lord and King, Henry!' And, despite all our efforts, there they were for all to see. I pondered on how they had got here. The Archbishop took the book, opened it and proclaimed,

'Glory be to the Almighty for His Hand has added a further chapter for the enlightenment of all mankind' and, as he spoke for the first time, we could hear music. It was the sound of angels more beautiful than anything anyone present had witnessed before. It was complex, the holiest of heavenly hosts singing dozens of individual parts harmoniously. It became louder but, as the congregation looked, they could detect no choir. It seemingly came from nowhere. No, not nowhere, but the heavens and it was overwhelming in its volume and its efficacy. It was beautiful. It would have been impossible not to be transported by this Holy intervention. The King and the congregation were happily absorbing this with perhaps only the Dukes looking on with a little apprehension and fear.

'Behold the vision as promised!' shouted Paracelsus, arms pointing skyward and then bodily slumping to the ground in tears and praising God. All gathered were then blinded by a sudden light after which Richard looked at Elspeth and pointed to the vast ceiling before them. It was clear on their faces already that they felt that they may have made a huge mistake. They presumed the Cataclysm to be a most fearful and violent event. Had they misunderstood the "clarification?" There was no reasonable explanation for what they were experiencing beyond it being supernatural and there was nothing threatening about what they were now a part of. The Dean vented forth in tongues, a direct gift from God which left those at the front of the congregation crossing themselves and prostrating their bodies. It was then that everyone present took in an audible breath. Probably as high as you could imagine, toward the north and south aisles, were two beautiful figures descending on clouds. The choir became more intense, the angels descending further. These two angels had soft, downy wings that moved as did their hands gesturing toward the altar and there was no question at all, they were flying. Peace bound together everyone in the congregation and many were now praying audibly. A third figure descended and it was immediately identifiable, to those who knew her, as Jane Seymour adorned in her wedding dress, smiling and glowing, but with the most disturbing disfigurement. It was as if her torso had been opened, in the way you might open a book, and a light shone out from it. It wasn't gory. No innards or blood just this open and illuminated womb. It wasn't that people were stupid, they just couldn't find any logical or scientific reason for this spectacle and neither would you try to if you were in a house of God. Many of the more astute members of the congregation were looking for ropes and pulleys, or any clear deceptions, but there were simply none to be seen. The angels and Jane floated downward smiling benevolently and benignly at the gathered audience. The Archbishop moved forward and began to read the aforementioned addition to the Lindisfarne Gospels ensuring that the King was now so near that he was practically part of this heavenly experience. There was still no reaction from Henry, at least nothing that was any different to everyone else who were all, including the Dukes, now on their knees. Some people were crying, in fact, sobbing, and some were wailing. It was the most bizarre atmosphere, especially when viewed from above.

'And so it came to pass' declared the Archbishop loudly and dramatically 'that unto the eighth King Henry came a vision whilst he slept. And in this dream, he was visited by angels and an image of his beloved wife Jane and the angel said "behold! You will have a child by this woman but he will not be of mortal fruit. He will be the King of Kings and shall be called Edward who will bring peace and prosperity to all." Christ hath returned and will defeat the beast and the Antichrist!' This was accompanied by a clap of thunder that seemed to make the building shake with debris falling from the ceiling and then, suddenly, an image of Pope Paul 111 complete with horns appeared, then vanquished by a sword, an image that faded as quickly as it appeared. Then, serenely, in the centre of all things, appeared a shimmering, glowing vision of Prince Edward presumably as he now looked, barely four years old. As only a handful of people had ever seen Edward, this was a presumption but this, certainly, fit the narrative. Women were wailing and beating their chests, men holding their heads swearing their allegiance to the returning Christ. A new age and, where the Antichrist (the Pope no doubt) was defeated. This, indeed, was a clarification which would leave every English man and woman in no doubt about their faith. Christ had returned in the same way he had ascended and would be a living God amongst the Tudor dynasty. The Archbishop continued the tale of Henry's dream as written in the, now extended, Word.

'Henry, you will know this prophecy to be true if the original Gospels of England appear before you in a house of God, at which time you must declare his coming to the world.' Then Paracelsus started to quote scripture,

'For as the lightning comes out of the east so shall the coming of the Son of Man be. He is coming on clouds and everyone will see him!' Of course, the timing was right. It had been written that people would start to turn away from their faith, nations would rise against nations, there would be famines and there will be an abomination that causes desolation. Richard thought of the famines in Italy, the rogue Pope. Was King Henry preparing us for this? Have we been misled by Rome?

The vision disappeared, the Gospels disappeared and silence followed. Everything rested on this moment. Even at this distance, I was watching the faces of Wriothesley, the Archbishop and Paracelsus. They, in turn, were watching the congregation carefully. Was this enough? Surely they are with us? they were thinking. I realised that this was a critical juncture. If this wasn't stopped, Henry, quite understandably, would now declare that Christ had returned, again by virgin birth, and was non-other than his son, the Prince. This, the greatest confidence trick in history was almost secured and there wasn't one person in the Cathedral who now wasn't completely open to suggestion with even Richard and Elspeth still trying to search their feelings to make sense of it all. That's why I needed them there, to test the effectiveness of this sting and, yes, Elspeth the Catholic nun had fallen for it. What hope was there for the vast uneducated and unwashed of England? It was a masterpiece and, perversely, I admired the perpetrators. However, this was to be the very moment when they would be uncovered, but there was nothing. The Mass continued, people whispering to the heavens with Paracelsus, the Archbishop and their minions consoling the new faithful. Come on, come on, I was whispering to myself and then I shouted it out loud as all was now lost. Sadly, I could not be heard and I could see guards approaching the west end to open the doors. The next steps would be akin to an epidemic, a religious plague. Once the doors were open and, even if just one person left, that would be it, the Tudors and Seymours holding unlimited power over Britain, Europe and, eventually the world possibly for hundreds or thousands of years. What had gone wrong? We rehearsed the plan over and over. Where the hell is he? I could see the doors creak open and there was already some movement of people. Had it all been in vain? Why on earth was I here if I fail to stop this? Why is this event not recorded in any histories if they are to succeed? Will events change? I could tell from my mindset that I was panicking which was of no use to anyone. I shouted again to Elspeth, Richard and Father Matthew. Nothing. They could not hear. Now I wished I had told them more. The Tudor Rose Boss in which I was cradled wasn't secure. It was the one thing that was still, definitely, on a pulley so I convinced myself that now would the time to hurl myself downward in a last-minute hope of disrupting proceedings. My most valued agent had let me down or he just needed a bloody clock. I tugged on the rope so that the pulley would release me and the Boss. I looked over the edge to see where I would land. It was then that I saw some movement from the south transept. Please, please let this be him. Why the bloody delay, get on with it man! Out of the darkness came a modified litter, a seat carried by servants if you like, and, at the front was the Queen. As the litter came into the light, it was King Henry sat upon it. This was enough to stop everyone in their tracks as he bellowed,

'Stop this at once!' Heads were spinning trying to work out how on earth the King could be both sat at the front of the congregation and also sitting on a royal litter emerging from the south transept. More supernatural visions? Not at all. The "King and Queen" of the congregation stood and walked toward the new royal guests. Those poor people in the congregation, what they had been through already and now they weren't sure who to bow to. "King" Robert and his "Queen" Wynnfrith, made excellent decoys as the real King watched all this nonsense from the shadows. Henry allowed them to stand by his litter. He turned to the Archbishop, the other clerics and Paracelsus.

'How dare you! How bloody dare you! You scurrilous demon's arseholes! You will burn for this. Burn!' It would be fair to say he was absolutely furious. Not surprisingly, the Archbishop and Paracelsus feigned ignorance insisting that they knew nothing of the visions until they took place. Seymour's man, who had undoubtedly engineered every detail of this, made for the door.

'Mouse!' The King boomed and I knew this was my signal to drop. Once I released the rope I was almost in free fall, the Boss hurtling down ahead of me as my hind legs and tail trailed behind me in mid-air. I was down in seconds and the boss landed on this scoundrel's head. He was still conscious but was immediately secured by two of the King's guards before he could make any headway. We all looked up as we could suddenly hear a faint ripping noise that gradually got louder. Heads were spinning trying to find its source. As everyone quietened, it was evidently coming from the very centre of the Cathedral. The congregation, now frozen, could see only two knife blades, one near the north aisle and one near the south travelling downward from the ceiling as if unattached. It was only when the knives had gone past halfway that their view of the quire and beyond became skewed and distorted and, for a while, it was hard to understand what they were looking at. Then, as clear as day, two figures were simultaneously, double-handed holding the knives cutting their way down a most detailed and elaborate backdrop. By the time they had reached the floor, Eirik and Thomas Farrier had absolutely destroyed the illusion revealing a cornucopia of gadgets, mechanisms, scaffolding and people wearing all sorts of strange outfits including those that blacked themselves out top to toe. The congregation had been looking at a perfect painting of the furthest half of the Cathedral in astonishing detail and perfect perspective. This had been placed in front of the quire splitting the Cathedral in two, stretched all the way from left to right. Sitting in the centre of the nave, they believed they were viewing the whole cathedral. The shock, now, amongst the congregation was palpable as they became very increasingly angry and upset.

'Join me Mouse!' commanded Henry. Robert picked me up and Henry took pride in the three Harry's standing side by side which, to be fair, was as uncanny a sight as what we had just seen.

'Viking and blacksmith by my side!' and Eirik and Thomas Farrier joined our ranks. The Archbishop and his sidekick were still pleading innocence whilst the mass of people that had been working behind the screen tried to flee but this was in vain. Many were in costume, others wearing complete black which scared the congregation as they now presumed them to be demons. Again, I thought how unbelievably easy society was to control at this time and how, unchecked, this deception would surely have succeeded. The cast, if they are to be called such, scattered in all directions looking very much like the proverbial rats leaving the sinking ship. They were shouting in several languages and pleading innocence. Silas had been carrying a rope in case he was needed to scale the walls to bring down this backdrop, but now thought to use it to lasso the legs of one of the escapees who was now nearing the exit. Yeomen secured several more. It was pandemonium and soon it was almost impossible to distinguish between the congregation, the Agents and the perpetrators. Richard left his seat to apprehend two young men who were shouting out in Italian. He grabbed them both, by the back of their dark jerkins, and handed them to the King's guards. All entrances and exits were now secured. Almost squeezed up against the ceiling was an enormous choir dressed in black, it was a sombre and intimidating sight.

Henry turned to address some of the rogues,

'My beautiful Jane and my son! My son!! How bloody dare you!' He pointed at the girl who had masqueraded as Jane Seymour 'you will burn for this girl and…' looking at the gathered mob of engineers, architects, artists, costumers, carpenters and illusionists 'you will suffer. God's teeth you will suffer! and you will tell all before you die! The Bible warned us of false Messiahs but this! God damn you all!!" His fury was unlimited and, certainly, at this point, I wasn't going to be the one to interrupt him.

'Scoundrels! You play around with the Word and the very name of Jesus Christ! In a house of God! And you, you!!' He had his eyes on Paracelsus and then, awkwardly, Henry descended from the litter. His servant helped to support him but Henry cursed him and knocked him aside. The King hobbled toward the shaking Paracelsus and took hold of him

'Thou buggerer of farm animals! Thou shitty arsed alien! You think to dupe the King?!! I know you, you venomous serpent!' And then the King turned to the congregation,

'This snail would have you believe that your world is ending in twenty years! Is that so?!'

Paracelsus, knowing full well that this was, but one, of his prophecies, said nothing so Henry decided to slap him hard on his fleshy head which, if nothing else, offered some light relief. Paracelsus grovelled, made promises, apologised but, by doing this, made things worse. So bad that I couldn't possibly repeat in full the King's response.

I was now upright on the King's litter dressed as he was which, to be honest, was now getting a little silly. As the, now crowded, population of the Cathedral looked upon me they couldn't work out whether I was part of the illusion or if madness had taken over the world in a single morning. The King turned to Wriothesley. A woman came out of the shadows pointed at Wriothesley and declared,

'This was the man that had my family put under house arrest. Threatened my children when all my husband wished for was to stop this evil.' Richard jumped up,

'Abigail!' he exclaimed and ran over to her.

'And, Your Grace, he falsely accused me of murder whereas it was he who was responsible for the unnecessary killing of a peasant in Stratford upon Avon' added Silas.

'Farmer and York idiot, join me!' ordered the King. Silas thought that York idiot wasn't a bad title when announced by the King himself, so promptly did as ordered. Another voice projected from the shadows of the north transept,

'to cover his wicked tracks, he had this woman tortured within an inch of her life, her husband dead.' It was Ham with Farrimond jointly supporting the incredibly frail Maud.

Then, forgetting to ask permission of the King, Silas ran over to embrace Maud.

The King then pointed at a singular priest in the congregation. On cue, Father Matthew unwrapped from a cloak the person sitting alongside him.

'This is Brother Bede, your Grace. Without the risks taken by this poor monk and his ally, Brother Bernard, no one would ever have been the wiser regarding these events.' The King invited them to move across to where he stood but hardly acknowledged this last revelation as he could not countenance the idea of monks being useful. The King then turned his attention to Wynnfrith, looking beautiful in her royal garb.

'And you, good washerwoman, bid your sister join us.'

'Yes, Your Majesty' answered Wynn. The most gormless expression developed on the face of Silas. The prince of last-to-know had only just realised that this was Wynn in costume and started to approach her but on clocking the King's displeasure, froze again.

There we stood. The Agents of the Word behind the King. What an uncanny development I thought but also knew that everyone in the room was in peril including us. This was going to be a secret that would hurriedly go to the grave with all present. Silas, astonishingly looking the King directly in the face, started to speak. How I was willing him not to. Keep it in Silas, keep it in. Please don't say anything! I was shouting in my mind.

'I trust Your Majesty's donkey is in good fettle?' asked Silas. No one, apart from Thomas Farrier and Shakespeare, had any bloody idea what this meant and, to most of those gathered, it sounded a bit vulgar. You could hear a pin drop in the Minster for a very long thirty seconds. And then,

'Ha Ha!, Ha haaaaa! He blustered. I like your fool, mouse. Better than mine! Might keep him.' The King then turned to me, his mood changing again and pointing at the vision that filled the rear half of the Cathedral.

'What on earth is all this?' and, as I looked, the contrast between the half in which the congregation were and the other half was stark and, for anyone who loved the Minster, it was also offensive and heart-breaking. It was very much "backstage" and I was possibly the only one there who even understood that concept.

'I have two allies, Your Grace, that will be able to explain every detail of this deception. However, it is paramount that nothing is moved.' I said although he wasn't going to give up easily.

'What's that damn thing?' he asked.

'A camerae obscurae Your Grace.'

'Well, henceforth it will be deemed unlawful!...and that?'

'A large glass, for magnification Your Grace.' He then noticed the prop worn by the woman pretending to be Jane which simply had a housed candle for light.

'And that?!'

An illuminated deceit, I think made of hollowed wood, Your Grace.

'Mmm, that too! Unlawful!'

'The candle too?' I dared to ask.

'Have to think on that one? Yes, yes ban bloody candles too!!'

Going to be a dark Winter ahead I thought. A woman dressed as an angel was trying to hide on the scaffolding but fell, screaming as she plummeted downward. One of her accomplices shouted,

'Betty!' as she landed on one of the platforms, hurt.

'Who the bloody hell is Angel Betty?!!' asked the King. Lost for words, as I didn't know if this was an attempt at humour, I simply told him that she wasn't an angel. As she lay there screaming, clearly nursing a broken arm, the King asked,

'Wings?'

'Swan feathers Your Majesty' and thought it wise not to mention that they were probably purloined by Wriothesley from Henry's kitchen. I also spotted thousands of printed pamphlets, presumably to hurriedly spread this "clarification" amongst the population of the City. I then asked the King what was to happen with all who were now locked in the Minster and surprisingly he asked my advice. This amused me and it lightened the King's mood somewhat. As I thought, my mind was cast back to those days and nights I had spent in the King's privy chamber in Lincoln. This is when the plan had been concocted. Yes, I thought, my days in the privy chamber staring out of my gilded cage at the King. That's where this plan was conceived.

The day after Henry had met with Wriothesley in Lincoln, Norfolk told the King that there were suspicions about a plot that may have been rooted in Seymour himself. I noticed that the constant gossip and rumours did little to ease the King's mood swings and he took to talking to, and confiding in, little King Harry more and more. The pressure built as he had a habit of saying,

'What am I to do mouse? No one to trust. Even my closest advisors seek only to feather their own nests. Will I ever get any intelligence that I can trust? How I wish you could speak to me!' And then he'd chuckle, walk away and then return and say it over and over again. I was bursting to put him out of his misery but held my counsel. That was until he said,

'Ah, dear mouse. I would give anything if I could confide in thee alone and, in return, you told me a truth. Any truth.' It didn't end there, he persisted and persisted in this mantra. So eventually I quietly offered,

'How can I serve your Majesty?' making sure to bow. I saw his head turn to sound an alarm so I quietly added,

'I will tell you any truth if you would just ask Your Grace' and to my chagrin, he started by asking about why I could speak and where I came from. By now I was exhausted with the whole crap and mouse game so, believe it or not, I told him. In the simplest, Renaissance translated version I could muster, I told him the truth. And how did he respond?

'When do I die mouse?' So, I lied. I simply said that, in this state, I had no historical memory which, if he'd challenged it, clearly wouldn't add up. He stopped asking. And that was that. There and then I decided to tell them about Brother Bernard, the pigeons, notes, the secret map, the Gospels. Everything. Whatever else you could say about Henry he was not stupid. I could see all this adding up in his head, it made sense to him. So my plan wasn't my plan, it was his. I just suggested the bit about using Robert as a stand-in.

'Is he as handsome as your King, mouse?' I remember thinking, all this shit we've just been through, and more to come, and his vanity is at the fore of the plan.

'Oh no, Your Grace! He scares even his servants! But I

do believe in the right costume he may serve as a decoy'. And that was that, and now here we are in York Minster awaiting his command and sentencing. He immediately issued orders for riders to go with haste to every Cathedral in the land instigating a law that stated the following "it is the sole responsibility of all Bishops to quell forthwith all talk, knowledge and physical evidence of the wickedness that is popularly known as the clarification on pain of death of the said Bishops."

He then asked Robert about York castle. Like Warwick, it was deteriorating but it would now have to be used to house everyone. Yes, everyone with a few exceptions. Wriothesley, Seymour's man, the Archbishop, the Dean, the Precentor, Norfolk and Suffolk along with the King's immediate retinue were to be under house arrest at the Archbishop's palace. Then he gave the command to arrest the Agents. I went cold and so did the rest of them.

'Holy Trinity is it?' he asked of Father Matthew.

'Yes, Your Grace.' he replied.

'Then you will be secured there until sentencing.' It didn't sound like it, but this was, indeed, a concession and we were immediately marched to the church.

A whole day had passed and, even though we did congratulate ourselves, very little was spoken. Kindly, the Queen had insisted on us being fed and our conditions were comfortable this, effectively being our home. She must have been terrified herself because her secret love would not remain secret for long. At around two o'clock in the afternoon a King's guard came to the door with Godwin and Bayard as I had informed the King that those two would be expert at explaining how the deceit had taken place. Behind the guard was William Fawkes who had given us such good service. I had happily agreed to keep him, Edward, the Shakespeare children, Culpeper and the Queen out of any conversation I had with the King so, as he entered, our interactions were formal. I then joined them and, under guard, we returned to the Minster and were allowed to examine the paraphernalia that filled half of it. There was now no one else there apart from the guard, William Fawkes and us three. William Fawkes reminded us that the King wanted a full report and explanation and I assured him that he would get one. There was a lot of muttering from Bayard and plenty of flatulence from Godwin, which was surely a good sign and, despite his aches and pains, he managed to negotiate the scaffolding. Added to this, not only was Bayard the world's leading expert on bullshit and deviant performances, he had travelled extensively and had seen some of this trickery before. Godwin helped to explain the practicalities and how everything had been made. I promised that I would relay all of our findings to William Fawkes who waited patiently.

'You do understand that the King expects plain speaking?' said William.

'That is exactly my intention' I replied and set about delivering his report whilst Fawkes sat and took notes diligently.

'It is probably wise to start with what the congregation were looking at. To the most suspicious eyes, sitting centrally looking west to east along the length of the Cathedral, everything looked as it always would. However, between them and the rear half of the building was stretched a thin canvas, on it a painting of the expected, usual view. So perfect in detail, colour and perspective that it was impossible to detect. Some slight movement was interpreted by some as hot rising air.

The angels. From where I sat, inches below the ceiling, I could see a short pelmet that was in front of the canvas, hiding the angels as they stepped over the canvas to start their descent. On the canvas were the thinnest of cuts that ran vertically down part of it. Each angel wore a brace around their waist (under their clothes) and this was attached to a hinged boom and, being directly behind them and passing through the slit, therefore could not be seen by the congregation. Behind, there had been constructed, for each performer, a huge cantilever meaning that if a weight was applied on the other end the angel would go upward and vice versa. The apertures were so cleverly engineered that they closed once the boom had moved past and opened when it returned. The over-application of incense masked the smell of coloured smoke used for the clouds.

Jane Seymour. She moved up and down in the same manner but was also wearing a prop simulating an open womb with a candle lit behind frosted glass. It must have taken many months to master this and also be able to mask the pain that the actress must have been in. The "womb" prop was also secured to the brace and boom that took her up and down.' It was at this point that I realised the audacious lengths these villains had gone too. Besides the King and the midwives, only Cranmer would have known that Jane gave birth to Edward by Caesarean section. That personal, inappropriate and tasteless addition to the performance must have hit Henry hard.

'The image of Prince Edward. This was a very crude projection using a Camerae obscurae, a recent device that can make you believe that an image has been transferred from one plane to another. For this to work the child actor must have had to have been suspended upside down and the image projected through a hole in a large, darkened box. The image would have been cast on the rear of the screen which made it seem ghostly from the front. A similar technique was used to create the phantom Pope.

The floating book. Smoke again and a mechanism, a machine based on Italian designs for moving parts. In simple terms, the book was cranked upward by someone hiding within the altar. Many of these ideas and devices can now be recognised by the illustrations on the document uncovered by Richard Shakespeare. If you examine the "Gospels" these are also a last-minute desperate forgery, most of the pages blank the perpetrators hoping that it would never be examined by the King.

The flashes of bright light. The perpetrators of this act timed all to coincide with the rising sun, in the east, behind them. Using those extraordinarily large lenses behind you, the sun was amplified many times and the light aimed directly through the canvas and straight at the congregation. Once angled downward, they became ineffective again.

The choir was there all the time but almost squeezed right up against the vaulting on the ceiling but behind the deceptive backdrop. I could see them, dressed entirely in black, from where I was on the ceiling. Thomas Tallis has been working on compositions of multiple parts for four, six or more people for some time although there were fifty or more in the choir creating a sound never heard before. I would suggest that this feat was masterminded either by Tallis or a student of his in allegiance with the Minster Precentor.

The thunder was no more than drums and rattled sheets of metal, and the debris simply small shards of light timber dropped from behind the pelmet.

To support all this skulduggery was an enormous scaffold stretching from earth to ceiling and across the breadth of the Cathedral. Technologies in scaffolding continue to develop at a pace and we have discovered that, as Michelangelo did in the Sistine Chapel, holes would have had to have been made in the walls of the Cathedral to support it.'

Not for the first time, William Fawkes winced. We noted the horror and disrespect of this dark scheme and pondered on how, if this had been successful, no one would ever have been any the wiser as the perpetrators would have had time to unravel this evil web. I asked Godwin to scoop up the printed pamphlets entitled "Christ returns!! Vision in York Minster. His Majesty's prophecy delivered." And that was just the start.

'We'd better get to work finding the printing press' said William Fawkes and I could see the look of disappointment on his face when I told him that it was likely that such pamphlets would have been printed throughout the land in readiness.

I emphasised that many of the participants, particularly the composer, would have had no clue that they were involved in something so treacherous but we both knew that sentencing would come from the King alone and no one else would have any influence. I could tell that Fawkes wanted to add something, he hesitated but then said,

'They're already dead, good mouse, almost everyone, Paracelsus too. Their only concession that it was all done quietly as the King wants all this finished with as soon as it can be and, no one ever be the wiser. He meets today with Wriothesley, the Archbishop and word has been sent to Cranmer and Seymour'. I said nothing. Godwin said nothing and neither did Bayard. History tells us that Paracelsus died in September 1541 but in his own country. Seemingly, Henry was going to do a really good job of keeping the Cataclysm neatly under the carpet for all time.

The report, admittedly, still full of questions, was completed by Fawkes and off he went to the King and we were returned to Holy Trinity.

23: God Himself

York, September 1541

The following day we awoke from sleeping on pews, the floor, the cellar and even some outside on the grass as the weather was fine. There was a heavy and complex atmosphere. Silently jubilant as we had achieved what we had set out to do but also dark as our discovery had resulted in the death of dozens the day before and the natural progression from that was that we would die today. All the same, we shared a light breakfast and resurrected those strong friendships and were now able to share amongst us the complete tale of the Cataclysm from start to finish as all were now there apart from Brother Bernard. Maud, still very poorly, doted on Silas and he did the same. Elspeth and Wynnfrith were delighted to see their brother but more so Robert who seemed surprisingly relieved that he was mended. However, there was an atmosphere around this issue that had made Silas distant. Eirik sensed this and also felt he needed to tackle it.

'I have offended you brother?' asked Eirik. Silas, of all people, wasn't one to bear a grudge but felt a great injustice had been done, especially now he was so close to Wynn.

'No. No my friend, just been the worst few days ever' he lied. Now, whether it was in response to this, or just to lighten the atmosphere, Eirik jumped up.

'You must see this!' he announced to all present and then opened his shirt. From a distance, Elspeth peered and said,

'Of course, the birthmark. An oak leaf'.

'Ha! No sister. Look closely' he said. Silas was bemused by this exhibition but chose to keep his counsel.

'This is the gift of that good man standing there, Thomas Farrier! See how he sealed my wound! With a branding iron shaped like an oak leaf. Haha!' Almost everyone was unsure as to why this was funny and Thomas Farrier was quite embarrassed as this could have looked like a good deed gone bad.

'Ah. I see you don't understand' continued Eirik 'when I was a small boy, the mark faded. Somehow, the blacksmith became aware of my birthmark story and, in saving my life, gave it me back!' Presented like this, it was funny and most people laughed although, it was a strange tale and split the Agents in two, some now increasingly suspicious of Eirik. He paraded his wound around and that was the end of it. Wynn mentioned that they had got behind with the washing which invited a few incredulous looks as we were all sure that we wouldn't see the day out. Abigail and Richard worried about the children but were assured that they would be looked after, the King had given his word. And then, from Abigail, tears that became infectious. Following that, silence. There was an unbelievable bond between all present but now we had run out of things to say. That was until Silas said,

'Is everything going to be alright now then?' His naivety was, in some ways, quite comforting but I couldn't lie.

'Silas, between us we have stopped a deception that would have given the Tudors and Seymours almost eternal power and the faith you all hold so dear would have been replaced by this lie. Yesterday's deception, now uncovered, probably seems like a passing inconvenience but it would have set in motion a new world where dictators would entirely control all things, possibly for all time. And, although it hurts me to tell you this, it is highly unlikely Henry will put to death the three main culprits.' Almost everyone in the room took immediate issue with this, so much so you'd have thought it my decision. It took a while to calm them down.

'Within weeks, Cranmer and Wriothesley will play their ace card, revealing the Queen's infidelities and the King, being so fickle, will place all his efforts, and theirs, into putting the Queen and Culpeper on trial, to death and then finding a new Queen. Henry will still need Seymour, Prince Edward's uncle, to look after affairs once he dies. Of course, you can be certain that the King will exercise his wrath on these miscreants but no one will hear of it and, of course, they will insist that the clarification was only a response to his dream and that they sought to serve him only. Norfolk will be immediately out of favour as yet another of his nieces, namely Catherine, has let the King down. She was fool enough to write to Culpeper of her feelings and I know these letters now sit with Wriothesley and, in turn, they will be used as bargaining chips by Cranmer.

'But surely it's only right these people are punished when so many innocents have died?' asked Elspeth.

'Absolutely. But you have to understand dear Elspeth that, above all else, this event has to disappear from history as quickly as possible. Wriothesley is known throughout Europe as Henry's trusted advisor and Cranmer is the Archbishop of Canterbury making him the architect of the new Church in England. Moreover, it was probably fair to say that Henry, in his role as Head of the Church could not function without his, usually benign, accomplice, Cranmer. Seymour is a renowned and successful military leader. Henry would have to concoct something astounding to cover up their deaths.' I replied. Then Bayard, of all people, chipped in.

'Not bloody right! The bastard! All those innocents in the congregation put to death!'

'Ah, but, my good friend, affairs of state rarely touch upon fairness. If only you were King Bayard.' I meant this kindly and it did, for a few moments, introduce some levity.

'All of that, sadly, is out of our hands my good friends. The King will do what he wishes about this and he will do as he wills regarding us. Please, please think on the good you have done this past few months' I said, 'and, I don't really know what happened to the congregation. We can only believe what we are told, there may be some still alive.'

'And all will be well now in England' added Wynnfrith. This is where I drew the line. I didn't have the heart to tell any of them of what was to come. The very fact that England still had the "old" and the "new" faith was enough to cause mayhem for hundreds of years. Henry's son Edward imposing the Protestant faith, Mary ruthlessly reversing it and Elizabeth trying to patch up best she could. I almost felt it was a blessing that at least some of my friends would not be alive to witness this after all they had been through. It doesn't matter what I, or anyone else, think about faith or religion, it has been, and will be manipulated to meet the needs and politics of those who seek to control and manipulate the masses. It's what drew me to these people. Either through simplicity or good heart, they understood the core message of love and forgiveness and they would stick to it come what may. Thank God they had no idea of the effect that Henry's initial division of the Church would have on societies to come for hundreds of years and, that such deceptions would be repeated in their future, not least in the Nazi propagandists that sought to create a Jew-free version of the New Testament establishing Jesus as the saviour of the Aryan race. A lie told well, and often enough, invariably and sadly becomes the truth. I hadn't the heart to delve into this so perked up and answered Wynnfrith's question.

'That it will Wynnfrith!' I replied. Then, Father Matthew accessed his seemingly endless supply of beer which certainly helped to raise spirits. Richard wanted to say something about the events that had taken place in the Minster.

'I confess, most humbly and embarrassed that I was taken in by the deceit.'

'Anyone would have' said his friend Thomas Farrier 'it was, indeed, spectacular and convincing.'

'Could such deception ever have a purpose? In theatre, entertainment?' asked Richard. Bayard was ready to, excitedly, offer his opinion but Father Matthew delivered a rant on the devil's work, how this must never be repeated, illusions being the tools of darkness. So, Richard Shakespeare let it go but he never let it out of his head, sure that the astonishing gift of illusion was fascinating, no matter how dark and that it could be implemented in the field of entertainment and education.

Soon after we heard footsteps. We were scared. Very scared and now that we were all assembled in the church garden, we felt incredibly vulnerable. At least there weren't dozens of guards. We could just hear shuffling and, as our heads turned toward the doorway, we could see the huge silhouette of our King. He had limped in on his own, a single guard waiting outside. This was unheard of. We were quite capable of harming him so this was a considerable risk on his part. We all fell to our knees, staring at his feet.

'Seat!' he commanded and Father Matthew obliged. He huffed and puffed for minutes before he spoke again.

'Be seated all of you.' So we sat.

'What a bloody rabble! Look at you! What an unfortunate mismatch of miscreants and misfits!' He annoyingly alliterated. How on earth did you find each other?' I presumed the question rhetorical but Elspeth, now boasting a return to her shaved head, decided to answer.

'We found each other fighting your cause, the cause of Jesus Christ and God himself!' Oh no, she wants to be a martyr and making our deaths that much more painful by the second, I thought.

'Mmm,' he paused, thinking and then said 'all very well coming from a rebel nun. A nun who would rebel against her King!!' he retorted very loudly. She didn't reply.

'But I see your sincerity. Long and hard I have thought on this and I have thought…yes…I have thought that your motives, generally, to be good. He looked at Father Matthew 'you, priest. You still have plenty of trinkets about your church to befuddle your congregation I see. You in league with the Pope?'

'My allegiance, Your Grace is to you, but before that God himself and, in my heart, I only think of the good teachings of Christ. I care not for "old" nor "new" Your Majesty, just truth.' he replied calmly and reverently.

'Been taking lessons from Thomas More methinks! Trying to lull me with clever words priest!!' Bayard's head went down as he remembered his recent trickery involving the supposed head of More.

'Be assured your Minster will be repaired, the culprits will fund it but I will have all excesses of Papism removed and that includes your shrines!!' He then calmed a little and added,

'You know they're all dead?!' This was clearly said as a threat, an attempt to assert his authority and he looked to see if we would bow to his power.

'So, little King Harry. What are we to do here?' for God's sake I thought. Why the hell is asking me. The first thought in my mind was to ask for a thousand pounds each, a pardon and an endless supply of lady mice and the priest's beer. Must think of something smarter, I told myself.

'This may surprise His Majesty, But I do understand the need to keep recent events secret. Any attempt to resurrect them and, or, monopolise on them would cause chaos. Have you considered other options apart from simply killing everyone?' I tentatively suggested. The expression on his face was extraordinary. It was almost as if this was a completely ridiculous suggestion. Pardon people? What for? All the same, he gave it some thought. Mood change coming. He stood and shouted so all York could hear,

'Have you any idea what a bloody mess this is?!! And who has to clean up the shite?! Again!!'

Wynnfrith was out of her seat which made me very nervous. He was trembling, partly through anger but visibly, also, he was in pain. She approached the King. Not allowed. She knelt in front of him, also not allowed. She then looked him in the eyes and took his hand and then it occurred to me that, of course, she now had nothing to lose and, being Wynn, for a few moments she had decided to put herself in the place of this moody and confused tyrant.

'God himself knows the secrets and troubles of your heart and has wonderful plans for you. If you could only follow His Will, Your Grace. Be at peace, and place your burdens at the foot of the cross.' I looked upon him and he had visibly mellowed. He touched her long silken black hair as a father would a child and he fought back a tear. Seemingly, even the senior clerics in the land had failed to minister to this man. He reacted, but softly.

'Ah child, if it were only so simple. I have half of Europe trying to bring me down and potential rebels everywhere in England and more threats in Scotland and

Ireland. How I pray for peace! The labours I have had just to secure an heir to the throne.' As he said this it would have been hard not to sympathise with his lonely burden of authority but, unfortunately, Wynn was right. Here was a man who had never given up to God's will, everything had to be on his terms. Ironic, in that he was a most scholarly theologist, possibly as well read as anyone in Europe. Not much use when you feel isolated, I thought. He had now calmed so we all sat staring at his feet waiting for a decision.

'Agents of the Word? Mmm, a little pompous but it has a ring. What use have I for those who would put their faith above their King?' I was certain, for a moment, that he thought again of his friend Thomas More who he had beheaded for that very reason and, most probably, had regretted it afterwards.'

'I would have you all swear an oath to God himself!' This, in itself, was very curious and then there was a pause.

'Yes, yes! To God himself. You will become known henceforth as the "royal secret agents of the word." Mmm. Yes. Very good' he muttered, self-congratulatory.

'You will be my agents and the agents of the Tudor line.' However good this sounded, I knew that my beloved colleagues would need more. Many of them would choose death over allegiance to anything that was considered corrupt.

'If I may, Your Grace' asked Silas 'what would be expected of us?'

Henry hadn't completely thought this through although I was astounded at this incredible concession. He muttered and thought. Got to his feet, hobbled, sat down again and muttered some more.

'Let me ask you' he said quite sternly, 'what do you say you stand for?' Robert, without apology, shouted out,

'Integrity!' and then Thomas Farrier answered,

'Faithfulness'

Then Wynnfrith,

'Kindness'
Elspeth added,
'Self-control'
'Goodness,' offered Silas and Eirik said,
'Forbearance'
'Love' added Father Matthew to which Richard added,
'Gentleness'

'Joy' was Abigail's offering. These words seemed to flow from the Agents as if they had been rehearsed. Pleased with themselves they felt that this was sufficient until another voice added,

'Peeze!' Bede was determined to contribute and in doing so shocked everyone present. There was an awkward pause as they waited for a response from Henry. Yes, I thought. Of course, peace.

'Hahaaaa!! Galatians – the fruits of the spirit! Yes! one of my favourites too! Against these there are no laws! Haha!!' he blustered. Favourite? I thought. None of these words are in this man's vocabulary! More like death, torture, back-stabbing, control and blackmail. I stopped myself. No point in being bitter. Although, I simply couldn't understand how a man who knew the Word so well could completely bloody ignore it! Still impressed, he thought a little longer.

'You will be the guardians of right and wrong!' he declared as if he had just invented the wheel. I saw Elspeth look up which had me thinking for certain that she was going to blow this kindness away in one sentence

'And who decides what is right and wrong Your Grace?' and without hesitation he replied,

'you along with Jesus Christ. That's good enough for me'. Bloody hell, I thought. He actually understands these people. He had managed to work out that, in all his years of rule, he had only met a handful of people of good conscience so had decided to take advantage of this grubby crew who seemed to know right from wrong. I could feel the pressure release in the room. Henry stood, smiled (not a pretty sight) and invited all to kiss his lumpy hand. He turned to leave and said,

'I will arrange for a formal oath to be taken. You will now disappear into the shadows until you are needed. Have no doubt that you will know when you are required!' He started to walk away and awkwardly turned again.

'By the way, I'm keeping Tallis. Fine musician….Oh, and if you ever speak of this Cataclysm or our agreement you will lose your heads along with those of all your family.'

There was no jubilation or celebration, I suppose everyone was trying to work out whether they had been conned or not. Realistically, Henry had managed to find a compromise possibly for the first time in his life and the comment about Thomas Tallis reassured us that there may not have been a complete cull after all. Elspeth hugged her sister and then her brother and then, curiously, Robert hugged Eirik. We looked at each other knowing that our fellowship was, at least for now, at an end and, in doing so there was a tangible sadness in Holy Trinity Church.

'Take heart my friends' said Father Matthew 'we shall soon be together for a wedding!' This was meant only as a light-hearted jest and it received cheers. Wynn and Silas were so embarrassed that they looked only at their feet, red-faced. I couldn't help thinking it would probably be another two months before they would hold hands, but progress is progress. I was now perched on the edge of a small table and felt the need to make an announcement.

'My beloved modern-day disciples. Your goodness alone thwarted this evil deed and I would urge you never to change, always be who you are' now looking at Bayard 'but perhaps get rid of all your pins' then to Silas 'find a map of York with all the cellars drawn on' but they weren't in the mood for humour so I concluded 'I must go. I am happy for you to say goodbye but I have no choice but to return from whence I came.' There were a few tears but nothing more. No one wanted to speak until Robert muttered something. Elspeth asked him to speak up.

'Not what angels look like anyway. Not at all.' We were all bemused not only because it came out of nowhere but, out of all of us, Robert was the least inclined to faith. No one challenged him although Wynnfrith did, for a moment, concluded that he must have had an angel of his own tucked away somewhere. Surely not? She thought.

As we left the church we noticed a single rose on Lizzy's resting place with one small note that simply had 'C' written on it. However it had got there, it was from the Queen. We paused to acknowledge this kindness and Elspeth led us in prayer for this much loved little girl.

We were now into the evening of my last day so I asked them all to accompany me to that place behind the walls at Micklegate Bar where I had first arrived. Edward entered carrying a box. I was overjoyed to see him and so clambered in. As we walked in groups around the streets of York for the last time I marvelled at the impact these misfits had had on me and acknowledged the depth to which I would miss them. Far in front were Farrimond and Ham, their silhouettes almost contradicting one another and, to their left, Godwin and Bayard almost blocking out the sun completely between them. I saw that a friendship had developed between Thomas Farrier and Father Matthew. When I say friendship, in truth it was possibly more as they had constantly exchanged glances as we sat in the church. How they deserve each other, I thought and hoped that they could negotiate the intense bigotry of the day to establish a meaningful relationship. Wynnfrith wobbled side by side with Silas, naturally dragging his feet which meant that they would touch, then separate and this would repeat over and over. I so wanted him to put his arm around her but, as I said, this was probably still months away. The Shakespeare family walked happily together enjoying the sights of this wonderful City, Richard still mumbling about entertaining peasants and they were joined by Maud who was faring better already. Erik was with Elspeth and, apart from his muscular frame, you really wouldn't tell them apart. This issue of him being related or not would crop up again and again with some very interesting revelations but, for now, they were family. I had said farewell earlier to Brother Bede and, in doing so, reminded everyone that, without the two monks, we would have had nothing and they were all to remember this. Robert walked with me. I thanked him, acknowledging that he had probably taken the greatest risk over the last few weeks and, as I did, he bade me farewell as he headed for Mrs Grindem's with a smile on his face.

Eventually, we passed through the gate at Micklegate Bar and I asked Edward to gently place me in the mud alongside the City wall. As they were reluctant to leave straight away I explained to them that, once there, I would simply disappear. Being the nosey buggers they were they wanted to watch. So, there I was with an audience which wasn't good as my bladder was full.

'Don't worry we've seen you pee before iron balls!' shouted Edward knowing full well he was at a safe distance. I felt the need, again, to say some last words.

'Don't be alarmed, as I will simply fade away.' They watched intently 'any time now' I added. Nothing.

'Bye!' Still nothing. This was becoming very embarrassing.

'Farewell, my good friends!!' A gust of wind animated nearby leaves, twigs and general detritus and it swirled around me picking up pace. My vision became blurred and I was disorientated and, as it calmed, I realised, still, nothing had happened. I looked over at my friends who were bent over with laughter. All I'd managed was a pee. It took me another ten minutes to realise that, not only was I not going anywhere, I couldn't even remember where the hell I was meant to be going. As Edward picked me up he said,

'what a load of nonsense mouse!' and laughed. I laughed

too.

'Come on, we've got a little time to tidy up at the workshop before curfew.' said Godwin and this was like music to my ears. My heart danced. I was still an Agent of the Word. No. No, a Royal Secret Agent of the Word and I was going to sleep in my workshop. How glad I was, this all seemed perfect to me and, enduring the constant mockery of my non-disappearance only served to cheer me up.

I was placed, wearing my little leather apron, at my bench and, as best they could, everyone peered in and applauded. I lit a small candle as a small crowd had noticed the commotion. The shutter slammed shut and I was, again, The Micklegate Mouse, alone and happy.

Epilogue

Lindisfarne, October 1541

Peter stood in defiance against the bracing wind that was continuously battering the northeast coast. On Sundays, after church, he had to himself the only two hours in the whole week that he could call his own. He had borrowed the family's small boat and made his way to the abbey at Lindisfarne, or Holy Island as locals called it. Here, he could feel the spirit of the monks, many now dead. He thought again, as he looked at the ruins of the abbey, of the demise of Brother Bernard and the secret he had kept so long. There were no longer soldiers here, just builders moving the stone from the abbey to the new castle. Almost as if to recreate the excitement that these events had inspired in him, he had brought along that pathetic scrap of paper that had been left behind. He held it up to the wind almost daring it to steal it away from him, showing the Latin letters to the sky. It was then, for the first time, that he realised that there was also something on the reverse side. He held it in both hands now scared it might blow away. Yes, it definitely had something on the back.

Now, whether it was this, or simply the frustration of owning this for months, or even the mysteries and adventures that had been concocted in his mind during that time, no one, including Peter would be able to say. But, at that very moment, he believed in his heart it was his duty to make way for York to see if there was any sense in what he now held.

THE END

Notes

Almost all the locations in this book are real although I do often use the names that would have been used in 1541, for instance, Wolverdington is now Wolverton. I would encourage readers to seek out these wonderful locations, many unspoilt. The stunning Holy Trinity Church, Goodramgate, York wouldn't be a bad place to start.

2021 will see the publication of 'The Micklegate Companion' which illustrates a tour around York revealing the many locations cited in this book and the two that follow. It will also contain 4 original watercolour illustrations that accompany the series.

The characters are a mixture of real people and fictional ones although, clearly, I've taken some artistic liberties with the likes of Edward Fawkes, Robert Hall and the Shakespeares. And, of course, the historical backdrop to the events is genuine with an added, fictional, plot twist.

Other books by Robert William Jones

1514 the Cataclysm is part of a trilogy, the other two books are:
1542 The Purge
1543 The disfiguration

One of his musicals *'A week in Space'* is also available on Amazon for just 99p and backing tracks and lyrics are available free through the website.

'Be a Teacher!' is a collection of anecdotes and stories from Rob's 40 years at all levels as an educational professional, will be available January 2021.

About the author

Rob holds a degree in both History and Art & Design and for his postgraduate studies, concentrated on British History. He taught both subjects for many years and his students ranged from early teens to undergraduates. Later in his career, he specialised in the application of new technologies in special and alternative education.

Rob started writing when he ran his own business in which he wrote scripts for plays and musicals that were used eclectically, but most often in theatre groups internationally and for major tour operators like Tui, First choice and Airtours. He has also written for national music magazines. Rob has also been a fine artist most of his life and, as well as designing backdrops and costumes for Jester Productions, he has received commissions that have ranged from magazine work and book covers to church interiors.

More information can be found at:
www.rwjauthor.co.uk

Printed in Great Britain
by Amazon

59071683R00185